John G. Morris

Life Reminiscences of an Old Lutheran Minister

Part 1

John G. Morris

Life Reminiscences of an Old Lutheran Minister
Part 1

ISBN/EAN: 9783337038458

Printed in Europe, USA, Canada, Australia, Japan

Cover: Foto ©Raphael Reischuk / pixelio.de

More available books at **www.hansebooks.com**

LIFE REMINISCENCES

OF AN

OLD LUTHERAN MINISTER.

BY

JOHN G. MORRIS, D. D.

PHILADELPHIA:
LUTHERAN PUBLICATION SOCIETY.

CONTENTS.

PREFACE.

An autobiography is not the most popular style of writing, and it has even been said that some men write the history of their own lives because nobody else will do it. This may be true in part, when men are ambitious of notoriety without any merit; but when a man writes for his own amusement and that of his immediate friends, it is a wholesome recreation from severer studies, and should not offend the delicate sensibility of any one. Men may say what they like; there is no doubt of the fact that most persons prefer reading a candid man's account of himself rather than that furnished by any one else.

I have nothing very remarkable to relate concerning myself, yet that which concerns me may hereafter be interesting to those immediately connected with me, and some of the facts which I shall state may perhaps be of some interest to those outside of my circle of friends, if they should ever have an opportunity or desire of reading these pages.

Many little incidents which would properly belong here are recalled in my "Fifty Years," and I did not wish to repeat them by transferring them to this book. Indeed, that whole volume may be regarded as one of "Reminiscences," only not quite as personal as this one. This is more private and professional; that, more public and historical. This is intended for my family and special friends; that, for anybody who will take the trouble to read it.

It has been my pleasure for many years to jot down everything of this character as it occurred to me, and then enlarging upon the same facts at irregular intervals and adding others, so that repetitions may be observed, and possibly contradictions.

If the whole had been written continuously such imperfections might have been avoided, but I have not taken much pains to remove them from these pages.

THE AUTHOR.

Baltimore, 1895.

CHAPTER I.

I HAVE abundant leisure at present, and have been fond of scribbling all my life. The six quarto volumes of my own newspaper articles, and numerous manuscripts which I have carefully preserved, will give full evidence of this propensity. I have amused myself for many years by jotting down these reminiscences for my own gratification and that of my family and other friends who may take the trouble of reading them, if they should ever appear in print. If they serve no other purpose, they may perhaps throw some light upon the inner history of one section of our Church during the transition period in which I have lived, and with which I was more or less closely associated.

I was born in York, Pa., on November 14, 1803. My father was Dr. John Morris, who settled in that town when the Legion of the Revolutionary army to which he belonged was disbanded in that place in 1783. He served as surgeon's mate during the war, and was commissioned as surgeon some time during its progress. From a fragmentary diary of his in my possession it appears that he came to this country in 1776 from Rintelm, a village in the Duchy of Brunswick, in Germany, and as he says, "I immediately joined the American army." This shows that he did not come over with the Hessian troops in the service of England against the American colonies, but as an independent adventurer.

He was assigned to duty in Col. Armand's Partizan Legion, and participated in all the adventures of that corps until the close of the war. His German name was Moritz, but I have heard my mother say that he was advised by the American officers to change it to Morris, so that if he should be taken prisoner by the English he would not be suspected of being a Hessian deserter and shot. His commission as full surgeon, signed by B. Lincoln, Secretary at War, and by Elias Boudinot, President of the Congress of the United States, dated Princeton, July 25, 1783, is still in my possession. I have also his certificate of membership of "The Cincinnati," signed by George Washington, in 1783, and the diploma of the society, also signed by Washington, at Mount Vernon, October 31, 1785. Being the only survivor of our family, this diploma entitles me to membership, but I have never availed myself of the privilege. These documents, however, have secured me membership in the "Society of the Sons of the American Revolution," and they have been of benefit in other ways.

Various other papers, diaries and letters of Revolutionary interest, mostly written by my father, have become my property, and are sacredly cherished. Among them is a highly complimentary letter from Col. Armand (Marquis de la Rouerie), dated York, November 25, 1783, of which I here give a literal copy from the original.

(Copy.)

YORK, *November* 25, 1783.

DR. JOHN MORRIS,

Sir,—At the instant the Legion is disbanded, it becomes my duty to give you my thanks for the attention, cares, intelligence, propriety with which you conducted yourself in both capacity of second and first surgeon to the first partizan legion under my command. I cannot be silent on the bravery which you evidenced on all occasions when you accompanied the legion to the enemy. I shall add that your conduct in general has merited and obtained the esteem and attachment of all the officers. I am happy in this opportunity to express myself those sentiments for you. I have the honor to be, Dr. Sir, your most obedient, humble servant,

ARMAND, MARQUIS DE LA ROUERIE.

When the Legion was ordered to York for disbandment, my father there met Barbara Myers, whom he married, and of whom I am the youngest child.

I have no recollection of my father, he having died in 1808, but my mother lived until 1837. He settled in York, after his honorable discharge from the army, and remained there all his subsequent life. He once made a tour to what is now Tuscarawas county, Ohio, then a region almost uninhabited by civilized people, and regarded as a very long and perilous journey from York. He went for the purpose of inspecting some bounty lands received from the government for military services, and also of settling there if prospects were favorable. But on his return from this tour my mother informed me that before he dismounted from his horse he said, "Child, we will stay at home."

His practice was extensive, and he was the only educated physician in York county for some years. To accommodate patients from a distance, and who were able to pay well for his services, he set apart three or four rooms as a hospital in his house, which he built of brick, in which all his children were born. It is still standing, on the south side of Market street, between Beaver and Water streets, nearly opposite Dr. Jacob Hay's residence.

His diaries show that he was a truly pious man. They are filled with prayers, meditations, Scripture quotations, and among them is a very creditable German poetical eulogy on Rev. Jacob Goering, who baptized me, and who died in 1807. His biography was written by Rev. Dr. Chas. A. Hay in 1887, and published by our Publication Board in Philadelphia.

My mother was one of the most saintly women I ever knew She was a diligent and daily reader of the Scriptures, and of pious German books popular among good people of those times. She never purposely neglected public worship, and had daily prayers in the family as far back as I can remember. Under God her maternal teachings and prayers and blameless example have influenced my whole life.

I have heard it said by some who knew my mother in the days of her young womanhood that she was remarkably handsome, and I myself used to gaze with the proudest admiration upon her clearly-cut, classical side face. I never saw one more symmetrical, or one that came nearer to the artistic ideal of feminine beauty, and she was as good as beautiful.

The only children of the seven born to my parents who were ever known to me were my brother Charles, whose name will frequently recur in these reminiscences, and my brother George, who died unmarried in York in 1856. I was the youngest of the family. All the rest, except Charles and George, died before I was born.

The first school I ever attended was taught by an old man named Miller. It was kept in a small building behind Mr. Schmucker's church, and was, I suppose, the parochial school. I could not have been over eight years old, and I do not remember how long I was a pupil there, neither do I remember when I was transferred to the York County Academy, but it must have been at a very early age. My brother Charles taught me my first arithmetic, and I have not forgotten the boyish fun I tried to make out of " carrying " the amount of one column of figures to another. He bore with my nonsense for a while, but soon had enough of it. Michael Bentz, who will be remembered in York, must have gone there as parish schoolmaster and church preceptor at an early period, for I went to his night school, kept in the small building behind the church, when I was very young. All the other pupils were older than I. His discipline was not rigid, for when one of these lads was rebuked for carelessness, or punished in any way, he would take his hat and walk out, and that was the end of it.

I began Latin and Greek in the York County Academy under the tuition of two New England teachers named Merrill. They were very imperfect linguists, and allowed us to do as we pleased, and we made no progress until Samuel Bacon, in many respects a very remarkable man, and a man named White, took charge of the school. These two men served at different times, and I was a pupil under each.

Mr. Samuel Bacon came to York as a Yankee schoolmaster, and after having taught several years joined the army as a commissioned officer. He was wounded in a duel with another officer; some time after he resigned and returned to York, where he studied law and was admitted to the bar, and married the daughter of Jacob Barnitz, Esq., one of the most respectable gentlemen of York. Mr. Bacon became a zealous Christian, and officiated as a lay preacher in the Episcopal church. He subsequently went to Africa, and founded a colony of colored emigrants, and may be regarded as the originator, or at least a prime mover in the work of African colonization. His biography was written by a New England author.

James Steen afterwards became teacher, and under him I made some progress.* It must have been in 1818 or 1819 that Samuel S. Schmucker, who had just returned from the University of Pennsylvania, or it may have been from the Theological Seminary at Princeton, where he studied some months, took charge of the Academy, and under him I was prepared for college. I need hardly state that he was the son of the venerated Rev. Dr. John George Schmucker, at that time, and for many years after, the pastor of the only Lutheran church at that time in York. I little thought that in less than ten years after I would commence an association with my schoolmaster in the prosecution of most of our church enterprises of the last fifty years or more. He must have been about twenty-one at that time, and was looked upon as a promising young man. He did not go into the company of the young people of the town, and hence he was not a favorite. He was studious, and loved his books more than society. He was probably the best educated young candidate for our ministry of those days, and plainly far in advance of all of them in his knowledge of English, and in ability to use it in the pulpit. When he was licensed to preach there were no vacancies in Penn-

---

*Thaddeus Stevens, about this time, was teacher of the Female Department of the Academy.

sylvania, and the present system of Home Missions and individual enterprise was unknown. In those days candidates were few, and vacancies fewer still; but none ever thought of opening a way for himself, if he did not find one. Mr. Schmucker accepted a call from New Market, Shenandoah county, Va., at that time a poor, forlorn, half-anglicized hamlet, but still where many of our people were kind, hospitable and devoted to their mother church. I shall have occasion to speak of this place again. This was the only pastoral charge Mr. Schmucker ever had. He remained there four or five years, until called to be the first professor of the Theological Seminary at Gettysburg in 1825.

Most of the boys of what may be called the first families in York were pupils in the Academy during my time. Two of them became members of Congress, five or six were lawyers and physicians, and others were men of business, and, while several of them became good citizens, they lacked energy and decision, and were satisfied with living a humdrum, indolent sort of life, content with mediocrity in all things. The children of some of them are very respectable people. In September, 1887, the hundredth anniversary of the York County Academy was celebrated. I was invited to make a speech, in which, among other things, I said that I was probably the only surviving pupil of the school of the period preceding 1820, when I left it; but after my address an old gentleman, whose name I forget, was introduced to me, who said that he also had been a pupil before 1820. I gave the audience a number of reminiscences, and mentioned the names of many of my school contemporaries and acquaintances, not one of whom is living, but many of whom became influential citizens and reared large families. I am the only one of that crowd that studied for the Lutheran ministry.

Some of the boys went to dancing school, but my mother would. not send me, neither had I any inclination that way. I never in my life stood upon a floor to dance. I conceived a special distaste for this amusement when I saw that the stupidest boy in our school was the best dancer in the company. I had no ambition to learn an art which required no brain, and nothing but agility of heel.

A few of the boys occasionally used profane language, but this habit I never indulged in. One of them tried hard to get the rest of us to drink liquor occasionally.

I remember attending a prayer-meeting on Sunday afternoon for some weeks at the Episcopal church, then served by Rev. Mr. Armstrong. Several other boys also went. No meeting of a similar character was held on Sunday, although Rev. Mr. Schmucker for many years had one in the old school-house behind his church on a week night, which was attended by a dozen or two old pious members.

I seldom missed Sunday morning church from my earliest days, although I then understood very little

of the German sermon. I was taught this duty by
my pious mother, and made it a matter of conscience,
although I felt no special religious interest in the
service. Perhaps it was habit, or the result of
domestic training; but it was good, whatever may
have been the motive.

One Sunday morning a boy, five or six years older
than myself, led me down to Loucks' dam to fish,
and every toll of the bells from the town churches,
which I heard distinctly, and which really seemed
louder than usual, sent a pang to my heart, for I
was consciously neglecting a duty, and acting contrary to my mother's wishes. Even to this day,
whenever I pass that place in the cars to Harrisburg, the recollection of that Sunday morning comes
up painfully. I do not mean to say that I feared
offending God so much as I feared wounding my
mother's feelings, if she had known it.

She and several other pious women used to hold a
prayer-meeting in her house, attended by not over
five or six. I, of course, was always present, and
took a boyish, although I will not say a religious,
pleasure in it. I was then about thirteen years of
age.

At a very early age I acquired a fondness for reading plays and books in general. Such as were suitable
to boys of my age were not numerous. My brother
George had a collection of modern plays, and these
I read more diligently than I studied my school lessons. I once ventured upon the composition of a

play, but laid it aside, and never heard of it until I had grown up, when one of my brother's friends told me how he had showed it around, and what hearty laughs they had over it.

The older young men of the town used to act plays in the upper room of the old court house. I once had a subordinate part in " She Stoops to Conquer," assigned to me as a boy. My brother George acted Tony Lumpkin capitally well.

I was always fond of spouting scraps of poetry, many of which I had committed to memory, as well as some larger extracts from Shakespeare, which I can recite at the present time, although I have forgotten many other passages which I committed since those juvenile days. Thus I began very early what is now called elocution and voice culture.

My juvenile reading was of course desultory. We had no large daily papers or illustrated weeklies or monthlies. Of course I went through Sanford and Merton, Robinson Crusoe, Thaddeus of Warsaw, and other popular books of that character. I read novels of the older school, for the modern school had not yet opened, and committed passages which, in my uneducated taste, I thought fine, some of which I can repeat at present, although I had not a good memory. Even about my fifteenth or sixteenth year I ventured on Milton, but I was not yet grown up to it, but Goldsmith, Boswell, Cowper, and other English authors of a like and unlike character were greedily read. I found Johnson's prose

2

too heavy for me, excepting his Rasselas, which I gloated over. A good portion of Swift was gone through; some of Addison, Sterne and other old English writers, and some of later years, as Pollock, Montgomery, Kirkwhite, Campbell and others. I tried Hume, but could not master him, and Gibbon was too heavy.

I had learned German well enough to relish Kotzebue's plays and others of that school. I liked Gellert, but I could never get through Klopstock's Messiah, and I felt disposed to take off my hat and beg his pardon when, some years after, I stood at his grave in Altoona, Denmark.

Later on, as I grew up, and during my student years, I read some of Scott's, Cooper's, Irving's, Dickens', Thackeray's, Macaulay's, Disraeli's, and many other novelists, and have continued to cultivate English literature to a small extent ever since. I once sat in the same chair at Abbottsford which, it was said, Walter Scott occupied whilst writing many of his books, but I was not conscious of drawing any of his inspiration from it. Cook's Voyages, Plutarch's Lives, Mungo Park's Travels, Anarcharsis, and a number of other travels and voyages were read, either before I went to college or during my college years. Goldsmith's Animated Nature, a book which naturalists now laugh at, was the only book on that subject to which I had access in these remote times, and it was perhaps the reading of this which imparted to me a taste for studies of a kindred character, which I have pursued with some interest in later years.

I could not have been more than fourteen years old when I made an electrical machine, with a large bottle for a cylinder, and astonished my companions and others with plain experiments. I got tired of the affair, and have never since had any especial fondness for physics, and that is because I had never been taught it at school. In my day there was not a single article of apparatus used or blackboard illustration given. It was the " day of small things " in pedagogics in York County Academy, but wonderful improvements have been made since those times, and some good scholars have received their first training there.

I had a fair voice for singing, and learned " the notes " after a fashion. I took lessons on the flute, when I was a boy, from Michael Bentz, but never played well, yet he put me in the " York County Band " before I was fifteen. I abandoned my musical practice when I went to college. I learned enough of vocal music to " raise the tunes " in a religious meeting. For years I " led " the singing in my week night meetings, which my church chorister did not feel himself bound to attend. That minister is deficient in his education, however learned he may be otherwise, who cannot, in an emergency, " raise the tune " in meetings, and there are not a few of that unhappy class.

We boys raised a soldier company, and our arms

were at first light pikes of tin attached to the end of
a long staff, but afterwards we got guns. I became
quite an expert in the manual exercise and in company drill, and have not forgotten it to this day. I
also practiced sword exercise pretty thoroughly, and
was strongly inspired with youthful military ardor.
To this day I delight in looking upon military
parades and hearing martial music, and I involun-
tarily catch myself in closely watching and criti-
cising the precision of movement and correctness of
step.

Our school debating society was vigorously carried
on nearly every season, but like all juvenile societies
of that character we soon quarreled and broke up,
to be renewed with the same results.

One of my boyish recollections is seeing the York
Volunteers, composed of many of the first-class
young men of the town, set out on their march to
Baltimore, to resist the invasion of the British. The
company took part in the battle of North Point,
September 12, 1812. I distinctly remember how the
mothers, wives, sisters and lady friends of these men
wept as the company marched out of town to the
tune of " The Girl I left Behind Me." I also remember the day of their return, a few months after,
when there was great joy in York.

None of us boys were allowed pocket money by
our parents, and this I think was not a commendable
feature in the training of boys in those days. I hold
that they should have a moderate monthly allow-

ance. It will save them from temptation, instead of leading them into it. Only one of our number had money, and we had reason to believe he did not come honestly by it. I do not mean to insinuate that he was a regular thief, but he had good opportunities at home of getting money without asking for it. Neither were the boys of those days dressed as genteelly as those of the present generation, though our parents were not poor; but times have changed. Quite recently a little boy in my family, who was much better dressed than I was at his age, insisted upon putting on a clean shirt and his Sunday trousers to go and see a base-ball game played by country boys in the neighborhood. This trifling incident brought up the memory of the olden times when his grandfather was not dressed as well on Sunday as he was in a suit which he would not wear at a base-ball game. Few of us had even such an article as an overcoat in the winter.

There was no German or French taught in the village or country schools, nor some other branches now considered indispensable. I learned French later in life, and improved in German, the rudiments of which I picked up from hearing it spoken a good deal in York. I never acquired a fluency in speaking French, for although I read it almost as well as English, owing to lack of intercourse with French speaking people my ear was never properly educated to catch the words of persons who rapidly speak that language. I hold that no one can learn to speak a foreign language fluently and correctly without daily conversation with natives. Hence I do not think that many of our young Americans who go to foreign universities to prosecute medical or scientific studies are much profited by the lectures they hear in Paris or Berlin or elsewhere abroad. They do not know the languages well enough to understand the professors. I have been surprised at not a few of my acquaintances, and other young men who have heard lectures abroad, how imperfectly they spoke German or French, and I am sure they understood but little of what the professors said; but they had the name of having studied abroad, and that was something.

In those early days there were several annual events which excited the interest of us youngsters. These were the " Fairs " and the " Battalion Days." The first was a feeble imitation, or rather a resemblance of the annual fairs in Germany, at which sales of all kinds of goods are held, and which are attended by respectable merchants from distant places for the sale of their various manufactures. But the "fairs" formerly prevalent in the German counties of Pennsylvania were nothing but country frolics, and the only traffic was in ginger-bread, small beer, raisins, oranges, and other small affairs. There was a dance at nearly every low tavern, and other immoralities were freely practiced. The town was crowded with country people, and all the thieves and other vulgar folks enjoyed a rich harvest. The stalls for the display and sale of the numerous articles were in and about the market house, and there the crowd assembled. We schoolboys also claimed the privilege of going to the "fair," but I do not remember whether we had a holiday or not.

Speaking of these fairs reminds me of a little incident worth mentioning. Some years ago one of our young ministers published an article on Luther, which denied the tradition that Luther's mother was attending a "fair" at Eisleben when her son was born. Our writer, knowing something of a Pennsylvania fair and its demoralizing influence, maintained that Luther's mother was a pious woman, who would not go to such a place, and therefore that was not her motive in going to Eisleben. This was printed in our most popular church paper, and the absurdity of it was not exposed by the editor.

The Battalion Day was a sort of annual parade of all the militia in the county, but it was a military farce. It brought large crowds to town, and the store keepers and tavern-keepers and cake-women and small-beer venders reaped the profit. On this day we had holiday, for it was a day of universal interest.

Some reminiscences which would be of no special interest to anybody lead me to make the following observation: If I had the training of boys I would do all in my power to encourage them by kind words, even when they failed in any public exercise, unless the failure was the result of idleness, and to applaud them when they did well. It is a great help to a boy who is struggling along in his studies. If he has no sympathy from his superiors he desponds, unless he has uncommon energy and self-will. I speak from painful experience, and I might tell a ta'e of youthful sorrows founded upon this fact. I have taken a different course, and while I tenderly rebuke carelessness and neglect of books, yet I applaud every honest effort to do well, and every instance of success in those young persons most nearly associated with me. It cheers and encourages them, and excites a commendable ambition to learn, but to be constantly scolded, and sometimes laughed at, blunts their tender sensibilities and begets indifference. They lose all interest in their books and become sullen and discontented.

CHAPTER II.

In September, 1820, at the age of seventeen, I entered the Sophomore class at Princeton College. Some other York boys had been there before, and two were still students when I went. My examination was not severe, and far below what is demanded at the present time at any respectable college. I was an inexperienced country boy, never having been from home, and cherishing all the crude ideas and rustic oddities of an obscure village lad of seventeen who had never been among strangers. This sudden introduction among a large number of young men, every one of whom I thought superior to me in every respect, intimidated me, made me feel awkward, and exposed my rusticity to a ridiculous degree.

The Pennsylvania village boys of those days had not the advantages of travel, sight-seeing, and intercourse with strangers which most of the sons of respectable families now enjoy, but we were kept at home, and our verdancy was nursed with care. It is true in those times there were no cheap excursions to places of interest as at present, and young people seldom left their village or rural home even to visit the largest neighboring city. We seldom had intercourse with strangers, and our country manners were not improved, nor any self-reliance cultivated or encouraged.

My brother Charles accompanied me to Princeton, which then required two full days' travel to reach from York.

I remember my trepidation in the presence of the Faculty, in the examination room, and also my exultation when informed of my admission. I leaped down three or four steps from the door to the campus in one joyous bound, and rushed across the street to the hotel where my brother was waiting in painful anxiety for the result. I heard several students who were standing around, and who observed my exuberant delight, say, " That fellow has got through, surely." I was wild with joy. In 1886 I pointed out that identical spot to my grandson, Charles R. Trowbridge.

Verdant and rustic as I was, I soon found some like myself, and a little more so. I, however, soon acquired respect, for I stood well in my classes, and had companionable qualities which were useful to me. From the very start I took an active interest in the " American Whig Society," and won its prize of $30 for declamation. I, however, returned it to the society, as some others had done before me. This was considered liberal and honorable, and the act secured me additional respect.

During the two sessions of the Sophomore year I ranked among the "First Graders," with several others. The "Grade" was awarded upon excellency of recitations only, and in some classes there were as many as five or six of equal rank; but in my first Junior session I lost my first grade, but got the second. This was because I failed in mathematics, which I never liked, and did not diligently study. Another reason was that I " stumped," that is, failed, in Bible recitation one Sunday afternoon.

The studies of the Sophomore class were not equal in grade to those of the Freshman in most colleges of these times, and some branches were not taught at all which are now considered essential. The text-books were not as well edited as at present; the apparatus was not as extensive, and the work of teaching was performed by fewer men, and for the most part in a very perfunctory manner, at least so I thought.

I indulged in no vulgar college mischief, and no dissipation, both of which I considered ungentlemanly, irrespective of their immorality; but I do not think I was deterred from them by any religious motive. I remembered my mother. I was, however, once unduly influenced to join in what was then. called a " rebellion " against the authorities, together with a majority of the students; but we were finally subdued, and were let off very lightly. The college exercises were interrupted for a day, but upon reflection we relented, and confessed our error rather than be suspended from college. It was a rash, stupid and inexcusable affair, without cause or provocation of any kind. We thought we were entitled to a holiday on some occasion, and the Faculty refused, upon which we held an indignation meeting, and resolved that we would not attend recitation, which was "rebellion." We were led into the mischief by an influential young man, and blindly followed his dictation. He afterwards became a lawyer of high character, and a distinguished general in the Union army.

Since I have come to years of discretion, and capable of taking an impartial view of things, I believe that in nine out of ten cases of college disturbances the Faculty is right and the students are wrong. The rebellions are usually the result of indiscretion and false pride, and deserve the exercise of severe discipline.

This was the only offense for which I was ever "called to account" at college. My conduct mark was always No. 1, although I had many temptations in another direction. There were many dissipated fellows around me, yet I never yielded to their wiles nor indulged in their frolics. My allowance from home did not justify any extravagance of this kind, and besides I always "remembered my mother."

My room-mate for a while (the word "chum" was not used at Princeton in my time) was a young man three or four years my senior, and quite an erratic genius. He was dissipated, but yet a genial, talented fellow. Strange, that over thirty years after I should be called upon to marry him to a foreign woman, with whom he had lived illegally for several years, and that a few years after that I should be summoned to a court in another State to give evidence in the case of his divorce. He was quite distinguished for his legal attainments, but having an adequate income, and being careless of business, he did not succeed in practice.

One hot afternoon, while some of the classes were at recitation, we heard the cry of fire in the village, but we did not move. Dr. Green, the President, came to us in great trepidation, and exclaimed as loud as his feeble voice would allow him, " Mr. Stockton's house is on fire." This we regarded as a call to the rescue, and the way we heeled it to the West End, where the house was situated, was a lesson to veteran firemen. We rushed in and dragged out all the furniture we could lay hands on, and finally, with the help of the townspeople, we extinguished the fire. Some of our boys, suspecting that there might be something in the cellar worth saving, found their way into it through the smoking ruins, and soon appeared, begrimed with dust and cobwebs, bearing in their arms lots of bottles of wine, and as there was no cork-screw in the company, the heads of the bottles were broken by a knock on the fence. Some of our zealous firemen did not get home till midnight, and not a few others were unfit for study next day, owing to severe headaches contracted from their hard work at the fire!!!

Some contemporaries of mine at Princeton became distinguished men, and some who were modest, pious and exemplary young men did not keep the faith when they entered upon public life. When I came to Baltimore I found one who had been one of the "Religiosi," as they were called at college, practicing at the bar, besides holding a high position in the court, but he had abandoned his religious profession, as well as his moral life. I could say the same of others, but it gives me more pleasure to say that most of that class of men maintained their integrity to the end, as far as my observation extended. One of these young lawyers at the Baltimore bar, who had graduated with high honors at Princeton before I went there, was a student distinguished for his piety and Christian earnestness. He became skeptical, it was said, from reading philosophical writings, and lapsed into infidelity. He may have been a student of theology, but of this I am not certain. It is said Dr. Alexander would never give him up, but believing him an elect child of God he would be brought back by divine grace; in other words, he could not finally fall away because he was predestinated to eternal life! He did not return, whence it follows either that he was not predestinated, or if he was, that the elect may "fall from grace."

I once tried an experiment to ascertain whether fellow-students at college, who were not particularly intimate while there, remembered each other after a separation of thirty years.

I had often observed, in his seat in the Senate of the United States, a member whom I knew at college, though not as a familiar acquaintance, for he was two classes ahead of me and belonged to a different college society; but I ventured one day in Washington to introduce myself, hardly expecting to be remembered by him, but to my surprise and gratification he recognized me after thirty years' separation, and said, " I not only remember you, but have kept trace of you ever since you went to Baltimore." This was Senator Pearce, of Maryland.

There was a very different experience which I had on another occasion. I once rather familiarly accosted a minister, who had been a classmate in the Theological Seminary at Princeton, and with whom I recited and heard lectures every day for eight months, and ate at the same table, and yet to my surprise, and another emotion which I need not mention, he did not remember of ever seeing me, and of course did not know me, although only ten years had elapsed. I turned upon my heel, and muttered in tones loud enough to be heard, " Don't know much of anything; bad memory."

*   *   *   *   *   *

How hard it is to get rid of college slang phrases! Some of these uncouth and unclassical expressions cling to me to the present day. I can tell a Princeton man among a thousand if he uses certain words and sentences which were peculiar to that college exclusively.

*   *   *   *   *   *

One of my room-mates for a season was William Buchanan, a younger brother of James Buchanan, then a member of Congress, and afterwards President of the United States. My room-mate was a young man of fine talents, but died soon after entering upon the profession of law in Chambersburg.

This fact was the ground of my acquaintance with Mr. Buchanan when he was Secretary of State under President Polk, and subsequently President himself. When he was a young man living in Lancaster he also practiced in the York county court, where he was a close acquaintance of my brothers Charles and George. He was Mr. Polk's Secretary in 1846, when I went to Europe. I asked him for a private letter to some of our representatives abroad, in addition to my passport. He refused at first, because, as he said, it was unusual and undiplomatic for a cabinet officer to give such letters to private travelers, but he would give it to me as a special private favor. These wily politicians want all their favors to have a special value. I dare say he gave this special favor to every respectable gentleman who asked for it. I spent several hours with him at the house of a mutual friend in Baltimore when he was on his way as embassador to St. Petersburg. I saw him frequently during his Presidency, when he always inquired concerning my brothers and other York people. Once during his Presidency he and I occupied the same seat in the car between York and Baltimore on the return from a visit to Lancaster.

During my time at Princeton it was customary for some one to write an Honoriad upon the graduating class—a sort of poetical picture gallery, describing the character of each man according to the preju- dice, or at least the immature judgment of the writer. I was mischievous enough to write one on the Juniors, in which, in doggerel verse, I depicted the character of each member according to my view. I made several copies of it, and deposited them in such places where I knew they would be found. The excitement was great, but I was not suspected except by one man, and I managed to silence him. The affair soon blew over, but I was apprehensive of discovery, which would have been anything but pleasant. Very few, however, took offence, for I gave most of them such exalted char- acters, and painted them in such flattering colors, they were rather pleased than otherwise. It was an inexcusable piece of mischief, but still it hurt nobody. I still have a copy of that Honoriad among my papers. I once read it to a gentleman who afterwards became a high officer of government, who thought it a good juvenile piece of mischievous nonsense in rhyme.

There were the ordinary bullet-rolling, cracker- firing, and what was called " funking " (burning in the college entries a ball composed of all sorts of villainously offensive materials), and I do not re- member that any rascally perpetrator was ever dis- covered. Regularly, every summer session, some

3

buildings on the campus were destroyed by fire. The scamps who played this villainous trick were not as honest as a young student who committed the same offense nearer home, but who, when converted from his evil ways by God's grace, made restitution to the college treasurer.

One mean trick was often perpetrated. The morning prayer bell was rung so early that many students jumped out of bed, and rushed into the "Oratory" without washing, or without even dressing, being satisfied with throwing a large plaid cloak around us, which was universally worn at that time. During the night some scamps would steal into the unlocked rooms and blacken the faces of the fellows asleep. In that plight some of them would go into prayers, and the effect may be imagined.

There was little or no intercourse between the students and the people of Princeton. We were not allowed to go outside of the campus in study hours, and there was no social visiting of ladies, as far as I know, except one. A young Virginian engaged himself to a lady of one of the "first" families in town, and married her soon after his graduation. He was obliged to get permission whenever he went to see her. Of course this rigid rule was often broken.

There was no intercourse whatever between the professors and students, except in the class-room, and that was stiff and magisterial. A cold distance was observed at all other times. Nobody kindly advised us or sympathized with us, and thus the honest ambition of many a studious young man was checked, at least not encouraged, when a word of friendly recognition or paternal advice would have imparted fresh vigor to his efforts, but there was nothing of this kind. Nothing was ever done or said to inspire us with a love for our studies, or with an honorable desire to become first-class scholars. I never heard of a student being invited " socially " to a professor's house.

I am not a pedagogist, but I think it a great mistake in the method of education to show no interest in students outside of the recitation room except to watch and report them. This is the way we were treated, and feeling that no confidence was put in us, we became perhaps more mischievous on that account. Our rooms were visited every night at eight o'clock by a tutor, who gravely went round with his hat in his hand and opened every door without knocking, peeped in in a perfunctory and policeman style, and next morning reported the absentees.

The style of religion was of the Presbyterian Puritanic type, of exceeding rigid morality but of no fervor. The pious students were called the " Religiosi," and many of them were exemplary young men. The ideas of most of them on the sanctity of the Sabbath, as they called the Lord's day, appeared to me, young as I was, to be very strange.   They would not write letters even to their parents on that day, for handling a pen implied work, and they would not study their Monday's lessons, because that was not religious work; but some of them, ambitious to be ready with their recitations on Monday morning, would gossip and talk nonsense all Sunday evening until the clock struck 12, and then they would apply themselves lustily to their books, and study hard for several hours.   They were conscientious, but it set me to thinking on the peculiar training which these pious young men had on the subject of the Lord's day. I find fault with no one.   I am not their judge, and will not be their censor.

There were occasions of special religious interest, but there was nothing like the Inquiry Meetings, which have since become so popular in the churches. When a student seemed to be religiously moved he was exempted from recitation, that he might have time for meditation and prayer.   The spirit of re- vivalism, which manifested itself in New England, was not cherished in Princeton.

The Sunday exercises were worship in the morn- ing in the " Oratory," when Dr. Miller and Dr. Al- exander, from the Seminary, preached; at other times Dr. Green, the President, and other members of the Faculty, performed that service.   There was Bible recitation in the afternoon, besides the repeti- tion of the Westminster Catechism.

*   *   *   *   *   *

One of the college exercises was declamation in the "Oratory" every day after evening prayers. One day a classmate and I were to speak. I had committed a humorous speech, such as was not often heard there. I was to come first, and I begged him to let me declaim last, for I knew that the whole crowd would be in a roar, and that he, following me with his selection, would appear to a disadvantage, for I wanted him to have a chance, knowing that he was ambitious of being an orator. But he would not consent, and the result was as I had expected. They were loud and uproarous in their applause of my selection, and the poor fellow was not listened to, for they had not done laughing at my nonsense when he was half through with his declamation.

At that time all the students and Faculty wore academic gowns at prayers, church, and sometimes on the street.

There were two literary societies in college, the American Whig and the Cliosophic, between which there was an active rivalry. Profound secrecy was observed as to the proceedings, and none but members were ever permitted to enter the halls, even when there was no meeting. There was great effort made to induce new students to join one or the other, and this was called "huxing," which sometimes resulted in ill feeling and angry words. There were no Phi Beta Kappa societies, or other fraternities with Greek initials. I now believe that they create jealousies, envies and clannishness.

I think it was at Princeton that I first began to keep a diary, which I kept up, at intervals, for many years. It is a good thing, if properly done, for in after years it brings up many a reminiscence of importance, or at least of interest. Sometimes also it realizes what has been said: " The remembrance of youth is a sigh," but the " olim meminisse juvat " is still good. Anthony Trollope, in his entertaining Autobiography, Chap. III., says: " Early in life, at the age of 15, I had commenced the dangerous habit of keeping a journal, and this I maintained for ten years. The volumes remained in my possession unregarded—never looked at—till 1870, when I examined them, and with many blushes destroyed them. They convicted me of folly, ignorance, indiscretion, idleness, extravagance and conceit. But they habituated me to a rapid use of the pen and ink, and taught me how to express myself with facility." I presume that most young diarists can say the same.

*   *   *   *   *   *

There was a college celebration of the 4th of July, and I remember being chosen to deliver the oration in the Presbyterian church in the town.

*   *   *   *   *   *

It was here also that I began copying into a book, which I yet have, every short poetical quotation of a striking character which I could find, prose extracts, beautiful similes, strong or otherwise remarkable expressions. This I have found of good service all my days, and I would advise every young man to do the same or a similar thing. Even advanced students would derive benefit from it. Later I used Todd's Index Rerum, and the advantage was great. These manuscript books have brought to mind many a fact, date, quotation or expression, that otherwise would have been forgotten.

* * * * * *

I do not know how it is at colleges now, but at Princeton we answered to our names four times a day, twice at prayers and twice at recitation.

Riding on horseback or hiring vehicles was forbidden on pain of suspension.

Among the students there were many, of course, from the most wealthy and influential families. I have met many of them since who were filling responsible positions, and some of them have risen to eminence. Others have lamentably decayed, and I have had the painful experience of being asked for a small gift of money by a former classmate to buy bread for his hungry family. This man was not intemperate, but beggared for lack of brains and energy to gain a living by his profession, for which he was never fit. But he had no force of character, was respectably connected, destitute of talent, married, had a number of children, had no practice, exhausted the patience and liberality of his kindred, borrowed from his friends, and was wretchedly poor. Instead of trying to make a professional man of him they should have put him to a trade, but the proud family would have scorned the idea of having a mechanic of their number. I could give other melancholy examples of decayed fellow students whose history is deplorable.

COLLEGE LIFE AT DICKINSON, CARLISLE.

About the year 1820 Dickinson College, at Carlisle, Pa., was resuscitated by the Presbyterians, under the Presidency of Rev. Dr. John M. Mason, a celebrated minister and theological writer of New York. He had been paralyzed, and walked feebly with the use of crutches, and his speech was sensibly affected; but his was a mighty genius, which flashed out brilliantly on many occasions.

My brother Charles, who controlled my movements, thought that all Pennsylvanians should patronize colleges in their own State, and besides, Carlisle being much nearer home, he concluded to transfer me to that institution. Accordingly, having spent the whole of the Sophomore and one-half of the Junior years at Princeton, I entered the Senior class at Dickinson, without examination, and graduated in 1823. My certificate of good standing at Princeton secured for me this privilege; besides this Prof. Vethake, who had been one of the professors at Princeton during my time there, but who, a short time before, had accepted a position at Dickinson, was perhaps partial to me. There were nineteen of us in the class, and it was the first that was graduated under the new government. It was afterwards said that sixteen of us became ministers. The one who became the most distinguished as a public man, though not as a scholar, was George W. Bethune, who was an eminent minister of the Reformed Dutch church, and one of the most popular men in the country as a preacher, lecturer, platform orator and poet. He was a genial, whole-hearted man, and he and I kept up an intimate acquaintance until his death. He was a man of infinite wit and humor, and a universal favorite. His biography has been published, and extensively read. He died in the West Indies, and his remains were brought home for burial. He was not studious in college, and seemed to be indifferent about learning. I have seen him scribble verses during recitation, and he was usually unprepared in his lessons. But in after years he made himself a good scholar. His wife was an incurable invalid, and he had no children. He had abundant leisure for study. He was ungainly in person, and far from being " one of your handsome men." In all other respects he was a model man.

There were others in that class who rose to some distinction, such as John Young, who became President of Danville College, in Kentucky; Erskine Mason, son of the President, W. R. Williams, and others.

In college Dr. Mason taught rhetoric, and lectured on Horace like a preacher does on a chapter of the Bible. His instruction was rich with facts and anecdotes of the most interesting character.

His paralysis affected his mind to some extent, and made his reading imperfect, although his thoughts were usually solid and often sparkling.

Vethake taught mathematics, astronomy and chemistry. Spence taught Greek, and McClellan metaphysics. He was an eccentric genius, and many humorous stories were told about him. He was careless about his personal appearance, and slovenly in his dress, and rather indifferent about the common courtesies of life; but he had a kind disposition, and was indulgent toward his pupils. One night he was present at an exhibition of nitrous oxide gas in the court house, got up by two strolling Yankees. I took the gas and immediately began spouting Shakespeare vociferously. Next day on entering the class-room I stumbled and nearly fell. McClellan was in his chair, and exclaimed, " Morris, still under the influence of gas?" He seldom preached, although everybody was delighted in hearing him, and I believe that was the reason he rarely gratified them. The following story is told of him: One Sunday morning he was on his way on horseback to a country church, where he had been announced to preach. Some people, not knowing him, overtook him, and after riding together for some time he asked where they were going. " We are going to hear Prof. McClellan, of Carlisle, preach; he's a mighty preacher, and we advise you to go with us." Instead of fulfilling the appointment, he turned his horse's head towards town, and did not go to preach.

We were allowed many more privileges than at Princeton, and the effect was salutary.

Dr. Mason was an enthusiastic admirer of Alexander Hamilton, and ministered to him after he was shot by Burr. He would take every occasion to bring Hamilton into his lectures, and once, where Horace says of some one, " Idem extinctus amabitur," he applied these words to his favorite with deep emotion, and even with tears.

He would sometimes stop in the campus and look at us playing foot-ball, and once said, " Ah, young men, I wish I could play with you!" We all revered the feeble old man, even if we did sometimes laugh at his foibles.

The Rev. Benjamin Keller was at that time pastor of the Lutheran church, whose service I often attended when he preached English. Little did I then expect that before many years I would become intimately associated with him in church work, as I afterwards was. Although he was not what was called a strong man, yet he was what is better, a good man, and had the esteem of everybody. He did much better service in the church than many a man more gifted and more learned, and has left a name fragrant with memories of the most pleasing character. It was in Mr. Keller's church where I first heard the Rev. B. Kurtz preach, with whom in after years I became so closely connected. I had once seen him before at my mother's house during a Synod at York when I was a boy. I was too

young for him to notice me, for I was 11 and he was
24 years of age. In subsequent years we became
co-workers in many church projects. He acquired
a wide influence in the church, and in many respects
he was a strong man.

As far back as I can remember, I had what may
be called the religious sentiment deeply implanted
in me. My mother's teaching, prayers and example
impressed me strongly, and even in the gayety of
youthful life God was not altogether absent from my
mind. I was a conscientious church-goer all my
life, but I never until this time made what is ecclesiastically called a profession of religion.

It was at Dickinson that my mind was fully made
up to be a practical Christian, but it would not be
important to say what were my previous exercises
of mind before I came to the final decision. A considerable number of students took the same position.
The lamented death of James Mason, a son of the
President, who had graduated somewhere else, but
who was now living with his father, had a powerful
influence on our minds, and to that melancholy
event was traced the deep religious interest that
ensued. He was a young man, highly esteemed,
although few of us knew him personally. We all
attended his funeral, and as some of us were carrying
the coffin out of the house the deeply afflicted father
uttered, in a deep, sepulchral tone, " Tread softly,
young men, tread softly, for you bear the body of the
Holy Ghost!" It was like a voice from the tomb,

and the effect was most impressive. I have often referred to this incident and quoted these words at the funeral of young men. Among the men whose attention was specially turned to practical religion on this occasion, and who united with the Episcopal church, was Samuel R. McCrosky, who afterwards became Bishop of Michigan, and who, after serving in that office many years, resigned it, and retired under a cloud.

We students held prayer-meetings in college, and most of us there made our maiden effort in leading in public prayer.

I joined the Belles-Lettres Society in college, and in fact re-organized it, for it had fallen into deep decay. I wrote an installation address to the candidates when admitted, but I do not know whether it has been retained.

It was at Carlisle that I began my career as a newspaper scribbler, which I have rather vigorously kept up ever since. I think it was in the Carlisle *Volunteer* that my maiden piece appeared, and it was upon the momentous theme of " The Time Lost in Visiting the Ladies!" When I saw my first contribution in print, I felt much bigger than on any subsequent like occasion.

On the occasion of some public exhibition of the college, I forget what, I made a speech upon a subject then agitating the public mind; I think it was the invasion of Spain by the French. I depicted the glories of ancient Spain in such rainbow colors, and so vehemently abused Napoleon, that some intemperate fellow in town, who was captain of a militia company, was so fired with military ardor and other exciting agencies, that he declared that if there were not a few objections in the way he would march his company to the relief of Spain, and drive the infamous invader from the country. Next morning his ambition was cooled off!

My graduation speech was on The Feudal System, a dull, dry subject, which I did not understand, and for which I got no credit, for it was a very stupid affair.

The academic gown was not worn at Dickinson as at Princeton, but what struck me as queer was that when Dr. Mason rose to confer on the class the degree of A. B. he put on his hat, and removed it as soon as the ceremony was over. Upon mentioning this fact to some one, he remarked that English judges when they sentenced a criminal to death always put on a black cap, and he mischievously observed that there might be some analogy between the two cases.

After graduation I went home; and now came the struggle. I had not fully decided to study for the ministry, and my conflict of mind was painful. I need not here give the details, but I finally determined for the pulpit, and then my mind was at rest.

There was nothing supernatural or even extraordinary in the circumstances of this, my '' call to the ministry.'' I thought that I had the religious qualifications—that is, I was a sincere believer, and wished to do good in the best way I could. I was in perfect health and of vigorous constitution. I had some of the attributes of a good speaker, and I thought that by culture I might make a fair preacher. I had means of my own, so that I need not be a burden on the Church; my brother was very anxious that I should study for the ministry, but neither he nor my mother ever urged it upon me. The Lutheran Church had less than 300 ministers at that time, and her sphere of activity was constantly enlarging, whilst the ministry was not multiplying in proportion. Providence had cast my lot within her limits, and I concluded that this was the field for me to work in, and I entered. This is the only " call to the ministry " I know anything of. The Church needed my services, I thought, and I cheerfully offered them. I regarded her need as equivalent to a call from her, and hence I concluded it was the divine will. The way to success in several other pursuits was open to me, but I was led into this way, and herein I continue, cheerful and contented, and perhaps to some extent useful.

From that time I gave myself entirely to the work, and made preparations accordingly. The question was, where should I study theology? There was no Lutheran Seminary, and my brother and I concluded it was not best, for the present at least, to go to Princeton. He wrote to Dr. Demme, of Philadelphia, and requested him to take me as a private pupil, and especially to learn German, which was at that time considered indispensable for a Lutheran minister, and should always be. But Dr. Demme declined, and we looked around. It was finally determined that I should go all the way to New Market, Shenandoah county, Va., where S. S. Schmucker was pastor, who made known his willingness to receive students as a sort of preparatory school for the seminary which he and a few others were meditating at that time. Here I was, fresh from college, and with a pretty fair education as it was considered in those days, but I was utterly unfit for any sort of business which required tact, calculation or attention. An errand boy in a country store had more knowledge of keeping accounts and managing things in general than I, with all my Greek and Latin. I have painfully felt this deficiency all through life, and just here there is a defect in our training. I have discovered that those of our ministers who had served in stores or any other secular business before they entered the ministry were always the best business men in Synod. They alone were competent to examine accounts, adjust mileage, disentangle knotty skeins, and give good advice on pecuniary matters. How much better it would be if every minister had a year's schooling in a commercial college, a bank or counting house. It would prevent many a stupid blunder in after life.

Mr. Schmucker was to be at Frederick shortly, in attendance on the General Synod, whither I went to meet him and to make arrangements, which I did.

He had prepared me for college, and he was now to become, for a while at least, my theological tutor. I was taught the orthodox system of faith from my earliest youth, and never was tempted to accept any other. I never had any difficulties of that character to encounter. It was my mother's faith, and I observed its sanctifying influences in her godly life, and that was enough for me. The peculiarities of the Lutheran faith, especially on the sacraments, were not taught me when I was young, and when I first came under the influence of teachers in later years I was led to the opposite direction, and I said and wrote and printed some things which I have regretted a thousand times. But I have changed my mind; it was a slow and gradual change, and perhaps on that account the more wise, and certainly the more permanent, and I am glad to witness so many evidences of a similar wholesome change in many of our ministers.

The first clear oral illustration of the Lutheran doctrine of the Lord's Supper was given to me by the Rev. Dr. J. G. Schmucker, of York, Pa. This was, I think, before I became a theological pupil of his son, who was trained by his father in the same faith, and vigorously maintained it in what is called the first edition of his translation of Storr and Flatt's Theology, but he afterwards abandoned it, and adopted the New England Zwinglian views. His teaching gradually brought me over to his opinions, for I was not well established in true Lutheranism;

4

but when I became free from his influence, and pursued independent research, I settled down in the true faith. This is the case with many others who were students in the seminary when Dr. S. S. Schmucker was theological professor. He himself became aware of this departure from his teachings before he died, and it grieved him exceedingly. He had done much towards securing the support, and perhaps also procuring parishes for some of these men, and he thought it hard that they should repudiate his instructions. Two of his three sons who entered the ministry became decided Lutherans of the straitest sort; his brother-in-law, the Rev. Dr. C. F. Schaeffer, was all his lifetime a staunch defender of the true faith; two of his sons-in-law, the Rev. A. Geissenhainer and the Rev. Dr. B. Sadtler, were equally devoted to it; some of his pupils, such as the Rev. Dr. Ziegler, Reuben Weiser, and all of those in connection with the Synod of Pennsylvania, as well as some others, subsequently repudiated the teaching of their professor on the subject of the sacraments.

Mr. Schmucker undoubtedly rendered great service to the Church in her struggles during the earlier period of his life. He had numerous followers, but they did not all adhere to him. He exercised a commanding influence in those days, and was easily regarded as the first man in the General Synod. He was the founder of the Seminary and College at Gettysburg, and of other auxiliaries to the benefit of the Church.

CHAPTER III.

BEHOLD me now installed in a straggling obscure Shenandoah county village of 400 inhabitants, who were exceedingly plain and uncultivated for the most part, but the majority were good specimens of American German thrift and frugality. There was no trade except that furnished by two small stores. The surplus farm products were conveyed to Fredericksburg or Alexandria in cumbrous wagons. There was one school, two or three physicians, and there was no use for a lawyer. There were no beggars, and few flagrant crimes were committed by the white inhabitants. The slaves were generally well treated by their masters, who were of German descent. There were several families in the hamlet and several in the neighborhood of a culture advanced beyond that of the majority. They were all hospitable and kind. There was little of what was even then called wealth. The state of public morality was far above that of many other villages in Virginia where the German element did not prevail. There were few cases of gross, habitual intemper-

ance, and I do not remember a single arrest for a
gross crime during my residence of twenty months.

The church was in a low condition before Mr.
Schmucker took charge of it, a few years previous
to my going there.   The preaching had been exclusively German by the former pastor at least, and the
service had not been frequent.   The settlement of
the young minister was quite an event in the vicinity.
He was the only really educated pastor for 25 miles
around; his style of preaching was so fresh and interesting; he was so gentlemanly and neat in his
appearance and withal so good-looking, and unmarried besides, that he attracted general attention.
The parish consisted of several other small congregations, so that there was service only twice a month
in the village church.

There was a Methodist church, which had not
then arrived at perfect sanctification, and an old-
school, hard-shell, iron-clad Baptist conventicle,
which had not had all its actual sins washed away
by immersion.   It was served occasionally by an
honest old farmer named Hershberger, whose English was not of the purest classic, either in accent,
pronunciation, emphasis or grammar.   Immersion
and predestination, neither of which he understood,
were his unvarying themes.

There was a settlement of Tunkers in the neighborhood, the principal preacher of whom was a good
old man named Keagy.   He was universally respected for his blameless life, but he had not studied

theology. I occasionally went to their meetings in
the country, and whenever Father Keagy led the
worship he would sing a long metre tune to a common metre hymn, or vice versa, and the style of the
music may be imagined. Whenever he preached
English he always introduced Nathan's parable of
the ewe lamb, but the good old man's interpretation
was original and queer. He took the word ewe for
the popular diminutive e-wee, and absolutely thought
that Nathan was speaking of an e-wee, little bit of a
lamb!! And yet nobody silently laughed but myself. I presume most of them thought it was all
right.

This is the original home of the Henkel family,
whose name has figured in the church for many
years. Old Paul Henkel, the patriarch of the family,
was living when I went there, but died a few months
afterwards. He was a venerable old gentleman,
and had done some good missionary work in the
earlier part of this century in Virginia and North
Carolina. He had not, for many years, attended
the old Pennsylvania Synod, of which he had long
been a member, and became specially estranged
when the Eastern Synods joined the General Synod,
which he regarded as a sort of antichrist. Four or
five of his sons were ministers, but I never saw any
of them (the preachers) except Ambrose, who lived
at New Market, and Charles, whom I met afterwards
at Germantown, Ohio. There was a great deal of
energy, and some talent, in the family. They kept

themselves aloof from the Eastern Synods, and were the originators of what was called the Tennessee Synod, and maintained that they were the only genuine Lutherans in the country. I am speaking of seventy years ago. Since that time some members of the Henkel family have become very useful men in the Church, and have contributed a good deal to its theology and literature by the printing of useful books. There are several laymen of that household who have become influential men, and are patrons of higher education and of progress. Several of them have become eminent physicians and men of great worth. Some years ago some members of that family published, at their own venture, an English translation of the Book of Concord. The Church was hardly ready for it, but the enterprise showed commendable zeal in the good cause. It was not well translated, but still creditable for that day and for the men who executed it. I presume that Prof. Jacobs' new translation will entirely supersede it, but still let all honor be given to the Henkels for their pluck and energy.

About the year 1877 several of the surviving members of the family, on their own responsibility, began the publication of a weekly religious journal called "Our Church Paper," which has sustained itself to the present day.

I had never before lived in a place where there was no first-class school, no reading room, no newspaper printed, no debating society, no band of music, no musical parties, no picnics or excursions, no public lectures, not even a show or exhibition of jugglers.

It was a strange transition for me, who was fresh from the refined society of Carlisle, to be thrown among these people, and yet I by no means underestimated their worthiness. Providence led me there, and perhaps I learned practical lessons of life which have been of service ever since.

Mr. Schmucker was a widower at that time, and had much leisure. He was a laborious student, and was engaged in translating Storr and Flatt's Theology, which was published at Andover. He was often absent for four or five weeks, during which I read such books as he gave me, but without order or system and perhaps much profit.

My fellow students were John P. Cline and George Schmucker, both of that county; Samuel K. Hoshour, of York county, Pa.; Wm. Keil, an honest, uncouth German, and John Reck. Cline was a man of good common sense. He had learned the carpenter trade, and was a robust, large-framed man. He and George Schmucker had never been out of Shenandoah county, and knew little of the outside world. They still cherished many of the prejudices and errors of the people among whom they had been brought up. They believed in ghosts, omens, dreams, and witchcraft, but gave up these silly notions as they advanced in intelligence.

Cline became a very useful minister, and served

churches in Maryland and Virginia, and died after more than thirty years of successful work. He left a large family not unprovided for, and one of his sons is in our ministry. He was a man of solid character and blameless living. John Reck was a brother of that most excellent of men, Abraham Reck. He was faithful in his work, and died in Ohio some time afterwards. He was the oldest of us except Keil, and of more religious experience. He had been reading with his brother at Winchester, and had also preached. He came to us under the influence of some feelings and opinions, which he abandoned before long. George Schmucker was the son of the Rev. Nicolas Schmucker, of Shenandoah county, and a cousin of our teacher. He had no education when he joined us, and was exceedingly rustic, but he had some brains and improved fast. He died in 1886 in southeast Virginia, and belonged to a small Synod of very staunch Lutherans. A son of his is in our ministry in Ohio. Samuel Hoshour was from York county, Pa., and had studied some Latin and Greek. He was not destitute of talent, and was an earnest Christian man. He was subject to severe attacks of hypochondria, and would sometimes alarm us and the neighborhood by his exclamations of anguish and fear. After serving several parishes he joined the Campbellites, was rebaptized, went to Indiana, was elected professor in one of their schools, and became quite a great man among them. He died in December, 1883. Keil was a

German oddity. I judge he was nearly forty years of age when he joined us—sincere, rather intelligent, by turns good-natured and violent in his temper. He made good progress, for he was incessantly at his books, and always ready for an argument. He died in northwest Pennsylvania.

I have thought it well to give these faint sketches of men who, seventy years ago, prepared for the Church in such a group as this.

After some months of study Mr. Schmucker allowed us to preach in the country school-houses, and I regard it as a useful discipline for sober-minded students. We held Sunday-School, and once had as many as 85 scholars. We also had prayer-meetings in the old log church and in private houses, and we had some curious experiences with a few women who we thought were "under conviction." We practiced the old "pray on, sister," system, and were real Methodists as far as that went, and with the same unstable results.

These untrained young men were, of course, obliged to learn the elements of higher education, and our teacher, to save time, I suppose, by not having more than one class, put us all together; and here was I, with my college diploma in my pocket and graduated with honor, absolutely reciting Greek grammar and the elements of natural philosophy and other primary school studies with young men who did not know the letters of the Greek alphabet nor the first principles of any science! I was often indignant, and the reminiscence is painful to this day. I once alluded to it in a meeting of the Seminary Directors years afterwards. The professor evidently understood my allusion, but made no reply.

On one occasion when I was speaking in a prayer-meeting a woman fainted, which, of course, occasioned some disturbance, and our Methodist friends said that there was now evidence that there was some life in the church, for a woman had fainted under the preaching!!! But when shortly after I stopped in the middle of a prayer because I was dreadfully annoyed by the holy groaning of a Methodist brother, they changed their minds, and denounced us as cold and dead!!!

It was at a Sunday afternoon Methodist meeting where I first saw old Paul Henkel, whom I was surprised to see there, and who was seated, by way of honor, "in the altar," as they called it. A Boanerges named Reily, of gigantic stature and build, and with lungs corresponding, declaimed. It was like the "voice of many waters" tumultuously rolling over rocks on the seashore; he yelled and screamed to about a hundred of us as if he were addressing five thousand at a camp-meeting. The effect upon Mr. Henkel's nerves was singular and ludicrous. He writhed in his chair as if sitting on hot coals; his countenance was distorted into shapes the most absurd; he seemed at one time to be laughing, and then again crying, and appeared to suffer an agony unspeakably severe.

During a portion of the time spent here I conducted a Latin correspondence with an old Princeton friend named Buzzard, originally from Georgetown, D. C. He afterwards moved to Ohio, and changed his name to Franklin. He was a mathematical genius, and I believe was an engineer in Ohio. Thirty-five years after this, when I was in the Peabody Institute, a young man and young lady came in and introduced themselves as his children, they having called at his particular request. It was gratifying to be thus remembered by an old college friend. His son was an Episcopal student of divinity, and the daughter was soon afterwards married.

I wrote several sermons for one of our boys, and also a love letter, which I was happy to learn resulted in a complete reconciliation, for he and his lady friend had quarreled; but they were never married.

At that time in Virginia every able-bodied man was obliged to turn out and work one day upon the public highway, or get a substitute. We all turned out, I for the fun of it, and worked some hours in loading carts and digging dirt. If I had hired a substitute, I would have been denounced as proud and having no religion. I made a holiday of it, but I can now say that for one day I was a highwayman in Virginia!!!

I should have said that during the twenty months I stayed at New Market I read a good deal in Buddaeus and Hollaz, went through Prideaux, Campbell's Gospels, Horne's Introduction, Reid's Philosophy, Mosheim's Church History, Bible History, Jahn's Archæology, and some others not remembered, besides writing frequent compositions, essays, skeletons, etc., etc. Our teacher gave us a short course of lectures, of which we took notes, and all this in addition to the Greek grammar and elements of natural philosophy aforesaid. He had studied for some time at Princeton Seminary, and introduced among us, his pupils, some practices prevalent in that school. One of them was the observance of the first Wednesday of every month as a day for special prayer and meditation. All study was laid aside, and it was a sort of half sacred, holy day, which was, however, not observed by himself, nor by us to any special profit. I looked upon it as a piece of affected Puritanism, and paid no regard to it.

On going to Princeton Seminary afterwards I found the custom in vogue. The Book says, " Six days shalt thou labor," but these people say, " No, that is not right; five days shalt thou labor in one of the weeks of the month, and in that week thou shalt have two Sabbaths." For years I could not shake off the unscriptural feeling that the first Wednesday of the month had a sort of sanctity attached to it. I think we had better be satisfied with divine ordinances, and let human inventions alone.

I do not think it was ever introduced at Gettysburg by the same professor.

At New Market game was plenty. Even bears

and deer were shot in the neighboring mountains; squirrels, quail and pheasants abounded within a mile of our house, but I presume things have changed since the increase of population and the introduction of the railroad. But strange to say I never saw a fishing-rod, or anybody using one in the Shenandoah.

Our teacher once showed us a Review of Buckland's "Reliquiæ Diluvianiæ," which had lately come out, and created an immense sensation, and as late as July, 1880, I wrote a little article for the *Observer*, of which the following is an extract. One of the young Henkels had sent me a pamphlet describing a cave, which gave occasion to it:

"I was a boy resident of New Market when Buckland's Reliquiæ Diluvianiæ first appeared. This was many years ago; but having read a review of that book, I was fired with an enthusiasm for cave exploration and the collection of what we then considered antediluvian remains, and certain evidences of the Noachic deluge. That idea is long since exploded—not that of the deluge, but that cave bones afford any proof of it. Well, several other stout young fellows and I were told of a cave several miles south of the village, and, arming ourselves with pick-axe and shovel, we started one Saturday afternoon on a scientific tour—and we knew about as much of science as we did of the Telugu language. But we entered and digged, and collected a pile of bones, but whether they were human, or reptilian, or bovine, or lupine, or asinine, we did not know; but we were desperately fatigued. We did not proceed very far, for we were afraid that some spiteful gnome or Shenandoah county spook (for they were believed in at that time) might rush out upon us from some Tartarean crevice, for so ruthlessly invading his subterranean dominion."

In the summer of 1882, more than fifty years after my residence in New Market, I visited it upon the invitation of a society connected with the Polytechnic School to deliver an oration. I was kindly received by everybody; I visited the old graveyard and the old house in which I studied, and various other places of interest in the vicinity, among them the cave, a few miles distant. I met several children of my old fellow-student, John P. Cline, who died some years ago. The town has made some improvements. We have two churches entirely English, and there are good schools, and several newspapers are published by the Henkels.

The following little incident might as well be mentioned in connection with my New Market career. It is one of many:

A young man of the village asked me to be his groomsman. We rode in company to Woodstock, the county seat, to get the marriage license. The clerk of the court required him to prove that he was 21 years of age. What was to be done? We were twenty miles from home, and the wedding was to take place next day. We were in a quandary. He at length thought of some old woman who was acquainted with his family, and he hastened to her for relief. She said she was willing to swear that his sister, younger than himself, was 22, but she would not swear that he was 21!!! I do not remember how it was arranged, but, at any rate, we got the license.

During a vacation at New Market I visited the Natural Bridge, and stopped one night at Lexington, at the house of Col. McClung, who kept the hotel. Dr. Alexander and his wife were on a visit there, for the Colonel was his brother-in-law. I introduced myself to the Doctor, observing that I had often heard him preach at Princeton when I was a student at Nassau Hall. He was very cordial, and expressed his gratification that I was studying theology with one of his former pupils, S. S. Schmucker. He made many inquiries concerning our Church.

That part of Virginia had been the field of his early labors in the ministry, where he was a popular young man. He told me many interesting incidents of his youthful career, and among others the following: He said he was once preaching in that neighborhood, and all of a sudden he came to a dead stop. He had lost his thread of argument, and did not recover it for about thirty seconds. There was an awful silence in the congregation, for apparently a deep impression had been made. Every eye was intently fixed upon him, and with almost breathless interest they waited for what was to come. He himself was confused almost to fainting, but he proceeded to talk in a bungling way, until he completely recovered his usual tranquillity. After service the most influential and intelligent gentleman present, Col. ———, approached him and congratulated him warmly, exclaiming, "Capital! wonderful! I never heard it so well done before! Just at the proper time—just long enough! What a deep impression it made! Wonderful!" Mr. A. inquired, "Why, Colonel, what do you mean?" "Why, sir," he replied, "that pause, sir, that pause! Never heard it so well done! Really, Mr. A., I did not know you had that much rhetorical art!" I do not know whether he informed the Colonel that the pause, which was so impressive to him and others, was a blundering act of forgetfulness, but he told the story to me with great glee. When I became a pupil of Dr. Alexander, several years afterwards at Princeton, I remember him telling the class, in his homiletical lectures, that if we should "lose the thread of our discourse," not to stop, but talk right on at random, for we would soon recover, and few people would observe the blunder. He did not, however, tell us the anecdote above.

A singular case of kleptomania was developed just at that time in that vicinity, which was talked of by everybody, and made a great noise. I would not speak of it, but it concerned an old classmate of mine, who was a Presbyterian minister in that county. His young and highly accomplished wife took anything she could lay her hands upon, however trifling. Even while singing pious hymns at the bedside of the sick, she would take thimbles, needles, napkins, medicine spoons, and everything which she could conveniently hide. A terrible malady—for such it really is. I have known several cases of this infirmity, and I suppose they are very hard to cure.

In 1825 our teacher married his second wife, and, having been previously elected professor in the Theological Seminary that was to be opened some months afterwards in Gettysburg, he never returned to New Market to live, but staid with his father-in-law, seven miles east of the village. Hoshour and I were the only students left, and the teacher would occasionally come to town to hear us recite, after a fashion. I do not remember why I did not leave before, but I presume it was vacation time at other Seminaries, and I thought I might as well spend a few months there as anywhere else. I am certain it was not for the benefit of the teaching.

He resigned his place as pastor, and Hoshour was chosen in his place, and accepted it. He was anxious to visit his friends in York county, Pa., before he began his pastoral work, and he and I bought a horse, and we traveled to York, "ride and tie," as it was called. One of us was to ride six miles ahead while the other walked, and would find the horse at a designated place, but usually we kept in company. My luggage had been sent ahead by stage.

Thus endeth the chapter of my career at New Market.

STUDENT LIFE AT NAZARETH.

The question again was, What is now to be done? Our own Seminary was not opened, and I did not care about going to Princeton just then, and I would not listen to several propositions that were made to me from other quarters to settle as a pastor. Upon consideration it was resolved that I should spend the winter among the Moravians, studying German and Hebrew. I thought that a pure German was spoken by them, and probably nothing else, and that surely one of their men would teach me Hebrew.

I took letters from the Moravian minister at York, named Leffler, and proceeded to Lititz; but they would not take me as a pupil, and advised me to go to Bethlehem. I went to Bethlehem, and had no better success; thence to Nazareth, where I was received. A young man named Shulze, who has since become a bishop,* agreed to teach me Hebrew, and I expected to learn German more from conversation than from books; but I found that English was almost exclusively spoken by the divinity students, and I, of course, learned little more than I knew.

My mother, who had a most exalted idea of Moravian piety, inspired me with the same sentiment, and I went among them with the expectation that I would there be about as near heaven as any place on earth. From report I was led in advance to admire the simplicity of their manners, the uprightness of their lives, and their missionary zeal, but I found they were people of like passions with others. They were trained to regard themselves as foreign missionaries whenever and wherever the church required their services. There was no question, "Shall I go? Does the Lord want me among the

* Died in 1885, aged 80 years.

heathen?'' but every one felt himself already called to the work, and only waited for Providence, through the church, to designate the field. One day word came that a missionary was wanted in Barbadoes, in the place of one who had died. The lot fell upon Mr. Zorn, who immediately set to work, and was ready in less than two hours. But Brother Zorn was a single man, and at that time they did not send out unmarried men. Brother Zorn was not engaged, and had no preference—perhaps had never visited any lady. The church soon settled that matter, and, by lot it was declared to be the Lord's will that Sister Elizabeth, at Bethlehem, should be Brother Zorn's wife, whom he had probably never seen. They were married, and went.

While I did not find the heaven on earth I so ardently expected, I spent a very happy and profitable winter among them, and still cherish pleasing remembrances of that remarkable people. In those days none but Moravians lived in Nazareth and Bethlehem, and perhaps in Emmaus; but at present, and for some years past, they have sold lots and houses to people of other churches, and the distinctive and exclusive Moravianism of these places no longer prevails. We have several churches there, and several of our ministers live there.

It was in January, 1825, that I went to Nazareth, and remained there several months. Mr. Shulze came to my room in the hotel where I boarded, and heard my lessons. I became acquainted with no persons except the divinity students, and some of the teachers, and a few retired old ministers. The students were a cheerful set of young men, whose manners and habits were very different from what I had been led to expect, and which would have given great offence to many persons. My training was of a contrary character, and perhaps not more consistent with the Christian profession. Their observance of the Lord's Day was very different from what I had been taught, but I would not say that my teaching was more Scriptural. None of these young men visited young ladies, in which recreation so many theological students of other schools lose so much time, and, some of them at least, are beguiled into premature and injudicious matrimonial engagements, or what is worse, into the violation of previous ones. A sad history might be written on this subject. These Nazareth young divinities could not become engaged, for they saw no young ladies, and besides, as the church arranged such affairs, they had nothing actively to do with it. Hence, there was no precious time lost in writing frequent letters of doubtful propriety, no money spent for presents which should have been laid out in books, no dressing beyond their ability to pay, and no extravagant patronizing of confectioners' shops. I wonder whether some of our young men, who have hurried into such tender alliances, have not wished that the church had had the arrangement of such matters, at least as far as their case was concerned.

I never ascertained what was their curriculum of theological study, never having been invited into the lecture room, and seeing no programme. They were very orthodox, and recognized the Augsburg Confession as their Creed. Their own ecclesiastical history is interesting; the labors of Zinzendorf in this country were abundant and successful, although our own earlier missionaries contemporary with him here do not always speak most favorably of him (see Hallische Nachrichten); but perhaps this may have arisen from jealousy, and supposed interference with their work.

When I was at New Market I read Heckenwelder's book on his labors among the North American Indians in Pennsylvania, which interested me exceedingly. I conceived a romantic admiration of him and his fellow-workmen. One day when I was straying through the beautiful graveyard, I saw the name of Zeisberger upon a tomb-stone, and it was the grave of the veritable man whom I revered for his missionary zeal.

Whenever there was a death in the congregation it was announced from the steeple by a dirge from the band, and on festivals, New Year or Easter, there were solemn religious services held in the cemetery, with instrumental music; and yet this people, with all their purity of life, their self-denying misssionary activity, their unaffected piety, would not be regarded as good Christians by some because they did not practice a puritanic observance of what is called the Sabbath, instead of the Lord's Day.

I laid a pretty good foundation of Hebrew, but I made no progress in German, for I seldom heard anything but English spoken except from the old people, and I saw few of them. The public service and worship were in German.

I left them with regret, having conceived a very exalted idea of their purity of life and Christian zeal.

THE GENERAL SYNOD AT FREDERICK, MD., IN 1825.

I was a looker-on at the meeting of the General Synod at Frederick, in 1825, at which only three Synods were represented,—Maryland and Virginia, united in one at that time, West Pennsylvania and North Carolina; and there were only eight clerical members! Times are changed, and we with them!!

At this meeting the Rev. Benjamin Kurtz, at that time pastor at Hagerstown, Md., was appointed to go to Europe to collect funds for the Theological Seminary which was to be established. He went, and never was any work more laboriously and conscientiously performed than this mission. He was absent two years and brought home about $12,000 in money, collected with great difficulty, and a large number of books, many of which were of no value, and now encumber the shelves of the Seminary library; but Mr. Kurtz was in duty bound to accept everything offered to him. The history of this mission is interesting, and will be found in the early volumes of the Lutheran *Intelligencer*, in my "Fifty Years," and in my History of the Seminary, in the *Evangelical Review*, 1876.

Rev. B. Kurtz stated to Synod that a certain Mr. Rowles, a Yankee schoolmaster, in Hagerstown, who had wormed himself into the good graces of Rev. K., proposed to write a history of the Lutheran Church in the United States. He could not read nor speak a word of German; he was not reared among our people, and was an entire stranger to our theology, church polity, and everything else that a historian should know. Mr. Kurtz injudiciously encouraged the man in his presumptuous purpose, and urged the Synod to do the same; but Mr. S. S. Schmucker, more keen-sighted and intelligent on this subject, and aware of the utter incompetency of the man for the work, quietly and adroitly got rid of the whole affair, and without offending Mr. Kurtz, by offering the sensible resolution that Mr. Rowles be requested to spend several years in collecting materials for his history!!! This was the last of it.

I remained until after the meeting of the Synod, when Mr. Schaeffer, the pastor, requested me to preach. I now occasionally meet a rather oldish gentleman who reminds me of that sermon of over 60 years ago. He says my text was, " Woe unto them that are at ease in Zion." He remembers more about it than I did, or cared about doing myself.

After I had preached this sermon somewhere—I will not say where—the pastor rose and flattered his people by the assurance that the sermon just preached could not be applied to them, for everybody knew they were not "asleep in Zion," but wide awake, and then he proceeded to enumerate their Christian virtues and convinced them that they were the best people in all the country round. It was easy to convince them of that, and no wonder their minister was a very popular man. A few years after, our Synod met in the same church, and when, at the preparatory service, I made some common-place remarks on the questions, What am I? What am I doing? Whither am I going? the pastor rose and answered my questions for his people by saying that they were a very good people, doing their duty, and were fast on their way to heaven!!! Blessed people! Happy pastor!

STUDENT LIFE AT PRINCETON SEMINARY, 1825–1826.

I left Nazareth in the Spring of 1825, and a short time after proceeded to Princeton, but I could not be admitted because I had neglected to take a cer-tificate of church membership with me. This was indispensable. I immediately wrote to York and the Rev. J. G. Schmucker sent me one, although he had not confirmed me; but the Faculty at Princeton were satisfied with it, thus showing it to be a mere form. This consumed four or six days, for the mail did not travel as fast in those days as at present, and there was no telegraph.

I was admitted to the Senior Class, as a sort of "Irregular," not having pursued the same course with it in its last term; but I enjoyed all its advantages and was to all intents admitted "ad eundem," on a perfect equality, without, however, the privilege of graduation. I was also accorded the favor of attending the lectures of all the other professors, omitting some of the hours of the Senior Class; for instance, Dr. Hodge's Hebrew and Greek, and a few other subjects, which I had gone over, and in one of which I was really in advance of the Senior Class. I do not mean that I knew it better, but because they were just at that time studying it, and I had already gone over it. I met here eight or ten men whom I had known in Princeton and Dickinson Colleges, so that I felt perfectly at home, and went to work with a will. I was soon elected a member of the Round Table Club, a sort of intellectual aristocrats, some of whom were not superior to others outside. We met once a week to discuss high theology, and it was considered quite a distinction to be elected, and of course it created jealousy in others. The number was small, very select and very consequential! I do not know whether the Club has been perpetuated. As well as I can remember no minutes of proceedings were kept, and secrecy was observed. I do not think it ever amounted to much, but there was a ludicrous display of learning and an affectation of profound wisdom.

Professor Hodge had a private class of more advanced students of Hebrew, which I joined, and I remember the surprise which my pronunciation and accent occasioned the first time I was called on to recite. I gave it the deep, guttural, sonorous tone, according to the German style, and they the flat American, which deprives it of half of its energy.

Soon after I entered, I was sent for one morning by Professor Hodge, much to my surprise. I went to his study and found that he wanted me to help him in some German translation he was making for a theological journal he was editing, but I could render him very little assistance.

In 1880, a life of Dr. Hodge, by his son, was published, which is a model biography of a model man. How charmingly it delineates the character of that most excellent man, and how attractive the book to all readers of taste and intelligence!

In an old letter of mine to my dear friend, the Rev. Dr. C. P. Krauth, Sen., I find the following account of a visit I made to Dr. Hodge, several years after my student life at Princeton:

"I was received with great kindness by the Professors, and am staying with Dr. Hodge, who insisted upon it. You know that for seven months he has been upon his back, on account of a diseased thigh joint, but he still lectures to his class who are seated around his bed, whilst he reads and expounds . . . He is an enthusiastic admirer of Germany, and you may well imagine the tenor of our conversation. We spoke of men, manners and things, professors and students, books and authors, church and state, mind and matter, kings and subjects, nobles and ignobles, orthodox and heterodox, and many other things. He tells me that a man may become as learned in a garret in America as in a garret in Halle, and that the only advantage in going to a German university is in learning the men and the state of opinion in the theological world, the modes of instruction, and the benefit of seeing and conversing with distinguished scholars . . . He says that Gesenius reads his printed Isaiah to his class, and when asked why he does not recommend his pupils to buy the book and read it for themselves he replies, 'How many can afford to do it? perhaps ten in three hundred.' . . He told me many anecdotes of the professors, their affairs, sayings, quarrels and jealousies. When he saw Marheinecke, of Berlin, the latter said of Halle, 'Da herschet die lebendige Dummheit.'"

Drs. Miller, Alexander and Hodge were the only professors in my time, and they were the excellent of the earth. Dr. Miller lectured on Church History. He knew not a word of German, and could not avail himself of German writers, even at that day, unless they had written in Latin. His lectures on other branches were good, but his manner was cold and unsympathetic, and did not arouse the enthusiasm of his pupils. Dr. Alexander, as a lecturer, was of a different character, and Hodge, then a comparatively young man, was sprightly and attractive.

One hot summer afternoon, during one of Dr. Miller's lectures on Church History, he was interrupted, and the rest of us excited to a laugh, by a loud, sonorous snore, which came from the son of a college President. The Doctor stopped, and remarking, with a deep-drawn sigh, "Ah! how much we have to bear in this world," proceeded with his lecture.

On a visit to Princeton some years afterwards I congratulated the Doctor upon his healthy appearance. "Yes," said he, "I feel much better since

I've quit drinking!" Observing my surprise, he continued, "For some years, by the advice of my physician, I drank every day just one glass of the best wine I could buy in New York, but I have quit it, and feel much better ever since."

I had scarcely got well settled at Princeton when I was invited to preach at Philadelphia by the people who subsequently became St. Matthew's congregation, but I refused. I was afraid that perhaps I might be tempted by the flattering prospect of things to rush into the ministry before I had finished my Seminary course. I was urged to accept the call, for it really amounted to that, by S. S. Schmucker, who had heard of it, which perhaps was well meant, but which displeased me much, for I was still writhing under some unhappy reminiscences.

Theological questions were discussed in general meeting in the presence of the professors, who would then sum up the arguments and give their own opinion. On one occasion I prepared myself particularly well, and was highly complimented by Dr. Miller, far beyond my deserving. This brought me into some trouble, for after that I was frequently requested to open the discussion of questions by men who had been appointed, but I constantly refused, for I knew I was not competent to the task, and was afraid of losing the good character I had gained. Some of the questions discussed at these meetings were, "Is Adam a federal head of his posterity?" "Is regeneration the effect of moral suasion?" "Is God bound to execute his vindicatory justice?" "Are the prophecies relating to the future condition of the Jews to be understood literally or figuratively?" and others of a similar character. There were not a few clear-headed, intelligent and well-educated young fellows among us, who handled these questions with great ability.

On one occasion I remember that the question was of a profoundly metaphysical character. Some of the disputants complained that it was too abstract and unpractical. The well known theologian, George Bush, who had not yet become a Swedenborgian, was present on a visit, and in reference to the complaint made about the subject coolly observed that "dogs bark at strangers," and then went on to discuss the matter most learnedly.

There is a queer incident related of this eccentric genius in the "Life of Hodge," p. 53. He was once overwhelmed with a fear of the desertion of God because he had killed a mouse.

High Calvinism was in the ascendency, but there were also a few Hopkinsians. I was considered as thoroughly unorthodox, because I could not adopt the extreme Calvinistic views on predestination and their Puritanic (not Calvinistic) opinions concerning the sacraments and "The Sabbath." They did not like it at all when I asked them why they did not adopt Calvin's opinions on all subjects, particularly on the Sabbath, the Lord's Supper, and other points. On the Lord's Supper they were Zwinglian, but really most of them knew very little upon the subject. These men were honest and upright, as far as I knew, and general harmony prevailed among them, although often there were fierce theological conflicts.

More than three-fourths of them were beneficiaries, of whom some dressed much better than I did; others were meagre enough in their wardrobe, but that depended upon the church which supported them. To one of our dandy charity students I once loaned $40, but he has forgotten to return it to this day. He never amounted to anything in the church, and for many years he was a clerk in a government office in Washington. He never was elected as pastor of any church.

As I said before, the students were men of blameless lives, but their views of some subjects seemed strange to me. Many would talk on all manner of matters on Sunday, and laugh and joke, and yet these same men would not write a letter to their parents even on that day, because writing implied work. I never argued the question with them, for it did not concern me. I have before stated a similar fact in relation to some pious college students in Nassau Hall.

Some of our own church ministers who lived in towns where Presbyterianism prevailed also conceived similar views of the sanctity of " The Sabbath," as I experienced some years afterwards. One Sunday morning during very hot weather I was sitting in the front parlor of one of our ministers in a prominent inland town. The shutters were closed, and I threw them open to enjoy fresh air. The pastor rather violently remonstrated, as though I had committed a grievous fault, and said, " Don't you know it is the Sabbath, and what will the Presbyterians say who pass by here on their way to church when they see my shutters open?"

I also remember once giving offence to a professor of one of our colleges because in a Wednesday night lecture before the students I said " I did not think it was a violation of the ' Sabbath ' for a man to shave himself on that day." *Sancta simplicitas!*

It was a fact then as it is now among theological students, that more than three-fourths of them were engaged to be married. There was consequently much writing that was neither theology nor sermons. I know of two who compared their letters to their absent friends to determine which could write the most ardently and lovingly. It is said that one of them acknowledged himself conquered before the half of his competitor's letter was read. I am satisfied from observation that these premature and often inconsiderate engagements sadly interfere with the happiness and success of theological students. Many precious hours are wasted in vapid correspondence; much annoying anxiety is suffered; jealousies and rivalries are often aroused; in not a few instances the long engagements end in separations. Not a few young men, as their education advances and their experience is extended, discover that the choice of their juvenile years was not judicious, and they change their minds to their own discredit and the disappointment and wretchedness of the lady in question. Some, in mingling with society, find ladies more refined, intelligent, handsome, and perhaps better endowed with worldly goods, and reject their first love, and thus occasion scandal. These early engagements also influence some men to leave the Seminary, and ask for license before they have finished the prescribed course of studies. Some of these men who were very poor were engaged to ladies of some means, who were the chief agents of securing their support. Perhaps it was the only return they could give, though it had necessarily to be confined to one of the sisters. I do not know what the others thought of it.

There was an ardent home mission spirit among some of them, and one of them, who had been up in eastern Pennsylvania, came back burning with zeal, and proposed sending missionaries among the Germans of that region to rescue them from their heathenism! I modestly asked whether the men whom he thought should go spoke German? I set forth so many other practical difficulties in the way that the plan was given up, although I did not think it was ever seriously entertained. I admitted that the state of practical piety in that region might be improved.

I conducted a Bible class and a Sunday-school in the country, and preached several times in a school-house.

I remember that my rather animated style of un-read preaching was wonderfully pleasing to the Jersey country people at that school-house. It was not more than a mile or two from the Seminary, yet the people were not more enlightened than the same class in Pennsylvania, who did not hear a Seminary bell every clear day in the year. They did not attend the Princeton church, and were well satisfied with the plainest kind of talk, especially if it was not read and was animated.

I remember that several of the students once staid all night at the house of the Rev. Mr. ———, the Presbyterian preacher, at a village a few miles east of Princeton. I think it was called Frogtown. There was a large, old-fashioned eight-day clock in the house, the strike of which was loud and sonorous, but which did not disturb the family, for they were used to it, but the terrific clang awoke me every time the clock struck till after midnight. I then silently arose, crept to the noisy machine and stopped the pendulum. This disarranged the routine of the whole house. The girls slept longer than usual, the breakfast was later, and everything else went wrong. They wondered what had happened to the clock, and they never found out.

Besides the lectures in the Seminary various other exercises were assigned to us. I remember that I was appointed to prepare a skeleton on " O death, where is thy sting?" Also an essay on Memoriter Preaching; The best Manner of Managing the Voice;

6

A Critique on Archbishop Secker as a Sermonizer. I also attended some lectures in the Middle class, and I heard Professor Patton, of the college, once a week on Greek tragedy.

I do not remember that one of the students read German, much less spoke it, except a German Reformed student from Eastern Pennsylvania, who spoke a barbarous dialect. It had not yet become the style to learn German.

I was one of four elected to make Bible Society speeches in the college chapel, where a few years before I had attended worship so often; but, alas! in a different state of mind. I made a decided hit, and the whole of it consisted in a story I told of an old Armenian bishop. I did not speak ten minutes, but I got much credit for what was really a poor performance. I dramatized the story, and gave it in my best style. It takes very little to move some audiences, especially when you go out of the old, horse-mill round, and give them something fresh in matter, but especially in manner.

About this time, an English elocutionist, named Barber, came along, who had classes in the Seminary. A report was started in town, by some women, that there was something wrong about his character. An indignation meeting was held in the college chapel, and Plumer and I were the only men who stood up in his defence. Plumer, in his speech, most effectively recited Shakespeare's "Who steals my purse steals trash," and so on. This was the same William S. Plumer who became a distinguished minister, author and professor, and who died in Baltimore, Md., in 1879 or 1880. When Plumer was pastor in Baltimore, 18 or 20 years before his death, he and I were very intimate. He went from there to be Professor in the Seminary at Allegheny City, Pa., where he was at the breaking out of the Rebellion. He was supposed to sympathize with the rebels, and he was compelled to leave that place. He was afterwards Professor at Columbia, S. C., until that school was disbanded. He came to Baltimore for medical treatment, and died in one of our hospitals. He was an eminently good man, and the writer of many good books.

I had frequent conversations with some students about joining our ministry, as furnishing opportunities of doing good which they thought their own church did not afford, but nothing ever came of it; and it is just as well, for I very seldom, in subsequent life, saw much good coming out of this sort of marriage with people not trained in our ways.

There was very little intercourse between the students and the town's people, and no visiting the ladies, for most of the students had ladies elsewhere to whom they owed special attentions.

During the spring vacation I did not go home, but remained and studied, excepting a short tour I made as far up the North River as West Point. On the boat I met a young man with whom I got into conversation, and found out that he was a student of one of our ministers in Pennsylvania. He was very verdant in experience and knowledge. He knew nothing whatever concerning the Church elsewhere, and uttered some very un-Lutheran sentiments. Some years afterwards I met this man in the Pennsylvania Synod, but he never was of any account. He defended the Zwinglian view of the Lord's Supper in an article in *The Review*; he neglected the Synod, and his name was finally dropped. On this voyage I saw another man of bad distinction. He was a small, thin, slovenly dressed man, who spoke to nobody, and seemed anxious to avoid everybody. He was brisk in his movements and restless in all his demeanor; he had a keen, piercing eye that really glistened; long, flaxen hair hung in negligent profusion over his shoulders; his face seemed wrinkled with care, and general inquietude marked the whole man. IT WAS AARON BURR! The boat passed within a mile of the bank of the Hudson, where, 22 years before, he killed General Hamilton in a duel, and that must have been a painful reminiscence.*

* During the meeting of The American Association of Science, at Boston, in August, 1880, the Hon. R. C. Winthrop invited four of us, Rev. Dr. Rogers, of London, Rev. Dr. Dalrymple, of Baltimore, Judge Speck, of St. Louis, and myself, to his magnificent villa in Brookline. Among his fine collection of pictures is a portrait of Alexander Hamilton, and while we were admiring it the conversation turned upon Aaron Burr. I happened to mention that I had seen Burr in 1826, on a steamboat, on the North River. Mr. Winthrop remarked, "I was on that boat at the same time and also saw Burr."

CHAPTER IV.

I HAD spent seven months at Princeton Seminary, and the class graduated. This was in 1826. I returned to York, and in October I went to Winchester, Va., where the Synod of Maryland and Virginia met, to be licensed. My examination was not severe; it was over in less than an hour. Mr. Krauth and Mr. D. F. Schaeffer principally conducted it, and I was unanimously accepted. I was asked to read the first few verses of Genesis in Hebrew, which I knew by heart, and the analysis of every word. I was asked only one question on the analysis of the first word, by a man who evidently knew nothing about it. Mr. Krauth was the only man present who could read the language. Mr. Schmucker was absent. They insisted upon my preaching, and I gave them a sermon on "Awake, thou that sleepest," etc. I was the only licentiate at the Synod in Winchester. In those days they were more rare than at present.

Immediately after my licensure, a party of a certain congregation disaffected with their minister, who was one of the best men living, but of whom they wanted to get rid because of his faithful preach-

(85)

ing, absolutely asked me whether I would come among them and establish a schismatic organization; but I was not the man to be employed in such a dis-honorable, unchurchly proceeding, and gave them my opinion in terms which did them good, I hope, although, of course, they were offended at me. I wrote to the minister and informed him of the con-spiracy against him.

On my way home I spent several days with Mr. Krauth at Martinsburg, where he was pastor, when an intimacy grew up between us, which continued to his lamented death at Gettysburg, in 1867.

In my "Fifty Years," p. 101, I have spoken at large of this honored, godly servant of Christ, whom I admired and loved more dearly than any other man, except my own brothers. He was a widower at the time of my visit to him, and a severe reader of miscellaneous books. He was highly respected by the people of every church for his perfect single-ness of heart, irreproachable conduct and amiable disposition.*

I also stopped at Hagerstown and preached for Mr. B. Kurtz. It was on this occasion that I at-tended the first church fair I ever saw; it was held in his lecture room. They have become almost universal at this present day, substituted sometimes

---

* In the Spring of 1885, his son, John Morris Krauth, of Get-tysburg, sent me a file of my letters to his father, written 40 years ago, from which I have drawn some interesting reminis-cences. I sent them to the Historical Society.

by excursions or dramatic and musical entertain-
ments, which fifty years ago would have been considered theatrical and of course highly objectionable. I returned to York and preached for Mr.
Schmucker in the large church. This was a trial;
all my old companions and other persons among
whom I had been reared were there; my mother
was there, but not a word did she say before or after.
I knew, however, that she was praying for me.
The only person besides myself who was at all apprehensive was my brother, Charles A. Morris,
whose sensitively nervous nature was sò excited by
fear of my utter failure that it was with difficulty
that he could force himself to church, and when
there he took a seat near the door so that he might
escape in a hurry in the event of my coming to a
dead halt and being compelled to leave the pulpit
in disgrace. It was the severest trial of his nervous
system that he ever encountered. I do not think
he slept a wink that night, and I am sure he ate
nothing during the preceding day.

Charles A. Morris was as pure a man as ever
lived. From his earliest youth he was devoted
to God, and through his long life of 82 years he exemplified all the virtues of Christianity. For over
50 years he was a Sunday-school teacher, and was
never absent from his post except when out of town,
which was seldom, or when he was sick. He was
most faithful and conscientious in the preparation
of his lessons, and usually wrote them out, as well

as his numerous addresses to his school. He had all the Sunday-school helps in the way of books and papers, and I found large piles of manuscript upon this subject among his effects. From his early manhood he began to be a helper of the poor, and I have a letter from one of the most eminent of our old ministers, who had become poor, acknowledging a liberal donation from him. This was many years ago, when my brother was yet a young man and not himself rich. The same may be said of many other deserving persons whom he aided in the same way. Multitudes of letters were found thanking him for timely donations. I once made a rough calculation, based on reliable data, and came to the conclusion that in the course of his life he gave away for charity over $80,000. One of his gifts to Pennsylvania College, at Gettysburg, was $20,000, besides other large sums to the Seminary. Many of his benefactions in money were not known until after his death.*

The Seminary at Gettysburg had in the meantime gone into operation, and I concluded to enter as a student and "wait for a call."

I did not offer myself to any vacant church, for I did not know any; vacancies were rare in those days; and again I resolved not to "run in advance of Providence." I thought that if the Lord wanted me anywhere He would open a door for me, and be-

---

* See Drs. Baum's and Weiser's estimate of him in "Fifty Years," p. 268.

sides I could afford to wait. There is a difference of opinion upon this subject among good men, some maintaining that a man wanting a place, whether he is at the time a pastor or not, is authorized to offer his services and secure the influence of brethren to get him the place. Others say wait for a direct call, without previous " candidating," as it is now designated. I know one vacant church which quite recently has had 43 applications, every one of which, except one, came from men who were pastors, and every one of whom thought it was the will of God that he should go there.

I entered in the fall of 1826 as a licentiate, and the only one in the institution, and thus for the third time I became the pupil of S. S. Schmucker—first, in the Academy at York; second, at New Market, Va., and third, in the Seminary. The present edifice (old building) had not been erected, and the recitations were heard in the old Academy.*

The men whom I met there as students were:

1. Henry Haverstick, who had been a fellow-student at Dickinson. He was a man of small stature, and gifted above the ordinary. For several years he was a useful pastor, and then conceived the idea of going to Germany to study. He went in 1832 or 1833, and remained nearly two years. I advanced him $60 for a series of letters he engaged to write for the *Observer*, of which I was editor.

* See my History of the Seminary, Evan. Review, Vol. IV., No. 4, 1876.

2. Lewis Eichelberger, afterwards pastor at Winchester, Va., then professor in the Theological Seminary of South Carolina, and who died during his service in that school. At Winchester he edited two volumes of The Lutheran Preacher in 1853-5. A list of his other writings may be seen in my Bibliotheca Lutherana. They consist of four pamphlets and six or eight review articles. He was a sensible, earnest man, rather prolix in his talk and preaching, but companionable and devoted to his work. He died in January, 1884.

3. David P. Rosenmiller, a York boy, whom I knew in our juvenile days. He served as pastor in several places in Pennsylvania. He was one of the northern pioneer ministers in southwest Virginia and North Carolina, and had much of what the Germans call "world experience." He began his studies with F. Schaeffer, of Frederick. He was a laborious worker, and secured the esteem of all his brethren. A son of his is in the Episcopal ministry. He died in September, 1880, while attending the East Pennsylvania Synod at Allentown.

4. Jacob Kaempfer was an honest, clear-headed, uncouth countryman—I believe from North Carolina. I remember seeing him when I was a student at New Market. He became one of those honest, plodding, unpretending, useful country pastors who aim only at doing good and serving their generation acceptably to God and man. He lived in York county, Pa., where for several years he was suc-

cessfully employed in the service of the Bible Society.

5. J. Galloway was a Presbyterian, and entered the ministry of that church. He studied at our Seminary because, I believe, his parents lived at Gettysburg.

6. David Jacobs did not finish the full course of two years on account of ill health and because of his appointment as teacher in the preparatory department. He died several years after. I do not think he was ever licensed. He was a brother of the late Prof. M. Jacobs, of Pennsylvania College, and uncle of that learned and worthy gentleman, Prof. H. E. Jacobs, of the Philadelphia Seminary.

7. Nicolas R. Sharretts was of Carlisle. He began his studies with Dr. J. G. Schmucker in York before the Seminary was opened. He died in Indiana county, Pa.

8. George Yeager, of Pennsylvania. He settled in Kentucky, where for a number of years he careered conspicuously in a very limited sphere.

9. Benjamin Oehrle, of Pennsylvania, who died a few years after he left the Seminary.

10. Daniel Heilig, of Pennsylvania, who settled in West Virginia, and was seldom seen afterwards.

11. Jonathan Oswald, of Maryland, became assistant to Dr. J. G. Schmucker, of York, and served the neighboring churches for many years. He devoted much of his time to the study of prophecy, and published a book on the subject. In his later years he

undertook the translation of the Hallische Nachrichten, a portion of which was unfortunately published by the Book Committee in Philadelphia,
through the influence of a friend. It was behind
the times in translation, and the remnant has never
been published.

12. Samuel D. Finckel became a very useful minister and filled several positions with credit to himself
and benefit to others. He was a capital German as
well as English preacher. His last pastorate was in
Washington, where he received an appointment in
the War Department, which he held for many years
before his death. (See " Fifty Years," p. 325.) He
has a son in our ministry, and several other sons are
influential laymen in the church.

13. William Artz was of Hagerstown. He went
to North Carolina, and remained there all his life.
He died in 1875, but was not in the ministry at his
death.

These are the men whom I found as students at
Gettysburg. This was the first class, and the year
was 1826. We lived together in great harmony, and
enjoyed ourselves wonderfully. I recited Rambach's
German *Moral*, but attended few other classes. I
wrote and read in my room at Mrs. Hutchinson's,
South Baltimore Street. I preached once in the
Presbyterian church, which was at that time located
on the street leading to the college. There was very
little English preaching in our own church. Mr.
Herbst was pastor, who never preached English, and

Prof. Schmucker seldom occupied the pulpit. Dr. McConaughy was pastor of the Presbyterian church, where we sometimes went, and occasionally we strayed into a small Methodist church "round the corner."

Charles McLean was the talented and eccentric pastor of the old Scotch Seceder church, but who at that time was *exscinded*, but still retained the church. We sometimes went to hear him. There was no effort made to instil into our mind any special fondness for the Lutheran Church.

Some of our boys taught Sunday-school in the country, and some of them preached in the Poor House.

The professor's theological course was constructed pretty much on the general plan pursued in that day. I do not think, however, that he taught Dogmatik this first year. The whole course at that day was only two years, which amounted altogether to about twenty months' instruction. He was very anxious to swell the number of his pupils, and admitted men for six or seven subsequent years who were entirely unprepared. He had occasion to regret it in not a few instances afterwards. He was often deeply mortified at the small number, and the almost constant wrangles with the teachers of the preparatory school, or Gymnasium, as it was called, for inducing some of the pupils to enter the Seminary before they were fit.

There was no pastoral supervision exercised over us, no paternal or encouraging word was given.

The professor's salary was originally fixed at $500, a sum which would about pay house rent at the present time, but it was soon increased, though it did not amount to $1000 for several years. He had the inconvenient reputation of being a man in what was called " good circumstances," although his income was not large.

The Seminary was not regarded favorably by the older ministers of the Church in Eastern Pennsylvania and New York. They were displeased that so young a man was elected professor; they doubted his church loyalty, because he had studied in part at Princeton; they were mortified that a Seminary should have been established by a set of young men comparatively, without their assistance, and then again, most of them were unfriendly to the General Synod, under whose auspices this institution was begun. The result was that very few of the earlier students were from the churches served by the leaders in Eastern Pennsylvania, although some very good pupils came from that quarter.*

I do not think our professor pursued the proper course for gaining the confidence and support of these men. I know that he excited prejudices against them among his students, and it required years to eradicate this unfavorable opinion of them from my own mind. He had good reason not to admire them, for they violently opposed the General Synod, which

* See my History of the Seminary, in Evang. Rev., Vol. IV., No. 4, 1876.

he as resolutely and ably defended. Indeed, I think it could be easily shown that the salvation of the General Synod from utter annihilation was entirely owing to his perseverance and energy. There was no journal at that time in which he could defend it, but he was indefatigable in his correspondence and skilfully rallied the scattered and disheartened forces. His influence, however, in this direction, extended no further than to a few synods in the central section of the church, and to one or two ministers in North Carolina; but he succeeded in maintaining the institution, and lived to see it grow into a large and influential body. While he was a man of power in some directions, he had not the faculty of securing friends to any cause by personal courtesies or acts of polite kindness. He knew how to retain adherents, especially among some of the younger clergy, but he failed in overcoming the opposition and prejudices of older men. Even some of the younger men whom he controlled, did not, in every instance, sanction his action.

At this period, Professor Schmucker, as he was then called, had not yet outlived the theological influence of his father, who had trained him in a sound Lutheranism. In subsequent years he indirectly taught his pupils to esteem the symbols of the Church very lightly, the result of which was that some of them regarded them with a feeling bordering on contempt, and not because they had studied them, but because they had *not!* The effect was what might be expected on uninformed minds. Some of his pupils became extreme anti-creed men, whilst strange to say, the effect upon some other young men was directly the reverse. They began to study the books which the professor sought so sedulously to depreciate, and the result was that they became sturdy Lutherans, and among these were a few of his nearest relatives.*

* For a fair and candid exhibition of the state of the church in that day, see Prof. H. I. Schmidt's "On the Lord's Supper," New York, 1852.

CHAPTER V.

I HAD not been at Gettysburg over a month or so, when I was invited by the First English Lutheran Church, in Baltimore, to preach for them several times. I do not know who mentioned my name to them, but neither I nor any of my relatives had anything to do with it. I accepted the invitation, and came to this city in the fall of 1826, and preached three or four times. I returned to Gettysburg, and soon after a call to the pastorship followed. The salary was $500 a year. After consultation with my brothers and others, and proper religious consideration, I agreed to go, and on February 4, 1827, I preached my first discourse as pastor, on Acts x. 29: "I ask for what intent ye have sent for me?" This congregation had recently erected a small church in Lexington street, but had no previous pastor in that house of worship.

I was totally inexperienced, and the idea of going to a city where, in my verdancy, I thought all the people were intelligent and refined, and where they were accustomed to the best style of preachers, created dreadful apprehension in my mind. I do not think the young ministers of the present day are troubled with such fears. They seem ready to go anywhere, and to preach without any timidity to any congregation. I believe this is owing, in part, to their larger intercourse with society than we of the olden time enjoyed, which is an important part of education. A wider range of acquaintance with men, the facilities of travel, and the progressive spirit of the age, have given young men more self-reliance. I had the foolish idea that anybody in a city was a good judge of sermons, and I was alarmed when I saw smart-looking young people come to my church, and this most unfounded conception led me into some inexcusable blunders. I soon found that city people are not more intelligent than country people, nor better judges of what is good preaching. I also knew that I would have no ministerial brother to sympathize with me heartily, advise or correct me. There was no other English Lutheran church, and the one which called me was still in an embryonic condition. I knew that I would have many difficulties to encounter and hard work to perform. I was apprehensive even of opposition on the part of some Germans, and of indifference from other quarters. It was an enterprise environed by difficulties all around, and I, a verdant country ministerial boy, was expected to overcome them.

I had one advantage here, and that was that my relations were very respectable and influential people. Dr. Keerl, a physician and druggist of high character and considerable wealth, and his four sons, all of whom were much older than I was, and were my first cousins. My almost daily association with them brought me into contact with many other persons of similar standing, which proved advantageous to me as a young minister. The only other Lutheran ministers in the city were the Rev. Dr. J. Daniel Kurtz and John Uhlhorn, joint pastors of the German church in Gay street. I have given sketches of both of these men in my " Fifty Years," pp. 21 and 95. These men received me with polite coldness, but did nothing to encourage my project, for the fact was that most of the persons engaged in our enterprise had been members of their congregation. Dr. Kurtz was aware of the necessity for an English church, but it was not his interest to show any decided approbation of ours. He was well aware that many young German Lutherans, and even whole families of the more respectable portion of his church had left, and joined other English churches, and he was too honest to put any obstacles in our way. Whilst he would perhaps not directly advise any one to leave his church and join ours, yet I am sure he would not have thrown obstructions in the way of their going. Some of their influential members opposed us directly, but I had the satisfaction, not many years after, of receiving some of these very men and their large families into my church, where some of their descendants remain to this day as most efficient members.

It pained me to hear of not a few influential families, with which I became acquainted, who had been reared in the old German church, but who now belonged to other denominations. Some of these encouraged me, but they were too comfortably folded elsewhere to come back to our flock, and I never asked one of them to do so. Indeed, I sometimes avoided families where I was invited to tea, lest I might have been suspected of wanting them to return. Dr. Kurtz and all his family except one member subsequently joined my church.

Before I proceed to write the particulars of my long pastorate of thirty-three years, I will give here an abridged sketch of our history, which was printed as the preface of a little book I published when I resigned, or a short time before. In their proper places I may also give a sketch of the other English churches in town, all of which were offshoots of the old tree which I planted.

BRIEF HISTORY OF THE FIRST ENGLISH LUTHERAN CHURCH.

The necessity for an English Lutheran Church in this city was deeply felt for some years before the first was actually established. It was a subject of much anxious thought and deliberation among many friends of the cause, and on the 27th of October, 1823, the first regular meeting for business was held at the house of David Bixler, in Howard street. This meeting was attended by David Bixler, John

Reese, Thomas Henning, Michael Klinefelter, George Stonebraker, Joshua Medtart, Jacob Deems and Frederick Seyler. They came together with a determined will to carry out their purpose, and in their laudable enterprise they had the sympathies and prayers of not a few energetic ladies. A subscription paper was drawn up, and two days after another meeting for further consultation was held, and a resolution passed to inform the Synod of the project in contemplation, at the same time requesting that body to appoint ministers to preach in succession. A committee to collect funds was appointed, as well as to address a letter to the vestry of the German Lutheran Church, soliciting aid in the erection of a house of worship.

It does not appear that any minister visited them till August, 1824, when the Rev. Mr. Krauth, then of Martinsburg, Va., complied with their urgent request and spent several days among them. At a meeting held August 30, 1824, which Mr. Krauth attended, measures toward a permanent organization were taken, and a committee was appointed to rent a room in which to hold religious service. Day now began to dawn. A room was soon secured, and though it was an humble place, hope revived in the hearts of these devoted children of the Church. This room, which was occupied by a school during the week, was situated on the east side of Howard street, near the corner, north of Pratt. About the same time measures were taken to secure a lot on which to erect a permanent house of worship. During this time, for a period of seven or eight months, the little flock enjoyed the pastoral services of the Rev. Jacob Medtart.

In the meantime the lot on which the church stands * was secured, and active preparations were made to build. In the fall of 1825 the corner-stone was laid, on which occasion the sermon was delivered by the Rev. D. F. Schaeffer, of Fredericktown, who was assisted in the other solemnities by several other ministers.

After Mr. Medtart resigned, various clergymen from other places and from the city were invited to preach.

On the 28th of May, 1826, the new house of worship was consecrated. The sermon was preached by the Rev. Dr. Endress, of Lancaster, Pa. It was a day of pious rejoicing and thanksgiving, and the people said with Solomon, 1 Kings viii. 13, "We have built thee an house to dwell in—a settled place for thee to abide in forever."

On the 16th of July, 1826, the Rev. William Jenkins, a licentiate of the Synod of North Carolina, was elected pastor, but difficulties occurred which prevented his acceptance of the call. This created new perplexity, and for a while the people were

---

* This was the church on Lexington street, on the north side, between Howard and Park streets, which was burned down in 1872, during Dr. Barclay's pastorate. The site is now occupied by large business houses.

disheartened. They looked around and lighted on their present minister, who was then a young student at Gettysburg, without experience or knowledge of the world. With fear and trembling, and only on the advice and persuasion of older brethren, he accepted the invitation to preach, and on Sunday, December 17, 1826, he preached his first sermon as a visiting minister. On Thursday night after he preached again, and at a meeting held after service he was elected pastor. After much deliberation he accepted the call, and on Sunday, February 4, 1827, he preached his first sermon as pastor of the church from the words Acts x. 29: "I ask therefore for what intent ye have sent for me." On the 3d of June of the same year the first celebration of the Lord's Supper was held, and as it may be a matter of interest to some, the names of the communicants are here given:

Andrew Walter, David Bixler, John Reese, Anthony Goverman, Erasmus Uhler, Frederick Seyler, John Brown, Joseph Clark, David Martin, William Ross, John Schriver, Abel D. Chase, T. Sederborg, Jesse Reifsnyder, John S. Bridges, Augustus Hack, William Hack, Garrett Altvater, Magdalena Bixler, Elizabeth Wehrly, Catharine Uhler, Ellen Brown, Catharine Martin, Rochena Utz, Ann Wampler, Margaret Bauer, Rachel Waltemeyer, Elizabeth Miller, Elizabeth Bruner, Mrs. Moal, Mrs. Deems, Miss Elizabeth Brien, Mary Deems, Mary Bixler, Ann Simpson, Isabella Altvater.

A Sunday-school was organized soon after the settlement of the minister, and various other church societies were formed. The congregation gradually increased, and we were greatly encouraged.

In 1830 the first organ for the church was purchased, and in the same year the parsonage was built.

In 1832 it was found necessary to enlarge the church, and nearly $1,000 were subscribed for the erection of galleries, but at a subsequent meeting, June 25th, it was resolved to extend the building towards the street, which was accomplished at considerable expense, and forty pews were added to the capacity of the building. At the same time the present lecture-room was excavated and furnished. Before that we held our weekly lectures and Sunday-school in the church, and afterwards, until the present room was finished, the Sunday-school and other extra meetings were held in the room immediately behind the church, which was erected for that special purpose.

These improvements greatly increased the debt of the church. Money was borrowed to meet present liabilities, and effectual measures were adopted to pay the amount.

One measure pursued was the establishment of a Sinking Fund, which was vigorously conducted by the young men, which produced the first year $976.02; the second year, $969, and in two years and a half they raised $2,580. This, of course, did not include the larger subscriptions of the members. In addition to all, $325 were realized from a concert of sacred music given in the church.

About this time also the Council, with the advice of a majority of the congregation, raised the price of the pews, excepting in the case of widows, who retained their pews at the old prices.

The efforts of the ladies in raising funds for the church should not be overlooked. They on several occasions relieved the treasury by timely contributions, and besides this displayed their interest in the church by the purchase of lamps and furnishing the pulpit.

Most of the additional pews were rented as soon as the house was finished, and have continued to be occupied, for the most part, to the present day. Gas was introduced into the church in 1838.

In 1839 an unusual religious interest was felt in many churches of this city, and during that year eighty persons joined our communion. Some have removed, some belong to other Lutheran churches in this city, some have not remained faithful to their vows, some have died, and some continue with us to this day.

Nothing of special religious interest occurred for several years, though the services were well attended, the number of communicants gradually increasing.

A considerable degree of anxiety was beginning to be felt from another quarter. Nothwithstanding the liberal contributions of the church for the preceding five or six years, the actual debt was increasing. Besides the annual ground rent of $300, the debt now amounted to nearly $9,000. In 1845 a congregational meeting was called, the gratifying result of which was that before the expiration of two years the larger portion of this debt was paid. So great was the relief extended that the Council passed a resolution of thanks to the congregation for their liberality.

In 1848 the church was frescoed, and a part newly painted, at an expense of over $600. New chandeliers were also purchased.

In 1850 a debt of $2,053.75 was paid by subscription, which was another instance of the liberality of the congregation.

In 1851 the lecture-room was furnished with new settees, and the aisles were carpeted.

In 1854 the ladies of the congregation undertook to raise funds for the purpose of improving the front of the church, and a committee of gentlemen was appointed to co-operate with them, which work was satisfactorily accomplished during the year ; the church was closed for several months whilst these repairs were going on, but divine service was held nearly all the time in the lecture-room.

In February, 1857, on the 30th anniversary of the pastor's settlement, a subscription of $1,500 was made towards putting a new roof on the church, and for other necessary repairs.

In 1858 the new organ was purchased at the price of $1,500, which amount was raised by the laudable energy of several of our young men.

Two legacies have been left to the church, one of $500 by the late William Wehrly in 1849, which has been properly appropriated, and another of $1,000 by the late Frederick Seyler in 1857, which is not yet due.

Including the cost of the original building, the alterations and repairs, the erection of the parsonage, ground rents, subscriptions, donations to benevolent societies, and general support of public worship, it is estimated that $75,000 have been expended by this congregation since its organization 32 years ago.

The pastor has baptized 1,204 infants and adults, confirmed 458, buried 217 infants and 270 adults, administered the Lord's Supper publicly 128 times, married 508 couples, delivered over 4,000 sermons. During 32 years' service he has not been prevented from preaching by sickness in a single instance.

I furnished the above statement for a paper published in town. After my resignation in 1860 the Rev. John McCron was elected pastor, and this resulted in a division. More than 100 members left and bought a Presbyterian church in Eutaw street, now St. Mark's, and elected the Rev. Dr. T. Stork, of Philadelphia, pastor. Rev. McCron was succeeded by the Rev. Dr. Joseph Barclay. During his ministry the old church, which had been enlarged twice while I was pastor and renovated several times, was burned down. The lot was sold, and the present edifice, corner of Lanvale and Fremont streets, was erected.

I now proceed to give some of the particulars of my pastoral life. There was no such thing as installation in those days, and I began my work without it. I had a pleasant home at Mr. George Stonebraker's, 42 Hanover street, and I wish to leave on record my appreciation of his kindness to me. I lived with him from my coming, in February, to my marriage, in November, and was treated as one of the family. When I asked him for a final settlement he refused to receive any compensation whatever. He was a kind, amiable man, and was considered rich for those days, and had no children. Both he and Mrs. Stonebraker died long ago. Mrs. Stonebraker married twice after her first husband's death. I buried her three husbands, having also married her to two of them. Mr. Stonebraker intended leaving a legacy towards building another English Lutheran Church, but he wrote the will himself, which was so awkwardly and illegally worded that the court declared that part of it void, and the Church got nothing.

I began with only 28 families, and even visiting them frequently did not consume much time. I could in one day see them all. I had but few official acts to perform, excepting preaching twice on Sunday and lecturing on Wednesday night, and of course had abundant time to study, which I used faithfully, especially in the preparation of sermons, one of which I wrote out fully every week, and thoroughly elaborated the other. I made it a matter of prayer and conscience not to go into the pulpit without giving the people the very best I could furnish, although much of it was deficient enough. I added to my library constantly, and even fell into that morbid habit peculiar to some young men, of multiplying books without judgment or taste. I often attended book auctions, very common in those days, and bought books for which I had no use, and piled up my shelves with what I afterwards sold as mere lumber. I sold off three or four very considerable collections of books in my time, and of course always at a loss. But when I went to Baltimore I had not as good a working library as some of the beneficiaries at Gettysburg now have.

I did an act, some years after, which I have regretted ever since. After having accumulated about a peck of written sermons and skeletons I committed them to the flames, and made a fresh start. I regret this now, not that they would ever have been of any service to anybody, but that I should now like to see my pulpit productions of long, long ago. Perhaps I might have used some of them over again, as I do now with my present stock on hand. I have preached some of them as often as three times to the same people, and so little striking was there in any of them that it was seldom that the repetition was discovered, or at least I never heard of it excepting once or twice.

I soon became acquainted with the very few ministers then living here, excepting some of the Methodists. Among the members of this denomination, who were physicians besides, I had some good friends. Dr. Roberts, Dr. Bond and some others I knew well. But John Breckenridge, Helfenstein, Hamner, especially Duncan, Musgrave and Backus, when he came, were particular associates. I also became well acquainted with the leading working laymen of the various churches, for I at once entered vigorously into the working societies, where I learned to know these men. I also joined several literary associations, and this brought me into contact with many of the intelligent young men of the city. I was President of the Baltimore Lyceum, and also of the Young Men's Bible Society, and afterwards of the State Bible Society. This was not, however, at the beginning of my career.

I will here mention another of the institutions to which I belonged during my pastoral life. It was a Conversational Club, which met in the homes of the members. It was composed of such men as Hon. Jno. Barney, John P. Kennedy, J. H. B. Latrobe, Rev. Dr. Burnap, Dr. Wynne, Brantz Mayer, and other literary characters. A subject was started and it was talked out, or a member would relate an incident or tell a story, on which the rest of us would make remarks, and thus the evening would pass enlivened by wit, brilliant talk, and social intercourse. There was nothing but cold water furnished for refreshment, not even cigars. We usually met in splendidly decorated parlors, where smoking would have been out of order. In *Harper's Monthly*, Vol. 25, p. 336, 1862, there is a notice of this club.*

I must now go back some years to my earlier pastoral life, for I am recording these events as they occur to my mind, without observing any order or chronological sequence, and hence I may be found repeating or enlarging upon some facts already mentioned. When I came to Baltimore in 1827 English Lutheranism was.not known, and the people who talked about it judged us by the standard of piety held by the German Church. I will not say there were no good people in that church, but they were not demonstrative in their piety. They

---

* " Dr. Wynne, in a sketch of John P. Kennedy in the above mentioned *Harper's Monthly*, says: 'I saw most of Kennedy while his townsman in Baltimore at a literary club, of which we were both members, composed of four doctors of medicine, four doctors of divinity, and four gentlemen distinguished for literary attainments. This club, styled the Monday Club, met alternately at the house of the various members in the winter, and during its existence was the most agreeable re-union in Baltimore, and was almost certain to command the presence of any distinguished stranger who chanced to be in town. Kennedy was the most constant in his attendance, and, with the exception of Dr. Morris, a Lutheran divine, was perhaps the best talker.' "

did not mingle with other Christians; they manifested no interest in the religious activities of the day; they were not recognized as a working, Christian people. When we came, bearing the same name, we were estimated by the same rule, and of course we had little sympathy until we became better known. In some places we are suffering from the same cause to-day.

I had but few active, working men, and they were not young men, and hence not known among the workers in religious societies. I suffered considerably from this source.

Some of my people were tainted with Methodist emotionalism, which was cherished to a much greater extent at that day than this, even among that people themselves. Not that any of my members felt disposed to join that church, but they thought that style of religion was preferable to our staid orthodox faith and unostentatious practice. They seemed to think that piety consisted more in feeling than in godly living. This gave me some trouble at first, but I finally brought them round to the sober gospel. An eminent Episcopal minister, who subsequently became bishop, told me the same was true of his congregation when he took charge some years before me.

I held private prayer-meetings with them, and the efforts of some of them to pray were awkward enough; but the most of them improvised, and almost from the beginning I had a goodly number who took part in that exercise. It was something altogether new that a Lutheran should "pray in public," and hence we were called "Methodists" by some who did not wish us well. This was kept up for many years in private houses, and on Sunday morning in the lecture-room in the church. In the course of time a female prayer-meeting, conducted by my godly wife, was also established, which was maintained for many years. My first catechetical class was begun about a month after my settlement, and 48 young people were present. This was encouraging. I confirmed ten of them after three months' instruction.

My first communion was held on Whitsunday, June —, 1827, and there were 40 communicants. Most of them had been confirmed in the German Church, in town or elsewhere. Some were people who had moved to town from other places.

On November 21, 1827, I was married to Miss Eliza Hay, of York, Pa., and immediately went to housekeeping on a salary of $500 a year. I do not mean to say that I lived on that amount, for I paid a rent of several hundred dollars out of it. My salary never exceeded $1,500 a year and the parsonage that was afterwards built. My perquisites never amounted to over $300, so I can safely say that in thirty-three years of my ministry in that church I paid out of my private income more than $15,000 for the privilege of preaching the gospel to that people. I was compelled to be liberal in my donations, as well as to "entertain strangers" to an unlimited

8

number.   When I resigned, in 1860, they made me a present of $1,000, but I had previously spent of my own money for building an addition to the parsonage, by which I secured a small room for a study, which I had not before.

I thus proceeded amid hard work and many difficulties to build up my church.   I spent much time upon my sermons, and kept up a constant system of reading.   I went to see my people often, and whenever I observed that strangers attended my church twice in succession I would enquire who they were, and if I was told that they belonged to no church I went to see them, but I did not intrude myself upon them.   I timidly told them who I was, and as I had seen them twice in our church, and hearing that they had no other church connection, I ventured upon a visit to them.   I was always politely received, and in not a few instances the result was happy.

I made it a matter of conscience never to interfere with another man's work.   It is mean and unprincipled to try to wheedle or steal away another minister's members.   There are some who are wicked enough to do it.   A very pretentious chap once settled in Old Town, when I was temporary pastor of the Third church, who boasted that in a year the half of my congregation would join his, and he even had the consummate effrontery to ask one of my elders to leave us and go with him.   In two years this clerical popinjay was completely used up, and was compelled to leave his fine new place of worship and go, he knew not where. He joined some other denomination and passed into oblivion. Some few, who call themselves Lutheran, are duped to leave the church of their fathers, though they may have been well cared for; but I have found that usually pride or selfishness is at the bottom of it, and in most cases they soon wish themselves home again. I remember losing two men because I would not sanction their unedifying attempts at exhortation, and because they could not succeed in being elected to church offices. They went where one of them soon became a lay preacher and the other a class leader, but neither ever amounted to anything.

A year after my settlement I had so secured the confidence of some of the religious societies, and among them the Bible Society, that I was sent to Frederick and Hagerstown to enlist the co-operation of the societies in those places in our design of furnishing every family in the State with the copy of the Scriptures. A committee began the work of exploration in Frederick during my visit, and the Rev. Mr. Schaeffer, of our Church, on hearing that they intended passing by his house, well knowing that he had Bibles in various languages, insisted upon their coming and seeing for themselves. This he did for the purpose of preventing superficial work on the part of the committee, and also to give them a reason for going to the house of the Romish priest. This priest attacked me and the whole work. I went to hear his denunciation on Sunday afternoon, but it amounted to nothing more than the usual jargon about a mistranslated Protestant Bible. He said he would favor a distribution of the Douay Bible, which of course he never did. I took notes of his harangue, which I afterwards gave to the Rev. Dr. Johns, Episcopal minister, afterwards bishop, and in ten days after I received a pamphlet in which the priest's arguments were all refuted. He never replied.

Exclusively English churches were very rare when I began my work. In our prominent cities there were none but Mr. Bachman's in Charleston, Mr. Mayer's in Philadelphia, Mr. Mayer's, in Albany, and mine. There were others in the interior of New York, one or two in Maryland, Virginia, and perhaps in North Carolina; not more than a dozen, I presume. Let it be remembered that at this time there were not more than 250 or 300 Lutheran ministers in the whole country, but now (1895) there are over 5,000.

The mode of worship in all our churches in which English was preached exclusively or occasionally was framed pretty much after the plain Presbyterian style. There was no such thing as we call liturgy, although in a few of the German churches there was a slight semblance of it. For a long time there was a desire expressed to reform our bald and spiritless mode of worship, and several liturgies were prepared by committees, but none met with general acceptance.

ORDINATION.

I was ordained at a synodical meeting in Frederick in 1827, just one year after being licensed, which was quite unusual, and at the next meeting of Synod, at Shepherdstown, 1828, I was elected a Director of the Seminary at Gettysburg, being the youngest man in it, and at the same time I was chosen a member of the ensuing General Synod. At its meeting in Hagerstown, in 1829, they elected me Secretary. I served as a Director of the Seminary for many years in succession, as well as Trustee of the College at Gettysburg. In 1843 I was elected President of the General Synod, which met in my church in Baltimore, and just forty years afterwards, in 1883, I held the same office at the meeting in Springfield, Ohio.

The *Observer*, when it got into the hands of Dr. Kurtz, vigorously opposed every approximation to responsive liturgy, chanting and clerical gowns; but the liturgical interest finally prevailed, and resulted in the adoption of that which was extensively, but far from universally, adopted by English ministers of the General Synod. Many others would have liked to introduce it, but it could not be done without creating excitement in their churches. The wish of many, it seems, is to be as much like every other neighboring sect as possible, thus losing their individuality, and of course the esteem of all others; for that church that merges its life in the general heterogeneous mass around, and abandons its ancestral memories, merely to be like others, loses its own, as well as the respect of its neighbors.

I know it is not an easy thing to introduce the full liturgy in an old established church. There will be the cry of innovation, but, led by a judicious use of parts of it, and a gradual introduction of the whole, on some occasions, will insure it success. The most effectual mode, however, is its use in the Sunday-schools, where the pupils and teachers will become accustomed to it, and reasonable parents will not oppose it; and this, I am glad to know, is practiced to a great extent. For more than fifty years this subject came up in the General Synod; the committee reported a form, which was discussed for several hours, and then was postponed until the next meeting, much to the relief of those opposed to a full liturgy. What is strange and unbecoming, is that men who would not introduce a liturgical form of worship into their churches, even if one were adopted, are most active in the adoption of one, and have been conspicuous members of committees. Perhaps some of them are personally favorable, but they fear their congregations would not be, and hence hold back at home, whilst at Synod they speak and vote in favor of it. The action of the General Synod of 1885 was more decisive; a liturgy proposed by a committee of the General Council, the General Synod South and our General Synod, was adopted, but I doubt whether it will be generally introduced.

In my verdancy, when I first came to Baltimore, I expected that some of the young anglicised Germans, who joined no other church, and some who had, would cast their lot with us. I was disappointed. Very few of them came, except the children of those parents who came, but none, or very few, whose fathers and mothers still continued with the old Church. I was compelled to depend upon strangers, or wait until our cause became more popular, or prejudices were removed, or opposition ceased. My church and people were too obscure and unfashionable to make it the advantage of gay young people to join us, but still I received quite a number of young people who had not settled in other churches. Among the names of the communicants of the first four or five years there are not over a dozen of persons whose parents or near relations had not been brought up in the German church in Baltimore or in the country; only four or five whose parents still belonged to the old German church, but were so completely English as not to understand German; there are a dozen or so names of persons who are not of German origin at all, and never were in connection with any Lutheran church before, but who fell in with us because they liked us. Of the large number, however, of Americanized young Germans who had strayed away from the old Church, and whose parents still held a nominal connection with it, there were very few who cast their lot with us.

We have great reason to complain that so many of our people have strayed away to other churches, but it is comforting to know that a large number from other churches, or "from the world," as it is called, have joined us.   Every English name in our churches is a gain.   There are no original Lutherans with English, Scotch or Irish names in this country.   Now it is a question worth considering, which are the most numerous, those of our own people whom we lose, or those of English name whom we gain?   I know it is said that some Episcopal churches are almost entirely made up of stray Lutherans.   I am satisfied, after some investigation in Baltimore at least, that this is a gross exaggeration.   There are some families of ours here and there, and some ambitious young people, to be found in other churches; but I am convinced that the number is not as large as represented, though still larger than it should be, and further, that there are not as many defections now as there were some years ago.   Just in proportion as good English preaching is introduced among us, and an efficient ministry exercises its functions, and our churches become enlightened and prosperous, the '' departures '' diminish.

Some years ago I made a careful comparison between the number of our ministers leaving us and the number of ordained ministers of other churches joining our Synods.   The latter was the larger, though, excepting a few cases, the loss was not to be deplored, nor the gain to be commended.   (See '' Fifty Years in the Lutheran Ministry,'' p. 382.)

Those young ministers who take charge of English churches in cities, or establish new ones and expect to build them up for the most part by accessions from the German churches, for the most part will be disappointed, except in neighborhoods where there is no other English church, and where the German young people are numerous. The German pastors generally oppose the founding of English churches, and by their influence many of their young people are kept away; but still there are cases in which energetic efforts succeed in building up churches composed for the most part of young German members, who, when well and properly trained, make good members. Our English Lutheran churches receive fewer from the " Missourians " than from other German churches, although their young members generally speak better English than German. But the most strenuous efforts are made to keep them away; and severe church discipline is threatened, if not exercised. Unless the Missourians form English churches, the third generation of their members will be lost to them, and I fear to the Church entirely.

It was only after Father J. Daniel Kurtz resigned his place in the old church, and moved up town, that he and his family (excepting his son) came to my church, and they all continued active members of the English church until their death. On my resignation they went with St. Mark's people, in the communion of which they died. The old gentleman died before I left Lexington street. Two of his grandchildren had joined us some years before.

My reading during my ministry was somewhat miscellaneous, and I always had one, sometimes two, books on hand, to be read at different times. I always thought that variety was good; one solid and another lighter book. I thus mingled theology, biography, history, biology and periodical literature. I was a diligent, but not a hard reader; some people thought so, but I knew better, and yet I did not idle away any time. I took long walks into the country for exercise, and was always ready for my Sunday work by Saturday noon, so that I might have Saturday afternoon for myself. I once stated this fact to a Presbyterian minister, who thought it capital, and said he would adopt it and no longer sit up late on Saturday night to prepare his sermons, and perhaps sometimes be writing the amen when the church bells were ringing on Sunday morning.

There was no Sunday-school when I came, but we immediately established one. Upon the death of our first superintendent, John A. Bentz, it came into the hands of Dr. Wm. A. Kemp, who for over 30 years conducted it, and the continuation of it at St. Mark's, most efficiently and faithfully.

There were several seasons of special religious interest in the old " Revival " or " New Measure " times. As the result of one of these meetings I once confirmed 80 persons. Some of them were admitted in the midst of the excitement, and with little religious experience or instruction, and not a few fell away. Others continue to this day. This "revival" system, as it was called, has fallen into desuetude, although it was very generally practiced many years ago. None practice it at present except the Methodists, and many of their ministers disapprove of it. I would be far from saying that no good whatever resulted from it, but I do know that when carried to an extravagant extent, as was done in many places, it distracted congregations, created dissension among members, and aroused opposition to the minister. The system would not be tolerated now in many places where it was once very popular. The word of God abideth the same forever, but is it too bold to assume that God may sanction the demonstration of it at some times and places by the employment of peculiar ways and measures which He would not approve of at other times and places? I do not believe that it is the unbelief of the people that has stopped the "revival" system, but that God now employs a less demonstrative plan of carrying on His work.

Some of the most efficient members who were brought in, of non-Lutheran parentage or name, were men whose children having died I had been invited to bury, through the instrumentality of some of my own members. There was one of them, lately deceased, a faithful, godly man, who was perfectly churchless and careless. He lost a child; a friend of his, and a member of my congregation, requested me, for his sake, to officiate at the funeral. My remarks so impressed the parents, who were then young, that

they both began coming to church, and in a short
time both applied for membership; they were confirmed, and the father and the daughter, when she
grew up (the mother is deceased), became most
active workers in the church.   I mention this fact
just to show what effect a few words dropped at a
funeral may have, and that a minister does not
always spend his time in vain by serving people who
have no claim upon him.

I have read of one eminent preacher who maintained that preaching funeral sermons, and I suppose
he included discourses in the house of mourning
before the interment, was lost time; but I do not
think so, if the service is properly, and not mechanically, done.   But I will not here enter upon the
discussion.   I will only remark that from the perfunctory manner in which it is often done I have no
doubt it is lost time to both preachers and hearers.

There is much of this " outside " work done by
some city ministers.   People who are not church
members, and not even in the habit of going to
church, nor of contributing to its support, seem to
think they have as much right to a minister's services as anybody else.   I have attended more funerals
and performed other clerical services for others than
for my own people, and without compensation or
even recognition; and thus it is with some others.
I know one city minister of our own Church who has
an immense Sunday-school, for the most part composed of children of outsiders, very few of whom

ever go to church, but they all call upon him for any service they may want done; and the result is that he has an enormous amount of work on hand, for which, in many instances, he does not even receive thanks. He is a diligent worker, and does not seem to groan under his heavy burden.

Years ago I gave a series of Sunday night lectures on the Evidences of Christianity, which I thoroughly studied. I devoted several of them to the objections which unbelievers make, and stated them strongly, so that my triumph in refuting them might be the more impressive. Against this my cousin, who came to my church every Sunday night, advised and argued that among my hearers there were doubtless some who were not firmly established in the faith, and who, hearing these objections for the first time, would cling to them, and would not be convinced by my soundest argument. In other words, that Satan would take advantage of their inexperience and persuade them that I had put a powerful weapon into their hand. They would feel the force of the objection, but would not appreciate that of the refutation.

I think he was right, for I do not believe that sermons on this subject, before an uneducated audience, are of any benefit. The living, practical power of the gospel is the best argument in favor of its divine origin, and if that is forcibly demonstrated and practiced there will be no need of external reasoning, which, if not well put, will do more harm than good.

During my earlier ministry, having no colleague
of our own Church to associate with on familiar
terms (Father J. Daniel Kurtz * was already too old
a man to be the companion of a " boy minister,"
and Uhlhorn not being precisely to my taste, though
one of the most brilliant men I ever met), I became
the almost daily associate of the Rev. John M. Duncan, a very eloquent divine of the Reformed Presbyterian church in Fayette street, where the Rev. Mr.
Leyburn afterward so successfully labored. Though
Duncan was much older than I, yet we took to each
other very kindly. He was avoided by the few
Presbyterian clergy, and I had no brother Lutheran
clerics, and so we suited well together. I did not
consider him exactly orthodox on some points, but
we did not allow our differences to interfere with
our social relations. I had not then recovered from
my country timidity and bashfulness, and as he was
the most prominent pastor in the city, I seldom ventured to oppose his peculiar views. He was not a
scholar in the modern sense, nor a well-read theologian outside of his own school, but he was a powerful preacher, who, for many years, drew large
crowds of hearers, and outside of the Presbyterian
church he was a very popular man. He was the
nephew and namesake and pupil of the celebrated
New York divine, and afterwards President of Dickinson College, John Mason, whose name adorns my
diploma. He was trained in the strictest Calvinistic

* See my " Fifty Years," p. 21.

school, but later in life abandoned it, and was excluded from the Synod for some alleged un-Presbyterian doctrine, but a majority of his people still clung to him, and after a long trial in the courts the retention of the church property was awarded to the Duncan party. It was at this trial that I for the first time heard the celebrated lawyer Mr. Wirt, who concluded his defense of Duncan's party by quoting from Macbeth those famous lines:

> "Besides, this Duncan hath borne his faculties
> So meek," etc.

It had a powerful effect, and the audience in the court-room vociferously applauded.

I was not as intimate with John Breckenridge, my former tutor at Princeton, and who was pastor of the Second Presbyterian church when I came here, as I was with his brother, Robert J., who succeeded him some years after. He was a very remarkable man, and one of the ablest that ever occupied a Baltimore pulpit. He conducted a monthly magazine, in which he severely exposed the errors of popery. A man named Maguire, the keeper of the almshouse, conceived himself officially assaulted, and was persuaded to prosecute Breckenridge for defamation. The trial excited great interest, but after it had proceeded to a considerable extent, and after Breckenridge's counsel was heard, the State abandoned the prosecution. The State's attorney was Geo. R. Richardson, of whom I have previously spoken as my fellow-student at Princeton college. Mr. Pres-

ton, of Kentucky, and brother-in-law of Breckenridge, and Mr. Crittenden, both United States Sen-
ators from that State, were present one day, and the
latter addressed the Court.

I heard afterwards that a note of sympathy and
encouragement which I had addressed to Breckenridge during the trial was highly valued by him.

ANTI-POPERY.

About these times there was a widespread excitement on the subject of popery, and many Protestant
ministers wrote and preached against it.   Through
the influence of a Presbyterian minister of this city,
though not a pastor, a meeting of clergymen was
called to organize a regular crusade against Romanism.   The design was to preach sermons and to cir-
culate writings on the subject.   The meeting was
pretty well attended, and a plan of operation was
proposed.   I had not much confidence in it, for the
reason that the Romanists would not come to hear
our discourses and our own people did not require
any special instruction on this subject, for they were
in no danger of apostasy to Rome; but particularly
I soon discerned what I should have known before,
that none of the men who attended the meeting,
except two or three, had ever studied the subject, and
that their harangues would do the cause more harm
than good.   They were in no sense familiar with the
controversy, and had never read any book attacking
or defending Rome, and were not even acquainted
with the titles of books treating of this matter.

Nothing was done, although the sermons of a few of us were strongly spiced with anti-Romanism for some time. For myself I have so acquired the habit that I seldom let pass an opportunity of giving Romanism a hit, but it is done mildly and kindly.

About this time I published a sermon on " The Necessity of the Reformation," which was violently attacked by the Romish press here, and which created considerable sensation.

The only other minister not of our Church with whom I was intimate in my earlier years was the Rev. Albert Helfenstein, of the German Reformed Church, then situated in Second street, and which was known as The Town-Clock Church. He was a man of blameless life, but not successful as a preacher. He was succeeded by the Rev. Mr. Heiner, who revived the expiring church, but died before he was fifty. After several colonies had gone out of my church, and called pastors, I of course had associates of our own faith, with all of whom, ever since the first one came, I have lived in perfect harmony, except perhaps with one who was afterwards expelled. After the Rev. B. Kurtz came to Baltimore, in 1833, to edit the *Lutheran Observer*, which I gave into his hands, and which he successfully edited for many years, although his Lutheranism did not suit my taste, we worked together for the most part very pleasantly. He was a hard man to preach to—impatient, often inattentive, and always severe in his judgment on my sermons. He

9

once most injudiciously attempted to found another English church without ever saying a word to me about it, and I only heard of it after he had commenced. I do not think that his own judgment heartily approved of it, but I have reason to think he was urged on by a disaffected and troublesome member of my own church. He opened a preaching place in an upper room at the corner of Gay and Baltimore streets, but soon abandoned it for want of encouragement. He was the last man who should have undertaken such an enterprise: he was not in robust health; he had not the time nor the disposition to carry on such a work; he had not the social nor pecuniary backing such an undertaking in a city requires; he had not the sympathy, much less the prayers of anybody, except those of one man. It was an inconsiderate project, and soon utterly failed. He never alluded to it afterwards. The failure was humiliating, and no doubt he was ashamed of it all his days subsequently. He was a strong man in many respects, but a very broad school Lutheran, besides which other influences, adverse to our system, were brought to bear upon him, and the result was that after the death of his son, Theophilus, not a single one of his children or grandchildren attended the Lutheran Church. With the *Observer* under his control, Dr. Kurtz was for many years an acknowledged power in the Church. He had a large following among the ministers and laymen, and always advocated a high standard of practical piety. The generation over which he exercised so much influence is nearly gone; a few linger, but every one, I believe, has abandoned the church polity and dogma he so strongly defended. Other men have come upon the stage, and their more churchly views are now maintained.

For many years my most intimate clerical associate in town was the Rev. Dr. Dalrymple, of the Episcopal church, a fair classical scholar and a genial gentleman. In theology he was a very low churchman, and on the sacraments especially a Zwinglian. He was a bachelor, with some queer ways, and kept a fine establishment; he was a man of profuse hospitality and sociable temperament. He had the largest private library in the city, and yet he was not what we call a student. He was not even a close reader, but kept his books as ornaments, and was extremely careful in their preservation. He, Philip Tyson, and I traveled together for years in succession to the meetings of the American Association for the Advancement of Science, and enjoyed each other's company vastly. He died in 1881.

During the last few years the ministers of our churches in town have been young men for the most part. They were very active as pastors, and generally they were successful. Very few of them had time to prosecute any special course of study, but I believe they carefully prepared their sermons. They had little time for mere social visiting, and I had very little time to enjoy it.

This would seem to be the place to mention the fact that I have never had any personal controversy worth mentioning with any of my clerical brethren. There has been coldness of intercourse with a few, but it never degenerated into personal rancor or complete alienation. With two men who treated me very unkindly after doing them favors I have had no social intercourse for some years. They do not live here, and I seldom meet them. God forgive them for their unkind conduct towards me. Among the many who have attacked me, and most of whom I have never noticed, I will make reference, as an example of an odd controversialist, to one who fiercely assailed my " Fifty Years." I gently corrected a few of his errors. He wrote to me that he had something more to say, and begged me to let him have the last word!!! I promised not to notice him, so that he "might enjoy the triumph of having silenced me." I knew well enough that the more severely he abused the book the more readily it would sell, and it gave me pleasure to allow him such a cheap enjoyment, for the poor, "underrated" soul had not much of any other kind. I was told that this same man attacked me in a western paper ten years afterwards.

I once had occasion to call an impulsive but I believe honest minister to account for a remark he made seriously affecting me. He vehemently disavowed any evil design, expressed deep regret for having given me any uneasiness, made apologetic explanations, and begged pardon for his indiscretion. I was satisfied, and we are good friends.

Most ministers complain of the difficulty of imparting enough of interest to their week-day services to attract their own members to the meetings. I believe that this is a universal complaint. I have tried various expedients; one was to invite written questions and answer them. This did well for a time, but by and by questions of an objectionable or personal character came in, and the design was frustrated. I once undertook to explain difficult passages of the Bible, and that succeeded pretty well for a time. I lectured on the geography and natural history of the Scriptures, and various other methods were temporarily employed. That which brought most people together was propounding a question and inviting members to express their opinions upon it. This brought out some sensible remarks, but sometimes incompetent persons would annoy us with their ill-digested talk, and sometimes we had a regular theological controversy. I believe the best plan after all is faithfully to preach the old-fashioned gospel.

FIRST CORNER-STONE.

The first corner-stone I ever assisted at laying was that of St. Matthew's, in New street, Philadelphia, under the pastoral care of the Rev. C. P. Krauth, Sr., and the first consecration sermon I ever preached was in that church when finished, on July

18, 1830. I have spoken of this gentleman before, and shall have occasion to mention him again. I would never grow weary of lauding his exalted virtues. He and I lived together on most fraternal terms until he died. We loved each other as brothers. He was a man of brilliant mind, and he had a wonderful faculty of acquiring knowledge. During his residence in Philadelphia of many years he was a most industrious reader, but too miscellaneous, and he remembered everything he read. It was only after he went to Gettysburg that he applied himself to those branches which he taught. As a teacher he was too indulgent, of which some of his not too industrious pupils took advantage.

STUDENTS IN MY HOUSE.

During my long pastorate I had as pupils in their preparatory course several young men to whom I shall allude here. The first was Charles A. Hay, for many years professor at Gettysburg in the Seminary. The whole Church knows his character as a teacher, as a gentleman, and as an active Christian. His attainments in his department of theological science were extensive, and his success as a teacher in his earlier years is now acknowledged by all his pupils. He was a modest, unpretending man, whose sterling qualities were universally known and esteemed.

There was another man who for several years was a pensioner upon my bounty, but he never succeeded in our ministry, either as teacher or preacher. He failed lamentably in both spheres. He was unhappy in several other relations, and left us for another church "for a consideration!" He was helped out of some difficulties, and paid his benefactors by the offer of his services, which were accepted. My brothers and I spent more than $1,000 in bringing this man out, but he accomplished nothing. The reason why we took him up was that his mother had been a nurse and "help" in my mother's family for many years, and took care of me when I was a child.

I took another young man off a tailor's bench, and supported him until he was fit to go to Gettysburg, where my church maintained him for several years. He was then an humble, promising boy. But he never advanced as a preacher, and was employed in teaching in female seminaries. After he ran a career among us he "departed," not exactly out of this life, but into the Episcopal church, of which he was a lay member. He became a merchant in a neighboring city. I met his brother-in-law in 1895, who told me that he died many years ago, but, he added, "he never amounted to anything."

Disappointed ambition plays the mischief with some of these fellows who have no grace in their hearts and no brains in their skulls. Some of them are vain enough to think themselves entitled to high consideration, and when they do not receive it, because unworthy of it, they behave themselves unseemly. They complain of not being "appreciated."

I once had another chap in my house for over nine months, who had a Scotch name, but his mother being a plain Pennsylvania country girl, this boy acquired from her a broad half-German accent. I soon got tired teaching him the elements of education. My folks at home nursed him through an attack of measles, but he never had grace enough to say "thank you." He is now somewhere in the west, but not in our ministry.

I had still another young man with me for several years who was well educated. He was licensed by our Synod, and held one or two good places, but was led away by some delusive inventions which he foolishly thought he had made, and from which he hoped to accumulate an immense fortune. He strayed off to a foreign country, where he died in poverty.

TEACHING.

I never taught school in my life, and never filled the exalted position of teacher as a profession, unless my lectureship at Gettysburg may be thus regarded. I have taught some men privately, but without compensation, and had a number of pupils in elocution and a few other branches, which was more pleasure than labor.

Some years ago I was prevailed upon to give lessons in Hebrew to some young men in town who were not students of theology. We met early in the morning, and continued it for some weeks, but most of them grew tired of it and would not study, and I refused to attend any longer. I had two other students in Hebrew, one a candidate for the Presbyterian church, who afterwards for many years served a church in Washington, where he died, and the other was a candidate for the Episcopal ministry, who became a worthy and influential divine in Virginia. I had made considerable progress in Hebrew, but unhappily, like too many others, I neglected it in after life. I usually carried with me a neat little Hebrew Psalter, and read it diligently while traveling and at other times, but that also gradually was given up. I ceased to be a daily reader of the Hebrew Scriptures, which I now very much regret. The copy of the Hebrew Psalter I gave to the Rev. Dr. Brown, of Gettysburg.

I once took a few lessons from an unwashed "wandering Jew," who I found knew very little of the grammar, and he soon ran away from his boarding house, forgetting to pay his bill, and also forgetting to return a fine copy of Buxtorf's Dictionary which I had loaned him.

A foreign Romish priest advertised for pupils. I went to him several times, but soon found that I knew more Hebrew than he did. He could not analyze a single word, nor could he translate a single passage in Genesis without the help of a modern version. I sent him $5 and quit, after two or three hours of lost time spent with this wretched humbug.

For several months one winter I met five or six

highly educated ladies, and read German with them. Several of them, having studied it previously, read Schiller pretty well.

DIFFICULTIES.

Like other pastors, I presume, I had my difficulties and drawbacks, arising from various causes. Lack of success was one, and yet I never had reason to complain for lack of Sunday hearers, although I had sent off two colonies. My difficulties and discouragements arose from the objectionable conduct of some of my members, the lack of interest in the higher spiritual life in many of them, the lack of liberality in their contributions to church objects, their indisposition to personal effort in church work, the absence of refined fraternal affection in some, the meagreness of my support, the absence of many from the usual week-night service, and many other reasons which need not be specified.

I never got into any personal difficulty with any of them until the breaking out of the rebellion, of which I shall speak hereafter, but I once gave irreconcilable offence to a family by marrying some parties connected with those families to whom they objected. On one occasion of this kind several valuable young men, closely related to a party I married, left my church, although there was a subsequent reconciliation. They never forgave me. They had no ground of offence but pride, and I never regretted what I did. The party brought into the family by the marriage was as good as they were any day. Sometimes a member or two would leave me without any ostensible cause, but on examination I would discover that there was some young man or woman in the case, or family pride. Sometimes the arrival or settlement of a popular preacher in town would draw off, for a while at least, some of the lighter material; but in the course of time they would come back again, finding that the solid gospel bread of the old home was, after all, the most nourishing.

When Fuller, the eminent Baptist preacher, came here, he had large audiences and created great sensation. He was a strong man, and an effective pulpit orator. Whilst his church was in course of erection some of us ministers invited him to our pulpits as an act of courtesy to a stranger of distinction, but he was careful not to say anything about his Baptistic notions. When he got his new church then he began and turned the heads of some people who submitted to immersion. I had no trouble on this account, except with one family, of which two very weak sisters were somewhat infected with the error, but they did not leave us. I was requested by some of my people to preach one or two sermons on the subject of immersion. I studied it thoroughly, and wrote every word. After preaching once or twice I never had any trouble afterwards. Everybody was satisfied that our mode was Scriptural, and we had peace.

Dr. Fuller was a sociable gentleman, of mild and agreeable manners. He narrated a little incident to me, which I think worth inserting here. In his younger days he once preached to a country congregation as a visitor, on which occasion the nabob of the county, Col. Blank, was present. When Fuller descended from the pulpit the Colonel advanced towards him with tears streaming down his face, and threw his arms around the preacher's neck, and amid sobs and deep penitential sighs hailed him as the instrument of leading him to Christ, professing his faith in the strongest language, and declaring his purpose to lead a godly life. The preacher was delighted at the sudden and remarkable conversion of so influential a gentleman, and welcomed him most cordially, but he was surprised that the happy event created no excitement or even any uncommon interest in the people. On returning to his lodgings in the carriage of his host, he was the more surprised that no allusion whatever was made to it. He at length opened the subject himself, and spoke in raptures of the conversion of Col. Blank. The only reply he received was, and it was a damper, " Oh, we have often witnessed that scene; he always acts it when he is drunk!" Fuller collapsed.

The most humiliating experience I ever had arose from the wicked conduct of a man whom I received into the church by baptism. He had been trained among the Quakers, and was at this time connected with an influential daily paper. He was respectably married, and had several children. He became a "praying member" and an active Sunday-school teacher. A few doubted his sincerity, for they had known him in business before his professed conversion. Less than a year after this man became an incendiary of several prominent public buildings, and to elude suspicion he set fire to his own printing office. He was never arrested for these crimes, but the universal belief was that he was the perpetrator. Some time after, he was apprehended in the act of purloining letters from the post-office, where he had free access as the manager of an influential daily paper. He was tried, convicted, and sentenced to jail. After a short time President Van Buren pardoned him on condition that he would leave the country. It was given out that he went to South America, where it was said he died. There is reason to believe that his professed conversion was all a sham to cover up his iniquity. He selected my church as the stage on which he played his hypocritical role because there were several of his relatives who were members of it, and whose good opinion it was important to him to secure, and besides I was intimate with him myself, for he did me some acts of kindness. This was the severest blow I ever received from a church difficulty.

I never had any serious difficulties with my Council. We often differed, but amicably. With a few exceptions they were moderate and judicious men, who always treated me most respectfully. I never took any active part in the financial affairs of the church, it being a matter which, unfortunately, I did not understand, and with which, as a minister, I had nothing to do. I had no reason to leave the " Word of God and serve tables," and yet it is a grand qualification in a minister to have financial aptitude and business tact, but he has no occasion to exercise these gifts if he has a sensible and judicious Council.

I have had, like most other men, some troublesome men to deal with. I remember one who had taken offence at me merely because I did not succumb to his unreasonable demands, and he was determined to create a disturbance in the church, vainly presuming that he would have a following. One morning as I was preaching as usual he suddenly arose, left his pew, which was near the pulpit, walked out, making all the noise he could with his heavy tread. I took no notice of it, not knowing the cause of his sudden departure. He remained in the vestibule till church was out, and then began to speak harshly about me; but not a man coincided with him, which mortified him to the quick. He continued to come to church, and by kind treatment he was won back again, and continued my fast friend until the rebellion broke out, when he and a few others became my bitter enemies, and did not speak to me as long as they lived.

I have elsewhere said in this book that after I had

resigned the First church I served sever other churches in town provisionally. On one occasion one of these churches had elected a minister, and I of course retired. After I had preached my last sermon, on coming down the stairs in the midst of a dense crowd, one man said in a loud voice, so that he might be heard all round, and knowing too that I and another person dearer to me than my life would hear it, "Well, thank God, it is his last." I would not have noticed it on my own account, but I regarded it as a deliberate insult to the cherished person with me. I left her in charge of a friend, and called to the man that I wanted to see him in the lecture-room immediately. I asked one or two friends to go with me, and the way I belabored that fellow with hard words, yet within moderation, was such a lesson as he never learned before.

If I had paid any attention to the various reports I heard of what some said of me, and especially of each other, after I left the First church, I would have had nothing to do but to try to settle disputes and reconcile contending parties, but I kept aloof from all strife. Still it was some years before several of them looked kindly upon me. Their will was not my will, and they would not sustain any man who would not follow their lead.

One whole family left my church, which annoyed me considerably, but as it was not occasioned by any dissatisfaction with me I endured the loss calmly. The family was highly respectable, of increasing wealth, residing in what was then (1852) a fashion-able part of the city, and aspiring to social position, which had not yet been attained.

The plain fact is that my church was not fashion-able enough, nor did it contain the class of people whose society such persons affect, and hence the younger portion of the household gave their sober-minded and well-disposed parents no rest till they "took a pew" in a fashionable and influential church. The father had not been born nor reared among us as a church people, but the mother was of Lutheran birth and training, and all her own family was closely associated with our Church. The father wrote me: "I beg you to understand that the step is not induced by any want of respect for or attach-ment to you; on the contrary, for yourself and family, as also the church, my regard is as it has been, the highest, and my every desire is for your success and prosperity." Everybody in and out of my church who was interested in the least degree in this affair, or who was acquainted with the persons, attributed it to what I would call social ambition, but I have been informed that success in that direc-tion was not secured.

Occasionally an individual or two left my church, either led away by wives belonging to other churches whom they married, or by disappointment in not being elected into the Church Council, or by not "being made much of," or by an ambition to be-come "leaders," or by a desire to be among those who depend much upon excitement. I remember two men who left us, who were otherwise fair men, but who were of ordinary minds and no education. I heard of them afterwards as being class leaders or local preachers, and thus their ambition was gratified. I believe one of them did not hold out long. I have no doubt that he aspired to something higher among the people he joined, and being disappointed became " soured " and " lost his religion." None of the backsliders from my church went to the Baptists or Romanists.

One very fair man, extremely backward in education, and of no social influence whatever, but honest and truly pious, left my church because he had moved out of our bounds, and a Methodist church was near at hand, the people of which made a great deal of him, which flattered him vastly. He joined them, and was at once made an officer or class leader. He gave us the credit, however, of making a Christian of him, and, as I have heard, annoyed them by the everlasting repetition, when " giving his experience," of the account of an interview with me in my study late at night, when, as he said, he acquired new and clear views of Christian duty and doctrine. I meet him occasionally now, when he repeats the same story, and tells me he has often told it in class-meetings, which I can well believe. I also sometimes meet a Methodist brother, who never belonged to us, to whom it seems to be a pleasure to tell me whenever he meets me that his

10

mother was a Lutheran, and I always reply, "That's the reason why you are a pretty fair and respectable sort of a man now." He agrees to it.

I had difficulties of another character, and they arose out of my own preaching. Not a few persons congratulated me upon what they called my "self-possession," whereas they did not know that I was usually so abashed that I scarcely knew what I was saying and scarcely dared to look people in the face. I have more than often half resolved never to face my people again from the pulpit, so wretchedly poor and weak was my preaching, even after good preparation. I have sometimes been so utterly ashamed that I was almost afraid to give out the last hymn, and have left the church without venturing to speak to anybody, and expecting to hear that my services would no longer be required. I would go home, and on my knees beg God to give me some token by which I might know whether He wanted me in the pulpit any longer, for I was sure that my people did not. Was this a temptation? or nervousness? or incompetency? And how doubly humiliating to be told sometimes that some of these discourses, which brought me down to the very dust in shame, were "fine," "impressive," "the very best we have had for some time." Oh what wretched judges you are! you cannot appreciate anything good! you are controlled by your feelings and not by reason!

There was one period, soon after the wearisome controversy in the *Observer* on "New Measures," that some men, seconded by that paper, tried "to write me down." I replied once or twice, when a few friends took it out of my hands and vigorously defended me. One of them was asked by a very conspicuous opponent of mine "how much he was paid for advocating my cause?" He was too amiable to ask in return what he thought, "how much are you paid for letting loose your dogs upon him?"

I did not escape the fate of men who take a conspicuous part in church questions, and who fearlessly express their sentiments, and who will not submit to be governed by a leader. I never allowed men who treated me unkindly to know that I was aware of their ill feelings towards me, excepting in one or two cases, and I have had the satisfaction of doing a few of them some slight favors for which they asked. I wonder how such men feel when they are compelled to solicit acts of kindness of their brethren of whom they have spoken evil and whom they have tried to injure.

I have patiently borne many injuries, and did not resent provoking injustice done me, because I was afraid of hardening the hearts of such men against the gospel. I thought it best to suffer rather than give occasion to men to find fault with it, which they would have done if I had betrayed any unchristian retaliation. Those to whom I especially allude are all dead, and may they have found pardon of God in their dying day!

I may have mentioned it before, but I have never

been subpœnaed to give testimony but twice in court; one was to swear to the good character of a young man who was indicted in Baltimore County Court for some misdemeanor, and was acquitted, and the other was in a divorce case in Delaware.

I once got into a slight difficulty for having unguardedly uttered what everybody knew to be true, that a certain man who was a vestryman in a certain church was an unbeliever. He heard of it, and threatened me with prosecution. A prominent lawyer, whom he had employed, sent for me to come to his office and stated his case, advising me that it would not do for me, a young minister, to engage in public litigation with men like his client, and that even if I could prove the allegation (which he knew well enough I could do) it would produce an unhealthy and useless excitement. He proposed a method of settlement, to which I assented, and the matter was dropped. The astute lawyer was well aware that I had it in my power to show up his client in a way not favorable to his character.

During a religious stir in my church, two young men, not originally Lutherans, thought that I was not zealous enough, and by that they meant that I did not encourage religious extravagance, that is, groanings of others during prayer, and loud amens. They tried to get up a party against me, but failed. They threatened to leave, but did not. They both lived to be old men, and although they ceased to worship with us, they continued to be my strong friends.

CHAPTER VI.

I began scribbling for the newspapers even during my student life at Dickinson College, in 1822, where my first communication appeared in the Carlisle *Volunteer*. I never had the boyish vanity to mount the poetical Pegasus, and can say with a facetious friend of mine that '' he never wrote more than half a line of poetry, and there stuck.'' I have continued to indulge this scribbling mania all through life, of which the pages of the *Lutheran Observer* and some other church papers, as well as those outside the Church, bear ample witness.

BIRTH AND INFANCY OF THE LUTHERAN OBSERVER.

When the *Lutheran Intelligencer*, which had been published and edited in Frederick, Md., for five years by the Rev. D. F. Schaeffer, died in 1831, and the *Lutheran Magazine*, edited by Dr. Lintner, in Schoharie, N. Y , had also breathed its last in 1830, there was no English paper in the Church from January, 1830, to August, 1831, a period of eighteen months—'' *hiatus valde deflendus*.'' This was a condition of things not to be endured. The Seminary at Gettysburg had already been in operation four years; many of our congregations were fast becoming English; all the influential denominations had their church journals; many of our ministers wanted a vehicle for the communication of their thoughts; an English paper was properly regarded as essential to our respectability and progress; and the leading spirits among us, such as Krauth, Sr., B. Kurtz, Schmucker, Keller, Lintner, Heyer, Reck and others, besides some influential laymen, determined to resuscitate the deceased *Intelligencer*, or rather create a new paper worthy the patronage of our people. The questions now were, who should edit it, and where should it be published? Gettysburg was already beginning to be looked upon as the headquarters of the Church, a sort of Lutheran Wittenberg (with the old Wittenberg spirit left out), the Canterbury of our Zion, with few Lutheran residents and no mediæval cathedral. It was thought that the great organ should play its tunes (or at least have its bellows) in this obscure, out-of-the-way place. It was to be printed by " The Press of the Theological Seminary," as it was pompously called on the title page of a book, but which was not owned by the Seminary, but was the property of and run by a fourth-class German printer in an office 8x10 in dimensions. Well, the prospectus was issued, and the name *Observer* was given it, without any distinguishing prefix. This non-distinctiveness—this absence of a denominational cognomen—displeased

some of the Advisory Council, who insisted upon a
name for the infant which would indicate its family
relations and pedigree. But there was one potential
objection, which was simply this: the majority of the
Gettysburgers were Presbyterians—very respectable
people. We had lately come among them, and were
poor and of little account. It was politic to secure
their good will, and do nothing to offend them—not
to say a word or do an act that looked like sectarianism!!! It was argued by the leading man, who had
consented to edit the paper for a time, that the title,
Lutheran Observer, would awaken denominational
jealousy, and perhaps social discord. The others
would not yield, and to avoid a total collapse the
compromise was made of transferring the paper to
some other place, where the name Lutheran would
give no offence, and where probably a man could be
found who would maintain the dignity and honor of
that illustrious appellation. But it was not convenient for any of them to assume the work. They
then bethought themselves that there was a young
man in Baltimore who might be unwise enough to
undertake it. They knew that he was without experience, without capital, and without influence beyond his own small congregation. There were no
subscribers, no advertising patronage, no reliable
promises, and no guarantees in the event of loss.
They absolutely prevailed upon this ministerial
youngster to take the responsibility, with the implied
understanding that the Church was to receive the
profits and he to pay the losses!!

Well, No. 1 of the *Lutheran Observer* was issued in August, 1831, as a semi-monthly. The number of subscribers gradually increased, but I do not think it ever exceeded 1,000. I was overwhelmed with communications on all manner of church subjects, and many of them equaled anything that has appeared in the *Observer* since that day. I presume very few copies are extant at the present time, but they are dearly cherished by those who have them, and only because they give a fair history of the Church at that period, and because lovers of old books earnestly covet such antiquities.

It would be wasting time to specify the leading articles, but the reflecting man will see in those pages the germ of many grand enterprises in which we now rejoice, and which are now so vigorously defended by the present editor. "The boy is father of the man;" that old saying is exemplified in this case. More than one man of good sense and cultivated taste has said that these early volumes of the *Observer* are, to this day, instructive and interesting documents. The first volume was in 8vo. form, and the second in 4to.

I devoted my time to this business for two years without compensation, but I endured much vexation, gave offense to some subscribers whom I asked for the money they owed me, and brought down upon myself the "celestial wrath" of some clerical correspondents whose undigested and crude material I could not consent to publish. But this is the common fate of editors!

In 1833 the Rev. B. Kurtz, then out of health, wishing to cease pastoral and pulpit labor for a season, consented to assume the editorial tripod, and in that year the paper was transferred to him. He came to Baltimore, and for twenty-five years conducted it with varying success. He devoted his entire time and high business qualifications to it, and made it a power in the Church.

Editor No. 1, upon collecting all the money he could, without however making much exertion, had the magnificent sum of $60 as profit of two years' work. With part of this I bought a lot of shade trees, to be planted in front of the Seminary at Gettysburg, and the balance I distributed among a few poor widows of my church. The subscription book, which contained about $500 of unpaid subscriptions, I gave to some association in the Seminary, with the privilege of keeping all they could collect; but I believe they were not very successful, perhaps because they were not energetic. Old subscription books are at best poor stock. I was sorry to learn that the efforts to collect these unpaid accounts met with indifferent success, in many instances.

The full history of the *Observer* has been written, and any persons curious on such historic lore may profitably consult the paper in its issues of January, 1877, or my Bibliotheca Lutherana, p. 131.

OTHER ENGLISH LUTHERAN MINISTERS IN BALTIMORE.

I have spent the whole of my ministerial life in

this city, and my friends know it has not been a short one. It occurred to me to-day that it would be interesting, at least to me, to look back and see how many other English ministers of our church had lived here during my time. I cannot here do much more than mention their names, with perhaps a few observations concerning them.

I will begin with the First church.

After my service of 33 years, I resigned in 1860, and assumed the duties of Librarian of the Peabody Institute, a position of which I have spoken more at large at another place. After a long and rather lively election, the Rev. Dr. J. McCron, at that time pastor of the Third church, on Monument street, was chosen my successor, his competitor being the Rev. T. Stork, D. D. Dr. McCron came to us from the Methodists, among whom he had been an exhorter, or a local preacher, and schoolmaster. He had been a sailor in early life, and had seen a good deal of the world. He was socially a very agreeable man, and had some of the gifts of a natural orator. He could hardly be called a theologian, though a very popular preacher. He was born in England, of Irish parents, and hence always called himself an Englishman by birth. I gave him the title of " Our Irish Orator," which by no means offended him. No man could entertain a company of his friends more agreeably than he, and his society was courted by men who loved hilarious enjoyment. He was sorely perplexed during high secession times, at the beginning of the Rebel war. He did not know which side to espouse, for he had friends in his church on one side or the other, and he assumed the equivocal and dangerous position of sympathizing with both sides in turn. This course injured his standing in both parties. He however had warm friends who supported him cordially to the end of his pastorate.

In 1872 he accepted the position of Superintendent of the Female Academy at Hagerstown, but his gifts were not such as fitted him for educational work. After that he became pastor of the church at Bloomsburg, then at Pottsville, then at Middletown, Md., where he remained a short time, and then went to Philadelphia, where he preached to a small congregation. There he died in 1881, and was buried by some of his friends, and probably by the Masonic Fraternity. His remains were subsequently removed to Baltimore.

He was succeeded by the Rev. Joseph Barclay, D. D., who improved the cndition of the church. During his pastorate the house of worship and parsonage, on Lexington street, were destroyed by fire, after which the people resolved to sell that ground, and build a new house in some growing section of the city. The result was the elegant church at the corner of Lanvale and Fremont streets. Several years after, he took charge of a church in Dayton, Ohio, which he left in 1887, and returned to Baltimore. He was succeeded in the First Church here by the Rev. M. W. Hamma, D. D., who came here from a church in Brooklyn, N. Y. He is a first-class gentleman and an industrious pastor. He resigned on account of ill health in 1886, and was succeeded by the Rev. Albert H. Studebaker, D. D., formerly of Harrisburg, Pa., who entered upon his work with the energy which ensures success.

The first pastor of the Second Lutheran church, on Lombard street, was the Rev. Charles P. Krauth, who at that time was preaching to a small congregation at Canton, East Baltimore. He was under twenty years of age, and already gave promise of his subsequent career as a scholar and theologian. His death in 1882 was universally regarded as a most sad calamity to the Church, for he was by all looked upon as the most brilliant star in the whole galaxy. He bore the same relation to me as I did to his sainted father. We were the closest, warmest friends as long as they lived, although there was a considerable disparity of years. I became the father's friend when I was under 22, and Charles became mine when he was under 19. During all his life he was in my family almost as one of us.

Charles was succeeded at the Second church by the Rev. C. H. Ewing, a Presbyterian minister who joined our Synod. Then came the Rev. J. A. Seiss, D. D., who has since become quite eminent in the Church. His services as a preacher and a writer deserve a longer notice than I have space to give. He is now (1890) the pastor of an influential church in Philadelphia, where he has achieved his high reputation.

The Rev. Chas. H. Hersh was the successor of Dr. Seiss, but he died in less than a year (?) after his settlement. He was a godly and amiable man.

The Rev. Joel Swartz followed. The Rev Irving Magee succeeded him. He moved to Albany when he resigned, and thence went to the Presbyterians.

The Rev. E. J. Wolf came next. He is at present Professor in the Theological Seminary at Gettysburg. He was succeeded by the Rev. George Scholl, who has recently moved to Hanover (1883). He was succeeded by the Rev. L. Kuhlman in 1884. The Rev. G. W. Miller, D. D., was his successor.

The Third church (Monument street) was organized by some members of my church in 1841, who erected a small chapel about a year later. In 1843 the Rev. W. A. Passavant, at that time, as C. P. Krauth had been, a missionary at Canton, was chosen pastor. He was followed by the Rev. Appleby, who came to us from the Methodists. The Rev. James A. Brown succeeded him, afterwards the eminent theologian and profound thinker at Gettysburg Seminary, whose sudden paralytic attack deprived us of his invaluable services, and whose death several years after was lamented by the whole Church. The theological attainments of Dr. Brown were extensive, and his general scholarship universally acknowledged. His knowledge was accurate; he knew things thoroughly; his thoughts were clear as the atmosphere, and his temperament cool and calm as a morning breeze. No opponent could throw him off his guard, and he was a dangerous man to encounter in debate, unless your cause was manifestly right. He was not born within our fold, but from conviction entered it after he had attained to manhood, and heartily espousing our cause, he maintained it vigorously to the end.

Dr. Brown possessed a moral courage that nothing could daunt. If the whole history of his experience in South Carolina, at the breaking out of the Rebel war, and of his firmness in maintaining his principles, were told, it would excite the admiration of friend and foe. His courage in opposing the theological teaching of the man who had been his own professor in the Seminary eighteen years before, in a strong pamphlet, and showing his un-Lutheranism, deserves the highest praise. Many more characteristic incidents might be given.

The Rev. P. Anstadt followed. The Rev. A. W. Lilly, D. D., now of York, Pa., then came, in October, 1851, and during his time the present brick church was built, although it has undergone some enlargements and other improvements since he left, in 1855. He was followed by the Rev. Samuel Sprecher, now in the Presbyterian church. Then came the Rev. H. Bishop, who also died in the Presbyterian ministry in the west. When poor Bishop left the state of things was deplorable, and as the church had been so deeply reduced as to be unable to call a minister they applied to me, who was not then engaged, and I served them at a very small salary. During this engagement the church building was enlarged by extending it in the rear. I retired, and then, contrary to all the advice of judicious friends, they elected a strange genius named Graves, who flourished exceedingly for several years, capturing the half of Old Town by storm; but his sky-rockets all burned high in the air, and after a whiz and an emission of harmless sparks nothing came down but a stick. Exit poor Graves!

The Rev. I. C. Burke is the present laborious and successful pastor of that church.

St. Mark's was organized in 1860 by a band of nearly 100 members who left the First church when Dr. McCron was elected pastor of it. They bought their present house of worship from the Presbyterians, which was in a neglected condition, and in subsequent years and various times spent thousands of dollars in its improvement and renovation. The Rev. Theophilus Stork, D. D., then of Philadelphia, was elected first pastor, and served them faithfully, and built them up in every sense. He was not in good health, and soon was compelled to relinquish the work. He was what may be called an elegant preacher—he had the most refined taste, and was very careful in his pulpit preparations. He read all his sermons, and yet not very closely, but his elocution was good, and his composition so correct that he was listened to with great attention and profit. He was the writer of several popular books, which were widely circulated. His distinguished son, Charles A. Stork, who had been his assistant for some time before, succeeded him, and achieved by his talents and attainments a place among the very highest in our ministry. He accepted the position of Professor of Theology in the Seminary at Gettysburg, and was as eminently successful as a teacher as he was as a preacher and writer. His early death was lamented by all, and I think there were more extended newspaper notices and biographical sketches and reminiscences written of him than of any other of our ministers who have died. He was a universal favorite wherever he was known, and he left a void which it will be hard to fill up.

The Rev. Charles S. Albert, D. D., was elected his successor, and after a most prosperous ministry of 13 years, he was followed by the present worthy pastor, Rev. W. H. Dunbar, D. D.

St. Paul's church was dedicated in 1873, and the first pastor took charge of it in November of the same year. This was the Rev. J. A. Clutz, D. D., who after faithfully serving it about ten years resigned, to assume the office of Home Mission Secretary, for which his good business qualities fitted him so well. He was succeeded by the Rev. E. Felton, whose successor was the Rev. W. P. Evans, who left us for the Episcopal church after a four years' service at the church. The Rev. Chas. R. Trowbridge followed him as pastor.

Other English Lutheran congregations have been organized here in the last fifteen years, as follows: St. Luke's, Grace, Christ, Church of the Reformation, Messiah, Trinity, and Calvary.

If I were not speaking here exclusively of English preachers I would like to say a great deal of that meretorious servant of God, the Rev. Mr. Heyer, who labored most successfully in building up our German interest in Baltimore.

The first man who tried to establish a mission here was the Rev. Dr. Gustiniani, who was form· erly an Italian priest, had lived in Australia as a sort of missionary, thence went to England and got among the Wesleyans, and I believe came over here and joined our Synod. He wrote a book at my suggestion, and I named it "Papal Rome, as it is," by a Roman. This was in 1833. He was a man of fair education and undoubted Christian character. His ways were somewhat eccentric, and his church views not the most correct. It mattered not to him where he belonged, and he assumed all sorts of church liberties without any regard to synodical restrictions. He died in Cincinnati some years after.

A little congregation at Canton was in early years organized by the Rev. C. P. Krauth, who remained six months, and then went to the Second church, as already mentioned. Then came the Rev. W. A. Passavant, who continued about six months, and then took charge of the Third church. He was followed by the Rev. A. J. Weddell.

11

SCRAP-BOOK COLLECTIONS.

For many years I have been in the habit of pasting most of my newspaper contributions in a scrapbook, of which I now have six large 4to. volumes. I have found this plan very convenient. It is amusing, and often mortifying also, to leaf over this *rudis indigesta que moles*, which frequently brings up the saying of the Persian poet: " The remembrance of youth is a sigh."

Several series of articles were written, which I will mention here, and omit in the list of my writings at the end of this book.

" Eight Days in the Alps," in which an Alpine tour, in all its lofty enjoyments, hairbreadth escapes, perilous stumblings, bone-cracking tumbles, and numerous other queer adventures are faithfully portrayed. These appeared in the *Observer* of 1846–7.

" The Confessions of a Beneficiary " recited the privations, discouragements and final triumphs of an imaginary character, but everything was true in its particulars. The articles were not imputed to me at first, so real did I draw the picture; they reflected somewhat unfavorably on the condition of things in the Seminary, so that Prof. Schmucker felt constrained to deny that any young man who had begun active life " as apprentice to a housepainter, had ever been a student under his care." I was amused at his fruitless attempts to find out the author, for he took every word as historically true, and made no allowance for ideal word-painting or fiction founded on truth. I was gratified also that some reforms in the Seminary were the result of these "Confessions." They appeared about the year 1836.

A series running through many weeks, entitled "The Country Parson," "The Country Parson's Wife," and "The Country Parson's Daughter," attracted the general attention of the *Observer* readers of that day (1833–1834). They described characters, manners, experiences, and things generally. My description of an imaginary country schoolmaster, who frequently annoyed his minister by his unwelcome presence, was so true to nature that a man answering the description called upon his minister, and censured him severely for exposing him to the church. The minister replied that he was not the author of the article. "Well, then," said the culprit, "you must have told that *Observer* writer all about me, for nobody knows it but you!" The pastor protested, but the man went away unconvinced. Some years afterwards the minister told me this story himself. It was that thoroughly-read theologian and professor, the Rev. C. F. Schaeffer, D. D.

"Letters from a Garret" were continued several years, and excited considerable interest. In them everything of importance occurring in the Church, including some tales and other fancy sketches, was treated. Many letters relating to them were received, and every encouragement given to continue them. Giving of offence was carefully avoided, and yet some sensitive and suspicious persons thought they were alluded to, when in reality they were either unknown or their cases were entirely out of mind. During the publication of these articles the Rev. Dr. Cuyler, of Brooklyn, delivered a lecture at Gettysburg, in which he mentioned Mr. Garrett, President of the B. and O. Railroad. The simple-minded students thought he was alluding to my Letters, and raised a yell, which annoyed the orator, for he knew nothing of these Letters.

" Old Pictures Cleaned " was the title of a series, in which some facts relating to the Reformation not generally found in the popular books, and other obscure historical events, were illustrated. They included also some incidents of travel, which had been omitted from other communications.

" Over Sea Recollections " recounted the tales of a traveler, in which were grouped many facts of interest, and which at that period (1848) were received with general favor.

" Stray Leaves from my Journal " embrace sketches of tours made to Ohio in 1839. This was before the existence of railroads generally, and canal and stage coach travel are set forth in true colors.

" Loose Leaves from my Journal "(1847), " Pickings from a Waste-Basket " (1875), " Chips Picked up by the Wayside," " Letters from Baltimore," " Recreations of Luther," " Lutherana," " The Note-Book of a Naturalist," " Insecto-Theology,"

"The Necessity of the Reformation," "Scenes from the Youth of Spener," "Myrtle from our Fathers' Graves," "The Last Days and Burial of Luther," all of which were lengthened out in many numbers, appeared in the *Observer* and other church papers, besides a large number of single or detached communications on an infinite variety of subjects. I also furnished a large number of communications concerning Luther for *Our Church Paper*, published by the Henkels, of New Market, Va. They reached through several years, and they were always gratefully accepted by those enterprising men, who informed me that their subscribers read them with pleasure and profit.*

I was frequently attacked, and in a few instances with unprovoked severity, strongly sprinkled with malevolence, all of which the *Observer* of 1840–1850 published. The most bitter and wicked personal thrusts were aimed at me. I never condescended to reply to these vulgar assaults, although on one occasion friends of mine did vindicate me against an accusation which the author of it knew to be untrue.

The controversies in the Church were carefully avoided, and very few of my articles treated very demonstratively of the points in dispute among us. I uttered my Lutheran sentiments very freely, but I never had a theological discussion with any one in the papers.

---

* The *Workman* and the *Lutheran World* also contained many interesting and instructive letters and communications from the pen of Dr. Morris. C. R. T.

CHAPTER VII.

WHATEVER I may have done, like other boys, in collecting insects, plants, minerals and other " curiosities," it amounted to nothing practical or useful. I had no one to guide me, and there were no popular or elementary books on natural history to instruct me. Somewhere about my fourteenth year I had pretty well mastered the preface of Goldsmith's " Animated Nature," which at that time was considered a great book. I learned the construction of an electrical machine, with which I performed many common experiments. Thus for years I amused myself with such books and collected materials as I could lay hands upon, but understanding nothing about them I laid them aside for something more exciting.

It was not until after I had entered the ministry that I really began to study science, and I here desire to record my sincere conviction that, under God, my uninterrupted good health for many years is owing, in a great measure, to my pursuits of this character. My frequent ramblings in the fields and woods in search of objects, my researches upon the banks of streams and in the water, my exertions in climbing trees, ascending hills, beating bushes, sweeping the grass with the insect net, turning stones and logs, all contributing to the exercise of the muscles, the expansion of the chest, and to mental and bodily recreation, the agreeable interchange of lighter and severer studies, all aided in giving me a physical constitution which to this day has never been assailed by severe sickness of twenty-four hours' duration. Only once, or perhaps twice, in a life of fifty years in the ministry, have I been kept out of the pulpit by sickness, and then I was able to preach, but the doctor advised me to stay at home, especially as I had a good substitute.

It would be better for many a dyspeptic, weak-lunged, bronchitic, " delicate " minister if he had even a moderate taste for some science which compelled him to go out of doors! True, there is a popular prejudice against a minister giving much time to such studies, but I have always seemingly satisfied some of my kind friends who with grave countenances would impart a tender caution, by replying that my sermons were always the better after my long wanderings in the fields on Saturday afternoons.

Throughout all my clerical life I had my work for Sunday finished by Saturday noon, so that I had the afternoon and night to myself. I was never caught working at my sermons late on Saturday night, nor writing the last amen when the church bells were ringing on Sunday morning. I once stated this fact to a Presbyterian, who was much older than I, and he vowed he would adopt the good practice.

Entomology was my principal study, but to pursue this to scientific advantage a knowledge of the food plants of insects is necessary, hence botany comes in naturally. I made large collections in both departments, and every species was correctly and systematically arranged and labeled, by the help of my books or by fellow naturalists. And lest I might forget it I will here state a little incident, interesting in more than one relation. When I was at Charleston, attending the General Synod, in 1850, I saw, in Dr. Bachman's study, an immense herbarium, consisting of many thick folio volumes, and upon expressing an interest in them, especially after having been told that many of them had formerly belonged to Elliot, from which he had written his Southern Botany, the good Doctor intimated that he felt disposed to give them to any man who he was sure would take good care of them. I jumped at the offer; Mrs. Bachman seconded the proposition, and apprehending that some change might take place in their minds, I went out immediately and bought two large "store boxes," and hired a man to pack them up, and before night I had them on the wharf ready for the next packet to Baltimore! This was a rich treasure, for it contains many of Elliot's original labels and of Dr. Bachman's also. On one specimen of the "Poison Oak" is written, in the Doctor's own distinct chirography, "This specimen was once near putting an end to my botanical studies, for it poisoned me to a very dangerous degree." Strange to say, I was never affected by this plant, and yet some persons cannot go near it with impunity. None but an enthusiastic naturalist can appreciate such an apparently small affair as this which Dr. Bachman relates of himself.

The duplicate specimens in this herbarium were so numerous that I was able to make several good collections of Southern plants, which I sent to my botanical friends in Europe and to one in this country.

Many of the great books on these two branches were bought by me, and others too costly for my purse were consulted in other libraries.

General zöology also engaged my attention, and I had respectable collections of birds, the more common reptiles, large numbers of our land and fresh water shells, as well as marine, and some fishes. The best books on these subjects were also studied.

In several of these departments I had for many years the valuable co-operation of Dr. Melsheimer, of York county, Pa., of the Rev. D. Ziegler, of the German Reformed church, and of Prof. S. S. Haldeman, who has since abandoned natural history, and has become so eminent a philologist,* and many other naturalists with whom I became acquainted.

* Haldeman died in 1880. I gave a brief sketch of his scientific career in an address which I delivered as President of the Entomological Section of the A. A. A. S. at the meeting in Cincinnati in 1881.

I carried on for a long time a system of exchanges and correspondence with naturalists in our own country, and with Profs. Burmeister and Germar, of Halle; Erichson, Klug and Troschel, of Berlin; Mr. Riehl, of Cassel; the Sturms, of Nurnberg; Dr. Von dem Busch and Wilkens, of Bremen; Mr. Doubleday, of the British Museum, and others in England. These studies qualified me to some extent to give public lectures on the subject, which I have already spoken of, and which also led to my election as Lecturer on Natural History in the University of Maryland, where I never performed any service, and to a similar position in Pennsylvania College, where I gave short courses at various times. The difficulty in giving even a tolerably full course in the college is that there is no special provision made for an additional teacher on the subject, and the interruption to the regular curriculum which the introduction of extra lectures would occasion.

My numerous letters from the gentlemen mentioned above, and from other naturalists, form a valuable collection.

In the Seminary it is otherwise. I am paid for my services there, and for some years I have given annual series on "The Connection between Revelation and Science" to the Senior class, and also several times a pretty full course on "The Natural History of the Bible."

In the winter of 1878–1879 I attended a course of fifteen lectures on Biology in Johns Hopkins University. Every Saturday we had a lecture of an hour by Prof. Brooks, and immediately after three hours of work in the laboratory. These lectures were very instructive, and furnished me the most wholesome recreation.

My scientific studies, of course, brought me early into the acquaintance, correspondence and society of men of similar pursuits, both in this country and in Europe. I joined the American Association for the Advancement of Science, and have been absent very seldom from the· annual meetings. I there met many of the most distinguished American savans, with some of whom I have been on intimate terms for many years, such as Profs. Henry, Baird, Coues, Newcomb, Haldeman, Scudder, Riley, Silliman, Hagen, Baron Ostensacken, Le Conte, Horn, Lintner, Orde, Bethune, Saunders, Comstock, and many others in every department of science. Besides these, and many other members of the Association, there were many naturalists, especially entomologists, with whom I had frequent correspondence and personal interview. I particularly desire to mention Herman Strecker, of Reading, Pa., who is professionally a journeyman marble-worker, but is also an artist of high merit in drawing, engraving and coloring butterflies in a style of beauty and correctness which demands the admiration of all men of taste. By extensive and long-continued exchanges with naturalists in all parts of the world, he has brought together the largest collection of butterflies in this country, and which is exceeded by few private collections in the world. He has also described numerous new species, which have been adopted by other naturalists. He is a queer genius, and like all men of that character, does not receive the ardent admiration of every one; but all must acknowledge his uncommon artistic skill, perseverance and success.

Students of natural history, especially those who are also known to be field collectors, often receive valuable aid from other persons, who occasionally find something that is new and interesting to them. They kindly send or bring an insect, reptile, fish, bird, and sometimes a mineral or a flower, to ascertain what it is, or to do a favor to the naturalist, which is all very kind. Of course some things are now and then brought which are very common, but still unknown to the generous giver. But the receiver should express his thanks, for if he were to treat the gift indifferently he would not be likely to receive anything more from that quarter.

Strange facts are often referred to him for explanation, and many letters of inquiry are received, even from a distance. Once I got a letter from Ohio, containing an uncommon spider, of which the obliging correspondent wanted to know everything, and fortunately, with the aid of my spider books, I was able to satisfy him. Numerous similar inquiries are often made, or queer facts are communicated, and it is gratifying to be able to impart information, explain difficulties, correct errors, and encourage further researches.

In addition to this fascinating science I also paid considerable attention to microscopy, which afforded me much gratification. I have numerous figures of animalcules, zoophytes, and other objects, which I drew from the slides under the instrument.

Many years ago a French naturalist, Count Castlenau, deposited in what was known, at that time, as the National Institution, at Washington, an immense collection of beetles, filling over one hundred boxes. They had been neglected, and were fast going to ruin. Joseph K. Townsend, the ornithologist, who was at that time a clerk nominally in one of the departments, but really the working naturalist of the National Institution, engaged me to go to Washington to overhaul this collection, and if possible to preserve it from total destruction. I accepted the offer, and my compensation was the privilege of keeping specimens of the duplicates. The boxes were removed to Townsend's house, his family being absent for the summer, where I labored laboriously for five or six days during a severe spell of hot weather. I put the collection into fairly good order, and thoroughly cleansed all the boxes. I was satisfied with my compensation, for my own collection was considerably enriched. I do not know what has become of the Castlenau collection, but I presume it has been suffered to go to ruin. It was subsequently transferred to the Smithsonian, but it is doubtful if any portion of it is now in existence. Townsend was an enterprising naturalist, and crossed the Rocky

Mountains with Nuttall, the botanist, long before the discovery of gold in California. It was a laborious and dangerous tour. He wrote a very clever book on the natural history of that country, in which he also describes the perilous adventures of the long journey. From the Pacific coast the two travelers sailed for the Sandwich Islands in pursuit of plants, birds, and other objects. Among many other interesting incidents which he related to me I will relate the following:

An American missionary kindly entertained them, and did all in his power to promote their scientific pursuits. On Sunday morning Townsend, who was no strict observer of that day, tried to steal away from the house, gun in hand, after Sandwich Island birds. To his deep mortification the good missionary observed him, and remarked "Wait a moment and I'll go with you." "What!" said Townsend, "do you go hunting on Sunday?" "This is not Sunday," replied he, "it is Monday." And so it was. Townsend in crossing the continent had lost a day, and the missionary in going around Cape Horn had gained a day, and this accounted for the difference. Townsend was glad that with a good conscience he could now go hunting on that day, and that he had the missionary for a companion. I have often told this story, and yet there are a good many otherwise sensible people who cannot understand how it could possibly be that the day should be Sunday to one of them and Monday to the other.

Thus for many years I pursued these studies as an amateur, and acquired by exchange or purchase a fair collection of insects. At first I confined myself to Coleoptera (Beetles), but exchanged them for Lepidoptera (Butterflies), to which order I have confined my studies.

I have already mentioned that I was honored by the Smithsonian Insitute publishing two of my books; one was " A Synopsis of the Lepidoptera of the United States," 8vo., which was much sought after by young entomologists, who used it to name their butterflies, and which was highly spoken of by some French, English and German journals. The other was " A Catalogue of the Described Lepidoptera of the United States." The list of my publications, given in the following pages, contains other minor writings of mine on this subject.

CHAPTER VIII.

RESIGNATION AS PASTOR; LIBRARIAN OF THE PEABODY INSTITUTE.

AFTER a service of 33 years in the church in Lexington street, I had a good opportunity of resigning without compulsion or from exhaustion. I offered myself as a candidate for the position of Librarian in the Peabody Institute, and was elected. It was necessary that I should resign my pastorship, and this was a struggle. I had served that church 33 years, having built it up from the beginning, enlarged the house of worship several times, sent off two colonies, built the parsonage, paid off a large portion of the debt, and left everything in a prosperous condition. I was not compelled to go, nor did the people desire it, at least there were no outward evidences of it. I reasoned thus: "If I do not leave now and accept this respectable place, so well suited to my tastes, I may never have a better opportunity of bettering my condition. If I stay here much longer I will be considered too old to be called to any other church, and my own people will get tired of me and give me unmistakable evidences that I had better leave. Worn out among them, and no longer a young man whom any other church would want (for few men over fifty receive calls), had I not better quietly withdraw and give the church an opportunity of securing another man?" I consulted judicious men, in and out of my church, and they sanctioned my course. Many persons afterwards told me that it was a proper step, and thought I was the proper man to fill the place. The church had never supported me, and the deficiency was made up from my own private income to an amount of upwards of $15,000, at a low calculation. I thought I could get along on a smaller salary, for the Peabody gave me only $1,500, whereas the church gave me $1,500 and the parsonage. Not being a pastor, I would not have so many expenses.

Some persons found fault with me because they thought I was going to abandon the pulpit altogether for a secular office, but they were mistaken. I never intended to do that—I would rather have given up everything else. I was consecrated to the pulpit. I might for a season cease to be pastor, but never for a day to be preacher. Expediency might suggest the former, but necessity only the latter. My own conscience justified me, and I had the sanction of one whose opinion on such a subject I valued more highly than that of any other person living. My brother also sanctioned it, and my mind was at ease.

I left the parsonage in July, 1860, and bought the house on Greene street, where we have since resided in the winter. I preached no farewell sermon.

12

Immediately after Rev. McCron was elected in my place, by those who remained after about 100 of the congregation withdrew and organized the congregation on Eutaw street under the pastoral care of Rev. Dr. Stork.

Monument Street church, which was originally an offshoot from the First church, was then vacant, and I preached there every Sunday for a whole year. Several years afterwards I was elected temporary pastor of that church. I never lived in Old Town, not wishing to change my comfortable home in Greene street for the narrow and inconvenient parsonage on Monument street, and then again I did not expect to stay long with that people. I spent much time among them, and occupied the study in the church. Most of them treated me kindly, and my services among them are gratefully remembered to this day. They were, in general, a plain, sincere people, who never gave me more trouble than usually falls to the lot of most ministers, and many of them were greatly profited by my instructions. The majority had very vague theological, and some of them fanatical notions and very loose ideas of true Lutheranism.

During my pastorate the house of worship was enlarged and beautified, but I continued preaching every Sunday morning for several summer months, although the whole rear end was knocked out, and the scaffolds were standing in the body of the house. I did not leave my summer home, and I thought it just as well to come in on Sunday morning and preach to the few hundred who attended.   My reminiscences of that church are on the whole pleasant.

While pastor in Old Town I collected nearly $1,200 to build a chapel on the Bel Air road, near the city, at a place called San Domingo.   There are two or three breweries there, and the population by no means inclined churchwards.   We held Sunday-school there for some years, and tried to gather in the people by preaching, but the lager beer interest was too strong, and the enterprise was abandoned after my resignation and the property was sold.   I remember that the proprietress of the largest saloon offered us the use of a large upper hall for a Sunday-school anniversary, and in order to reach it we were compelled to pass through a large place that was crowded with beer-drinkers on Sunday afternoon, so that they were talking loud, laughing and jingling their glasses while we were singing and praying up stairs, and all the doors open.   We never could awaken any interest in our work among the people there.   Some of them would not even send their children to Sunday-school, and it was a queer excuse for the absence of the few who did attend that they sometimes gave, that they had to stay at home to help in the bar!

After my resignation, in 1866, they elected a man, against my remonstrance, who, by his extravagance of demeanor, almost ruined the church.   They were perfectly infatuated, but paid dearly for their error.

He was expelled from our Synod in 1876, and this congregation was in a deplorable condition. They then called on me to again take the oversight of them, which I consented to do until they would elect a man permanently, which they did in a few months afterwards. My last Sunday with them was January 19, 1877.

A few years before this, that is, in 1874, the Rev. C. A. Stork, D. D., went abroad, and I agreed to be his substitute during his absence. I began October 4, 1874, and concluded in July, 1875, when he returned. During his absence the General Synod of 1875 was held in that church (St. Mark's).

In January, 1879, the Rev. Mr. Dimm, the principal of Lutherville School, and pastor of the village church, resigned the latter position, and as there was no one else who could take charge of it on account of the small salary, I assumed the care of it. I agreed to preach but once on Sunday, and I continued this service to July 6, 1885.

MY LIBRARIANSHIP IN THE PEABODY INSTITUTE.

It is well known to persons acquainted with the history of this grand institution that Mr. Peabody, besides appointing twenty-eight men as Trustees, designated two hundred and fifty others, from whom vacancies in the Board were to be filled.

My name was on this latter list, and I was the first man elected as a Trustee to fill a vacancy, which was occasioned by the death of the Rev. Dr. Burnap.

I was much surprised and gratified by this mark of distinction, for there were many older and more influential men from whom a selection might have been made. Besides, I was not personally acquainted with most of the Trustees, and not on intimate terms with those whom I did know. I accepted the position, and attended several meetings of the Board before I resigned my church to assume the responsible office of librarian. At this time the institution was not in active operation; the building was not finished, and no books had been bought. The Trustees, however, concluded to elect a librarian, and after long deliberation I concluded to offer myself as a candidate, not, however, before I was certain that I would be chosen. I had assurances from a sufficient number that they would vote for me, and I gave in my name. There were four other candidates, but I received all the votes except a few. My chief competitor was John R. Thompson, the poet and editor. The salary was $1,500 a year, which was less than I received from my church, for there I had the same amount and a free parsonage, which was equal to $500 more. I had paid some attention to bibliography, and had become pretty well acquainted with books which were suited to a first-class reference library. I was elected on June 1, 1860, and entered upon my duties August 1, 1860. For some weeks I was diligently engaged in preparing rules for the government of the library, the modes and places of purchasing books, and making out lists of works to be bought. This list comprised 50,000 volumes, and the Trustees appropriated $500 for its publication in an 8vo. volume. This was the basis of purchases for some years.

In making this list I consulted the best English and American catalogues, and in studying library economy I had access to all the great works on that subject in English, French and German.

During my three years' service I spent over $30,000 for books, keeping up a constant correspondence with European and American dealers. I went to Boston and New York several times to make purchases, but especially to examine the libraries and to study their modes of management. I wrote voluminous reports for my Library Committee on systematic arrangement, cataloguing and preservation of books.

I had numerous applications from ladies and gentlemen for subordinate positions; most of them looked upon it as an easy place, where they might spend most of their time in reading. I selected as my assistant Philip R. Uhler, who is still connected with the institution, and has become Provost. During his absence at Cambridge, where he was a pupil of Agassiz in natural history, having previously resigned, but subsequently reassumed his place, I appointed Alexander Stork, who held the position for several years.

Some very unfounded prejudices against the Institute prevailed generally, which I did all in my power to remove, and to some effect. An opinion was entertained by a certain class of people that it was intended only for what they called the aristocracy, and not for persons of inferior station in life. This opinion was founded upon the fact that only wealthy, or at least influential men or leaders of men, were managers of it, but I took pains to invite reading men of all classes to partake of its benefits, and heartily welcomed all who did come. One strong argument that I employed was this, that if it was intended only for the upper classes very few of them took advantage of it, for there were hundreds of " first-class citizens " who never entered the house, and some of them living less than 500 yards from the building. It is a singular fact that there are thousands of respectable and intelligent men and women in this city who to this day have never seen the grand collections of books in that library. There are lovers and readers of books by the hundreds who never go there. The prejudice is not eradicated, but I fear it is on the increase. I could tell some of the reasons, but the subject is not interesting.

Uninterrupted sedentary labor, of seven hours daily, was not favorable to my health, and I became weary of the monotonous life. After the first year it was not much more than manual labor or mercantile business, cataloguing, letter writing, and buying at the lowest prices; this latter part was often humiliating, but I was compelled to submit.

. The entire management of the concern was left to

me and a member of the Library Committee. The other members paid no attention whatever to it, and some of them came into the library department once or twice a year. This member was not a scholar, nor had he any knowledge of the higher style of books. He did not know a word of Latin, Greek or German; he was unsympathetic in his nature, haughty in his manners, and most absurd in his pretensions. He knew no poetry nor literature nor science, and yet this man was my master in the selection of books and my superior in authority in all things. Never before had I been placed in such a humiliating position. I was mortified beyond expression at my enforced subserviency. I was often compelled to yield my better judgment to his imperious dogmatism to avoid a violent conflict. Never was my patience put to so severe a test, and I bore it all as a righteous divine chastisement. One member of the committee who would have sympathized with me was sick during all this time, and died. I sometimes complained to him of the manner in which I was thwarted and oppressed, and he used to say, " Bear it a little longer, until I get well, and you and I will work together harmoniously." Alas for me and for him and for the Institute, he never recovered. He was a scholarly gentleman, and in his death the Institute suffered an irreparable loss.

I was made to feel very soon that this member did not want a man of literary tastes as librarian, but a man who could drive the best bargain with the trade, and I often felt myself and the institution belittled by obeying his instructions in this regard; he wanted a man who could keep a ledger, and looked upon a literary acquaintance with books as a secondary matter. A man who could manage a factory, keep the operatives severely to their work, pay them off on Saturday evening, and keep the accounts straight, was his idea of the qualifications for a librarian. He never would listen patiently to any suggestion I might make, although he subsequently adopted many of them after I had adroitly made him think they were his own, but as coming directly from me he never would sanction them. He treated me and my assistant as if we were apprentices in a dry-goods store; he had no respect for our labors, and never gave us credit for anything we did; he was constantly finding fault. He would give orders, and then rebuke us for executing them, having forgotten that he had given them.

The man who without any linguistic knowledge would pretend to select the best editions of the Latin and Greek classics must have a high opinion of himself, and the man who asked me "whether the Septuagint was a Hebrew Bible," and often spoke of the "Opera om *i* na" of a great author, and suggested the purchase of a "Greek Lexington," is not the man for a Library Committee!!!

It may be presumed that my situation was anything but pleasant, and I longed for the day of my release, but only because my daily association with this man embittered my life. I could enumerate other grievances which I suffered, but I will forbear. Never did I spend three such unhappy years, and the remembrance of the mortifications to which I submitted, and the painful experience of my unhappy association with that man, is anything but pleasant.

I was previously told that I would have trouble with this pretentious individual, for his association with some gentlemen in the management of the Baltimore Library rendered him obnoxious to them. I was warned against his arrogance, but I thought that by conscientious attention to my duties, and the cultivation of a forgiving spirit, I might overcome his morose disposition; but from the beginning he treated Uhler and me like fourth-class clerks, and showed his contempt of us and his own perverseness every day. And yet, let every man have his due. He was a man of leisure, and devoted all his time to the Institute, from the day the first plan of the building was proposed to its completion. His residence was within a hundred yards of the location, and enabled him to be present constantly and to see every stone and brick laid. No other man had time or inclination to do this, and he doubtless was of some use. But unfortunately his service was rendered in a very offensive manner, for there was not a workman about the building, from the superintendent down to a hod-carrier, who did not take delight in using any other than polite language respecting him.

I often defended him against severe malediction. I have often heard others, who were his equals in authority and far superior to him in intelligence and influence, denouncing him without stint. But he was sincerely honest in his zeal, I believe, and may have saved many a dollar for the Institute; and yet his bungling errors cost it many more. He lived unloved and died unwept.

I left the Institute at the expiration of my term with the personal good will of every member of the Board, except this man; and even he, thinking possibly that I was poor, and needing support, gave me a parting stab by saying that they would perhaps give me a professorship, when he knew well enough there was no provision made for such an office, and never would be. My successor, who is a first-class business man, soon managed to get rid of this person as a member of the Library Committee, and has never encountered the humiliating difficulties which so severely taxed my patience. After my resignation I received a letter from Prof. Henry, of the Smithsonian Institute, of which I give an extract:

"SMITHSONIAN INSTITUTE, APRIL 6, 1867.

"Although your position in the Institute gave you an opportunity of doing much good in the line of your tastes, yet your resignation mnst relieve you from perplexities and annoyances ill suited to the constitutional habits and the essential requisites of a man of literature or science."

CHAPTER IX.

WHEN, in 1851, Dr. B. Kurtz and I, with our own
money and on our own responsibility, bought the
farm, now called Lutherville, consisting of a large
number of acres, for which we gave $7051, and which
we subsequently transferred to the Seminary Board
at the same price, to be sold in lots at an advanced
price, thus raising funds to build the Seminary edifice.
We retained 16 acres, he eleven and I five, with the
consent of the Board, as a sort of compensation for
the risk we ran and as interest on the money advanced.   I chose the five acres which I now occupy
and he selected eleven, embracing that section upon
which Mrs. Urlaub's house now stands.   I once heard
it intimated, to my deep chagrin, that this enterprise
of Dr. Kurtz's and mine was a pecuniary speculation.
Never was a greater calumny uttered.   Our design
was purely disinterested.   We ventured our money
for the good of the Church, and we suffered untold
anxiety and trouble.   Some men are incapable of
generous acts themselves, and think everybody else
like them, or are envious of the liberality of others
because it rebukes our own parsimony.

My house was the first one erected. It cost $4,000. All the ground was covered with a dense forest, and much preliminary and subsequent work and expense were necessary to bring the surroundings into proper shape and order. We moved out in the summer of 1852, and have lived there four or five months of every summer since that day.

From the Lutheran Observer.

"MY DEAR DR. S——: You ask me how I am spending the summer at my Tusculum at Lutherville. Well, a man who has a large and convenient house, situated in the midst of a grove of native forest trees, and surrounded by some of the cheaper embellishments of landscape gardening, with a soil producing in abundance all the fruits and vegetables of this latitude; with spring water, cold and clear; with arbors inviting retirement from the hot sun; with seats scattered over the lawn, under the shade of the wide-spreading beech and gnarled oak; with the fragrance of flowers; with the rose and morning-glory, and *Wistaria, Clematis*, and other climbing plants twining in graceful embrace over the columns of his cottage; with a plentifully supplied table; with a good appetite and a grateful heart to enjoy it; with a happy family; with a good conscience; with intelligent neighbors; with a good library; and—and—well, I was about to say, that a man with all these things should spend his time pleasantly and profitably; shouldn't he?

"But you ask me what are my special employments and my regular everyday pursuits? Well, as far as amusement is concerned, I receive my daily mail at nine o'clock, and then an hour is spent in reading the morning papers and my letters. Those of the latter requiring answers are immediately attended to. I go fishing three or four times every week, on which account my neighbors call me Old Izaak Walton! I give several lessons a week in botany to a lad of my family; I capture moths at night in my study—well, if they *will* come in and fly about my lamp, I think it well to *press* them to stay, and they do! I play croquet with my girls and my neighbors' girls and boys! I have even umpired the village boys in their game of base ball; I occasionally serve at the bat myself, but I pay a little Irish boy to run the bases for me; I strike tremendous sky-scrapers and clover-cutters, and my Hibernian boy makes many a home run. I play nine-pins with the ladies and gentlemen, and often make a ten-strike, so that I am always chosen first by the makers-up of the game. A sound philosopher once said: 'He that thinks any innocent pastime foolish, has either to grow wiser, or is past the ability to do so.'

"These are my chief amusements, but I do a great deal of work beside. I carefully prepare one sermon a week; I go to town several times a week; I read the principal reviews and monthlies and a few of the weeklies, beside skimming over more than a dozen of our own Church papers, especially the German; I conduct a considerable correspondence with friends and the press; I am writing several fresh lectures for next winter's campaign. I try to keep up with the current literature of the day, which I find it very hard to do; I am constantly making efforts to increase my collection of books concerning Luther, and of the productions of Lutheran divines in America; I spend considerable time in entertaining my numerous city visitors, for my place is so convenient from town! But they are always welcome. I give several 'receptions' in the summer, one of which is a strawberry party, to some of my city clerical friends, and the other to a company of scientific associates who annually come out for a day's recreation. I leave home occasionally with my family on a tour to the seashore or elsewhere, and especially to the meetings of the American Association for the Advancement of Science, at which I meet many distinguished men. This is the way I spend my summers here."

For four or five years I have been preacher for the small congregation here, because when my predecessor resigned there was no one ready to take the place, and I happened just at that time to have no pastoral charge. The congregation is not large enough to support a minister, and it suited both parties for me to step into the vacancy.

MY CAREER AS A READER.

From my earliest youth I was a "spouter" of selections from Shakespeare and other writers, and spread myself widely, as young declaimers do. My brother George, who had some taste in that line, often urged me to recite my pieces in our room before we went to bed. In this way I acquired a fullness of voice which has been of great service to me in public speaking during my whole life.

I always was assigned to leading parts in our academy elocutionary exercises at York, and when I was but a small boy I took an inferior character in "She Stoops to Conquer," which was played in the old court house at York by the young men of the town.

When public reading became a popular institution, twenty or twenty-five years ago, I entered into the ranks of professionals with energy, and have prosecuted the subject to a greater or less degree ever since. I studied it thoroughly with all the aid that the numerous books could furnish me, and wrote out a pretty thorough treatise for my own use, for I was called upon to teach the art, and had a number of private pupils. It became known that I was giving lessons to some persons, and I soon had more applicants for instruction than I have ever told, for some of them were under promise of secrecy. Some were teachers in schools, some were lawyers, several physicians applied, a few candidates for the stage, some ministers, and one aspirant for a seat in Congress, to whom I gave a very few private lessons, but when he was defeated in the nomination by his party he gave up elocution. I received very few of these applicants. I did. not want the reputation of being a teacher of elocution, and would not give the time to proper instruction. I took several, however, and one of them was an ambitious local Methodist preacher, but a truly good man, who came to my study on Saturday nights to learn to read hymns and the Scriptures, and insisted upon giving me a dollar for every lesson, which I did not wish to take, but he seemed to be offended at my refusal. He began too late to read, and with all my pains I could not break him of a peculiar nasal pulpit tone, which he very much regretted.

I gave two courses of ten lectures each in the Peabody Institute at $150 for each course. I had twenty to thirty pupils, but did not accomplish much with beginners, for I had no opportunity of giving each of them special instruction, which is absolutely necessary. The hour slipped around before I could hear each one read and correct their faults, and besides I always gave a lecture of twenty to thirty minutes duration. I have no confidence in general class instruction in elocution. Unless there is frequent reading by each pupil, teaching does not do much for practical reading.

For some years I have given, by appointment of the Board, annual lectures to the Seminary students at Gettysburg. Many of them have gone out as excellent readers of hymns and the Bible, as well as good declaimers.

Of course I have frequently been invited to entertain societies, private assemblies, churches, and home parties; I have gone to more than twenty different towns and read for the benefit of religious societies and literary circles, but seldom asked for any pay.

I could not mention the number of times I have read in Baltimore, publicly and privately, and have received the stereotyped notices of the newspapers.

This business, like all others, has been overdone. Many pretenders, of both sexes, have ventured upon this stage, and they fail ingloriously; while there are many also, of both sexes, who are wonderfully gifted, and some of them make a good living in the profession.

Of course I went to hear all the public readers who advertised in Baltimore, but I have never heard any tragedian on the regular stage. I should like to hear how some of the most eminent render certain passages in Shakespeare and other popular dramatists. An actor of some eminence once called at the Peabody Institute, and upon being introduced to him I asked him how he would read a certain pas-

13

sage in Shakespeare's " Julius Cæsar." He read it, and I ventured to dissent from him. When he heard my reading, and it was but a single line, he exclaimed, " By George, if I ever play Cassius I will adopt your reading, for it brings out the sense, which my rendering did not." This led to further conversation, and he gave me to understand that most actors read mechanically, without sentiment; it was their profession, and their only aim was to get through the part as soon and as genteelly as possible; that while the audience was sometimes moved to tears or other demonstrations, the actors were really indifferent to all the emotion they seemed to feel, or were really winking to other actors behind the scenery.

From many of these professional readers I learned much, but others taught me nothing. I introduced myself to some of them, and had some interesting and profitable interviews. Some of the gentlemen and ladies were cultivated people, and others were anything else.

Some of these men occasionally have strange and unpleasant experiences. I rememeber once hearing a first-class professional reader perform in a country town where I happened to be at the time. In reciting a humorous piece, which he did admirably, he was, of course, compelled to distort his face to bring out the full force, and this naturally set the audience into a roar, and a benchful of little boys seated just before him were particularly demonstrative in their applause. Before the noise had subsided the reader announced the impassioned defense of Cataline, which requires great physical exertion, loud and vehement declamation, the facial expression of anger, contempt and disdain, and necessarily occasions distortion of the features. These little boys thought he was reciting another funny piece, and laughed uproariously. The reader was in the midst of the most impassioned part, and was dreadfully annoyed by this untimely demonstration. I leaned over and told the scamps to hush, and that this was not the time to laugh but to cry, but they could not understand.

The reader committed an error. The transition from the broadly comic to the deeply tragic was too sudden. It was an offence against good taste as well as against mental philosophy.

I have tried to push forward some young aspirants to fame and money, and have secured places for them by letters and personal efforts. A few have paid their expenses and perhaps had little over, but I remember one occasion where I was compelled to make up a deficiency to save a candidate for elocutionary honors from very serious embarrassment. I was under no obligation to pay other people's debts, but I did it, to the great relief of those particularly concerned. I vowed to quit recommending adventurous and unfledged readers.

I know one very ambitious young man, with whom I read in private several times at his request. No one else was present, and the practice was pleasant. He aimed at being a professional elocutionist, and hoped to make a fortune by following the business. He began his career in a neighboring city, and failed in bringing out a crowd and did not even pay expenses. He became disheartened, and came to tell me that after earnest prayer he felt it his duty to enter the Methodist ministry, in which, however, he did not continue for more than several years, and then joined the Unitarians.

Another young man, engaged in a very honorable and useful profession, came to me for instruction, and said that he was a candidate for the Methodist ministry. I took him as a pupil, but charged him nothing. I lost sight of him for several years, and was then told that he had been refused license on the ground of unsoundness in the faith, and had gone to the Unitarian church. My gratuitous service was all in vain.

For several winters we had reading exercises conducted by me weekly in the Y. M. C. A. rooms, before the present building was erected. We usually had good audiences, and spent agreeable evenings. Some of my old pupils usually read; others I sometimes invited, and occasionally there were volunteers, some of whom did well, but others badly. So many of the latter appeared that the audiences thinned out, and I became weary of it and broke it up. There were some exhibitions of such presumptuous vanity and affectation as are seldom witnessed.

THE LECTURE PLATFORM.

It was about the year 1830 that the public lecture system was first introduced into Baltimore. It was a new institution, but it has since become universal, and has been pursued by some as a profession. Like many other good things, it was carried to a ridiculous extent, and many ambitious men, who had neither the qualifications of education, character nor graceful elocution, sought distinction and money in this field. Some secured both, and they became so popular as public lecturers that their services were engaged months in advance at high prices. Some clergymen especially acquired immense reputations in this department, and were invited to remote places to be heard. Others of smaller note set themselves up in the profession, but a few experiments demonstrated their incapacity for the work.

This "lecturing business" would make a good subject for a first-class article, but this is not my design at present.

I do not remember how it was that I became one of our earliest lecturers in Baltimore, but I am sure it was not of my own seeking or appointment, but I held forth on "The Honey Bee" as early as 1833 in what was then called Warfield's church, in St. Paul street, now standing back of a house which N. C. Brooks built for a ladies' school. This lecture, with various additions, has been repeated by me more than twenty times in various places, and frequently by special request. It interested people everywhere, for it is wonderful how few persons know anything about the extraordinary habits of that little insect. I had large painted illustrations (as I have for all my lectures), which add much to the understanding of the subject and to the relief of the lecturer.

The Smithsonian Institute in former years had regular series every winter. Prof. Henry invited me to give six or seven on "The Transformations of Insects" and allied subjects, which were attended by crowds of persons. One evening in riding over to the Institute in the same carriage with several Southern members of Congress, I mentioned that I was going to show that there was such a thing as slavery among a certain genus of insects, and that the slaves were black, as is well known to be the case among ants. "Make the most of it, Doctor," said they. "Not more than nature has done," said I, "and that is enough. Even you Southern slave-holders would not do what instinct leads ants to do, that is, steal your slaves from neighboring plantations and compel them to work for you." They were much gratified with this information, new to them, but I gave them to understand that in my judgment this slave-holding system of the ants did not justify human slavery.

I afterwards gave another series in the Smithsonian; subsequently I gave a course of six on "Insect Architecture," "Discoveries of the Microscope," and "Some Wonders in the Structure and Life of

Plants," in Dr. Butler's new church. Prof. Henry was in the pulpit with me, and made some remarks afterwards.

On numerous other occasions I held forth as lecturer in Washington at Dr. Butler's church or lecture-room, and once before the Washington National Academy on "The History and Progress of Natural History in the United States." They passed a complimentary resolution to have my lecture published, which was the last I ever heard of it, as I expected, for it was an impecunious concern, and did not last long.

Besides my regular and annual course in the Seminary and College at Gettysburg I have lectured in the College church and Agricultural Hall in the same town. On one occasion many years ago the students undertook to raise money for some purpose connected with the College, probably for Linnæan Hall, and they sent for me to help them out of the difficulty, if possible. I went and gave them two discourses on "Adventures in the Alps," and raised $80 for them. It was a small sum, but it relieved them of some pressing demand.

Many a poor church, Sunday-school or other religious enterprise have I thus aided on a small scale. My "Bee and Alps" lectures were in great demand, and though it is now thirty years since I was on the Alps, yet that lecture, with my pretty pictures, is still occasionally called for.

I gave the " History of the Hessian Fly and the

Wheat Midge, with the best Methods of Preventing their Ravages," before the Agricultural Society of Frederick county, Md., and also the York County, Pa., Agricultural Society.

Some years I have received as many as twenty invitations to lecture or read from different quarters, but I did not accept the half of them. I was seldom offered more than traveling expenses, but this was not the reason for declining. I did not like leaving home in the dead of winter, nor lecturing probably in a cold church to a small audience, if the weather should be bad, or the roads muddy, or the nights dark, nor being put, probably, in a cold room to sleep, nor being exposed in riding to the place from the railroad station, as was sometimes the case. I refused some invitations to places of easy access because my conditions were not complied with, which were simply that a good audience was to be secured in advance by the sale of tickets, and all matters previously arranged, so that nothing was left to me but to do my work.

The subjects of my lectures were generally scientific or literary. I never chose any of those so-called popular or *ad captandum* themes which some of our men delight in, such as matrimony and the like.

Colleges at which I have given single lectures are, besides Gettysburg, the University of Virginia, at Charlottesville, where by invitation of the Students' Christian Association I gave on Sunday night, in the University Hall, "Young Men in History," Newark,

Del., Allentown, Pa., and the Agricultural College near Washington. I have received invitations from the college at Westminster, Md., and Springfield, O.

The following are the places where I have occupied the lecture platform: City of New York, Philadelphia several times, Lancaster, York frequently, Gettysburg frequently, Chambersburg, Harrisburg, Hanover, Lutherville, Towson, Ellicott City, Frederick, Westminster, Richmond, Cumberland, Kutztown, Catonsville, Govanstown, Allegheny City, Selinsgrove, Pottstown, Hazleton, Mechanicstown, Reisterstown six times, Union Bridge, New Market, Salem, Washington several times, at Dr. Butler's church and two courses in the Smithsonian, Wilmington, and other places not remembered. I was invited to Wytheville and Marion, Va., Bellefonte, Pa., and many other places, which I refused.

The following is an extract of an article of mine in the *Observer :*

"The minister who has acquired a respectable reputation as a lecturer or reader, has an opportunity of extensively helping religious objects without any expense to them, *if he has inclination and time.* I know a man who has unfortunately for himself become somewhat notorious in this line, who this winter has had over twenty invitations to exercise his alleged gifts, and not more than two of them offered anything like compensation. They ask him to leave his own work at home, to expose himself to all sorts of weather, to run constant risks of his life on railroads, to wear out his clothes, to sleep in cold rooms and to submit to many other inconveniences, and the only return offered in most cases, is, 'your traveling expenses will be paid.' They expect a man to consent to an absence of two or three days from his church and family, to be willing to lose the bene-fit of a wedding or two, to invite some other minister to attend to funerals and other pastoral labors, to yield to the contraction cf a cold, to give up his books and warm study, and all for 'your expenses will be paid.' Nothing said about torn coat, bedusted clothes, exposure to the vitiated air, the vulgar pro-fanity, the rude jostling, and tobacco-puddled floor of a crowded car; nothing said about the risk of losing your carpet bag or breaking your limbs, or detention on the road, or *collisions*, or misplaced switches or perilous night travel! Oh! no; 'your necessary expenses will be paid.'

"This acquaintance of mine has had *some* rich experience in the lecturing business. Among many others he says that he was some time ago invited by a minister on the border of New York State, which would have required at least four days' ab-sence from home. 'Expenses would be paid' and yet the minister would not consent to sell tickets and ascertain whether he could secure an audience; he was not certain whether the people would come out, as it was a new thing, and was not even sure whether the 'expenses' would be made up.

"Another minister, living in a small obscure village, wanted to 'surprise his people,' and this is the way it was to be done. The lecturer was to travel over seventy-five miles and to arrive in the village just at night-fall and nobody was to know it. The bell was to be rung and the people would come without any previous announcement. Then the 'lecturer' was to enter the church, and thus 'surprise' the congregation! Happy concep-tion, most considerate minister! If the lecturer had been fool enough to go, he might have had about ten old women, and seven men, and four mischievous boys and two young darkies for an audience. Well, he did not go, and told the minister that he (the lecturer) could put him in the way of 'surprising' his people at a much cheaper cost, and that was by studying and preparing some good sermons and faithfully doing his pastoral duties, and if that did not 'surprise' them they must be ineffa-bly stupid! He has not heard from that quarter since.

"A peculiar and forcible argument was once employed by a country pastor to induce the lecturer in question to accept an invitation. The place was an out-of-the-way village, where perhaps two or three newspapers were taken, where the people had little or no intercourse with the outside world, where there was no social influence and no literary culture, and the last place in the world where a man could make a hit and acquire reputation. The argument urged by the minister was that a good lecture in his church would secure for the performer a good name, and thus promote his interest as a candidate for similar favors elsewhere! Jehoshaphat! a penny whistle to *trumpet* fame, and the bleating of a calf for an advertisement!

"Some of our lecturing friends are sometimes sadly disappointed in their audiences. One of them told me that he once went over a hundred miles to lecture and his subject was 'Matrimony.' It happened that the weather was bad that night and his whole audience was made up of four old women, two very old men and three very young boys, one of whom was a darkey, the most inappropriate audience for a discourse on *matrimony* that can be conceived. There was no fitness of things.

"Some men have adopted the lecturing business as a profession, and being popular and immensely puffed they make money by it. They get from fifty to a hundred dollars a night. Some men get more, but they are not lecturers by profession. They are eminent ministers or scientists. Tyndall was paid by this city $1,000 for three lectures, and more at some other places. Gough charges from $250 to $300 a night, and some few lady lecturers are paid high prices. Saxe came to Gettysburg for one hundred dollars and Lossing for sixty dollars, and of that sum they were obliged to pay a good per cent. to the bureau in New York.

"I hear some one ask, 'What is this bureau?' It is an office at which lecturers register their names, subjects and prices. The men at the office engage to furnish lecturers of any grade and price, and select from their list the men who they think will suit the applicants and send them, and of course they charge the lecturers for securing the engagement for them. Most of the business for the Northern States is carried on in this way, and frequently the people are sadly disappointed.

"If an ambitious gentleman has, or thinks he has, a good lecture, let him deliver it in Turkey Buzzard School-house, and then pay the editor of 'The Cross-road Literary and Political Trumpeter' to blow loud and long. Let the aspirant send the puffs to the bureau, his name will be put on the list, and he may secure several paying engagements, but his shallowness will soon be discovered and he be dropped. I have seen such laudations of some of our men in the papers which would have been worth at least one hundred dollars to them if they had 'put in' at the bureau. I would advise these men not to select Matrimony as a subject. They do not handle it delicately. They compel ladies to hang their heads in shame; they offend refined people, and cultivated audiences will not listen to them a second time. I know one man who broke down under the weight of a matrimony lecture. It was horribly offensive in its allusions and exceedingly commonplace in its treatment. He could not get on the bureau list, nor secure a hearing outside of his own narrow circle, and he wilted. Beware of lecturing on matrimony, whatever you may do about practically demonstrating it!"

CHAPTER X.

CHURCH CORRESPONDENCE.

FROM my earliest ministry an extensive exchange
of letters on church affairs has taken up much of my
time. I do not mean to intimate that it was all time
wasted; much of it, on the other hand, was useful
labor, for it concerned the Church; there was no
subject of great importance relating to her welfare
agitated in the central section of our territory that
did not come within the sphere of my correspondence. Many letters from beyond these central limits
on special church subjects were also received, most
of which required answers. I managed, however,
to keep free from controversies existing elsewhere,
or participation in any exciting subject; but in matters of peaceful interest and the general good, involving no quarrel, I took an active part. Hence
there were few of the most influential men of the
Church (until they became so numerous) with whom
I had not more or less intercourse by letter, and with
a select few, in earlier days, the interchange was
frequent.

I also received my share of anonymous letters,
some of which were outrageously abusive, a few ad-

visory or minatory, none complimentary. One of
the offenders in this business, whom I had often entertained at my house, was not aware that I detected
his handwriting, which he had not sense enough
carefully to disguise, but I allowed him to go to the
grave without letting him know that I had discovered that he was guilty of such meanness. He
played other dishonorable tricks upon me, but I said
nothing.

I never carried on a large correspondence on
church affairs with men abroad. Epistolary intercourse between us native Americans and ministers
in Germany has never been extensive. Inspector
Hoffman, at that time " Inspector " of the Basle
Missionary Institute, afterwards Superintendent at
Berlin, and I had a rather lively correspondence
concerning an unworthy German minister who
brought a letter from him. I saw him subsequently
at Basle, and we had a very satisfactory explanation
of the affair. Several other German ministers wrote
to me concerning some of their relatives in this
country, but this was merely formal business, and
not ecclesiastical. My scientific correspondence with
foreigners was much more extensive.

When I was in Germany I found that most of the
clergy whom I saw cared very little about the
Church in the United States, especially the English
portion of it, and hence did not trouble themselves
with correspondence. An improvement in this respect has taken place within the last twenty years,

and particularly at this time. Some of our Home Mission Societies are, at this time, carrying on correspondence with the heads of several Mission Institutes in Germany in relation to sending over young men to fill the numerous vacant German pulpits and mission stations among us. Our seminaries here cannot furnish the men, for the demands of English churches are more numerous than we can supply, and comparatively few of our theological students learn to preach German, and even if they can they prefer serving English congregations. Hence the necessity of sending abroad for young men, and it is this fact which of late years has awakened a new interest in the Church of this country among many pious people in Germany.

PRIVATE CORRESPONDENCE.

I frequently received letters involving the most private interests, confessions of secret sins, earnest entreaties for prayer, as well as importunate solicitations for aid. To maintain secrecy, which most of the correspondents requested, I never allowed my letters to be opened during my absence from home, or at any other time, even by my own family. Some of them involved affairs of great private interest to the writers, which I was compelled to regard as " professional secrets " as much as physicians are obliged to do.

Aid was given to many a poor sufferer whose name was never known to any one besides myself, advice to some in difficulty, warning to some in danger of ruin, visits of condolence to private sufferers and to prisoners. On one occasion, through private correspondence of this kind, I thwarted the wicked schemes of an unprincipled lawyer to defraud some heirs of their inheritance who were friends of mine. He heard of it, and pursued me with malice until he died.

SCIENTIFIC AND LITERARY CORRESPONDENCE AT HOME.

My studies in science necessarily brought me into contact and correspondence with many men.

Dr. E. F. Melsheimer, of York county, Pa., and I were fast friends for many years, until he died. He was a capital entomologist, and was of unspeakable service to me in my recreative pursuits. I visited him once a year for many years at his simple home, and always admired his inflexible integrity, his unpretending honesty of purpose, and his extensive and correct knowledge of entomology in particular and of things generally. He seldom left home, but devoted all his time to his studies and his practice of medicine. His letters were always valuable, because they embraced the results of his patient researches. I am more indebted to him in this branch of study than to any man of all my extensive acquaintance. Many of his letters will be found among my papers.

I became acquainted with that singularly gifted man, S. S. Haldeman, very early in my scientific pursuits. Entomology and conchology were his chief subjects when I first knew him, and his contributions to both these branches are invaluable. Our mutual visits and letters were numerous. He was a genial spirit, inexhaustible in his fund of information on almost all subjects, without the least display of pedantry or affectation. I learned much from his very instructive conversation, and he was ever ready to communicate by letter whatever he was asked. He had risen to eminence as a naturalist, at home and abroad, by his writings and discoveries, and was highly respected and honored as a perfect gentleman.

I first became acquainted with Agassiz in Newport, at the meeting of the American Association for the Advancement of Science, and somehow or other we "took to each other" at sight. I met him frequently afterwards, and visited him at Cambridge. We usually spoke German, and that may perhaps have contributed to drawing us nearer together. Sometimes he imperceptibly glided into French, but I did not venture on French with him, and drew him back to the language of the Vaterland, in which I could get along more fluently and correctly. He is a world-known man, and I need say nothing more of him here. His letters, which I have preserved, are highly valued by me.

For more than twenty-five years I was as intimate with Prof. Henry, of the Smithsonian, as any one could well be intimate with that extraordinary man.

14

Sometimes he was familiarly cordial, and then again apparently cold and repellent. But all who knew him kindly overlooked these peculiarities, for he showed this disposition indiscriminately to all his friends. I have passed him in the Smithsonian unrecognized by him when he was profoundly absorbed in some abstruse proposition in physics, or annoyed with the endless difficulties he encountered in the management of that institution. Upon meeting him a few hours afterwards, when he had perhaps worked out his philosophical problem, or had relieved his mind from some perplexity, he was cordial, and greeted me with engaging familiarity. I visited him whenever I went to Washington, which was two or three times a year.

Our exchange of letters was not frequent, but important. He sympathized with me deeply in my unpleasant relations at the Peabody Institute. I proposed to the Peabody Board that it would be an appropriate compliment to Prof. Henry to invite him to deliver the first lecture after the opening. They agreed, and he accepted the invitation. He gave considerable offence to the Board for his outspoken plainness on the inexpediency of spending large sums of money on buildings for such institutions. His friends are well aware of his opinions on that subject, and on this occasion he was very candid. Several of his subsequent letters to me alluded to this matter   I remember once rendering him a service for which he was very thankful. A large lot of rare German pamphlets of the times of the Reformation were sent to the Smithsonian library, the titles of which he requested me to translate. I did the work to his great satisfaction. Those pamphlets would be immensely valuable to any writer on the Reformation, for they are all originals. They are now in the Congress library.

In one of his letters the Professor says: " I think the lectures you gave at the Smithsonian were among the most interesting we have yet received, and without further notice I have directed that you be put down for a course of four, five or six lectures on insects, to be delivered next winter."

Prof. S. F. Baird, the distinguished successor of Prof. Henry, and I were on the most friendly terms of acquaintance and correspondence even before he went to Washington. He is a man of world-wide fame, and has rendered inappreciable service to the natural history of the country. His management of the Smithsonian for many years as Assistant Secretary and as head of the establishment, has secured the admiration of the whole scientific world. I may safely say that more than one hundred letters have passed between us, besides frequent visits, for I never go to Washington without calling on this most excellent of gentlemen at his office, and though almost constantly overwhelmed with visitors, yet I always have the entree, when some others are obliged to wait.

Dr. Thomas Stewartson, of Philadelphia, and I

had a long correspondence on the Ailanthus Silk Worm, but it resulted in nothing practically beneficial. Mr. Grinnell, of the Department of Agriculture, and I had frequent interchanges of letters on this same subject.

W. T. Harris, of Cambridge, Mass., one of our early entomologists, and an eminent writer, favored me with many letters, some of which I have carefully preserved.

That rare genius and thorough entomologist and general scholar, Benjamin D. Walsh, of Rock Island, Ill., was an active correspondent of mine. He was an Englishman, and a graduate of Oxford. I do not know what induced him to come to this country, but he here achieved great reputation as a writer on this subject. Poor Walsh was fatally injured in a railroad accident, and died deeply lamented. He gave me much more credit for my work in this department than I was conscious of deserving.

Mrs. Mary Treat, who has acquired a fair fame in the science, and I exchanged a number of very pleasant letters. She is a keen observer and a diligent student. She has written numerous articles for the journals in a very piquant, attractive style, and her researches into the Ants of Florida have greatly enhanced her reputation.

Hon. Isaac Newton, at that time (1865) Commissioner of Agriculture at Washington, entrusted to my care a number of the eggs and cocoons of the Ailanthus Silk Worm, urging me to come to Washington without delay. I reared the worms and distributed the eggs very generally, but the culture or "education" of this insect, as the French call it, was never prosecuted to any great extent in this country, which I think was a mistake. This commission, of course, occasioned frequent letters between Mr. Newton and myself, and not a few visits to him; but he was not the man to feel interested in such a subject, and paid little attention to it.

In the Reports of the Department of Agriculture for 1861 and 1862 will be found two papers on the "Cultivation of the Ailanthus Silk Worm," for which Mr. Newton sent me $60. These papers brought me over 50 letters from various sections from Canada to Bermuda. They enquired for further information, and not a few of my correspondents, presuming that I was a dealer in the "article," sent orders for eggs, worms, cocoons, and even the seeds of the Ailanthus tree. Even several years after the papers appeared, I received "orders" which have remained unfilled to this day. I never before got into such a scrape. Not a few of the letters came from ladies, some of which I politely answered. I highly delighted one of them, who had published a volume of poems, by quoting some of her own lines. She complimented me highly upon my cultivation of literature in connection with my writings upon the Ailanthus Silk Worm, and thought it an agreeable diversion of study. I did not tell the good lady that the lines I quoted were about all I knew of her book. Brackenridge Clemens, of Easton, Pa., wrote extensively on Sphingidæ and Microlepidoptera. His work on the former family has been accepted by all cultivators of the science, and by his permission it was transferred to my Synopsis of the North America Lepidoptera. He also kindly furnished for that book the analytical table of the families of Heterocera. This brought us into lively correspondence, and I once visited him at Easton. He died before reaching middle age.

William Stimpson, a young man who did great service in Marine Annelida, and died as Curator of the Academy of Sciences at Chicago, and I were very intimate. I first met him in Washington, and exchanged many letters with him.

Townsend Glover, a singular genius, for a long time entomologist in the National Department of Agriculture, was one of my most highly prized friends and correspondents. We saw each other three or four times every year, and always to my advantage. He was a most capital artist, as well as naturalist, and beautifully illustrated several orders of our insects.

That distinguished geologist and eminent scholar, Principal Dawson, of McGill College, Montreal, and I have exchanged some letters on entomology, in which he felt some interest. He asked me some questions, which I was fortunately able to answer. I have frequently met him at the meetings of the American Association for the Advancement of Science. He is the author of " The Origin of the World," "Acadia," and of a large number of papers on various classes of invertebrate animals. He has lately been most worthily knighted by the Queen of England.

Benson J. Lossing, the author of a number of American historical works, biographies, etc., was one of my correspondents. I had occasion to ask him some questions, which he politely answered, and this led to others from both sides. I have met him on several occasions; once at Gettysburg, where he delivered an oration.

I find that it will take up too much room to enlarge upon this subject, and hence will curtail my remarks. The following gentlemen have been my correspondents for years: Prof. A. S. Packard, now of Brown (?) University, who has described many of our insects and furnished many useful papers and books. A. S. Grote, now of Buffalo, is one of the best authorities on Noctuidæ, who has for more than twenty years devoted all his time to the study of that family, and has achieved wonderful success. His writings are numerous, and eagerly sought after by students. W. H. Edwards, now of Coalsburg, W. Va., is the author of the most elegantly illustrated work on our diurnal Lepidoptera ever published, and of numerous single papers. J. A. Lintner, of Albany, a son of my old clerical friend, the Rev. Dr. Lintner, gives his exclusive attention to our science. He is connected with the New York

State Museum, and has contributed valuable papers on our fauna.

Samuel H. Scudder, of Boston, is one of the most learned and thorough entomologists of the country, and his writings are highly prized by all lovers of insect study. Wm. Saunders and the Rev. Mr. Bethune, of Canada, are intimate friends of mine and valued correspondents.

C. V. Riley and J. B. Smith, of the Agricultural Bureau, and the Rev. G. D. Hulst, of Brooklyn, and many other entomologists, exchanged frequent letters with me.

Prof. A. J. Cook, of Michigan University, Lansing, Mich., is the author of a most excellent book on the Bee. Years ago I sold him some valuable German entomological books, and ever since I have exchanged occasional letters with him. He is also distinguished in microscopy.

Herman Strecker, of Reading, Pa., who has the largest collection of Lepidoptera in this country, and it may be said the largest private collection in the world, has been a valued correspondent for some years. These and others not mentioned here have for years been my correspondents. Indeed, there have been few leading entomologists of the country with whom I have not had a greater or less epistolary intercourse. In earlier life Prof. C. B. Adams, a conchologist of high distinction; T. M. Brewer, of Boston, the well known öologist; G. W. Fahnestock, of Philadelphia; Townsend, Brevoort, Titian Peale and others, were constant correspondents.

There is no more proper place than this to mention a fact or two of no great significance, but still of some small interest to·myself. I never met the elder Audubon but once, and that was in Baltimore. I remember his features and manners very distinctly, but I had little opportunity of conversation with him. When in the British Museum in 1846, in London, where I had, through Doubleday's influence, the unobstructed entrance into those departments not open to the public—I mean the working and artists' rooms—one of the professors remarked that behind that screen—pointing to one—I would find a fellow countryman. I went, and found one of the young Audubons painting a copy of an Arctic animal for the Book on American Quadrupeds, which the brothers were bringing out. I introduced myself, and he received me very politely, especially when I told him that I was a good friend of his father-in-law, the Rev. Dr. Bachman, of Charleston. I spent a pleasant hour with him.

Some years ago I undertook to make a sort of bibliographical list of all the writings of natives of Maryland, no matter where they now live or when they had written or published their productions. Brantz Mayer and others aided me, and I was compelled to go through numerous catalogues and get information from various quarters. I was also obliged to write to a number of gentlemen then residing elsewhere for correct lists of their writings, and this brought me into pleasant relations with a number of first-class men. I continued the work until the matter was nearly exhausted as far as my resources went, when I gave all my papers over to the librarian of the Historical Library, who has made large additions.

I have among my letters an autograph from President Fillmore, who wrote to me in response to a request of General Howard for a speech of his, but he says he does not remember having ever delivered such a speech.

Harris W. Hall, a literary character of Philadelphia, furnished me with a list of his own writings and gave me information about others; and thus I might go on and mention a long list of other gentlemen with whom I exchanged letters on this specific subject.

I knew that celebrated bibliophile and bibliopole, Sabine, of New York, pretty well, and also his namesake, of Boston, who wrote the " Loyalists of America." I was of some service to the latter in furnishing him a few items for the second edition of that book.

With numerous other gentlemen, I was invited by that most industrious worker, the Rev. W. B. Sprague, of Albany, to supply material for his book, " The Pulpit of America." I furnished letters for this book concerning Dr. J. G. Schmucker and Dr. E. Hazelius, which may be seen in my " Fifty Years," pages 11, 66.

With the gentlemen at the head of most of the

great libraries of the country I had frequent corres-
pondence or personal interviews, such as Poole,
Jewett, Trumbull, Spofford, Saunders, Schroeder,
Cogswell, Vinton, Sibly and others.

MY FOREIGN CORRESPONDENCE.

This was extensive in the course of years, although
the number of persons with whom I exchanged letters was not very large.　I should like to say more
concerning some of them than I will have room for.

The family of the Sturms, of Nurnberg, were very
able correspondents.　The father and two sons were
authors, artists, engravers, printers and publishers,
and issued many beautifully illustrated volumes on
insects and plants, and did all the work themselves.
After some years of correspondence and active exchange of objects, I saw them at their home in
Nurnberg, and was delighted with their society.　I
have many of their letters.　They gave me many of
their writings.

Herr Dunker, at first of Cassel, where I saw him,
and recently of Marburg, is one of the great paleon-
tologists of Germany.　Although I never studied
that branch, yet I exchanged many letters, particularly on American works on that subject.　I shall
never forget the Sunday I dined with him, and the
company at his table.　He also gave me a number
of his writings.

Herr Schaeffer, of Ratisbon, was a great writer
on Lepidoptera.　I never met him, but exchanged

many letters and specimens. He began to write English to me which was not the most idiomatic, and when I told him he might thereafter write in German he was delighted beyond measure. Some of his writings may be seen in the Peabody Library, and show his wonderful learning in his department.

Mr. Riehl, of Cassel, with whom I carried on an active exchange and correspondence before I saw him in his own house in 1846, was a bachelor, and treasurer of some great railroad, and treated me very kindly. Being with him on Sunday morning, I told him I was a church-going man, but he would not go with me. I met him at dinner on the same day at the house of Prof. Dunker, where was also present the Oberst-Lieutenant of the Hessian army, who told me that his father had served in the Hessian army against the Americans in the war of the Revolution, and moreover, he added, " My father left one of his legs there." I remarked that his father had better stayed there himself, as many of the Hessians did. " In that case," he replied, " I would not be the General of the Hessian army." " True," I rejoined, " but if you had been born there you might have reached a higher position." " And what is that?" he eagerly asked. " You might have been President of the United States," I answered, but this was something he could not understand.

With Drs. Von dem Busch, Schmidt and Wilkens, of Bremen, I also had made exchanges before I saw them in their own houses. The latter two lived in splendid style on "The Wall," as they call a fine avenue there. The intelligent wife of one of them spoke a little English. They seemed surprised when I refused to smoke in their elegantly furnished parlor.

Profs. Germar and his nephew, Schaum, of Halle, Erichson, Troschel, and Klug, of Berlin, were frequent correspondents of mine, all of whom, with many more, I subsequently met in their own country.

It was while I was in Germar's house one day in earnest conversation with him I heard the singing of a juvenile choir in the street, and upon inquiring into the meaning of the performance, he told me it was a company of boys from a charity-school singing for their support. The *carrende* years of Luther came to my mind. I hurried out, listened for a moment, and then I astonished the leader by putting into his hand a Prussian thaler note. Prof. Germar told me that a few kreutzers would have been enough, but I was too full of Luther for such a trifle.

Guerin de Merreville, of Paris, was my principal French correspondent, and especially upon the Ailanthus Silk Worm. He gave, or afterwards sent, me all his writings on this subject, and besides speaks in exalted terms of my Synopsis of North American Lepidoptera in his Magazine of Zöology. When I saw Guerin afterwards in Paris I found he could not speak a word of English or German, but we got along pretty well with my imperfect French. I found him on the fifth story of a very large apartment house. I presume he was a bachelor.

Mr. W. Doubleday, of the British Museum, was a valued correspondent for several years before I met him in London in 1846. He was the most American Englishman I ever encountered, and he told me that if he had a self-sustaining position he would settle in the United States without delay.

When I entered that department of the Museum in which he was engaged, and inquired for him of a person whom I saw, and gave him to understand that I was an American, he said, " You will find Doubleday more of an American than an Englishman." " I admire his taste," I remarked, and the man smiled. I spent many pleasant hours with Doubleday. He died a few years afterwards.

I exchanged letters with a number of other scientific men in Europe; many of their letters will be found in my various collections.

CHAPTER XI.

THE DIETS, AND ACADEMY OF LUTHERAN CHURCH HISTORY IN
AMERICA—ANSWERS TO QUESTIONS—MINISTERS' LEAGUE—
PREACHING IN STRANGE PULPITS—GOOD ADVICE FROM
MEMBERS—EVANGELICAL ALLIANCE—FLIEDNER, OF KAI-
SERSWERTH—CONSUBSTANTIATION.

FOR several years before the first Diet was held,
in 1877, there had been much discussion in the most
of our Church papers on the expediency of holding
what was called a Colloquium, to which all Lutherans were to be invited. The design was to discuss
amicably those points on which the several sections
of the Church were presumed to differ, particularly
the teachings of the symbols on the nature of the
real presence in the Lord's Supper, altar and pulpit
fellowship with the denominations around us, secret
societies, and so on.

On all other points there was no difference, or at
least none which divided us.

Any one who desires to learn the history of this
protracted controversy must consult the *Lutheran
and Missionary* of that period, *Der Lutheraner*, of
the Missourians, *Die Lutherische Zeitschrift*, and
other Church papers. The *Observer* took no active
part in the controversy, but was contented to furnish

its readers with occasionally a general view of the field of battle and the utterances of the most distinguished warriors.

There was a display of much theological learning, of ancient and modern church history, of logical acumen, of narrow-minded sectarianism, and, in many instances, of bitterness and rancor. It was amusing to see that good and amiable brother, Brobst, making his politest bow to the Missourians, and burning the most fragrant incense in their nostrils, and acknowledging his most hearty acquiescence in their theology, yet spurned from their presence and derided for his inconsistency merely because he belonged to the " heretical " Synod of Pennsylvania. It was no matter to the Missourians how thoroughly orthodox a man might be in Lutheran theology, yet if he did not adopt their procrustean practice, and come out from all Church associations, he was utterly condemned and repudiated.

The Iowans were a little more liberal, for they consented to maintain a sort of step-sisterly connection with the General Council by sending delegates; but they have not as yet united with it, nor will they until the Council abandons some of the notions and practices which it has derived from American training or European unionism.

There was no prospect of a settlement of these differences, and it was thought by some that a general Colloquium would heal all difficulties by reconciling all parties. It was considered the grand panacea for the Church's sores. Some men on both sides were in favor of it. Even the Council as a body seemed inclined towards it, and made certain propositions to the General Synod, which the latter body rejected, and decided it was not best to hold such a meeting, presuming that the desired result would not be attained. This was done at the meeting of 1875, in Baltimore, Md.

This settled the question of a Colloquium. It was then I proposed to hold a Diet, hoping that in the course of time, and by the annual assembling of men of all schools, and the discussion of subjects of general interest, asperities might be softened, doctrinal differences adjusted, and personal estrangements reconciled. I called it Diet, and not Congress, Convention or anything else, because it was a new term in modern church language, and because it was appropriate. The name pleased everybody. The question now was to bring it about. To refer it to Synods I knew would occasion endless differences as to time, place, persons and everything. To consult a large number of men individually would require immense correspondence and labor, and would result in no uniformity of opinion. To call a large meeting was inexpedient, troublesome and useless. After having ascertained the opinions of some influential men of various sections as to the expediency of the measure, and having published some of them in the *Observer*, and received favorable responses through this and other papers,

15

I concluded that the Church was ripe for the movement. Some good men were doubtful of its success, as they are about everything that is new, but
even these finally approved of it when they saw the
programme adopted and the expression of the very
general favorable opinion. Having thus secured a
favorable public sentiment, I then consulted Dr.
Seiss, and we agreed to take the responsibility of
selecting the time, place, subjects of discussion,
essayists, officers, rules—in a word, the entire and
exclusive management of the whole affair. We
apprehended some opposition, but we disarmed it by
making it plain that this was the only way, under
the circumstances, that the Diet could be brought
about. Our men, whose opinion was worth hearing,
were satisfied, and we have never heard of any complaint, publicly. So well satisfied was the Diet with
our management that we were appointed by the body
to make arrangements for holding the second and
the third. The Doctor and I went to work, and
nearly the whole of it devolved on me, for having no
pastoral charge at the time I had more leisure. I
wrote more than forty letters and cards concerning
the first Diet, and perhaps more for the second. We
selected the subjects and the essayists, and I announced them. Nearly all promptly accepted. We
had not much difficulty in agreeing upon the themes
and men. Each of us proposed a certain number,
and the exchange of a few letters settled any difficulties. We yielded mutually. Dr. Seiss and I

through life have been warm friends, and worked harmoniously or differed gracefully. The difficulty was in adapting subjects to certain men, but we finally succeeded, to the general satisfaction of the parties. A few objected to the themes selected for them, and in one or two cases we made a change: but generally they acquiesced. What determined our selection of some men in preference to others of equal claims and rights was location, synodical relation, ecclesiastical influence and personal considerations. We soon heard from various quarters that offence was given because certain first-class men were overlooked. This we expected, but we had determined not to enter upon any public defense of our conduct, for we were well aware that some would be displeased no matter who would be preferred. One of the English papers of the General Synod opened upon us, and charged us with sectional partiality, and (the editor) declared that " he would have nothing to do with the Diet," and he never has had since; and let me gently add that the Church has had, for five or six years, very little to do with or for him. A German editor of the General Synod, apprehending perhaps a failure of the enterprise, and wishing to clear himself of responsibility in advance, gravely told his readers that he " had nothing to do with getting up the Diet," and he never will have!!! But he spoke kindly of it after it had been held and had become an acknowledged success. Of course the papers in the Missouri interest did not speak favorably of it, but they had no influence outside their own circle.

To our surprise and gratification one hundred ministers and theological students attended the first meeting, although it was held between Christmas and New Year. And the result is before the Church!!!

I have kept a large number of the newspaper articles which were published upon the subject, and they are nearly all commendatory, reflecting the general opinion of our influential and thoughtful men.* The arrangements for the second Diet were very like those for the first, most of the labor for which I also performed. This also was a success, as we hope all those to come may be.

Full reports of the proceedings were made by the daily papers of Philadelphia, which were copied into several of our own Church journals and widely read. Five or six leading papers of other denominations gave large space to the proceedings, and spoke very favorably of us. All the papers read at the Diets, accompanied with the remarks of others present, were published in neat volumes.

A new feature was introduced into the second Diet. Two " speakers " were appointed to follow each essayist, so that we might be certain of having the matured thought of three competent men at least upon every theme.

* Preserved in the Archives of the Lutheran Historical Society in the Seminary at Gettysburg, Pa.

The fault of both meetings was that the number of essays was too large, the essays too long, for most of them exceeded the prescribed forty-five minutes, and consequently the time was too short for the discussion. The following communication written by me, which appeared in the *Observer*, gives a fair exhibition of the first meeting:

IMPRESSIONS OF THE DIET.

I never saw a more happy, I may say, jubilant company of men than on the close of the first day of the meeting. Every one saw that the experiment was a complete success, and hearty congratulations were exchanged all round. Men of different synods, schools and *tendencies* greeted each other with the heartiest hand-shaking, and joyous smiles beamed on every face.

The first session was opened with some apprehension : it was not known whether half of the essayists had arrived; it was feared that sufficient notice had not been given; it was uncertain whether even the neighboring ministers would be present; it was known that some worthy men were not satisfied with the arrangement; but when in the course of the morning our rural brethren were seen coming in by dozens, many intelligent laymen taking their seats, and many ladies gracing the church by their presence, all apprehensions vanished, and we began in our hearts to sing the *Gloria in excelsis!* and when, at the end of the second day the names of precisely *one hundred* Lutheran ministers were recorded as present, it was hard to subdue a very emphatic expression of *Bless the Lord, O my soul!*

I have not taken the trouble to ascertain how many synods were represented, but I can easily determine *ten*, and probably there were more, and this shows that the conjectures of some of our friends that Christmas week was an unseasonable time, were unfounded. You could not collect a larger number of ministers, paying their own expenses of travel and entertainment, at any other season. Philadelphia, too, was just the place, for there are over 300 Lutheran ministers within three hours' distance.

This meeting has disappointed two classes of men: first, that class which was not favorable to it. They have no doubt bit their nails in holy ire, and will take their vengeance on us by depreciating its character, and will make ugly faces at its "unionistic" tendencies. The other class are those who were fearful of a failure as to the number of attendants and lack of interest. They have been most agreeably disappointed, and have joined with us in the exclamation, *Laus Deo*.

Most of us have heard of dissatisfaction in various quarters, but nothing more will be said on that point. *We could not do otherwise* in this first Diet. We could not make it general; it was intended to be territorial, and not universal. It was thought that men from a great distance could not come at their own expense. It was not certain whether even those near at hand would make it a success. We could not possibly select more than a small number of essayists, not because of a paucity of men, but because we could not protract this first Diet longer than three days; but why *other* men were not chosen in place of those on the programme is not for me to say. It is thought they were all competent men; but knowing that even these good reasons why some other men were not selected will not satisfy them, I had better say nothing more about it. I might get myself into a difficulty.

There never was a meeting held in our Church in which more respectful feeling, more tender regard for the opinions of others, more fraternal sentiment, were displayed than in this. There was not an unkind word uttered from beginning to end. There was an utter absence of all harshness of expression or show of fretfulness. There were not even signs of impatience or any evidences of disappointment. The fullest liberty of speech was allowed and indulged, and very strongly divergent views were expressed, but everything was said and done in the kindest, most gentlemanly spirit. The most decided Lutheran doctrines were maintained by some men of the General Synod; the most ultra pulpit and altar exclusiveness was advocated by some men of the Council; the very highest confessional standpoint was assumed by some of both bodies – and whilst lively discussion grew out of all, yet there was no acerbity of feeling, but on the contrary the most amiable temper and mutual respect displayed all through.

Profound research, patient investigation and thorough scholarship were shown in most of the essays, equaling in all these qualities according to the judgment of a competent critic present, those of the Episcopal Congress and of the recent Alliance at Detroit.

The discussions also brought out much talent and mental acuteness. There was no attempt at making speeches—that would have been out of place—but there was hard logic, forcible reasoning, ardent feeling, occasionally enlivened by smart repartee and flashes of genuine wit. Indeed, such was the prevailing good humer of the house that the president was compelled more than once to subdue the demonstration of hilarious mirth.

It was a grand occasion. So well pleased were the men that they were reluctant to vote a final adjournment, and no wonder that a committee was demanded to make arrangements for another Diet. We have some experience now; we shall be able to avoid some errors in future. I do not mean that our selections hereafter will give more satisfaction, for we cannot choose everybody, and unless we do some will consider themselves *unappreciated* and complain *through their friends*, as heretofore. One of the men stated that wherever *four* Germans met there were *five* opinions; I have sometimes thought that it was pretty much the case with us, the descendants of Germans; for we find a fearfully harassing discord of opinion as to who should be selected to read papers at a Lutheran Diet; but let the committee do their duty fearlessly, and the majority of us will be satisfied even if our names should not be on the list.

The expediency of a third Diet was much spoken of in some circles, but there was no hearty acquiescence among some leading men outside of the General Synod. A few of them did not attend either of the previous Diets, and one reason was that they have no confidence in our Lutheran orthodoxy and will not associate with us ecclesiastically. I really believe, however, that one reason for the indifference of others of the Council to a third Diet was that they were wearied to exhaustion by the interminable theological discussions at the meetings of their Synods, and did not desire a repetition of it. That feature has now been removed, but that is a recent event, and they have not recovered from the fatigues of a few years ago.

Here will appropriately come in a notice of the ˙

ACADEMY OF LUTHERAN CHURCH HISTORY IN THE UNITED STATES.

This is one of my creations, which at once secured the approbation of all our ministers whose opinions are worth anything. I called my good friend, the Rev. Dr. B. Sadtler, especially into consultation, and had informal conversations with other ministers in Baltimore and elsewhere in whose judgment and church loyalty I had any confidence.

The result was the following, as copied from an article to the *Observer* of September 12, 1894:

A LUTHERAN HISTORICAL ACADEMY FORMED.

At St. Mark's Lutheran church in Baltimore, Md., last week, an organization for the "Cultivation and Promotion of Studies in the History of the Lutheran Church and her Missions," was formed. This organization is a result attained through the personal efforts of Rev. J. G. Morris, D. D., LL. D., and we may truly call him father of it. A constitution was adopted and officers elected. Dr. Morris was chosen president, and Dr. F. Ph. Hennighausen secretary and treasurer. The vice-presidents are Prof. Wackernagel, Dr. Edw. T. Horn, of Charleston, S. C., Prof. Graebner, St. Louis, and Dr. Swensson, President of Bethany College, Lindsborg, Kans. The Council is composed of the officers of the Academy and the following persons: Dr. E. J. Wolf, of Gettysburg; Dr. Sadtler, of Baltimore; Dr. Seiss, of Philadelphia, and Rev. C. F. Dallman, of Baltimore.

The following persons participated in the organization: Drs. Morris, Hennighausen, Miller, Sadtler, Studebaker, Hartman, Scholl, and Revs. Felton, Schmidt, Dallman, Zimmerman and Garland, of Baltimore, with Prof. Turner, of Lutherville, Dr. Yonce, of Roanoke, and Rev. Hartman, of Altoona.

Thirty-nine others of the Lutheran Church in America, having sent in their assurance of interest and co-operation in the work and their willingness to aid the movement in every way possible, were duly elected members of the Academy.

The next meeting of the Academy will be held in Philadelphia about Easter. Announcement of exact date will be made later. An initiation fee of twenty-five cents was fixed. Any person belonging to the Lutheran church may become a member of the Academy upon the payment of this fee. The applicant is to be nominated by some member of the Council. The design of the Academy carries it above any distinctions which may be found amongst Lutherans. Its purpose is purely historical, and in the interests of the entire Church in America—the Church of the Reformation. It is therefore hoped that all differences will be forgotten in the co-operation and prosecution of the work of this Historical Academy of the Lutheran Church.

A Constitution was adopted, and I immediately proceeded to solicit contributors of papers to be read at the first meeting in Philadelphia. Some declined for various reasons, some promised conditionally, but a sufficient number to make up a first-class programme promised and kept their word. We met on Wednesday morning of Easter week, 1894, in the lecture-room of Dr. Seiss' church, and about eighty ministers and theological students and others were present during the first session. The papers were:

1. Sources of information concerning the history of the Lutheran Church in this country, by myself.

2. The education of ministers by private tutors before the establishment of theological seminaries, by the Rev. Dr. B. Sadtler.

3. The influence of language in modifying the early history of the Lutheran Church in the city of New York, by the Rev. Dr. J. Nicum.

4. The English Hymnology of the Lutheran Church in America, by the Rev. Dr. M. Sheeleigh.

5. The early history of the Lutheran Church in Reading, Pa., by the Rev. Dr. Fry.

6. The influence of rationalism in the Lutheran Church of America, by the Rev. Dr. G. F. Spieker.

7. The causes of the extinction of Lutheranism in the Swedish Lutheran churches on the Delaware, by the Rev. S. E. Ochsenford.

8. The Economics of the Lutheran Church in America, by the Rev. Prof. Graebner (read by proxy).

There were other papers on the programme, but the

writers were not present. The meeting was considered a success, and we resolved to meet again next year, 1895.

The second meeting of the Academy was held in the same place as the first on Tuesday and Wednesday, April 16 and 17, 1895.

Omitting all preliminaries and incidentals, which may be learned from the Church papers of the time, I will proceed to give the programme, which will interest more readers than other routine details:

1. The history of local churches urged upon pastors, by J. G. M.

2. The history of the educational work of the Kansas Conference of the Augustana Synod, by the Rev. C. A. Swensson (read by proxy).

3. The significance of the Lutheran Church for Christianity, by the Rev. Dr. J. B. Remensnyder.

4. Early history of the Lutheran Church in Georgia, by the Rev. Dr. D. M. Gilbert.

5. The early history of Charles Porterfield Krauth, by the Rev. Dr. A. Spaeth.

6. Deaconess work in America, by the Rev. Dr. G. U. Wenner.

7. Pennsylvania and the Lutheran Church in the seventeenth and eighteenth centuries, by the Rev. Theo. Schmauk.

8. What an American saw in Scandinavian countries, by the Rev. Dr. M. W. Hamma.

9. Shadow of Luther in the Orient, by the Rev. Dr. W. E. Parson.

10. Missourianism in Germany, by the Rev. H. Walker.

11. Lutheran bishops of Denmark invited to consecrate bishops for Episcopal churches in America, by the Rev. F. P. Manhart.

12. Liturgies and set forms of worship, by the Rev. Dr. Seiss.

" The presentation of this program," writes the Secretary in the *Observer*, " is sufficient evidence to show the reader of this report that the meeting could not have been anything but profitable and interesting. The large number who were present showed the appreciation of the matter presented by the closest attention from beginning to end. There is no doubt of the fact that these meetings will become more and more interesting from year to year. That was a happy idea of the venerable President to inaugurate the movement, since it affords Lutherans an abundant opportunity to learn more of the history of the Church, and to appreciate the potent influence of the Church as brought out in her rich history of nearly three centuries in America."

ANSWERS TO QUESTIONS.

My judgment on various points of church order and law has often been asked, and only because, I presume, some people think I have some knowledge in such matters from long experience, for I have no claims upon the character of a church lawyer.

The Council of a country church unceremoniously

voted the minister out, and some of the members applied to me for my opinion on the proceeding, which I gave as follows, and published it in the *Observer* January, 1880:

CAN A CHURCH COUNCIL DISMISS A MINISTER?

A few weeks ago the above question was sent to me by a layman of one of our Maryland country churches, which I answered substantially in the following way:

He put me to some disadvantage by not informing me whether such an act had really been done, or was contemplated; nor did he tell me where it had occurred, nor did he say a word about the constitution of the church, nor of the character and conduct of the minister; but he simply put the naked question to me, and I replied accordingly. I said:

1. If the constitution of your church gives the right to the council exclusively to *elect* the minister, then they have the right to *dismiss* him after due trial, for they are virtually his only constituents.

2. If the congregation, however, voted to discharge the minister, it becomes the duty and business of the council to execute the sentence by informing him of it officially; but in this case they would only be the agents of the congregation, and hence it would not be their exclusive act.

3. If the congregation universally had become dissatisfied with the minister, and no longer attended the services, and withheld their support, and yet did not wish to eject him by vote, but feeling that the welfare of the church demanded his removal, then the council might, by *universal consent* of the church, advise him to retire; but they would have no right peremptorily to *send him away*. Even locking the church against him, or renting the parsonage to some one who might issue a writ of ejectment, would be unlawful and revolutionary, as I will presently show.

WHAT WERE MY REASONS?

1. I presumed, of course, that the *church* or congregation *elected* the man, and *they alone* had the power to compel him to leave. You might as well maintain that the commissioners or orphans' courts or any other county officers, have a right to dismiss the sheriff or any other officer elected by the people.

2. The council is elected to discharge certain duties prescribed in church constitutions and in our Formula of Government, but no authority is given to them over the person of the minister. See Formula, Chap. III., Sec. 6, and Chap. IV.

3. No minister can be dismissed by the congregation, even much less by the council *for any cause*, without giving him an opportunity of defense. See Form., Chap. XII.

4. Even if the minister had behaved badly, or if his usefulness were at an end and the church were declining, and it were extremely desirable to employ another minister, not even in that case, nor *in any other conceivable* case, has the *council* the exclusive right to discharge him.

4. No minister who has been regularly elected can be discharged without a majority vote of those entitled to vote, and hence the council has really as such nothing to do with it.

5. If any complaints damaging to the minister are made to the council, or if they themselves make the charges, he must be cited and tried and found guilty, before any action for his dismissal can be lawful. See Form., XII.

6. Even if the minister is tried and condemned by the council, their action is not final until he has had an opportunity of being heard by the synod to which he may appeal. Form., III., 6. The synod has no right to compel a church to retain a minister, but it claims the privilege of examining accusations against him and vindicating his rights when they are assailed. The *congregation* may keep him or not, but the *council* alone has no right either to reject or retain him.

7. A council has no right to hold a church meeting relating to church discipline or government without the presence of a minister. Form., IV , 3.

8. No minister dismissed by a council without law or precedent, should submit to such an oppressive decision, but appeal to the church or united parish which elected him, even if the combined councils of the parish agreed in his dismission. If the united congregations sustained the action of the councils, then perhaps he had better retire, but of his own voluntary act. But if the congregations stood up for him against the councils, or any one of them, let him hold on and have these disturbers of the peace turned out at the next election.

The act of a council in turning away a minister is an unwarranted presumption and tyrannous persecution. Such men disgrace the office to which they have been been unfortunately elected, and they should be resisted to the utmost. At the same time I will say that I would lose my respect for any minister or congregation that would tamely submit to such oppression on the part of the council.

I do not know whether my answer pleased the questioner, as I have not heard from him. Perhaps he was a member of the usurping council, and no wonder he did not answer.

I presume that most ministers of any influence are sometimes asked for advice on professional subjects by others than their own church members.

A very respectable minister, who I had reason to think did not like me personally, yet had some respect for my judgment in some matters, came to me once, even before I was out of bed (it was in the country, during a meeting of ministers). He had just received notice that the title of " D. D. " had been conferred upon him by a college of sixth grade and not of our Church. He was evidently gratified at this mark of appreciation, but still thought that he deserved notice from a higher source, which was true.   He was uncertain whether he should accept, because an acceptance would debar him from a similar recognition from one of our own more influential colleges.   I advised him to decline the proffered honor, and gave him good reasons.   I do not know whether he took my advice, but he is called Doctor, and many think he is entitled to it, and the result is he has never been thus honored by any of our institutions, though his name has been proposed.

I will select another instance of a queer character. The deacon of a church in a western State asked for advice in the following case: The parish is composed of four churches, and all the Councils form a joint body.   The pastor resigned at one of the joint meetings, without previously announcing his reason for calling the meeting, and his resignation was accepted.   He then recommended his successor, and said " he would wait for his back pay if we took his man; if not, we would have to pay him every cent before he would let us call another pastor."   " The Joint Council sent his man a call then and there. . . . He accepted and is now here.   Now some refuse to support him, claiming that the call was not legal, because the Councils elected him instead of the congregations."

" There is another point on which we want your judgment.   If three of our churches elect a pastor, and one rejects him, can the three compel the opposing church to accept and help to pay him?"

" Some also hold that the election was not legal, because the object of the meeting was not stated."

"There is a disagreement also as to the meaning of Sec. 5, Chap. VI., of the Discipline, and some maintain that it applies only to a parish consisting of one congregation and not of several."

"Please tell us what we must do to give a man a legal call; is it done by the Joint Council, or by each church, or by each Church Council?"

To this I replied in substance as follows:

"I never before heard of such conduct on the part of a minister; if you state it correctly, namely, 'that if the parish would call the man whom he recommended, he, the pastor, would wait for the back salary you owe him, but if you did not take his man, and prefer some one else, he would make you pay him every cent before he would allow you to call another pastor.' Now, I 'agree with him that a church should pay what it owes to a minister before another is called, but that a man should manage to get as his successor another man upon condition that you pay him his back salary is unheard of. I admit he might properly say 'you shall not call another man until you have paid me,' but to say 'take the man of my choice, and not of yours, and I'll trust you longer, but if you do not take him I will press my claim instantly and compel you to pay,' is coming nearer to what the apostle calls 'lording it over God's heritage' than anything I know.

"The Joint Council plainly transcended their authority by calling a minister without giving the whole parish an opportunity to vote. This is an act

16

of usurpation and presumption not sanctioned by our church law or usage. See Chap. VI., Sec. 5. No Synod would justify such proceedings, and no parish should submit to it.

"In regard to Chap. VI., Sec. 5, it is true that the language seems to imply that only one church is meant; but it has been the universal practice of our Church that when the parish consists of more than one congregation, and one of them dissents from the choice of the others, the whole number of votes should be counted, and if the candidate receives two-thirds of the whole he is declared elected, and the dissentients are expected fraternally to submit, just as in a civil election where a congressional district is composed of several counties. If a candidate gets a majority of all the votes he is elected, although one or even two counties may cast a majority of their votes against him. So in a church election, while each congregation votes by itself, yet the ballots of all together are counted as a whole, and if a candidate receives two-thirds of the whole, no matter from which congregation they come, he is declared to be chosen by the whole parish.

"In answer to your last question I would say that according to our church government the united voices of two-thirds of the churches of a parish is necessary to a legal call, and not the individual call of each congregation, and much less that of the Joint Council. The minister is called as the pastor of the whole parish, and not of any particular church of the parish, and therefore a united call from two-thirds of the legal voters is necessary to render it legal. It follows that your call of the present minister by the Joint Council is illegal, and not binding upon any one of your congregations. Your Joint Council violated the law in electing him, and he did the same in accepting it. The dissentient churches, as well as individuals, have a right to complain and to appeal to Synod for a vindication of their rights.

" You have not asked my advice as to relieving you of this difficulty, and hence I will not give it, and only remark that you are in a very anomalous position, from which I fear you will not easily be extricated."

I once received a letter requesting me to name six ministers in the order of their merit, in my judgment, who would be adapted to a congregation of commanding influence. Fortunately for me there was no mention of place nor of any other particulars, although I guessed. I took advantage of this lack of specialty, and replied that I could not possibly give a sensible answer without knowing whether it was a town, city or country church, whether German preaching was required, whether the congregation was intelligent, liberal and well trained, whether there was a parsonage and a flourishing Sunday-school, whether the post-office was near at hand and the roads good, and a number of other questions of like character.

I heard nothing of it after my reply.

A very worthy minister once came to me and complained that he could not read half an hour without falling asleep. He deplored this infirmity, for he was sincerely anxious to prosecute his studies, but encountered this serious difficulty. I advised him to consult a physician, for I had no doubt his somnolency proceeded from torpidity of his liver. It may have been indolence, in part, or lack of interest in his work, or dullness of comprehension, and yet he seemed ambitious of improvement. I apprehended the trouble was physical, and I could give him no better advice than to submit to medical treatment. He also complained of the difficulty of finding suitable, or rather satisfactory texts on which to preach. For this I kindly rebuked him, and said that Bible readers (and he should be one) would come across numerous suggestive and pregnant texts or themes, which he should note in a little blank book, such as every minister should have about him. In addition I suggested the names of several books made up of classified texts, but recommended specially that he should take up the Sunday lessons of the Church Year, which he would find in the Church Almanac. I added that for doctrinal sermons he might give a systematic series founded on the Creed, or the Confession, The Order of Salvation, and for practical subjects he should use the Epistles, the Lord's Prayer, the Sermon on the Mount, the Ten Commandments, and the whole Bible. I do not know whether he followed my advice.

A young man came to me for advice about studying for the ministry. He was a perfect stranger. I of course inquired into his moral and mental character. "Who is your pastor?" "I have none." "Of what church are you a member?" "Of none." "Where do you go to church?" "Nowhere." "Are you a professor of religion?" "No." "Do you read the Scriptures, or pray?" "No." "Have you any sense of personal guilt, and do you feel the need of a Redeemer?" "No." "What is your motive in seeking the ministry?" "Oh, I think it is a respectable sort of life." "And you expect to make money by it?" "Yes, enough to live on."

This is the substance of a long talk, and I never encountered a similar case. The man was not insane nor drunk, and the nature of my advice and admonitions may be imagined.

LUTHERAN MINISTERS' MUTUAL INSURANCE LEAGUE.

At the meeting of the Synod of Maryland, October 28, 1870, I introduced the subject indicated above, but not wishing to take up too much time in the explanation of it, I promised to set it forth in the Church papers, and then proceeded immediately to the establishment of the League, with the help of such brethren as would favor the measure.

The main feature of the concern is simply this: That every minister shall agree to pay to the treasurer the sum of $2, as soon as he shall be officially informed of the death of a member, to be transmitted to his widow or children or other legal representatives. Every minister in good health may become a member, and provision will also be made for the membership of laymen who may desire in this way to help the families of deceased ministers, but no layman, however, can derive any pecuniary benefit from the institution. He may give, but he cannot receive.

In order to have an amount of money on hand to pay for stationery, printing certificates, appeals, reports, and post-office expenses, there will be an initiation fee required not exceeding one dollar.

There will be no office rent, no salaried officer, no commissions, and no large sum of money in hand to be invested, so that the sum of $2 from each member will be secured entire to the family to which it shall be due. Thus, supposing that we had 500 members, the widow of the first deceased member would, forty days after his death, receive $1,000, and so in proportion to the number of members.

The League will be empowered to receive bequests and legacies, which may become a perpetual fund, from which appropriations may be made to relieve special cases of want and distress in clergymen's families, or the income of which may go to swell the amount of mortuary dues as often as death might occur.

A similar institution has been for some time in successful operation in the Episcopal and perhaps other churches, and this inspires us with the utmost confidence in commending it to the favorable consideration and acceptance of *our whole Church*, and specially because, while it provides a life insurance for all its members, the premium which secures the ultimate benefit is not paid to a board of managers, who for a pecuniary consideration invest it for the benefit of the insured, but it is at once transmitted by the treasurer to the widow and orphans of the deceased member without discount, expense or defalcation. Not only is it impossible that funds should be misappropriated or lost, but at the decease of any member all the surviving members are summoned to the relief of those who are dependent upon him, and thus the charity which each exercises towards all becomes a pledge that all will do the like for him, and so a sacred brotherhood is perpetuated, which is evoked into practical activity the very instant that death removes a brother, thus in effect realizing that mysterious promise: " Give and it shall be given unto you, good measure, pressed down, and shaken together and running over, shall men give into your bosom.''

Each brother by this plan, simply exercising the benevolence which we all owe, converts the League, so far as its provisions extend, into a guardian for those whom he shall leave behind when death removes him from his labor.

Inasmuch as the lnterest is mutual, it will obviously be the policy, and in some sense the duty, of each member to increase, so far as is in his power, the number of members.

At a subsequent meeting held in Baltimore a few weeks afterwards the League was organized by the adoption of a constitution and the election of officers, and it went into immediate operation. There was fierce opposition to it through the *Observer*, for every good scheme proposed among us encounters enemies; but it prevailed notwithstanding, and it worked wonderfully well for 15 years. It was found necessary now and then to change some of its features, to which there was no objection. Over $63,000 have been paid to poor widows, but at this time (1885) the membership has decreased, owing to the painful fact that during one period of six months nine members died, and the payment of dues so quick in succession was hard for poor men. A number of them withdrew their names. I have not much hope for the continuance of the League, which has been of such invaluable service to the families of many of our poor men.

There was much frivolous and some dishonorable writing about it in the *Observer*, and all along some men have been severely and spitefully averse to it who have nothing better to propose. They are not the men who usually have anything good to bring forward, but who stand off and take an unamiable delight in finding fault with other men who have left them behind in so many other things.

It gives me pleasure to state here that to the

Rev. F. Ph. Hennighausen is mainly due the credit of sustaining the League through its vicissitudes and perils.*

PREACHING IN OTHER PULPITS.

Whilst I never received but two or three calls from other congregations since I have been ordained, and have never served any other church but one for 33 years,† which very few of my brethren have done, yet I have been frequently invited to occupy other pulpits for a sermon or two or more. I presume the reason why I have never been often called as pastor anywhere else is, first, because I never was in the market, and by that I simply mean that I had no inclination to go, and employed no means to secure such attentions, and secondly because I presume I was not desirable, in other words, no church wanted me. That was sensible on their part, and I humbly acquiesced.

I have been called to other responsible positions at Gettysburg, but I would not go.

The fact of my not being elected to other pulpits was once pleaded, in his own justification and very much to his delight, by a minister of another communion. He was a good and sensible man, but a

---

* The Society has at present (1895) less than 100 members, and there are no additions.

† I served the Third church as *temporary supply* for several years, and I am now preaching at Lutherville because the congregation there is too weak to support a pastor.

dull preacher, a wretchedly poor speaker, and wearily inanimate. He never had a call for these reasons, and it was gratifying to him to be able to refer to my case as analogous to his own. He derived comfort from that fact, and although very anxious to make a move, for he had preached his church empty, yet he consoled himself by saying, " Well, there are other ministers in the same condition; there's M——, for example, and if he never was asked to leave his present place, I don't see why I should grieve about being overlooked!"

In my earlier years I preached in nearly all our own pulpits for *a hundred miles around*, and in some directions further still. I have attended frequent corner-stone layings and church consecrations and sacramental meetings, and in the olden times many protracted and revival meetings. I presume many of our energetic ministers can say the same of themselves.

I have never practiced what is called exchanging with other ministers. It was not common years ago, but I dare say it is a good custom when not too frequently indulged in. People like to hear a strange voice, and they sometimes gain by it. I have sometimes been asked by a few of my own people, who did not like to stray away from their own church, to invite to my pulpit some man of distinction who came to town, or to ask an exchange with some settled minister; but I never complied, knowing that their motive was shallow curiosity, and not a desire to hear the gospel. I replied, " If you want to hear the man, go, but I shall not make my pulpit an exhibition stage merely to gratify your whim!"

I have invited many men of reputation to preach for me, and some have come; but they were usually engaged in other more influential and fashionable churches, and we obscure Lutherans were compelled to put up with the plain gospel fare served up every Sunday by ourselves.

I have preached in many non-Lutheran pulpits in Baltimore, but that sort of courtesy, if it may be called such, is not practiced as it was many years ago, before the churches became so numerous, and when ministers were not as exclusive as many are now. Besides this, many men properly think they can do their own work as well as and a little better than others.

I have never been much annoyed by strangers asking me for the use of my pulpit merely to preach, and not for the presentation of a specific object. I refused every one, for I did not know whether they could set forth the gospel more forcibly than I did, and besides I was not willing to pander to the vanity and egotism of some of these men.

In the olden time it was almost a universal custom to invite into our pulpits members of Presbyterian Synods, Methodist Conferences and the like, which met in Baltimore. Very few city ministers do it now. I have several times been disappointed at the non-appearance of men appointed to my pulpit, and often, too, when they did come they were not of much account. One man once excited anything but a solemnizing emotion by speaking of *Mr.* Luther!! Simple as it appears to be yet it was a phrase that nobody had ever heard before, and it sounded supremely ridiculous.

I once preached five or six consecutive Sundays for a pastor who had gone on an excursion to the West. He never made any acknowledgment of my service, not even saying "Thank you, sir." After some time had elapsed I asked him "whether he ever heard that I had complied with his request to preach for him during his long absence?" He replied that he had heard of it, and said no more, not even offering to pay my car-fare to town. All this came from defective early training. It was not lack of respect for me, or an inappreciation of my services, but pure absence of culture; for this same man, a few years afterwards, came to consult me on a very important affair affecting his clerical standing. It was simply whether I would advise him to accept an honor offered him by a corporation for which he had not a high respect.

I have paid a few men more than their expenses for preaching for me in my absence, but I never was offered anything more than expenses myself except once or twice. Some men are very particular in paying just precisely your expenses and not a cent more. Thus I know a prominent church which gave a helping brother exactly $1.72, which he had paid for car fare, withholding the few cents to make it the even $2.

For many years it was not an easy matter to get a substitute in Baltimore if you intended to be absent a week or so. There were at that time not so many clerical editors, secretaries, dilapidated or churchless ministers as at present, and hence in the olden times we were compelled to ask men of doubtful ability to preach, and who could make a better boot or coat or horse-shoe than a sermon.

I once knew a very good and popular pastor of a city church—not Baltimore—who on nearly all occasions of his absence, and always at Communion, invited men of that class to help him. A medical professor was a member of the church. The minister had most injudiciously invited an ignorant quack doctor, whom somebody had licensed to preach, to help him. Our professor, who knew this ignorant pretender, refused to receive Sacrament from him, left the church with his family, and joined another of our congregations in that city.

I was once invited by a lay preacher to help him in some meetings he was holding in a small chapel in the country. I went, and expounded the parable of the Publican and Pharisee. He "followed with some remarks," and used the word "Republican" all through, much to my disgust and the amusement of the young people.

GOOD ADVICE FROM MEMBERS.

For many years it was my good fortune to have among my hearers several intelligent gentlemen who occasionally did me the good service of pointing out what they considered some faults in the style of my preaching or the matter of my sermons. In my early life my cousin, J. C. K., who attended my church every Sunday night, would now and then make judicious criticism, for he was extremely interested in my success. His remarks were always made in the kindest spirit, and I profited by them.

In later years another good friend was my mentor, who was well instructed in the Scriptures, but he was rather exacting; but I knew that his intentions were perfectly pure, and he aimed only at my good. I often took his advice, and improved under it. On one occasion I remember that my good friend Heyer was present when my critic and I were discussing a theological point about which we differed. I had presented my views in a sermon, to which he objected. He was a good talker, and rather able as a disputant. When he left me Mr. Heyer remarked that it was a great advantage to a minister to have such intelligent men in his church, who would rightly appreciate their pastor's good qualities, and yet who had the honesty to tell him his faults in a kind and fraternal spirit.

There are people enough in every church who are continually finding fault with the preacher, and who freely speak of these faults to others, but who have not the manliness to tell the minister himself. Some are afraid of hurting his feelings, and others delight in this style of church gossip; but the man who really respects his minister, and is jealous of his good name and popularity, would be doing him good if he occasionally pointed out an acknowledged blemish in his manner and matter of preaching. Captious criticism and brotherly counsel are different things, and blessed is that minister who has a kind, intelligent, pious friend, who will give him good advice when there seems to be occasion for it.

I have had one or two clerical brothers, who were engaged in other pursuits, as my hearers for months together, but who were not pleased with my preaching, and gave good evidence of it by their inattention. One of them ceased coming to our church, and went, I believe, to the Methodists, though he got his bread from our people. A good old lady once remarked to me, "The only two persons asleep in church this morning were two ministers."

Once in a lecture on a portion of Scripture I said that the passage was difficult, and that I was not sure whether I had caught the precise meaning. I presume my language was equivalent to an expression that I did not understand it entirely. One of my elders kindly said to me that I had better not have made it thus publicly known, for the people expect of their minister that he should understand the Scriptures thoroughly, and that they would lose confidence in him as a Bible interpreter if he ac-

knowledged his own ignorance of any portion of it.
My old friend was right.

EVANGELICAL ALLIANCE.

Somewhere else in this book I have stated, or
should have done so, that in 1846 Drs. Schmucker,
Kurtz and I went to London to be present at the
meeting of the Evangelical Alliance, which was to
convene in August, the history of which I need not
here repeat. We were. not commissioned as representatives of our Church, for the Alliance emphat-
ically declared that no men would be recognized as
representatives of any church or body; besides this
we were expected to pay our own expenses, which
we did.

Various interesting events grew out of this Alliance and its American branch. The following is
not unimportant, and may as well be introduced
here. I furnished it to the *Observer* twelve or
fifteen years ago:

THAT ALLIANCE EXPEDITION TO RUSSIA.

The American Evangelical Alliance appointed a commission
to proceed to St. Petersburg, with the benevolent design of in-
terceding with the emperor in behalf of the poor, persecuted
Lutherans in one section of his dominions. These people are
badly treated by the priesthood of the Greek church because
they will not abandon their Lutheran faith. Their rights of
conscience are interfered with, and their condition is rendered
deplorable. Measures altogether at war with the liberal and
enlightened spirit of the age have been cruelly pursued, and
these persecuted brethren of our faith have in vain implored for

protection against the outrageous proceedings of a bigoted priesthood.

The American Alliance has generously come to their rescue, and a commission of eminent divines and laymen from this country has already entered upon their embassy of love and pacification. Their truly Christian purpose is to endeavor to influence the emperor in behalf of persecuted *Lutherans*, for which we should give them all due credit, and pray that their mission may be successful.

The commission is composed of distinguished gentlemen of four or five Christian denominations, *but there is not a single Lutheran among them.* "Perhaps none of our men would go?" It might be so; but none were asked! "Perhaps they did not think any of us were fit to go!" Probably; but how did they know that? I know fifty of our men who speak more languages than any of the commission, excepting one, and who have all the fitness which any of them possess. "Perhaps they did not want a Lutheran to intercede in behalf of his Lutheran brethren?" Perhaps so, but it was unwise policy.

One of our ministers, whose tender susceptibilities were stirred up, who, in plain English, felt hurt at this manifest slight of his brethren in the ministry, wrote to the most eminent member of the commission, whom he intimately knew, and inquired why no Lutheran was honored with a place among those worthies. Was it intentional? was it an oversight? or what was it? The inquirer has kindly sent me the original reply, and here is the whole of it:

DEAR SIR: Your letter of May 18th, asking the reason why no Lutheran has been appointed a member of the Alliance deputation to Russia, has been received. It is neither intentional nor an oversight. We had to select such gentlemen who, besides their high standing and qualifications to represent the Evangelical Alliance in so important a mission, were able and willing to proceed to Russia at their own expense, the Alliance having no means to reimburse them. This fact, of course, cuts off many who would be as well qualified, and would have been as cheerfully elected. Do you know of a Lutheran friend of the

17

Alliance who would fairly represent your church, and be willing
to make the sacrifice of time and money for a good and noble
cause?   I shall be happy to bring him to the notice of the deputation.   I expect to sail June 3d and return in September.

This was as much as could be expected at so late a day, and
I am sure the noble-minded writer of the letter would have been
glad to have one of our like-minded men in his company.   He
is a most genial *German* gentleman, who fondly admires every
thorough-blooded Lutheran.

Well, after all, what is the most probable reason why none
of us were invited?   Shall I tell it?   It is only my op.nion, but
I think I am right.   The reason is obscurely shadowed forth in
this phrase of the above letter: *"If you know of a Lutheran
friend of the Alliance,"* etc.   That's the reason.   *As a church*,
we have not joined in the glory-hallelujah of the Alliance!
That's the reason; and I am candid to say, that we have no
right to complain.   And yet, strange to say, the very man
among us who, of all others, has taken the least interest in the
Alliance, was gazetted for a speech at the meeting that was to
have been held in New York last fall.

The fact is, we had better say no more about it.   If we are
ambitious of distinction among such influential associations,
we must cultivate a more friendly spirit with them, and let
them send deputations to Russia in behalf of Lutheran Christians without a Lutheran delegate among them.   I wonder
what answer they would give to the emperor, or to some
eminent Lutheran divine in Russia, who should chance to ask
them why there is no Lutheran on their committee?   Well, let
it pass.

The Alliance appointed for Stockholm in 1884 did
not meet.   In April of that year it was announced
that the Archbishop of Upsala and other dignitaries
and clergy of the church in Sweden had publicly
protested against the meeting, and hence it was

abandoned. It is presumed the reasons were that the English non-Episcopalians of various sects had already created some difficulties in Sweden by proselyting members of the State Church. The Committee in this country, of which Dr. Schaff is (was) the energetic head, even if not chairman, which I however presume he is (was), invited nearly fifty American ministers to attend that Alliance at their own expense, of whom only one, as far as I know, was of our Church—Dr. Wolf, of Gettysburg. He was willing to go, but evidently we could not consider him a representative of our Church. He was not appointed by any Synod, Faculty or Board, and although he would be a fit representative, if such a character were acknowledged, yet we as a people could not regard him in that light, and hence could not make church provision for his expenses. Besides this, some of us knew that the Lutherans in Sweden would not favorably regard this uninvited Alliance (uninvited by the Church authorities), and hence our highly esteemed Dr. Wolf would not be treated very hospitably by his own Lutheran brethren. They would look upon him as a colleague of those English and American churches who are spending large amounts of money in proselyting Swedish Lutherans to the faith of their sects, and hence would most probably treat him coldly. The Alliance was not held in Stockholm.

In December, 1887, a meeting of the American branch of the Alliance was held in Washington,

Wm. E. Dodge, Jr., of New York, President. It is said that over 1,000 ministers attended, and among them 40 of our own men, all General Synod ministers except one. No conspicuous position was given to any of us in the way of reading a paper or any other, except that one was invited to read the Scriptures and another to pray at the opening of a session. There was the usual howl from several quarters in the *Observer*, and grievous lamentation about being "ignored." Dr. Strong, the Secretary, came out in vindication of the Alliance, and disavowed any intentional slight of our Church. The fact is simply this, that we are to blame ourselves for being overlooked in such public demonstrations, because we, as a church, do not participate vigorously in these general union efforts; and yet I attribute it more to backwardness, or call it modesty if you choose, than to unwillingness or lack of interest in the great evangelical movements of the day.

FLIEDNER, OF KAISERSWERTH.

In 1849 Mr. Fliedner, of the Kaiserswerth School of Deaconesses, came to this country, and upon arriving at Baltimore, and learning that I was in York, Pa., went up to see me. Whilst we were there together, the guests of my brother Charles, President General Taylor passed through town. The train stopped a short time to give the people an opportunity of seeing him, and I was amused to see the sedate Fliedner taking off his hat and waving it lustily while joining the multitude in vociferous hurrahs. On expressing my surprise at such a demonstration from him, a foreigner and monarchist as he was, he replied he was carried away with the scene, and thought it was nothing more than right to do homage to the chief magistrate of the country.

After our return to Baltimore he visited some of our penal and charitable institutions, and one day he came home deeply distressed, and unsparing in his rebuke of " American " Christianity. He said he had just come from a visit to the city prison, where, among other subjects claiming Christian sympathy, was a young girl, entirely forsaken, and no kind heart to extend help or consolation or protection in any way. He asked, " Have you no Christian ladies here who visit these poor outcasts, to instruct them, and do other Christian offices to them ? " and when I replied that it would not be considered genteel for a respectable lady to go to a prison on any errand, or at least these ladies thought so, he asked, " What sort of Christianity have you here?" and well he might. I told him there are hundreds of ladies here in Baltimore who would liberally furnish as much money as was necessary to relieve such persons; that they would be found in large numbers at every meeting called to relieve human suffering, and freely contribute funds and furnish food and raiment for the destitute ; that they were constant attendants at public worship and other church assemblies and ordinances, but that it was

not the practice of Christian ladies here, with perhaps the exception of a few old Quaker ladies, in
person to visit women in jail.   He could not understand it, nor can I.

After the meeting of the Evangelical Alliance in
New York in 187? a number of the German delegates came to Baltimore.   Some of the German
ministers here made an arrangement for a religious
meeting in St. Matthew's church, at that time Pastor
Meyer's, after which we had a plain German supper
at a neighboring house, at which we spent a very
pleasant and profitable evening.   The strangers
present whom I now remember were Christlieb,
Kothe, Spies, Krummacher, a lay brother of Heng-
stenberg, and a few others.   I had a long conversation with Prof. Christlieb upon American church
affairs.

Not a few foreign clerical visitors of other times
were not precisely of the same caste of those mentioned above.   Some of them were not at all adapted
to the condition of things in this country.   I heard
one of them preach one Sunday, and before next
Sunday he committed suicide.   Several of them
enlisted in the army.   One came to my house whom
I was compelled to turn out.   One was, physically,
the lamest man you could meet, totally incapacitated
for pastoral out-door work; but there were many
good exceptions to these men, who have become
very serviceable in the church.

CONSUBSTANTIATION.

We have for many years been surprised, and somewhat vexed also, because very respectable and intelligent writers continue to charge us, as a church, with holding the doctrine of consubstantiation. We have repudiated it over and over again, and have quoted the absolute denial from many of our old theologians, but it all seems to be of no service. The imputation is repeated again and again, notwithstanding our proofs to the contrary. Even such a learned and respectable writer as Dr. Schaff, who knows better, allows the false accusation to appear in some of his books. The learned Prof. —— repeats it, and the minor writers follow the lead of their superiors without any further investigation, blindly assuming that it is all right.

In the preface to an English work on the Reformation, all the remaining copies of which were bought by our Publication Society, there is an implied, though not direct, charge of the same character, and as the book was offered for sale by our store it would not seem proper to leave that uncontradicted.

The Board of Publication requested me to prepare a series of extracts from our old dogmaticians, showing that our Church does not hold and never did hold that doctrine. I quoted from a number of them, in which I was assisted by Schmidt's *Dogmatik* particularly, and made a full exhibit of the subject. This was printed in the American preface of the book above mentioned and also in the *Observer*, but I have no doubt the same misrepresentation will be repeated, whatever we may say.

I cannot believe that these learned men would wilfully pervert the truth, and I account for their culpable errors by believing that they leave some of this work to be done by amanuenses who are not intelligent on these subjects. I know that Dr. Schaff, for instance, employed a number of copyists, who were called secretaries, to whom was committed the task of gathering material, and who were not always competent to do it properly. Even if this conjecture be true, it is no justification of the errors they perpetuate, for the principal should read the final proof, and should correct all blunders.

CHAPTER XII.

STYLE OF PREACHING.

I NEVER had an opportunity of hearing many of our ministers preach, except at Synod and other general meetings, and then for the most part it was the same men, for on such occasions usually the most prominent men are the speakers. At such times ministers are presumed to do their best, and hence their synodical sermons are not a good test of their style and manner at home. Some men have what are unhandsomely called '' crack sermons,'' which they parade on all unusual occasions, and to this I see no objection; but they should aim at making all their discourses '' crack sermons.''

There was very little doctrinal preaching as far as my observation extended, but mostly of the practical character that terminated in the hortatory. There were very few men who indulged in the boisterous, and not many who practiced or affected the highly florid, or, as it has been designated, the "spread-eagle" style. We had one or two who were famous in this line. They elicited the admiration of some hearers who were as superficial as the preachers, and they never accomplished any permanent good for the Church. They did not remain long in any parish, for the people grew tired of that style of preaching, from which they derived no instruction, and ceased going to church, and the flowery preacher was obliged to seek another field of labor.

Many of our preachers, who had any respect for themselves or their people, either wrote their sermons or studied them carefully. Some of them read them in the pulpit, which, however, never became popular among our people, and I know some men who failed in securing desirable places because they did not preach without their notes. This is a matter of taste and education, and many intelligent people, even among us, would prefer hearing a well-read discourse to any other.

I know one of our very best preachers, who at the beginning of his pastoral life, read his sermons, but becoming dissatisfied with himself he adopted the other extreme. It was hard work at first, but by perseverance he attained a fluency of speech and an elegance of diction, as well as a logical sequence of solid thought, so that he is now one of the most instructive preachers in our Church or any other.

Some men begin by writing and committing their sermons, but most of them tell me that after a few years they found it a laborious work, and besides it led them into a monotonous, sing-song delivery.

Some of our preachers are content with the preparation of an outline, or skeleton, as it is called, and trust to their readiness of speech to fill it up when they get into the pulpit. This is well enough for a man of experience, but dangerous for beginners. It begets sameness of idea as well as of words. It is hard for such men to get out of the well-trodden rut, and hence a discerning hearer can nearly always anticipate what the preacher will say, and frequently, too, the very language he will use.

I fortunately never, or very seldom, have heard any attempt made at profound preaching—I mean an affected metaphysics, or display of hard and obscure logic. There are a few among us who sometimes divide their themes into parts, in abstract language, and often use the terms objective and subjective very glibly, just as if the majority of their hearers understood them very distinctly.

I have also heard the use of some scientific terms, taken from geology or natural history, when it was very evident that the preacher was not very familiar with the subject himself. This bad practice has come into use especially since there has been such an outcry against evolution. But let us charitably presume that the preacher merely intended to warn his hearers against the dangers of modern infidelity, and thought it well to mention some offensive names or describe some objectionable doctrines.

I observe that the old plan of dividing a text cr theme into two or three distinct heads, with a few subdivisions of each, is almost entirely given up. Most sermons now are a sort of essay, with the text as a motto. There is very little direct exposition of Scripture, and very little Scripture quoted in illustration of the positions assumed. I think this is the character of most of the modern preaching in most pulpits. I look upon it as a deterioration, a grievous calamity. I have too little acquaintance with the popular sermon or skeleton books, to detect the practice of preaching other men's sermons, but I have sometimes heard discourses which I thought were a little above the calibre of the preacher. There was a compactness, a graceful or eloquent diction, a clearness of conception, a logical consistency, and an intellectual breadth which he never displayed on any other occasion, so that I did not think it unkind to suspect that he was ploughing with another man's oxen.

There have been detections of this trick, some of which will occur to almost every clerical reader. I know some who justify this practice on the ground that the preacher is bound to give the best to his hearers, and if he cannot furnish it from his own brain or heart, let him take good bread from another man's bakery with which to feed his own half-starved congregation. I more than once heard a very popular and influential editor of one of our leading Church papers stoutly defending this position.

Some years ago, during the lifetime of the Rev. Drs. Schmucker and Krauth, it was observed that not a few of their pupils quite unconsciously imitated their tones of voice whilst preaching, but it has not been noticed that any student, since the death of those two men, imitate the tones of the present professors! Now, I dare say this was quite unintentional on the part of those students; they fell into the habit without designing it; but such was really the fact. The voice tones of both those men were soft and musical—sometimes very touching. They had the effect of a tender melody upon sympathetic minds. You find yourself humming it without reflection, and so, I suppose, some men imitate the tones of others in speaking without being aware of it. Men with discordant, unpleasant voices are not thus imitated, but it would be well if those men who unconsciously fall into this habit would, with full purpose and intent, imitate the studious habits and entire consecration of heart of their instructors.

I think I could safely say that if some of our Lutheran preachers whom I could name were members of other communions, their reputation would be much wider than it is as Lutheran preachers. Church influence, the plaudits of the crowd, the frequent compliments of their church papers, the pride of sect, the power of a costly house of worship, and a fashionable and wealthy congregation, would give them a position in public favor which we cannot do.

I was trained to a high conception of the necessity of pulpit preparation, but I did not always live up to it. Sometimes I was careless, and this arose from the fact that my people seemed to be satisfied with my ill-digested discourses. But that is a dangerous gauge. Their being satisfied is no evidence that they were edified, which should be the aim of the conscientious preacher. They were content, probably, because the superficialness of the sermons cost them no thought to understand, and they were pleased more by a pretty off-hand sketch rather than by an argumentative, well-elaborated discourse.

I remember being at the house of a worthy minister when I was a very young man. He was called to preach a funeral sermon in the country, and just before he mounted his horse he came into the study and took out of a pigeon-hole of his table the skeleton of a sermon from a pile of dingy, yellow old manuscripts, without ever looking at it to see whether it was appropriate or not. Now, he may have selected it before, but from his manner I should judge not. It was done in a hurry, without any regard for the fitness of things. It struck me as a queer proceeding, and yet I do not know but that I may have done what is equivalent to it myself in later days. I do not think this preacher would have been so careless about his Sunday morning sermon to his own congregation; neither would I.

ARGUMENT FOR STUDY.

I have frequently urged upon our young men, in writing and conversation, the importance of pursuing theological and linguistic studies, and have encouraged them whenever I had an opportunity by speaking well, in the *Observer* and elsewhere, of their literary work. We shall want thoroughbred scholars in our colleges and seminaries, and the clergy are evidently looked to for the supply, although some of our professors are laymen.

My views are briefly expressed in a notice of the April number of the *Review*, 1880:

"That professor who is satisfied with his present attainments, and who is not constantly advancing in the literature of his department, is not fit for his place, and it is said there are some such men. They know no more now than they did when they assumed their duties, and are content. A professor should be a growing man, and if he once gets indolent he loses his influence, and would be much chagrined to hear what his fellow professors, the students and the trustees, say concerning him. He had better begin to study, or vacate his place for some more ambitious and industrious man who would keep far ahead of his classes and up to the times in his science. He should read all the new books and journals relating to his subject, and thus show that he is conscientious in his office and anxious to reflect credit upon himself and his college."

We have, on several occasions, had hard work to fill several important vacancies. I have known at least seven ballotings at one time, and those not between two candidates, but whether one should be chosen who was not quite up to the gauge. He was finally elected at midnight, after a long struggle, by one or two majority.

It would be well if we always had three or more competent men in reserve to chose from, in the event of vacancies, which are likely to occur at any time. I am sure that different arrangements would have been recently made in one of our institutions if we had had proper men to fill the place vacated without sacrificing other important interests.

I know well enough that some of our young men who are inclined to study plead want of time, occasioned by numerous pastoral engagements, but I am satisfied that in most cases this is a baseless excuse. If they only systematized their studies and time, and would devote more of it to their books, and not waste so much in gossip and useless visits and in newspaper reading, it would be better for them. The most laborious pastor of a large parish might have at least two whole days of the week at home if he were a systematic man, and these devoted to the study of one subject would make him a good scholar in a few years. As for his sermons, let him study them *inter equitandum* (on horseback or between times), and write them down on his tablet, which every man should have with him always.

Another reason why we have so few really first-class scholars is, because most of them aim at being encyclopedial, and not special. They range over the whole field of theology, and hence, whilst they may become capital preachers and respectable divines, yet they are not fitted as they should be to teach thoroughly one or two specific branches.

Let some whose minds or tastes lie in the direction of *Dogmatik* pursue that department particularly, and so of the Hebrew and Greek languages and exegesis, or church history, or homiletics, or any other special study. By such a course many of our diligent young men would become proficient, and would always have the best chance of being elected to desirable positions if they had any ambition in that line.

I have heard it said of one of our ministers, who lived many years ago in North Carolina, and who had not the advantages of a thorough early training, was a laborious student all his life, but he died before he had reached his 40th year. He always carried some books with him, and though he might have been on horseback the greater part of the day, yet wherever he stopped when away from home he spent half the night in study. He made considerable acquirements considering his slender opportunities, but unfortunately they were not devoted to the best interests of the Church.

Many ministers when they retire from active pastoral service, or those who are growing old, usually neglect study, or even diligent reading. They seem to be willing to rest after having done hard service, or their reading is confined to newspapers and, it may be, to devotional books, which is well enough. I find no fault with these men. They never were

18

diligent students, and it is too late for them to acquire a different habit.   But I wish here to record
my own experience, which differs so much from
that of many good men, and it is that I never was
more desirous of acquiring knowledge, never more
industrious in reading, especially in writing, never
more diligent in consulting books, and never spent
more time at my literary work than I do now, and
have been doing for some years.   I am more jealous
of my time, so to speak, than ever before.   I seem
to think time lost that is not devoted to research and
writing.   I have sometimes thought that it is morbid, and not healthy.   Not infrequently I get up at
one or two at night, go into my study, and work one
or two hours.   It is a bad habit at any time of life,
but at my time, now over 70, it is not at all to be
commended or imitated.   But a fit of insomnia seizes
me, and I reason that the time would be more profitably employed over my books than in dreamy semi-
consciousness in bed.   I do not feel any ill effects
from it next day for having had only five or six
hours' sleep, but can get to work next morning after
breakfast and work for hours without cessation.   I
never could study before breakfast.   Some men say
that it is the best time.   My experience is different,
and if I am much interrupted during the day, late
at night is the best time for me.

For over thirty years also I have been in the habit
of reading every night before I go to bed, and during all that time I have never fallen asleep without

extinguishing the light. It matters not how early or how late I retire, I must read afterwards. The length of time depends much upon the book I have on hand. I never venture upon anything which requires thought; usually the monthly magazines, but more generally a French or German novel, is just the proper thing.

I once mentioned this habit to an unorthodox clerical acquaintance, who jocosely observed that he had the same habit, but " always read one of his own sermons to put himself to sleep." " Yes," I replied, " and you are not the only man whom your sermons have put to sleep." He laughed heartily, for perhaps he was conscious, in part, of being the dullest, prosiest preacher possible.

STATE OF THEOLOGY.

On page 392 of " Fifty Years " I have given a brief sketch of " The State of Theology " in the Church for many years, but I did not mention the persevering efforts made by influential men in opposing genuine Lutheranism. They clung ardently to the name, and gloried in their ecclesiastical an-cestry; but they held that under that name they could be Calvinists, Zwinglians, or Arminians. Lutheranism with them covered a multitude of errors, hence they struggled violently in maintenance of the lowest church views, the loosest theology, provided a man was what they called pious, the most unchurchly revival methods, and even

extravagance in some of their meetings.   There
was what might be called a school of men, which
sanctioned the extremes of Methodism in conduct-
ing religious services, but only at night.   The day
services were orderly enough.   When a growing
attachment to the Symbolical Books and a more
sober, churchly feeling were manifested, these men
raised a terrific cry against " the substitution of
the Creed for the Bible," and even quoted the
children's song against popery, " We won't give
up the Bible," just as if the orthodox party aimed
at depreciating God's word.

Of course this school inveighed severely against
the use of a liturgical, and above all a responsive
service, and although very few of us ever thought
of introducing the gown, yet that also came in for
fierce animadversion.   One of the most influential
of them one day triumphantly told me that he had
good old Lutheran authority against the use of the
gown, for the writer, an old German theologian of
high authority, positively asserted that the clergy
should wear no distinctive dress from the laity.
Our American friend thought this settled the question, but when he was told that this old writer was
talking of every-day costume—civil dress in the
street—and not of clerical vestments in the pulpit
or at the altar, he was compelled to abandon his
ground, much to his chagrin, although I suspected
that his acknowledged penetration led him to see
the true state of the case before.   It was enough,

however, for his blind adherents, who followed him implicitly, and never examined for themselves.

This same school, or the leaders of it, also persuaded their followers that the mass, which in the symbols is sometimes used synonymous with the Lord's Supper, was the Romish doctrine of the mass, and that therefore the symbolical books teaching such a doctrine should be rejected. I sometimes thought these men knew better, but it answered a purpose, and that was enough.

The "odium theologicum" was cherished to a ridiculous extent. For instance, because I frequently attended the meetings of the Pennsylvania Synod to see old friends, and did not rail with others against the Missourians and "old Lutherans" in general, I was denounced as an opponent of the General Synod, and regarded as an "old Lutheran." But this spirit did not prevail for many years, for our men gradually became more enlightened, and of course more liberal; but the real secret of this change of spirit was a change of theological opinion, for genuine Lutheranism is progressing every year. Indeed, I am agreeably surprised in observing that most of our clergy are closely approximating the true doctrines of the Church, although the minds of many are not very clear on the subject, yet they strongly disclaim everything un-Lutheran. This change has been going on for a number of years through the introduction and study of distinctive Lutheran theology.

You will now find few respectable ministers of our Church who cherish the sentiment or spirit which prevailed extensively thirty years ago among some influential men of the General Synod. It was an un-Lutheran, unchurchly, semi-rationalistic spirit, which happily began to die with the death of its authors and abettors.

During the year 1880, or perhaps a little before, the *Lutheraner*, the organ of the "Missourians," came out boldly and strongly in defense of a phase of Calvinism quite startling to the Church. The doctrine was advocated in a long series of able articles, which excited much interest among the Germans especially. Most of the "Missourians" adopted the views set forth by their influential leader, Prof. Walther, but a few opposed him, and this led to the establishment of a new paper, edited by Prof. Schmidt, who was a strong defender of the old Lutheran faith.

Great excitement arose in these different camps of German theologians, leading to a general meeting in Chicago to discuss the question, the proceedings of which I believe have never been published. The result was the adoption of every proposition made by Prof. Walther and the total discomfiture of the opposing party, as far as voting was concerned. This led to a separation between that Synod of Ohio which had warmly fraternized with "Missouri," and the farther estrangement of a few others which had previously been on good terms with that Synod, if not in actual connection with it.

The English papers of our Church have not shown much interest in this controversy, as well as in many other affairs relating to the German churches. There was an immense amount of theological learning, acute logic, but, unfortunately, too much controversial bitterness, displayed in this discussion.

In the autumn of 1880 several articles decidedly in favor of the introduction of Episcopacy into our Church appeared in the *Lutheran*, which were written by the Rev. J. Kohler, an influential member of the Synod of Pennsylvania. He had some coadjutors who went so far as to call a meeting of all ministers who favored that measure, but the result of it was not propitious. The editor of that paper made no allusion to the articles, nor did the *Observer*. The whole matter has fallen into oblivion.

In the early history of the General Council certain rules and measures were adopted which have not stood the test of time. One was "Lutheran pulpits for Lutheran ministers, and Lutheran altars for Lutheran members." Whilst in general it must be admitted to be a true principle, yet some of the more rigid interpreted it as denying General Council pulpits and communion to all outside of that body, but they soon discovered that it could not be carried out. Others interpret it more liberally, for they never heartily accepted it, and when that wonderfully gifted man, Dr. Krauth, Jr., died, and his potent influence was no longer felt, the stringency of the rule began to relax. From several other

utterances of the Council in its early fervor there
are broad departures, and ten years hence they will
be entirely disregarded.   Extreme high-churchism,
by which I mean exclusivism, will never take deep
root among us, and many good men of the Council
have become restive under the enactments of its
first days.   The fever has abated, and more healthy
symptoms have been developed

And yet as late as 1883 some members of the
Synod of Pennsylvania, who preached in other
than Lutheran pulpits, during the meeting of that
body in Norristown, were very severely called to
account for this breach of what they called Lutheran
orthodoxy by some of their German brethren.   The
Synod, as such, did not sympathize with these ex-
clusives, and the matter was fortunately dropped.
It shows, however, that this exclusive spirit still ex-
ists to some extent in that Synod, but I apprehend
it is confined to a few foreigners, who happily have
very little influence.

This brings to my mind a little incident within my
own experience.   I once attended a meeting of the
General Council in Philadelphia—it must have been
about 1875 or 1876—when I preached for a prominent member of that body who had previously invited me by letter.   I resisted for some time, assur-
ing my friend that it would occasion him trouble,
and also upon the ground that it would seem to be
discourteous to members of the Council to invite an
outsider to his pulpit when there would be so many

of those present who would naturally expect to be invited. He insisted upon it, and I yielded. I suspect it was a species of banter on his part, for he professed to be very independent, and would not be governed by the restrictive rule. The next day one of the leading members mentioned the fact before the Council, in terms of strong disapprobation, that a member of the General Synod had been invited by one of their own body to preach in his pulpit. This displeased me at first, and I wrote to the gentleman, inquiring whether his objection to my preaching was based upon *personal* grounds? He replied in the most courteous manner, expressing the highest personal regard for me, and stated that he thought it was an act of discourtesy to the Council for any minister of that body, during the time of its meeting, to invite a non-member to preach when there were so many present who had superior claims to that distinction on account of their membership, but on no other ground. I think he was right, and told him so.

At the meeting of the Council in 1884, held at Monroe, an obscure town in Michigan, some of its members accepted invitations to preach in English Presbyterian and other churches in the place. Towards the end of the session the pastor of the place introduced a resolution of censure of those large-hearted brethren who considered it no sin to preach the gospel, even to Presbyterians! Now, here was a dilemma. The majority felt that it would be disgraceful to pass the resolution, and yet here was the rule staring them in the face, "Lutheran pulpits for Lutheran preachers," which rule these liberal Council men had violated. How to get out of the dilemma was the question. It was adroitly done by the leaders who control all the business, by moving that the resolution be laid upon the table, inasmuch as the "offenders" were not present to vindicate themselves, and it was not known in what manner these services were conducted, and above all, as the protest was not against the action of the General Council, but merely against individuals, therefore resolved that the paper be laid upon the table.

It was a dexterous way of getting rid of the troublesome affair, but they will have the same difficulty wherever the Synod or Council meets until the principle be abandoned or it becomes obsolete.

At a subsequent meeting of the Council it was resolved that hereafter no member during the meeting shall be permitted to preach in a non-Lutheran pulpit except by permission of the pastor *loci*. This amounts to a surrender of personal rights to the control of one man, who may not be favorable to the permission.

When I entered the ministry in 1826, what is called *distinctive Lutheranism* was not a subject of thought, much less of discussion. A few of the older clergy were probably orthodox on the sacraments, but they gave themselves no trouble about bringing their views prominently forward, either in their sermons or in writing. I know that Dr. J. G. Schmucker, of York, was a genuine Lutheran, for it was his explanation of the Lutheran doctrine of the real presence in the sacrament that first led me to reflection upon that subject, and which has more or less influenced my theological *Richtung* (tendency) ever since. Sometimes, owing to adverse associations, my faith was shaken, for at first it was not very firm; but when I got beyond the influence of living teachers, and began independent examination, the old Scripture doctrine would come back with double force.

I do not know one of the *mediæval* men of that generation, and by that I mean the men who were between the old men of the Church and us young men—such men as D. F. Schaeffer, B. Kurtz, F. Ruthrauff, A. Reck, C. P. Krauth, S. S. Schmucker, and a few others of the same period—I do not know one who laid any claim to more than the name of Lutheran except, perhaps, D. F. Schaeffer and C. P. Krauth, Sr. Some, years after, became more pronounced, but still it was a subject that gave nobody any trouble about propagating it. The same was true concerning men of that grade in the old mother Synod, except, perhaps, Mr. Demme, of Philadelphia, and a few others.

On the other hand, even after the Seminary was established at Gettysburg, systematic and sustained, but covert, attack upon the Symbolical Books was made.   The result was that the books were not regarded with favor by many of the ministers and students, and very many did not accept the doctrine of the sacraments as taught in the Lutheran Church. This continued to be the state of affairs for many years.   There were some that were true Lutherans despite these adverse circumstances.   Strange to say, not a few underwent a sort of reacting process, and absolutely were converted to the true church doctrine by the very agency diligently employed to deter them from it.   These men did not venture to be demonstrative, but so soon as they became free from the painful shackles by which they were fettered, they professed the true doctrine.

A large number, however, were Zwinglians (not even Calvinists) on the sacraments.   That is, they were not Lutherans, and were satisfied with opposing the doctrines of the Church without bothering themselves about any school of theology.

This unhappy state of things continued for some years.   At length that secretly begotten abortion, the "Definite Platform," appeared, and this aroused a wholesome controversy, not so much on the doctrines reprobated in it as upon the inexpediency of altering the Confessions and disturbing the harmony of the Church.   The discussion led many men to reflection upon the subject in general, and the issue was precisely the contrary from what was intended by the projectors of that mischievous experiment. From that day there can be traced a gradual change, and the more sure and permanent from the fact of its being slow. At present (January, 1884,) orthodox Lutheran ministers in the General Synod can be counted by the hundreds. As chief examiner of those students who have been licensed by the Synod of Maryland for more than 20 years, I have been gratified by the gradual improvement in this respect, very different from my experience of 35 or more years ago, when a student absolutely lost his temper at some questions on the sacraments I put to him, and intimated that those old doctrines had become "obsolete," "effete;" and I remember also how Charles P. Krauth, Jr., who afterwards became one of our mightiest men, sitting beside his fellow-student, rebuked him, in a subdued voice, for his impertinence and ill manners. He never amounted to much in the Church, and died early.*

Most of the other Synods, in which the American element predominates, also rejoice in evidences of improvement in this direction. Even in those in the General Synod, in which heretofore there was a lamentable looseness on our distinctive points, you will find men who are returning to the faith of the Church, and rejoicing in it.

My little treatise on The Lutheran Doctrine of the Real Presence in the Lord's Supper (1883) was kindly received by many, and I was surprised and greatly gratified to receive commendations of it from men of whom I did not expect it.

* For a full history of it, see "Fifty Years," p. 337.

I cannot more forcibly illustrate this wholesome change than by quoting the language of the same man in 1870 and 1883. "*Ex uno disce multos.*" In speaking in a printed book of the leader of the low Lutheran school, he says: "We are among those who endorsed his views, and cannot but regret that his clear, Scriptural and liberal views did not prevail in the Lutheran church. We still hope and pray that his . . . views will, after some time be past, be endorsed by the Lutheran Church in America." And hear this same man in 1883—in speaking of the same men and times, he says: "Our Church became the servile imitator of others. Her own glorious doctrines she either explained away or ignored altogether. In conforming to the views of others she had to reject her doctrine of baptism and the Lord's Supper. The glorious Confessions were thrown aside. . . . The great Confession of our Church was scarcely looked at, and the other Symbolical Books were only read to be condemned. . . . A wild, un-Lutheran spirit prevailed . . . but how great a change has taken place in our doctrinal position."

Hundreds of our ministers would make the same acknowledgment if any occasion rendered it necessary.

PROGRESS.

One of the most gratifying evidences of our growth in this country, and of advancing intelligence, is the large number of periodical publications

(every one of which is of a decidedly religious character), of colleges, theological seminaries, orphans'
houses and hospitals. There are also 24 academies,
most of which are under synodical control, and there
are 12 or 13 seminaries for females, which are conducted by individuals for their personal advantage,
but none of which, as far as I know, is under synodical management, and hence I would not designate
them as Church institutions properly speaking,
though highly worthy of mention in a chapter on
Progress.

When I entered the ministry there was not a single
incorporated college, that is, which had the power
of conferring degrees and was manned by a regular
Faculty; there was only one theological seminary
besides Hartwick, but this latter was of extremely
limited influence and patronage; there were but two
periodicals, and they were monthlies, one of which
was continued only one year, and the other maintained at a heavy loss; there were no orphan houses
and no high academies controlled by the Church,
and no schools of a high grade for the education of
ladies.

But what is the present condition of things? We
have now (1884) 90 periodicals, from weekly to annual, 31 of which are English, 35 German, 12 Nor-
wegian, 8 Swedish, 3 Danish, and 1 Icelandic.*

We have 18 theological seminaries, 16 colleges, 22
orphan houses and hospitals, and 11 schools for

* In 1895 there were 150.

females, although the latter are not really under Church control.*

These are interesting and cheering signs of progress, though it may be doubted whether the multiplication of schools, especially colleges and seminaries for theology, is the best policy. But this defect cannot be remedied, and all discussion upon the subject would lead to no good result, excepting enlightening the Church upon an acknowledged evil.

Whilst we have been making progress in some directions, yet we are still far behind in others. I have reason to think that very few of our clergy are *real* students; many of them, no doubt, are readers of popular books and newspapers, but I know very few are prosecuting higher studies, so that if there were vacancies in some of our professorships, for instance, it would not be an easy thing to fill them with *first-class men*. Ordinary men enough can be had, but that is not the kind that the present state of learning demands. Too few of our men buy standard books; even the English translation of Schmid's *Dogmatik* has sold very slowly; perhaps 1000 copies have been disposed of, and yet this book is almost indispensable to a Lutheran theologian.† The same may be said of the sale of some

* In 1895 there were 106.

† I am pleased to hear that a new and improved edition of this great work is in course of preparation by its learned translators.

other English books printed in this country, although of not such commanding interest to the scholar as Schmid.

Neither do large numbers of our clergy seem to feel any concern in extra measures for the advancement of the Church in influence and respectability. The Diets, for instance, awakened very little besides local interest. Some men even opposed them; but I never heard of any opposition worth listening to except from men who were not invited to read papers, and they were confined to one section of the Church.

Even when the opinion of influential men on certain matters proposed in the papers is invited, nobody responds. I know a man who, distrustful of his own judgment on several important subjects, asked for light, and no one deigned to notice his request, which led him to remark that his brethren were as stupid as himself, which was perhaps true!

D. D.'S IN OUR CHURCH.

Before the establishment of colleges in our Church, and before we had any authority of conferring literary honors, there were not more than six or eight of our men who bore these titles. One reason was that the number of our ministers was very small, and the other was that very few of them, comparatively, were thoroughly educated men.

But when our institutions were empowered to bestow these dignities and our ministry had been increasing for years, the titles of D. D. and A. M. were unsparingly conferred. It is not for me to say anything about the fitness of most of these men, but this I know, that of many of the men honored with the title of D. D. very few would be chosen by the same Board as teachers of theology in any seminary.

I know, and so do others, that not a few were thus titled for the services they had rendered or were expected to render the Church and college—some in accordance with the earnest solicitation of friends, some in compliance with their own importunate though secret requests. But all of our colleges have become more careful, and for the' last few years the roll of the distinguished has not been inconveniently increased.

I presume there is scarcely any influential member of our college Boards who does not every year receive a gentle request or recommendation in that direction, but there seems to be a set purpose not to spend any more of the college funds in buying diplomas for eminent theologians!

I opposed most of these nominations in the College Board, and it was because I did not want to aid in cheapening the title; and, secondly, because most of the nominees did not come up to my standard; and, thirdly, there were so many others equally entitled to it on the basis assumed by their friends, and why discriminate?

But some may ask, "How was it in relation to yourself?" It was just so. I challenge any one to say that I ever, by letter or any other way, accepted any of the college titular honors bestowed upon me. No such letter will be found noticed upon the Secretary's record nor anywhere else; and if my name sometimes appears in print with these suffixes, I have never authorized the use of them. Hence I felt free to vote against *Doctoring* some men whom neither I nor anybody else deemed fit for the distinction, but who were nominated for reasons very different from those of literary or theological qualification.

Dr. Schaff once told me that you would hardly make a mistake in calling every Dutch Reformed minister *Doctor*. It has not yet become quite as bad among us, but I know a man who once made the experiment at one of our Synods. He was rather a stranger, and did not intimately know all the men. He was corrected in only a few instances. I was once a guest of a highly esteemed Dutch Reformed minister, and I called him *Doctor*, which title he said he was not honored with. I told him the above incident in justification. He did not deny the truth of it. It would not do to reveal the proceedings of College Boards, but some queer stories might be told in relation to this matter. And yet, to the credit of many of our titled clergy, it may be said that they are equal, and in many cases superior, to the similar class of men in other churches. We have comparatively as many good scholars and thoroughly bred theologians as they have.

CATECHISATION, PASTORAL VISITING, AND OTHER
FUNCTIONS.

Every year of my pastoral life at the First church
I instructed a class in the catechism, and confirmed
those whom I could with a good conscience admit to
the full privileges of membership. I occasionally
gave great offence by rejecting some, especially the
children of Germans whose parents did not belong
to my church, but who sent their children to my
class because they understood English better than
German. They were generally very young, that is,
twelve to fourteen, and I soon found out that the
design was not so much Christian instruction with
a view to salvation as conformity to ancient custom
and mere ancestral habit. Now, whilst it is true
that some of these were deeply impressed with the
truth, and were confirmed by me, yet others merely
learned the lessons as they would a school task, and
the sooner it was over the better. Personal religion
made no part of the business, but it was a merely
mechanical process from beginning to end. Such I
did not confirm, and the parents were much displeased.

I sometimes preached a sermon on this subject on
the Sunday before I opened the class, in which I
carefully explained the whole matter, and I found
it always had a good effect.

Successful catechising is not an easy thing, and
hence it should be studied. From what I have
heard, it is frequently performed in a slip-shod sort

of manner, which is far from being edifying. Men who have never heard lectures upon it should care-fully read some treatise from which they might learn much. The only English book on this subject by any of our men which I now remember is one by Dr. Zeigler, which is said to be good.

I wish this old-time church custom were universal. I am persuaded the cause would gain much, and it is gratifying to hear that it is becoming more popu-lar in some new sections of the Church where it was formerly almost unknown.

I, however, admitted by confirmation some per-sons to membership who had never been catechised according to the good old system, and I presume this is the practice of most ministers. They may be persons intelligent in the Scriptures, familiar with our church customs, and truly pious, whom no man has a right to debar from any church privilege, even if in their case the old custom is not observed. The end of catechetical instruction is already secured in them, for they know the Scriptures, practice the Christian duties, and lead godly lives.

I have never insisted upon confirmation in the case of those who joined our communion from other churches; for, recognizing their church membership elsewhere, confirmation would have been a super-fluous form.

I remember a case or two of persons who united with us as a church for the first time, who were not of Lutheran parentage, and who objected to confirmation on the ground of its being a mere ceremony. I earnestly argued the question with them, and when I showed them that their objection was groundless they yielded. I found that the objection was based upon an unwillingness to come out singly before the church to make a confession, inasmuch as they had done what was equivalent to that before. In several cases I yielded as a matter of expediency, as no principle was involved.

Some men make a difference between pastoral and social visiting. By the former they mean a visit of a purely religious character, when nothing but religion was spoken, and which usually, when convenient, was concluded with prayer. By social visiting they mean a polite call, with inquiries into the condition of the family's health and gossip in general. If religion was introduced at all, it was merely adventitious, and was not more personal or practical than the necessity of getting a new organ or other church improvement.

How absurdly such men must feel when they go to make a *pastoral* visit and think that now nothing but religion must be talked of, and the following week at the *social* call there must be as little religion as possible introduced. This is mechanical, artificial, and unscriptural. A judicious mingling of both at all visits is the best course, and a sensible man can easily so arrange it. My pastoral practice for years was to have singing and prayer at the breaking up of every *social* gathering where at all practicable, and it always had a good effect.

I have known a few men who, on their *first* visits to their people, had prayers with every family. I know an elder who accompanied his pastor during his rounds to show him where the people lived, who said that "the pastor had him on his knees seventeen times in one day." Some of the good people rejoiced that now at last they had secured a good pastor, for he prayed with them on his first visit; but they never saw that pious exercise repeated, for he seldom or never called to see them again, and if he did the time was spent in frivolous talk.

It is not always judicious or opportune to introduce personal religious appeals to unbelievers, whilst it is very easy and natural to bring up the subject before Christians. What is more pleasing than to converse with such on their own personal religious condition and the affairs of the kingdom generally?

I once knew a zealous but verdant young minister who was very faithful in his pastoral attentions to the sick. He had noticed the absence from church for some time of one of the best young married women of his congregation, and upon being informed that she was sick, he hastened to her house to discharge his ministerial functions. He was admitted to the lady's chamber, and at once began his service for the sick, accompanied with the usual exhortations to resignation and the merciful designs of heaven in afflicting His most faithful people. He earnestly prayed that God would not permit this sickness to be unto death, but that she might speedily recover to resume her position in the church and Sunday-school and her family. He prayed for her young husband that he might be prepared for the terrible calamity which the terrible death of his young wife might bring upon him, and heartily commended all to the loving mercy of the heavenly Father. He observed a lack of sympathy in the company of friends in the sick room, and it was not until he had left the house that he learned that the young mother, her husband, parents, brothers and sisters, and the whole relationship were rejoicing in the happy birth of a bouncing fat baby, and that a preliminary funeral service was not exactly in order!!!

Of course the report spread, and the verdant parson was laughed at for his simplicity, though everybody gave him credit for zeal. He afterwards said himself that he heard something like an infantile whimpering under a snow-white covering by the side of the *sick* mother!!!

I knew an inexperienced young brother who once visited a sick woman, with whom he earnestly prayed. As he was rising from his knees at her bedside, she, with pious fervor, threw her arms around his neck, and almost drew him down. He was shocked next day to hear that she was suffering from *mania a potu!*

LUTHER MEMORIAL MEETINGS IN 1883.

The occurrence of the 400th birth-year of Luther, on November 10, 1883, awakened a very lively in-

·terest in our Church as early as the fall of 1882. The Synods which met at that season adopted measures towards a general celebration of the event, most of which have been very creditably carried out. A few Synods seemed to be indifferent about it, but they were those who were lax in doctrine or deficient in energy of every kind.

All through the year our church papers contained numerous articles on Luther. Scarcely a number was issued that did not set forth some trait of his character or some fact connected with his history. The *Observer* even published a biography in weekly portions, but I do not think the people grew weary of the theme, although there was necessarily much repetition of well-known facts.

During this year there were published independently of the church papers more than 100 books, tracts, sermons, poems, and addresses concerning Luther, and I suppose that most of them were read. Many of our ministers preached discourses to their people, so that much useful and interesting information was disseminated, and they were always ready to receive more.

The most popular demonstrations of this kind were the gatherings of a number of neighboring congregations in a grove, and on several occasions there were as many as 4,000 people present. These were held at places easily accessible by railroads, and it was not hard to collect large crowds. They were conducted on the picnic fashion, each family bringing its own provisions, but the religious exercises were of an inspiring nature. There were bands of musicians, besides church choirs, and in most cases an organ. Committees had been previously appointed to make arrangements, prepare program, select subjects, and appoint speakers. The programs were printed, so that there was no confusion. The subjects all related to Luther, and a specific portion of time was allotted to each speaker, which, however, was not always observed. The whole day was devoted to the demonstration, and the occasions were hugely enjoyed. Hundreds of people came on foot, and hundreds more in their own vehicles, whilst the majority came by rail.

The first one was held at Rupert, near Catawissa, Pa., at which I was present, and this was followed by many others in various sections of the country. I was invited to six, but owing to the distance I attended only three. Usually all our ministers from near and far were present. I began—but not quite soon enough—a collection of newspaper cuttings on this subject, with illustrations, from all the sources accessible to me. I bought the foreign journals, and many of our own country, which contained anything upon the subject, and in the course of some weeks I gathered an immense number of scraps, which I pasted in a large folio volume. I think this is unique, and it is essential to any man who desires to write an account of the extraordinary Luther celebration of 1883.

LUTHER STATUE.

The subject of a Luther statue had been barely mentioned eight or ten years before the fact materialized. I timidly proposed it in the *Observer*, not very sure of a favorable hearing.

I estimated the cost at $10,000, but my proposition met with no cheering response, and though chagrined I was not disappointed. I was then satisfied with bringing out my plaster statuette of the Reformer, which some of his admirers will perhaps remember, and on which I of course lost money. It was three feet high, and was modeled after various engraved likenesses and busts by a skillful artist in that department of work. There is a copy in the Seminary at Gettysburg, which was presented by a friend now deceased.

It was not until the approach of the Luther commemoration day of 1883, or a year or two before, that the erection of a Luther statue was seriously entertained. Several active laymen in New York, consisting of such ardent and liberal Luther admirers as Charles A. Schieren, now Mayor of Brooklyn, A. J. D. Wedemeyer, and J. Dobler, especially, laid hold of it with vigor, and a few of us in Baltimore fell in with the measure, among whom Gustavus A. Dobler deserves special mention for his energy and liberality in prosecuting the cause. We constituted ourselves a committee, for there was no one else to appoint us, and I have found in various analogous cases that this is the best way of accomplishing important enterprises. Secure the interest of a few persevering, intelligent, whole-souled men, and then lay your plans and proceed. You will soon find helpers, who will be glad that you saved them the delay and annoyance of framing a constitution and electing officers and pushing the machine into motion. This committee consisted of myself, G. A. Dobler, J. G. Butler and George Ryneal, of Maryland and the District of Columbia; A. J. D. Wedemeyer, C. A. Schieren and J. Dobler, of New York, and Daniel Fox, Esq., of Philadelphia.

Through the kind offices of Mr. Sutro I corresponded with the sculptor Prof. Lenz, of Nurnberg, and got his proposal for a life-size statue. G. A. Dobler also wrote to the foundry at Lauchheimer, and received very favorable proposals for a fac-simile statue of that in the Luther group at Worms. This was accepted by the committee at $4,500, to be delivered at any German port most desirable to us. The bargain was consummated by telegraph, and a considerable part of the money paid immediately, which specimen of American promptness greatly astonished and gratified the German artists. During the summer of 1883 one of our committee, Mr. Wedemeyer, during a visit to Germany, spent several days at the foundry, and gave all particular directions as to transportation. He had frequent consultations with the gentlemen connected with that great establishment, and all things were satisfactory. The work required longer time than we expected, and hence the unveiling was necessarily retarded. We hoped to have it ready by November 10, 1883 (the 400th birthday of Luther), but it did not arrive here until April, 1884. The steamship company charged no freight, and on my application to Mr. Garrett, President of the B. & O. R. R., he cheerfully offered to transport it to Washington. It is proper here to state that the Pennsylvania road had offered the same favor to me through one of its officers, but the statue was landed within a few yards of the B. & O., and hence the loading was more convenient.

The press reporters in the city, always looking out for something fresh, were much concerned about it, and I had numerous calls for information. We expected it by every German steamer coming to Baltimore for several weeks before its arrival, and the fact of the non-arrival was duly heralded with much earnestness, and thus the excitement was kept up. When it finally came it was welcomed with *eclat*, and the fact was telegraphed all over the country. The 21st of May was selected for the day of unveiling, and all our energies were directed towards that consummation. The pedestal had previously been contracted for, and everything was expected to be ready. For some weeks previous a sub-committee was busily engaged in selecting and engaging speakers and other persons to participate in the proceedings. Dr. Butler deserves the credit cf almost exclusively carrying on the large correspondence and attending to the numerous and often vexatious details. He worked faithfully for weeks in superintending the erection of the pedestal and all other necessary arrangements, and has the satisfaction of knowing that his onerous duties were well performed.

Some of the gentlemen invited to take active part in the services declined, and others were selected. We aimed at having nearly every section of the Church represented, and the individual selection was not an easy task. A few who were proposed by some members of the committee were rejected by the rest, for some of us were determined that no minister of our Church should speak on that occasion who had either opposed the enterprise or was indifferent to it, or who was unsound as a Lutheran, and for these reasons several otherwise respectable gentlemen's names did not appear on our program.

The public exercises were performed by the following gentlemen: On Sunday night (May 18) Dr. F. W. Conrad delivered an oration on Luther, of an hour and a half's length, in Dr. Butler's church. On Tuesday night Dr. J. Fry, of Reading; Rev. Dr. Gilbert, of Winchester, Va.; Rev. D. H. Geissinger, of Easton, Pa; and Rev. Dr. Swartz, then of Gettysburg, Pa., and Hon. Mr. Miller, of New York, delivered addresses in the same church, and Rev. Dr. M. Sheeleigh read a poem. On Wednesday morning, May 21, Rev. Dr. Hennighausen, of Baltimore, Revs. Mohldehnke and Wedekind, of New

York, delivered German addresses, and at the unveiling, in the afternoon of the same day, Hon. Mr.
Conger, U. S. Senator from Michigan, and I delivered orations in the open air upon the platform.
Chief Justice Waite had promised to unveil the
statue, but was sick. President Arthur previously
declined. The committee had not decided who
should draw the string until we were on the way
from the church to the platform, when I suggested
Mr. Corcoran. They agreed, and he consented.
An immense audience attended the ceremonies,
among whom there were over 100 Lutheran ministers. It was naturally expected that the fervor excited upon this subject would result in the establishment of some other Lutheran institution, but thus
far nothing has been suggested. I have no doubt
if some influential man of leisure and energy would
undertake something worthy of the Church he would
succeed, but he would necessarily have to encounter
opposition, unless he first secured the approbation
of certain gentlemen, who will not consent that any
individual should receive any credit for any specific
work done. Besides, the Church has so many other
enterprises on hand at present that it would be hard
to succeed in anything else, and yet who knows but
that something great will yet grow out of this statue
celebration.

Many queer incidents occurred during these numerous commemorations, and many good things were
said. Many of our own people learned more about

Luther than they knew before, and many outside of our pale were led to make inquiries, and some of these inquiries were of a very simple character. A lady of our Church told me that after returning from a celebration of November 10th she remarked to a Presbyterian lady neighbor that "she very much enjoyed the commemoration of Luther's birthday." "Why," replied the neighbor, "I never knew you had a son named Luther."

THE LUTHER STATUETTE.

In 1875, the year before the Centennial, several articles appeared in the *Observer* on the subject of erecting a statue of Luther in Fairmount Park, Philadelphia, as the Presbyterians had resolved to erect one of Dr. Witherspoon. I replied to the first article, highly approving of the object, and giving $10,000 as the probable expense of an ordinary work of art. The matter was not prosecuted further, but this induced me to have a plaster statuette of about 36 inches in height moulded. I thought it well to secure the interest and co-operation of several other men, and spoke to Dr. F. W. Conrad and Rev. Chas. A. Smith, formerly of our ministry, but then in the Presbyterian church, and both living in Philadelphia.

We went together to see the reduced model of the statue of Witherspoon which the sculptor had engaged to make for the Presbyterians. The artist was a Frenchman, whose establishment was in

Market street, and his name was Bailley. He agreed to make a mould for us at $300, but could not execute it for some months, until his return from Central America. This did not suit us. I returned home and engaged Dr. Volck, of Baltimore, on my own account, but subject to the final acceptance of the two men in Philadelphia. Dr. Volck made a sample, which I had photographed and sent to them. They did not approve of it, and thus I was thrown upon my own responsibility. In the preparation of the model the Doctor used all the acknowledged likenesses of Luther, and even sent to St. Louis for a mask of Rauch's well-known Luther bust in the Walhalla, near Munich, which he specially followed in making his own. I took this mask to Philadelphia and showed it to Conrad and Smith, without, however, telling them that it was Rauch's. They condemned it, but when I told them the origin of it they were much confused, and blamed me for leading them into such a mischievous scrape. It is not everybody who has had that degree of artistic taste or culture which would qualify them to judge in such a case.

I then proceeded alone, paying Volck $200 for the mould, and advertising the statuette. I employed an Italian image maker to mould the statuettes, paying him $5 for each, including packing. I charged $10 for the first copies, and I did not receive orders for more than about twenty, and of course lost considerably on the enterprise. Though

20

many of our ministers and people glorify Luther in exalted strains, very few of them were willing to buy what was considered by good judges an admirable statuette as an ornament for their parlors, studies or Sunday-school rooms. High art has made little progress among us, and hence there are few patrons. In one hundred years hence it may be different.

Wherever the statuette has been seen by artists it has been pronounced an admirable piece of work, and extremely like the universally accepted likeness by Rauch, but many of our people thought it *did not look like Luther*—just as if they knew anything about it. To such an *enlightened* critic, who was sure it did not resemble Luther, I once meekly observed, "It was so long since I had seen brother Martin that I did not remember how he looked." The critic wilted.

ELECTION OF PROFESSORS AND PRESIDENTS.

I have taken part in the election of most of our professors and other officers in the Seminary and in college, which in most cases occasioned no difficulty, for usually the candidates had been determined upon, and nothing was necessary but to vote them in. In a few other cases there was a difference of opinion, and several candidates were presented by their respective friends. I never, however, observed anything like fierce party strife, but everything was done in kindness and mutual respect.

I shall notice only several cases. Until 1830 Dr. Schmucker had been the only professor in the Seminary. He taught all the classes, and at a small salary. He might have continued to do it, for the number of students did not exceed 15, and for some years it did not reach that number. If he had done that, which it is true would have demanded a little more labor, the Seminary would have saved a good deal of money, and some unpleasant events might have been avoided. But there was an ambition to spread out. Dr. Hazelius was elected second professor, and this transaction turned out to be costly and injurious.

There were very few thoroughly educated theologians among us at that remote period, and what few we had were extravagantly extolled. None of us had ever seen Dr. Hazelius, who was the only candidate, but he had the reputation of being a good scholar, and had been teacher in Hartwick Seminary for a number of years. He was elected, and accepted without delay. He was as good, kind, guileless a soul as ever lived, and in his simplicity he thought that everybody was as honest as himself. He was of an extremely social nature, and it was not long before he felt himself uncomfortable in his new position, and wished himself back at Hartwick, or anywhere else. Besides this his salary was paid, for the most part, out of *the invested capital of the Seminary*, which was unwise and unbusiness-like. This in a short time occasioned embarrassment, but what else could be done? There was not enough revenue from investments to support both professors, and this fact annoyed the good Doctor painfully. He did not remain more than several years, and was then elected to the professorship in the Seminary of the South Carolina Synod. A leading member of that Synod wrote to me, inquiring about the qualifications of a minister who was spoken of for that position. Instead of giving him an opinion, I recommended Dr. Hazelius, who I knew was anxious to leave Gettysburg. My South Carolina friend was overjoyed to hear it, and they chose the Doctor immediately, and he went as soon as he could get off. He was in many respects an interesting man, and performed all his duties faithfully. He died at Lexington, S. C., in 1853, aged 76.*

I remember well that on one occasion the Seminary Board held an adjourned meeting in a gentleman's parlor in Gettysburg, and thirteen ballotings were held before a candidate received a majority, and then it was only one. It was midnight before we parted, and the only thing that secured a majority was the complete exhaustion of a few of the members. They wanted to leave town in the morning, and it was necessary that the vacancy should be filled. It was a severe struggle, but all was conducted in the best good humor. One man at length yielded, and the matter was decided. I do not think that the gentleman elected has ever found out what

* See Sprague's Annals and my "Fifty Years."

a protracted effort it cost his friends to elect him. All the rest submitted to the result gracefully.

We once had great trouble in persuading an elected officer of one of the schools to accept the position. We all voted for him, and the meeting was held in his own house. There was some diffi- culty in the way, and it was toward midnight before it was finally adjusted to the satisfaction of all.

When Dr. Baugher, Sr., was elected President of Pennsylvania College in the place of Dr. Krauth, transferred to the Seminary, I was one of the commit- tee appointed to inform him of the fact. The Board was still in session, and it was important to hear his decision before it adjourned. We proceeded to his residence, which was then out of town, on the road to the almshouse. We found him at home, and upon being ushered into his study, I without many words announced his election. Without uttering a previous word of acknowledgment he abruptly re- plied, " I will not accept it!" He appeared vexed at hearing it, but after some consideration he with- drew his declination and accepted the office.

I could recite another instance of difficulty and vexation and midnight election struggle, but I will forbear. Some facts in history had better be un- written.

The lamented death of Dr. Stork, who had so ably filled the professor's chair in the Seminary, rendered an election necessary. There were several candidates for the place, and there was the unusual number of 45 members of the Board at the special meeting called for this purpose. There was more excitement than usual, and the friends of the several candidates were very sanguine. Indeed, there were several members present who usually absented themselves from the regular meetings. One of the candidates received but three votes of the 45, and Dr. Valentine all the rest. There was some sharp disappointment and chagrin felt out of doors, not so much at the election of Dr. Valentine as at the complete discomfiture of their favorite.

A few members of the Board had concluded to bring forward Dr. Christlieb, of Bonn, and it would have been done if one of his advocates had not been suddenly called home during the meeting. I do not think that Dr. Christlieb would have been chosen, for the minds of the Board were set upon Dr. Valentine; and besides it was not known how Dr. Christlieb was disposed, and it was considered a hazardous experiment.

During the summer of 1884 Dr. Hamma, of Baltimore, went to Europe, and took occasion to call and see Dr. Christlieb. I gave him a letter of introduction to him, and a month afterwards Dr. Hamma wrote me that he had seen Dr. Christlieb, and casually spoke to him on the subject. He said that whilst he would like to labor for the Church in the United States, yet that he felt himself too old for such a move, but especially that he thought it his duty to remain in Germany to fight the battle of

Orthodoxy against the Rationalists; and I think his conclusion was sensible.

It has always seemed to me absurd to ask a learned German professor to come over here and teach (as he would be compelled to do) the elements of theology, or, it might be, the alphabet of Hebrew. He would spurn it with disdain, and denounce the day he ever consented to become the preceptor of young men in preliminary branches which they should have learned long before at the University. I know something about one celebrated German divine who was elected to a position in this country, and of whom it was really expected that he would teach the A B C of the German language to mischievous American boys and a few theological students. He did not come.

It might well enough suit a young man who had not yet acquired a reputation, and who could easily accommodate himself to our manners and church life; but to ask a man of European celebrity and long-established German habits to come over and lecture to our half-trained theological students is literally expecting a little too much.

I once heard a German professor of high distinction, in one of our Church Seminaries, openly declare in Synod that his pupils were not sufficiently advanced to be profited by his lectures, and for that and other reasons he resigned.

Dr. Valentine's transfer to the Seminary left the College Presidency vacant, and various gentlemen were named as suitable successors. On Wednesday morning, June 25th, 1884, the Trustees met, when after long deliberation the Rev. Charles S. Albert, of St. Mark's, Baltimore, was chosen by 19 votes to one blank. A committee was appointed to wait upon him next day in Baltimore, but owing to the destruction of a portion of the railroad by a flood, they did not see him until the following Monday. Mr. Albert declined the offer.

An extra meeting of the Board was called for July 15, when Dr. McKnight was elected, and finally accepted the place.

COLLECTING FUNDS FOR THE SEMINARY.

No wonder that in the early history of the Seminary and some other good Church institutions many serious blunders were made in the methods of collecting funds for their support. That business was not elevated to an art as it is to-day, and hard work was done in securing the requisite funds. Collectors were constantly in the field, and small donations were in order. Gifts of thousands were not known in our Church, and were not common anywhere. Benjamin Keller, Prof. Schmucker and Benjamin Kurtz were the most successful solicitors, although other men, such as Rev. Dr. J. G. Schmucker and a few others, did efficient work.

Prof. Schmucker's field was principally among the New Englanders, and B. Kurtz spent two years in Europe in this service. He was there when Rationalism was still popular. His cause was novel, his manners were engaging, but not polished after the European style, his preaching so simple and impressive that many were disposed to contribute small sums for the sake of the man, if not for the cause. After two years' hard work he managed to bring to the Seminary treasury not over $12,000, besides piles of books, many of which were of no account.

I think that I have recorded the fact somewhere else that our Board once voted a donation of some of these books to the Theological Seminary which a short time previously had been established in Columbus, O., with Prof. Schmidt as President. I met him in Frederick not long after he had received the books, and he complained grievously of the quality of the donation. He said with few exceptions they consisted of nothing but old German prayer-books and sermons, which he did not want, and of which he could make no use. I can easily conceive all this, for the selection was left to a gentleman who was not too favorably inclined to the Ohio Seminary, and who was only too glad to disencumber our shelves of a pile of useless lumber, and who thought besides that these useless old books were good enough for what, in his opinion, was a very small concern!

In connection with Mr. Kurtz's agency it may be worth while to state that his services were rendered gratuitously, but he still, and I think very properly, too, looked for something more substantial than a vote of thanks. I do not mean that he desired any pecuniary compensation, but he did intimate that some of the very nice fancy articles which were sold at a fair in Baltimore would be acceptable, and which he intended as presents to some of his female parishioners at Hagerstown, for he was then a widower. All the articles were sold, and he got nothing; he then said that he would be pleased to receive a few of the best and most costly books. The result of the whole proceeding was that he was presented with a duplicate copy of a *Hebrew Bible!* This was not the action of the Board, but of a single individual. I have the best reason to know that this fact mortified him to the very quick, and he spoke of it privately many years after as one of the most humiliating events of his life. He had too much self-respect to speak of it publicly or to complain, but it harassed him painfully for years, and he never entirely recovered from it.

Persons entirely incompetent to the work were appointed as solicitors, and I myself, when quite a young man, was inconsiderate enough to go out upon such an expedition. Why did not some judicious friend dissuade me from it?

I had no experience, and not another single qualification. I had not been in the ministry over a few months; I was not known, and in all respects the most unfit man for such a position. But I ventured upon the ill-considered enterprise, and the result may be foreseen. I hired a vehicle, went up as far as Winchester, and did not receive, even in promises to pay, as much as my expenses amounted to, but I paid these myself, so that the Seminary at least did not suffer. I have not gone out on such business since!

In the course of years the Seminary has received some bequests, though none very large; but by dint of perseverance I presume that over $100,000 have been collected in the course of fifty years.* Many subscriptions were never paid (and some money has been lost). The Board was not always judicious in the choice of its Treasurers; good, honest men they were, but they were not practiced financiers, and did not know how to invest funds wisely. The present Treasurer (1886) is the only one I remember who had the necessary business qualifications for that office.

The efficient services in securing funds for the Seminary rendered by Rev. Drs. Brown and F. W. Conrad deserve the most honorable mention. These gentlemen brought together considerable sums, but their labors belong to a later period of the Seminary's history, and my design in this chapter is to speak of the early times more particularly.†

---

* It was announced in 1885 that several large bequests were made, which have since been paid (1896), amounting to almost $100,000.

† See my History of the Seminary; *Evangelical Review.*

CHAPTER XIII.

WHEN Jenny Lind was in Baltimore I became acquainted with her, and exchanged several letters with her afterwards, one of which I gave to Brantz Mayer, who was an autograph collector. She had made up her mind to come to our church on Sunday in company with Consul Brauns, a faithful member; but when she saw the immense crowd assembled in the streets around Barnum's she timidly shrank, fearing that the unthinking multitude would follow her carriage, which would have been the case, to her great discomfort and our inconvenience. If she had come to our church there would have been such a rush as was never witnessed, so insane was the curiosity of the *ignobile vulgus* to see the great singer whom they could not afford to pay to hear.

I was offered tickets to her concerts, but never went. First, because most of my people, not know-

ing that my tickets were free, would have thought
hard of me for paying \$7 (the price); and secondly,
because she sung in a theatre, where I would have
been severely blamed for going. Two ministers,
one of our own Church and one a Protestant Methodist, both editors, were reprehended in one of the
dailies for going to a theatre to hear Lind sing.
Some of my good people said to me they were glad
I did not go, for I would have been included in the
censure by name; and so was I.

The opinions of thousands of people have changed
on this subject. Whilst it would not be safe for a
minister to go to a theatre to witness a regular dramatic performance, yet the public will now permit
him to go to a theatre to hear a lecture or a concert, or to be present at a college commencement or
a meeting in behalf of any good object.

EXCURSIONS.

The poet Rogers, of London, was in the habit for
many years of giving breakfasts to his foreign visitors, and to everybody else who was anybody. The
guests were sure to meet people of distinction in
every profession, and hence the honor of an invitation was anxiously coveted. Rogers was once much
amused at receiving a reply from an American lady
whom he invited to breakfast, which contained no
other words than " Won't I ?" He used to tell the
story with great glee, and he thought it exceedingly smart and characteristically American.

This was in effect my reply to a polite note from the high authorities of the Northern Central Railroad to accompany an excursion party as far as Watkins Glen, in New York. Most readily did I say "Won't I?" and we went.

The party consisted of two clergymen, some artists, newspaper reporters of course, and a few miscellaneous amateurs. They were all gentlemen of culture, and some of them of reputation, as for example, General Strother, of Virginia, the genial "Porte Crayon" of *Harper's Magazine*. The rest of us were no persons in particular in our own estimation, although a few of our artists are rising fast in public favor, and will be further heard of after a while. Every one of them has studied abroad, and the only sculptor among us is the only one who intends to return to Europe, the main reason of which is that a German lady of beauty and high social distinction captured his young heart, and he married her. She is the accomplished daughter of the most exalted Lutheran hierarch in the kingdom of Bavaria, whom we had the pleasure of meeting in Leipzig some years ago, whose official title now is *Oberconsistorialrath und Reichsrath, Dr. H.*

Our company was composed for the most part of young men who, when out of their studies and their editorial coops, are expected to be gay, and of right should be. Nature requires it, the gospel sanctions it. Most of them behaved like boys let out of school, and yet there was nothing undignified or unbecoming the gentleman. There was sparkling wit, sharp repartee, unctuous story-telling, classic quotation, extempore poetry, refined song, racy conversation, and everything exhilarating you could expect from a company of educated excursionists. Nothing offensive or discordant with perfect propriety was said or done. Every man seemed determined to contribute his best to render the occasion agreeable, and the most awkward among us put in his share to the general enjoyment, if in no other way than by creating a laugh at his bad puns or his unmusical songs. We were furnished with a car for our exclusive use, supplied with everything that could refresh the outer and the inner man, and as we had with us a high official of the railroad company, we *switched* off where we pleased, and were taken up by the next or any other train that passed. It was impossible for us to escape observation wherever we stopped, for the artists would disembark with their camp-stools and sketching apparatus to copy scenery, and would soon have around them a group of staring country boys wondering what these city men were doing, and then some of us, with rod and tackle, would *try* for a trout and catch only a chub, or one of us, with insect net, would break his shins over stones and rush through briars after a butterfly, to the wonderment of the group of rustics.

It was necessary also in maintaining perfect railroad discipline to telegraph ahead our coming, so that at every station of importance we were met by the

dignitaries of the place, by the editor, and road officer and subordinates, who were anxious to see these
great men from Baltimore, and all our names were
paraded in the next morning's paper with considerable flourish and *cclat*, various invitations to stay
and look round were extended, which we could not
accept, and after a brief levee on the platform, but
no long speeches, we were summoned to our car and
off we went with railroad speed.

To some of our company the scenery along the
Susquehanna was quite new, and the artists saw
many a place which they would have liked to transfer
to their sketch books. The towns wore the same unwashed, frowsy appearance, and presented so little
attraction that their names were not even asked.
The editors and reporters would occasionally inquire,
but I do not think these villages will find a place in
their published accounts of the excursion.

Of course conversation sometimes lagged, and
somehow or other men will sleep, and in their sleep
in a railroad car they assume most unclassical positions and utter most unmusical sounds. A few
piped gently, others groaned, some snorted outright,
and one burly fat man gave out all the dissonant
noises of a starting locomotive. Whilst some were
indulging in these innocent though annoying amusements some of the artists sketched their likenesses,
a little caricatured of course, which afforded infinite
fun to all around. What a wonderful talent in
sketching these men have! In a few minutes they

transfer to the paper a recognizable likeness of a man, with all the surroundings, which, though roughly drawn, is fit for a portfolio or a specimen of art. They talk most excellently with their pencils, and convey truer and sounder ideas, and better expressed, than many of them do with their tongues. The more careful sketches some of them took of scenes to be published in Harper's are exquisite gems, and it is a pity that they must be reduced in size and engraved on wood for that magazine.

On another excursion to which I was invited by the Baltimore & Ohio Railroad, the company was composed of such men as George Bancroft, Prof. Henry, Brantz Mayer, and some others. We proceeded as far as Wheeling, and thence by boat to Pittsburg. Bancroft's design was to trace the route of Braddock's army from Fort Frederick, in Maryland, to Pittsburg. Our first stopping place was at Harper's for several hours, then at Fort Frederick, and whilst we were surveying the remains Bancroft said it was just one hundred years ago, on that very day, that Braddock occupied that place.

We stopped all night at Martinsburg, where we were entertained by Hon. Mr. Faulkner. We tarried at many places between that and Cumberland, where we were elegantly entertained by Mayor Tucker and others. We dined one day with Mr. Weld at the Mt. Savage Iron Works. At Frostburg we made a long pedestrian tour, and according to Bancroft we found the road cut by Braddock for the

21

march of his army. When we arrived at Pittsburg as the party selected Sunday for the inspection of Braddock's field, I did not accompany them, but stayed in the city and preached.

This was a most delightful and instructive tour, which continued eight days. We had sleeping and cooking apartments on the cars, and stopped wherever we pleased. I was often alone on our wanderings with Mr. Bancroft, and often tried to draw out his religious and theological views, but could not succeed. It was a subject he avoided, but on historical and literary matters he was open, and let me say inexhaustible. For the remembrance of facts, places, dates, men, he was remarkable. It was a week of unmixed enjoyment. Prof. Henry, with his rich stores of learning, and Brantz Mayer, with his sprightliness and literary anecdotes, contributed much to the pleasure of the company.

There was another excursion on the Baltimore and Ohio given to a few of us of the Academy of Science. This was only free as far as the transportation was concerned, but we had a distinct train, under the direction of an officer of the company. Our caterer laid in a good stock of provisions, and we enjoyed ourselves to perfection. Our evenings were spent in the cars, when I would give a burlesque lecture on every insect that would fly to our lamps.

At some village on the Alleghanies we were visited by a well-educated German doctor, who was so enamored with the ale which some of the party had with them that he traveled with us nearly a whole day. I presume he had not enjoyed such fare as we fed him on for many a day. He and I had a dispute on Christianity, and by a happy question I so turned the laugh of the whole company upon him that he left us at the next station, having fared sumptuously at our table.

PRIVATE LIBRARIES.

Very few of our ministers of 40 or 50 years ago, or even much later, could afford to buy good libraries. The fact is that very few had time to study, and again more of them had not been trained to habits of study. The collections of first-class theological books were few until the establishment of the seminaries, and in the beginning there was nothing remarkable even about them, but they have improved wonderfully since.

Some of our professors and pastors have fair collections—I do not mean in quantity, but in quality—and several of them have large and rich libraries. That of Rev. Dr. Krauth, of Philadelphia, is the largest private library probably of any minister in the country, and it is exceedingly rich in the highest departments of literature. It has often been alluded to by scholars, and Dr. Thomas, the author of the Pronouncing Biographical and Mythological Dictionary, says that he found assistance from Dr. Krauth's library which he could at that time find nowhere else in the United States. The rarest and most useful books on Lutheran theology and *Symbolik* abound in the collection, which you can see nowhere else in the country.

Rev. Dr. B. M. Schmucker has a rich collection of works on Luther's *Liturgik*, some of which are unique.

My own special collection is confined to books on Luther, of which I now have some very rare and curious copies, and to books written by Lutheran ministers in America.

Some other men have made a specialty of collecting Lutheran pamphlets, proceedings of Synod and the like. The largest of this character of publications was made by Rev. Dr. Sheeleigh, which was purchased by the Lutheran Historical Society.

I have never aimed at collecting a large library. First, I could not afford it; secondly, I had no room for it; thirdly, I have observed that even owners of large collections are not always the most industrious readers, and if they are students at all they find that their books of reference are sufficient, and this is the experience of most students; and fourthly, I have always had access to fair collections, and since the Peabody and the Johns Hopkins libraries have been instituted, I have the use of every book I wish to consult.

I have expended hundreds of dollars on books, and imported large numbers from Germany, but I have sold off several collections, and never had over 2,000 volumes at any one time. That morbid dis-

position to buy books so common to young students
has happily left me long ago. My reference volumes
answer all my present purposes, and the books which
I read I get from the libraries, especially the Mercantile, Peabody and Johns Hopkins University
libraries.

Not a few of my later possessions are the gifts of
the authors, but years ago I also received as gifts
valuable books from de Menneville and Bossange, of
Paris; from Burmeister, Sturm, Ericson, Troschel,
Herrick, Schaeffer, Dunker, and other naturalists,
of Germany; Dr. Rogers, Doubleday, and others,
of England, saying nothing of many of our own
writers on this side. The number of pamphlets sent
me by the authors of them is very considerable.

THE REBELLION.

During the rebellion I was not a pastor, but
librarian in the Peabody Institute. Though the
congregation in Lexington street which I had served
so many years was for the most part on the side of
the Union, yet that would not have determined the
decided stand I took had I been their pastor. Before I knew which side my former friends would
assume I had openly proclaimed myself for the government, and on that ground I stood to the end.
Some of our city clergy of other churches held the
same position, others espoused the Southern cause,
and a few affected to be indifferent, and a few vainly
tried to accommodate themselves to both parties,
and thus lost the confidence of both.

It cost something to be an uncompromising Union man in those early days. For one or two days we were threatened with an order of expulsion from the city, and we were forbidden for a short time to display the Union flag, but a change of sentiment soon occurred.

Some men and women whose pastor I had been for many years, whose children I had baptized, and some of whom I had buried, whose friend and comforter I had been in trouble, and their welcome guest always, broke up all intercourse with me and my family, and would not even speak to me when we met. Some of them maintained this hostile stand for over ten years, until their death. It led some of them to leave our Church and connect themselves with congregations whose pastors and people were more demonstratively on the Southern side. A general notion also prevailed that the " aristocracy " and fashionable people belonged to that party, and this led some of those who sighed *to be respectable*, and whose personal merits would not have secured recognition by that class, to take advantage of this crisis to secure a standing among them. They succeeded to some extent, as long as their money and help were wanted, but they were dropped out of the ranks when the excitement was over.

It was for a considerable time regarded as a very bold, and by some a presumptuous act, to pray for the President of the United States. I remember on several occasions when I prayed in churches, not our own, that some people would abruptly leave the church, making as much disturbance as possible, and I am sure that if you had asked them what was the cause of the rebellion, not one-half of them would have been able to give an intelligent answer.

One of our Pennsylvania ministers, who was a very popular man, preached in one of our Lutheran churches, and gave great offence by praying that the Lord would grant success to our army and navy. He has never since been invited to that pulpit. Even the Union men thought he was too denunciatory for the pulpit, and feared that some of the party would be so grievously offended as to leave the Church.

To show the gradual improvement in public opinion in one of our churches at least, the pastor, who was not loyal at heart, came to me in great glee, and said "that there was no danger in praying for the President now!" He did not rejoice that he could now discharge a plain Christian duty unmolested, but that by so doing he would not openly offend his secession friends, and that he would thereby gratify his Union members!

I received a commission from the National Sanitary Board, and for some time discharged the duties required. I one day heard that a Pennsylvania regiment commanded by Col. Hartranft, since Governor, which was encamped near the city, had some sick men who needed attention. I went immediately, announced my benevolent errand to the Colonel through a subordinate, and was deeply mortified when word was sent me purporting to come from him that my services were not required, and he did not want to be annoyed by any such offers. Perhaps the man I sent in did not convey my message properly, or the Colonel was in a bad humor, or it may be that his reply was not properly reported to me. At any rate, I went away mortified that the benevolent design of the Commission should have been so inhumanly repelled.

Thousands of troops passed our village of Lutherville in the railroad cars during the war, and as we could hear the rumbling of the train and the yelling of the soldiers a mile distant, a number of us loyal citizens would rush down to the road and welcome them as they passed by waving the Union flag and giving them enthusiastic hurrahs. Their response came with a will.

Some of our neighbors did not share in our sympathies, and this unhappy disposition was near leading to what would have been a deplorable result. One evening as a train crowded with soldiers was rushing by, a rebel flag was displayed at a window not far below us. This imprudent act exasperated some of the men on the train, and one of them fired at a number of ladies standing in the window flaunting the hateful banner. Fortunately the ball struck the house and no one was hurt. It was an unjustifiable and cowardly act on both sides.

During the war our railroad from Harrisburg to Baltimore was guarded by troops, a company of whom were encamped near our village. This company was commanded by Captain Beaver, now Governor of Pennsylvania (1889).

We in the village * never felt ourselves in any particular danger from the rebels but once, and then our apprehensions were groundless.

One Sunday morning in going to church, in company with Dr. B. Sadtler and our families, we saw two dense columns of smoke apparently three or four miles distant up the railroad. We had heard of a small detachment of rebels being in the neighborhood, and when we saw the smoke the Doctor at once suspected that they had set fire to some barns or houses, and that in all probability they would pay us a visit before night. We went to church, however, and the Doctor performed the services, and preached with his usual dignity and calmness without betraying any emotion. When the service ended, and we came out, a young man had just arrived at the place on a horse all foaming with sweat, announcing the approach of the rebels. We hurried home, and most of us concealed our watches and other valuables. I hid a lot of such material under a wood-pile. We hid our horses out of sight, and calmly (?) awaited the enemy. I knew well enough that if I could have an interview with the commanding officer I could probably prevent his

* Lutherville, Md.

men from plundering us, for I believed that was all they wanted. He and his father had taken tea with me not many months before, and I could with success have appealed to his gentlemanly instincts. One of his subordinates had in the meantime robbed our post office, compelling the postmaster to deliver up the small amount belonging to the government in his hands, but "private property was respected."

Whilst we, with our families, were awaiting the approach of "the enemy," and feeling rather uncomfortable also, to our great gratification, instead of continuing down the turnpike leading to our village, they turned off into a lane about a half a mile above us, and that assured us that instead of paying us a visit the commander was leading his men towards his father's residence, five or six miles distant from us, which turned out to be the fact. Our apprehensions were relieved, and we went to bed that night in peace.

The commander of this marauding troup, Harry Gilmor, professed conversion to Christianity (1880–1882), and boarding one summer (1880) in our village, was a regular attendant at our church services. He died in 1882.

At a meeting called for loyal ministers, held in the lecture-room of St. John's church, Liberty street, about this time, I offered the following resolutions, but I was prevailed upon to withdraw them, as being too strong for some weak-kneed gentlemen present:

"WHEREAS, In the call for this meeting it was distinctly

stated that it was to be composed of *loyal ministers* only, and as that phrase is variously interpreted, and an unwarrantable latitude of meaning given to it by some, we deem it proper on this occasion to state precisely our understanding of it.

"1. We hold that he is not a *loyal* minister who gives no other evidence of his loyalty than by a cautious silence of expression *against* the government, without ever saying or doing anything *for* the government. We regard that negative loyalty as unworthy the honored name, and the men who practice it as not entitled to seats in this meeting.

"2. We do not regard him as a *loyal* minister who in the presence of loyal people seems to incline to *their* side, and in presence of rebels and traitors seems to favor *them*.

"3. We do not consider him a *loyal* minister who seldom or never in his pulpit offers prayers distinctly for the *President* of the United States, but satisfies his conscience and that of his disloyal people by praying only for 'those in authority,' without even the qualifying word 'legal' or any other word discriminating the *present* government.

"4. We do not hold him to be a *loyal* minister who only at this late day is loud in his profession of loyalty and in praise of the late murdered President, when the popular feeling is in that direction, and an outraged community demands a profession of national faith from the public teachers of religion, especially when some such teachers have written, uttered, defended and voted for disloyal resolutions.

"5. We doubt the loyalty of those ministers who give no other evidence of it, than taking a compulsory oath of allegiance.

"Having thus stated the *negative* aspect of the case, the *positive* is apparent and the public will know our definition of a *loyal* minister."

This was too strong meat for the majority, and they begged me to withdraw them to avoid confusion and the exposure of some of the weak brethren.

Nothing came out of the meeting.   Most of those present were opposed to the government; others better disposed were afraid of offending their rebel parishioners.   The few faithful could do nothing.

GIVING OFFENCE UNINTENTIONALLY.

I have carefully avoided hurting the feelings of my brethren when at peace with them, but in heated controversy it is unavoidable.   Some men regard a hard argument as a personal assault, and a smart repartee as a grievous offence.   But we sometimes say things either in animated conversation or in public speaking which are taken as personal thrusts or innuendoes when they are not thus intended, and this direct application of them is unwarranted and unjust.   Some men are so extremely sensitive that they seem to be always watching for something to find fault with, and especially in relation to their precious selves.

I once delivered an address upon an important public occasion in which I paid well-deserved compliments to various gentlemen who were associated with the occasion of the meeting.   To my amazement and sore chagrin, just one year after, one of the men whose services I had highly lauded, and for whom I had always felt and expressed great admiration, called me severely to account for what he termed " disparaging remarks " in my oration.   I vehemently repudiated the unfounded imputation, and showed him that he entirely misapprehended my language and design. I expressed my deep regret that he, with whom for years I had lived upon most intimate terms, should suspect me of taking advantage of my position to say anything disrespectful of a man whose talents, acquirements and character I had even boasted of for years. I felt deeply wounded, and spoke with emotion. After I had said everything in exculpation of myself, I took the opportunity thus furnished of turning the affair against him, and showing him that I was the more aggrieved party of the two. I charged him with treating me unkindly and discourteously in allowing this fancied grievance to fester a whole year without giving me an opportunity to heal it— that he did me a greater injustice in cherishing this unkind feeling intentionally than I did him in inflicting a wound upon him without design. I cited the law governing cultivated gentlemen in analogous cases, that an insult, real or presumed, should be adjusted or inquired into without delay, so that the parties may be reconciled by an explanation or apology, and that in the failure of an amicable adjustment they may cease future intercourse or resort to harsher methods of settlement, as ungodly men sometimes do. I demonstrated to him that in waiting a whole year before calling my attention to this affair, which he had frequent opportunity to do either by letter or intercourse, he was a more culpable offender than I was!

This view of the case took him by surprise. He

expressed himself as satisfied with my disavowal, but I was not invited to his house for several years after, though his treatment of me more recently is more courteous, and I hope he has been convinced of his error.

KÖSTLIN'S LIFE OF LUTHER.

When the two large 8vo. volumes of this work appeared in 1875, Dr. Krotel and I had some correspondence on the subject of translating it, but we wisely concluded that the work was too large, would take up too much time, would be too costly, and was not of that popular character which would suit our people, on account of the large extracts from Luther's writings, of which most of the book is composed. We dropped the matter entirely.

When in 1882 the abbreviated edition in one volume appeared, I immediately began the translation of it, in order to have it ready for the commemoration year of Luther's birth in 1883. It was the hardest German I had ever undertaken, and the work was slow. I then concluded to call in the help of some friends, and divided the work between four or five, and herein committed a great mistake. Only two of them were really competent, and one of them worked in such a hurry that much of his performance had to be gone over again, as was really the case of that of all of them, excepting one.

These corrections and improvements cost me a deal of labor of the most perplexing kind, and no wonder that some errors were overlooked and some inelegancies passed by.

The book appeared in the summer of 1883 in fine 8vo. form, and copies of it were sent to numerous editors, some of whom assailed the translation fiercely, pointing out some mistakes, and decrying pretty much the whole performance. I admit there was some ground for the reproof, but I attributed it all to my translators, but that I acknowledge was no sufficient vindication. Some contributors to several of our own church papers were also severe upon me; others defended the book, and upon the whole our church press was favorable to it, though a few scribblers struck at me personally when deigning to notice the book. Some of the errors were corrected in the stereotype plates, the price was reduced, and in about six months the third edition of 1,000 copies was still in demand.

The Scribners brought out an edition translated and published in England, which is said to be very fair, though, as a judicious friend tells me, it contains not a few errors in the rendering, and misconceptions of the original text. I presume that many copies were sold, as that house has it in its power to push forward any book it chooses to put on the market.

The fact is that thousands of readers became weary of this subject, as it was so frequently brought to their attention, and too many were satisfied with the superficial knowledge they had derived from the reading of some popular biography cf Luther, or from the hearing of sermons and addresses.

BAD TREATMENT.

I presume there are few of us upon whom some mean trick has not been played. I do not mean such small affairs as being cheated in trade, or over-charged in a purchase, or loaned money never being returned, or hospitality abused, or favors unrequited, or being evil spoken of by some to whom you have been kind. These are bad enough, but there are some things done to us occasionally which are so mean and contemptible, so utterly inexcusable and vulgar, so savoring of the sulphurous pit, that you cannot think of them with patience.

Some years ago I was roused up at midnight by a terrific knock at my door. A man stood below whom I could not distinctly discern, but in a hurried voice he informed me that one of the finest young men in my church, who lived more than a mile distant, was suddenly and alarmingly taken ill and wanted to see me. I hurried out to his house with locomotive speed, and when I got there, out of breath and half dead myself from the exertion, I found that I had been deceived. The young man was not sick. The thought then flashed upon my mind that I had been thus betrayed from home by burglars, who would take advantage of my absence to rob my house, and then the way I hastened home was a lesson to pro-fessional runners, but I found all right and my household undisturbed.

I concluded it was nothing but a mean trick, which no doubt afforded merriment to some sons of Belial. They compelled me to take some active midnight exercise, and that was fun for them, but most painful anxiety to me.

I will give another instance, which was not only unspeakably mean, but ungodly.

A long time ago a man imposed himself upon me as a guest. The best chamber in the house was given him, and the "best the market afforded" was daily set before him. After he had been with me several days, loafing about to no profit to himself or advantage to others, he asked me about the value of a certain bank's notes. I told him that they were not worth a button, the bank was smashed, and a bushel of its issues would not bring five cents. He then handed me a five-dollar bill of that bank, and said that a lady whom he had met in a distant State had given him that as a present to a little girl of mine. I took it, of course, remarking that Mrs. H——, who was a friend of ours, surely did not know the condition of the bank, but the dishonest bearer of the gift said nothing. The child was told that the note was worth nothing, and of course lamented it. About a year after this lady friend visited my family, and my little girl, in her childish simplicity, said, "Why, Mrs. H——, that five-dollar note you sent me by Mr. —— was not good!" Mrs. H—— was amazed and mortified and told her she had not sent a bank note, but a five-dollar

22

gold piece!!   What was the natural, logical, though unpleasant inference?   The fellow kept the gold and gave me the note, which he knew was worthless.

My name was once forged in a letter purporting to be an introduction from me to a country minister. The guilty scamp tried to impose upon the minister by getting money from him on the strength of the letter; but the latter was too shrewd to be deceived, and the rascal went away without any ill-gotten gain.   The forged letter and all the circumstances were published in the village newspaper, and the people were warned against him.

HOUSE ROBBED.

Every now and then, but not often, we hear of a minister's house being burglarized, which always reminds me of the remark of a Presbyterian bachelor minister, whose house had thus been visited by unwelcome guests.   He said to me, " What fools these fellows must be to rob my house at night, when I can't find anything in it in day-time!"

I had two such visits during my residence on Lexington street, Baltimore.   My study was in a building behind the church, and on entering one morning I found things in general confusion.   It had been entered by thieves, but there was nothing there they wanted, so that I missed nothing whatever. They removed some of my insect drawers from the cases, and left them uninjured on the table, having taken, no doubt, a lesson in entomology before leaving.

The second visit I had from these gentlemen was one summer evening just after nightfall. My family were in the country, and I had gone down town. No doubt I was watched, and as soon as I had gone the front door was opened with a night-key. My chamber was entered, and my drawers forced open. A heavy gold medal, worth $50 or more, which was presented to my brother George by the Masonic fraternity, was taken, together with a lot of other valuable articles. This robbery was committed by the son of my sexton, who was afterwards sent to the penitentiary for some other crime.

The third visit was made at my house in Green street. Nothing but clothing was taken, of which the ladies' dresses and shawls were subsequently recovered by the police.

CURIOUS WEDDING EVENT.

I once had a very embarrassing and at the same time provoking experience at a wedding. I was called upon to unite in matrimony, at the house of a friend, a couple who were strangers to me. When all was ready I took my position and invited the parties to rise, which they did. I had scarcely begun the service when the lady suddenly left the side of the intended bridegroom and ran to a chair, declaring she would not be married. This caper created surprise and confusion. The few friends present prevailed upon her to stand up again. I proceeded, and off she bolted again. They begged her to submit, and she did; but before I was half done she darted off the third time, and this insane manœuvre she repeated again several times over, until finally she stood long enough for me to conclude the ceremony. The secret was that she was a Romanist, and did not believe in the validity of my right to perform this service, although she had previously given her consent.

That night I went to the meeting of a scientific society, and in the midst of the proceedings a strange, out-of-breath man, rushed in, and asked me for the license, which I fortunately had in my pocket. The mother of the bride insisted on her being married over by a Romish priest that night!

KOSSUTH IN BALTIMORE.

(From a leading morning paper.)

The visit of Kossuth to Baltimore during the past week threw our city into a perfect furor. Our newspaper columns are full of Kossuth only and continually. Americans, above all people, perhaps, are disposed to give manifestations of popular favor to foreign visitors which border upon man-worship; and however worthy Kossuth may be, and however noble his cause, certainly the enthusiasm he has awakened here is quite equal to all he has a right to expect. To publish all his speeches, and all the speeches of those who visited him as committees of reception, would nearly fill our paper entire.

" A number of our Baltimore ministers paid their respects to him on Monday evening at the Eutaw House. We were not present, and learn that there were perhaps fifty ministers present. Kossuth is doubtless a sincere patriot—a man full of genius and full of the love of his country. His manifestation of religious feeling is perhaps greater than we have ever seen in any man of such political distinction.

" The address of Rev. Dr. Morris is one of the best that have been spoken to Kossuth since he came to America. We say among the best because it is full of religion, of the providence of God, of the Bible, of Protestant Christianity. It was delivered with great dignity and impressiveness. The address and reply are subjoined.

KOSSUTH AND THE CITY CLERGY.

" About seven o'clock a large number of the Protestant ministers of Baltimore waited upon the Governor, who was addressed in the following beautiful and touching address by Rev. Dr. John G. Morris, of the English Lutheran church, Lexington street:

"Gov. Kossuth—These, my brethren and I, appear as the representatives of the Protestant clergy of Baltimore to welcome you to our city. We have come as the ministers of Jesus Christ to pay our respects to you, a Protestant brother in the faith, an observer of the Lord's day, an admirer and lover of the Scriptures, and a worshiper of God. We have come to salute you as a defender of the weak, the helper of the oppressed, the advocate of human rights and the promoter of human liberty. We recognize you as an instrument designed by Providence to rouse the oppressed nations of Europe to a sense of their wrongs by so eloquently instructing us in the history of their sufferings. Your efforts, Governor, will affect not only your own unhappy country, but all Europe will feel their influence. When Hungary fell we all mourned, and followed Kossuth into his exile with our sympathies and prayers; but who knows but that Providence designs from that first fall to raise her higher than she has ever been, and from her present enslaved condition to make her more free than ever? God may have seen it necessary to humble her before exalting her. He often deals so with men; why not with nations?

"It was in the exile and apparent humiliation of Luther in Wartburg Castle that he forged that mighty weapon with which he dealt such tremendous blows on the enemies of the truth, and so gloriously carried on the work of the Reformation—I mean the German translation of the Bible. He was humbled only to be exalted—imprisoned and exiled only to gather strength for the coming conflict; and well did he sustain the fight, and nobly did he achieve the victory.

"It may be that Hungary is now humbled only that she may recover her energy—that youths just growing to manhood may be the better prepared for the struggle—that her warriors, statesmen and patriotic women may learn to look to Heaven for help. It may be that Kossuth was exiled and humbled that he too might fill his quiver with fresher and keener arrows, and prepare for himself a mighty weapon to be wielded with terrible energy in behalf of his cause. I mean a knowledge of the English language. It may be that he was exiled and humbled to teach him dependence on God, and to mistrust himself.

"There is one thing, Governor, which excites our admiration in your public speeches and conduct, and which will enlist the sympathies of millions of Christian hearts in our country. You recognize in all things the direct agency of God—and depend on Him for success in your cause—you have publicly acknowledged the Scriptures as the inspired Word of God. You have publicly recommended the religious observance of the

Lord's Day. You have in a quiet and unostentatious manner frequented the house of God, and have thus set an example to hundreds of thousands of foreigners, and of our own countrymen, who neglect the sanctuary. We admire you for all this, independently of many other grounds. We hope these principles will continue to animate your bosom, and characterize your brilliant career all through the land.

"Governor, you know what the Psalmist says: 'Except the Lord build the city, they labor in vain that build it.' Let that be your motto, and the God of nations will bless you in your patriotic efforts to deliver your land from the shackles of bondage. May God therein give you success. May He preserve your own life until the great work of Hungarian liberty shall have been consummated—yea, until all those everywhere groaning under the yoke of despotism shall have become free.

KOSSUTH'S REPLY.

" ' It is some twelve years ago,' said he, ' that for my decided attachment to the rights of a free press, which had never been oppressed except by the arbitrary laws of my country, I was put in prison by the Austrian government, where I lay three years. The first year they gave me nothing to read and nothing to write with. In the second they came and told me it would be granted me to read something, but that I must not make my choice of any political book, but only an indifferent one. I pondered a little, and knowing that a knowledge of languages was a key to sciences, I concluded that it might perhaps be useful to get some little knowledge of the English language. So I told them I would name some books which would not partake in the remotest way with politics. I asked for an English grammar, Shakespeare and Walker's dictionary. The books were given, and I sat down, without knowing a single word, and began to read the Tempest, the first play of Shakespeare, and worked for a fortnight to get through the first page.   (Laughter.)

" 'I have a certain rule, never to go on in reading anything without perfectly understanding what I read. So I went on, and by and by became somewhat familiar with your language. Now, I made that choice because I was forced not to choose a book of any political character. I chose books which had not the remotest connection with politics. But look what an instrument in the hands of Providence became my little knowledge of the English language, which I was obliged to learn because forbidden to meddle with politics. If I had come out of prison to England and America without this little knowledge of your language, I never would have been able to express even my thanks for your generous sympathy; but now I am permitted not only to thank you, but to explain my humble views—to explain the principles which under the protection of your Constitution afford freedom of thought and of conscience, and the protection of that freedom even to every stranger in your country. And if my humble, unpretending explanations can somewhat contribute to conserve your generous sympathy in republican hearts towards the oppressed nations of Europe, what a mighty instrument of welfare and benefit to mankind, because in the hand of Providence, that little knowledge which I acquired.'

"Kossuth went on to speak of the confidence he had in God, from the fact that every time he was crushed down to the earth, when he got up again upon his feet he was more strong and powerful than before—more competent for the fulfillment of his duties for his country and for humanity. Ten or twelve times they endeavored to crush him, and succeeded for the moment, but he never despaired, and subsequent events always proved that what God does is well done.

"Again he enforced the great principle of Christianity—brotherly love—in respect to nations as well as individuals. He was sure that the time would come when nations would acknowledge that principle as a rule of conduct, and that this nation was the one selected by Providence to lead on this new reformation. That glory was reserved not to a single individual, but to the United States, to become the regenerators of international policy, basing it upon the principle of Christian, brotherly love. (Applause.) Whatever might be the decision of this country now, whether willing or not willing to adopt that principle, it would sooner or later come to that point, when it would feel itself to be the executive power on earth of the laws of nature and of nature's God.

"Kossuth apologized for his inability to speak the English language as well as he could wish, and said that it was hard work for him to do it, notwithstanding the constant exercise he had. He was growing old, and old men did not easily advance in the knowledge of languages. Grammar was for children — scarcely for men. In conclusion he thanked them for their kind indulgence in listening to him so long with such attention, and though he was somewhat worn out, both in body and mind, never would he be so worn out as not to remember with gratitude the generous manifestation of their approbation and sympathy. Throughout this address, which occupied about twenty-five minutes, Kossuth was listened to with breathless attention in a crowded room.

" At the conclusion of his felicitous remarks the ministers were severally introduced to the illustrious stranger by the Rev. Dr. Heiner. The Episcopal, Lutheran, German Reformed, Presbyterian, Methodist and Baptist denominations were all largely, and some of them fully, represented. The number of ministers present could not be less than fifty or sixty. The meeting was one of high gratification on all sides, and will doubtless be long remembered. All seemed to be most favorably impressed with what passed, and the Governor himself appeared highly delighted with the interview. His remarks on the subject of divine Providence, especially with reference to himself, and the spread and final triumph of the principle of brotherly love among all mankind, were very beautiful and Scriptural.

" After the interview the clergymen were introduced to Madame Kossuth and Madame Pulzsky, who received and entertained them a while in the most handsome manner."

Kossuth had been in my church the previous Sunday. The most violent snow-storm of the winter prevailed, and very few people were present. I had not invited him to church, as a morning paper said, for I never employed such clap-trap measures to draw a crowd; but a few days before his arrival he wrote to Mayor Jerome to recommend a Lutheran church, and he mentioned ours.

Several years after, a large meeting of Presbyterian ministers assembled here. One of them, of my name, sought me out on purpose, as he said, to thank me for my address to Kossuth.

LISTS OF LUTHERAN PUBLICATIONS.

Some years ago (1876) I published a small volume which I called *Bibliotheca Lutherana*, wherein I gave the title of every book or pamphlet issued under the name of a Lutheran minister in the United States up to that time. It cost me considerable work, and was as complete as could be made. Dr. Sheeleigh kindly furnished a list of the periodicals of the Church, which enhanced its value as a book of reference on that subject.

Of course it did not pay expenses, which I apprehended, but I thought I would publish it as my contribution to the Church Jubilee, which was celebrated that year.

Nearly every year since that I have carefully made a list of every publication of book or pamphlet during the year, gathering the titles from 10 or 12 of our church papers. I took a sort of church pride in exhibiting the literary work of our men, and at first I was simple enough to think that many others would look upon it with some interest. But I was disappointed, for no person seemed to notice it, and only one editor, and he was not a General Synod man, ever made any allusion to it. I should, however, say that Mr. Stall, the wide-awake editor of the Year Book, prevailed upon me to let him insert the list one year as far as October, and wanted it for the next, but I replied that few or none would look at it, and he should not devote a single page of his admirable book to dead matter.

It is, however, gratifying to men of cultivated taste to observe the progress of literature and of authorial activity in the Church, and even though most of the publications are small, yet most of them give evidence of advance in generous studies.

For several years, between 1883–1886, the Rev. Prof. Frick, of St. Peter, Minn., also published a list, embracing more of the writings of Scandinavian ministers than mine did. I engaged him and Prof. Schodde, of Columbus, Ohio, to join me in preparing a list as accurately as possible, beginning with 1886, so that it is likely hereafter no publication of a Lutheran minister will be omitted. It is a matter interesting to very few, but it is a part of our Church history which should be written, even if it should only be read by a few.

July, 1889.—The above proposition, made to those gentleman, was not carried out, so that for four or five years we have had no annual list of our Church publications.

VISITS FROM FOREIGNERS.

I had the pleasure of receiving visits from a number of foreign gentlemen, among whom I will mention only such as now occur to my mind.

Koch, a German conchologist of great name, called at my house, but unfortunately I was just getting ready to go to a meeting, and he did not stay long.

Mr. Alexander, an English botanist, spent several hours with me looking over my herbarium, which at that time was very insignificant. He came over here to study the botany of the pine forests of the South. He called on his return, but I did not see him.

Prof. Von Raumer and his son, of Berlin, spent a whole day here. I went with them everywhere I thought worthy of a visit, even to the top of the Washington Monument. He was in raptures with that view. What he wanted to see particularly was a Methodist negro meeting. He wished to study it as a psychologist, for he had heard wonderful things about it, which are to us every-day events, but to a German philosopher they are simply marvelous. He

went (I could not go with him that night), and he
was overcome with amazement, and yet from his
description I should judge that it had not been a
very "lively" meeting; still the manifestations
seemed extraordinary, and he wondered "why the
government did not break them up!" He had
been to Washington, and I shall never forget his
criticisms on the group of statuary on the east front
of the Capitol, though this is not the place to record
them.

Zimmermann, a learned German entomologist, remained here some months, and I was with him or
he at my house almost every day. It was he who
gave me, as his own offer, a Paris clock worth $36
and a mahogany book-case for which he gave $40
for one specimen of an African beetle (Goliathus
cacicus).

Young Schaum, a nephew of Germar, whom I
met in Germany, was also here, and spent many
hours with me. I have many letters in my book
from him.

Years ago most of the young German ministers
who landed at Baltimore came to my house, and
some of whom I kept for several days. I believe
that now few of them are living.

CHAPTER XIV.

I HAVE held a number of positions in the Church
and out of it. The following list includes only the
most important positions of this character to which
I have had the honor of being chosen:

President of the Baltimore Lyceum.

President of the Linnæan Society of Pennsylvania
College, Gettysburg, Pa.

President of the Young Men's Bible Society of
Baltimore, Md.

President of the Maryland State Bible Society.

President of the Maryland Academy of Science.

President of the Maryland Historical Society.

President of the Society for the History of the
Germans in Maryland.

President of the Historical Society of the Lutheran Church.

President of the Academy of Church History of
the Lutheran Church in America.

Vice President for Maryland of the Society of the
Sons of the American Revolution.

(351)

In the Church I have served as President of the Synod of Maryland seven or eight times, and several times as Secretary; twice as President of the General Synod, and twice as Secretary; as Director of the Seminary for a period of over 60 years, and several times as President and Secretary; as a Trustee of Pennsylvania College for about the same time, and as President of the Lutheran Historical Society ever since the death of Dr. Schmucker.

I was once elected professor in the Theological Seminary, and also in the College, at Gettysburg, but I declined, not feeling myself competent for either position. It was a joint professorship, but I thought the pulpit was my proper sphere. Professors were scarce in those early days, and some of us young men did not think ourselves qualified for every position in church or state, as it is said many young men of these modern times do, fit for any position. One not very young man said to me himself that he felt himself qualified to fill any place in the Faculty of Pennsylvania College, from the President down. Somehow or other the Trustees differed from him, and he has never been offered any office in that college, not even a tutorship in *Prep!*

In 1870 I was elected President of the Maryland Academy of Arts and Sciences, which I held for a long time, but from which I retired to make room for another.

Many years ago I was elected Professor of Natural History in the University of Maryland, at Baltimore, which was an office without honor, work or profit. To secure certain privileges it was necessary to fill the Faculties, upon which a number of men were chosen to certain positions in the scientific and theological departments, not one of whom was ever called upon, and not even expected to perform any service.

About the year 1858 I was elected a Trustee of the Peabody Institute, but I have already considered my connection with that institution, and will not refer to it further.

I consider myself the founder of the Linnæan Society at Pennsylvania College, Gettysburg, Pa., and was chosen its first President. I was also one of the founders of the Maryland Academy of Sciences.

For some years I was nominally Lecturer on Zöology in the Gettysburg College, and several times gave partial courses of lectures. The College could not afford to pay me any salary, and my services were gratuitous, excepting for one series of lectures, for which $300 were raised by Rev. Dr. F. W. Conrad, C. A. Morris and Samuel Appold, the latter of Baltimore, each of whom gave $100. This was a proposition of my excellent friend Dr. Conrad, who suggested and secured the subscriptions from the other two gentlemen.

For many years I have been a lecturer in the Theological Seminary at Gettysburg, where I have given an annual course of lectures on the "Connection between Science and Revelation," and also on "Pulpit Elocution."

23

In 1886 a number of us in Baltimore established a Society for the investigation of the History of the Germans in Maryland, of which I was elected the first President, and have been re-elected every year since.

In January, 1886, a few of us founded a Baltimore County Historical Society at Towson, Md., of which I was chosen President. It was composed of very few members, and no interest whatever could be excited in the subject, and the Society soon became extinct.

For many years I had been one of the three Vice-Presidents of the Historical Society of Maryland, which office imposes no severe duties. At the annual meeting of the Society, in February, 1891, John Lee, Librarian, resigned. He received no stipulated salary, but an annual sum of several hundred dollars was voted to him. The Constitution of the Society requires the annual election of a Librarian, and as it is an unsalaried office, and as I had leisure to attend to it, I consented to an election. I go there during the winter nearly every day, and spend several hours in answering letters, opening documents, and receiving new books coming in, giving information to visitors who come to consult books or old records, and so on.

The Assistant Librarian, John Gatchell, attends to all routine work, and Daniel, the janitor, brings the mail and keeps the house in order.

On February 11, 1894, I was elected President of the Maryland Historical Society.

PARTIAL LIST OF MY PUBLISHED WRITINGS AND
MANUSCRIPTS.

Books.

1832. Catechumens' and Communicants' Guide,
16mo.
Exercises on Luther's Catechism, 16mo.
1834. Henry and Antonio; or, To Rome and Back
Again (Trans.), 12mo.
1839. Von Leonhard's Lectures on Geology (Trans.),
12mo.
1842. Exposition of the Gospels, 2 vols., 12mo.
1844. Year Book of the Reformation, five articles
in, 8vo.
Luther's Catechism Illustrated, 12mo.
1853. Life of John Arndt, 12mo.
1856. The Blind Girl of Wittenberg, 8vo.
Catharine Von Bora, 12mo.
1859. Quaint Sayings and Doings of Luther, 12mo.
Register of the First English Lutheran Church
in Baltimore, from 1827 to 1859, 12mo.
1861. Synopsis of the Described Lepidoptera of the
United States, 8vo.
Catalogue of Books for the Peabody Institute,
8vo.
1873. A Day in Capernaum, (Trans.) 12mo.
1876. Bibliotheca Lutherana, 12mo.
1878. Fifty Years in the Lutheran Ministry, 8vo.
1880. Diet of Augsburg, 12mo.
1881. Journeys of Luther, 12mo.

1882. Luther at Wartburg Castle, 12mo.
1883. Köstlin's Life of Luther (Trans.).
1886. The Stork Family.

Pamphlets.

1834. Sermon on the Reformation.
1841. The Study of Natural History—Address at Gettysburg.
1844. Address at the Dedication of Mt. Olivet Cemetery, Baltimore.
1847. Address at the Dedication of Linnæan Hall, Gettysburg.
1855. Martin Behaim—the German Cosmographer.
1860. Catalogue of the Described Lepidoptera of the United States.
       Two Articles on the Chinese Silk Worm (*Samia Cynthia*).   In Government Reports.
       Entomology (in American Museum).
1867. Address at the Reformation Jubilee.
       Luther's Visit to Rome (Year Book).
       The Theses of Luther (Year Book).
       John Calvin (Year Book).
       John Reuchlin (Year Book).
       Luther's Cell in Erfurt (Year Book).
1874. The Lords Baltimore.
1876. History of the Theological Seminary.
       Luther as a Pulpit Orator.
       The Literature of the Lutheran Church.
1881. The Table Talk of Martin Luther.
       By-ways in the Life of Luther.

The Asperities of Luther's Language.

Visits to the Sick-bed of Martin Luther.

1882. The Young and German Luther.   Bogatzki.

1883. The Lutheran Doctrine of the Lord's Supper.

Address at the Meeting of the A. A. A. S. at Cincinnati.

History of the Annapolis Tuesday Club.

Luther in Bronze at Washington.

1887. The Lutheran Origin of the 39 Articles of the Church of England.

1891. Address at the Muhlenberg Celebration at Selinsgrove.

1892. Conundrum No. 2.

1893. Address at the Laying of the Corner-stone of the New College at Gettysburg.

The German in Baltimore.

The Benefits of Historical Societies.

1895. Sources of Information on the History of the Lutheran Church in America.

My seven scrap-book volumes contain many of my newspaper articles of many years.   Besides all these I have numerous manuscripts, some of which may be worth looking at.   Among them are, Luther; a Drama.   Some of these scenes have been printed in some of our papers, and a few of them have been acted by amateur players.   The Life of Hans Egede, Preuss on Justification, From Night to Morning, a translation from Delitzsch, are included. The latter title is not his, but a fancy one which I gave it.   There is another manuscript, which is an abbreviated translation of a book by Melchior Nicoldi in vindication of Luther.

PAPERS READ BEFORE THE MARYLAND HISTORICAL
SOCIETY.

1861, April 4. The Old Stone Mill at Newport, R. I.

Dec. 5. The Ailanthus Silk Worm of China.

1863, Nov. 5. A List of the Inhabitants of Baltimore in 1752, with their Occupations, etc.

1864, Dec. 1. The Lords Baltimore as Authors.

1865, Nov. 2. The Dinners of the Maryland Historical Society.

Dec. 14. A Descriptive Catalogue of the Publications of the Maryland Historical Society.

1866, May 3. A paper on the Lords Baltimore, and their connection with the Province of Maryland.

1867, April 4. A Paper upon the very frequent use of foreign words, both in speaking and writing.

1868, Jan. 2. An account of the Tuesday Club, of Annapolis, which existed in 1745, *et seq.*

1872, June 10. A Contribution to a History of Maryland Literature.

1873, May 12. Investigation in regard to the Lord Baltimore portrait, now in possession of Titian R. Peale.

1884, Dec. 8. The History of the Society of the Cincinnati.

PAPERS READ BEFORE THE SOCIETY FOR THE GERMANS IN MARYLAND.

Some of these have been printed in the Proceedings.

Sketch of the Life of Prof. Seyfurth; printed in No. IV., p. 17, of Proceedings.

Arrest and Trial of J. D. Smyth, an English Loyalist, by Germans of Fredericktown, during Revolutionary times, in 1776, No. IV., p. 35.

Humane Treatment of their Slaves by the Germans of the Shenandoah Valley.

Biographical Sketch of Rev. John Uhlhorn.

Abbé Domine's wonderful discovery of Indian Antiquities.

Sketch of Conrad Weiser.

List of German Books relating to Maryland.

Account of liberal bequests and donations of foreign born German citizens to charity and education in America.

LEARNED SOCIETIES OF WHICH I AM A MEMBER.

Corresponding member of the Academy of Science, Philadelphia.

Corresponding member of the Academy of Science, Boston.

Corresponding member of the Society of Natural History, Nurnberg, Germany, with diploma.

Corresponding member of the New York Lyceum.

Corresponding member of the Iowa State Historical Society.

Corresponding member of the Society of Northern Antiquarians, Stockholm, with diploma.

Corresponding member of the Royal Historical Society, London, with diploma.

Member of the American Association for the Advancement of Science.

Member of the National Society of Sciences, Washington.

Member of the American Philosophical Society, Philadelphia.

Member of the Brooklyn Entomological Society.

Besides these I have been chosen a member of eight or ten minor and local scientific societies.

CHAPTER XV.

THE sturdy figure and resonant voice of the Rev. John G. Morris have so long occupied a large place in the life of the community and of the Church that it is difficult to realize the absence and the silence that have followed the active living. The closing years of this patriarch of the Church were in no wise different from the rest. They were also filled to the brim with busy labor, in many directions, for the Zion he loved so well, and to which he gave the very best that was in him of love, loyalty, service, for the many interests that claimed his thought and his efforts. The years, as they passed, brought no perceptible change, outwardly. By the grace of a loving Providence Dr. Morris retained his physical vigor, his mental forcefulness, and his strong personality unweakened even to the last. One by one the earthly ties were being severed, however, and the waiting, almost impatient, spirit was finally released to join the throng of loved and loving ones in the great host of the glorified.

The last few birthday celebrations of Dr. Morris that showed him prominently to the public, as a most vigorous man, in spite of the great age to which he had attained, were very full of enjoyment to him.   As the eighth decade of his life passed by, it became more and more the custom of his friends, not only in the city, but at distant points, to unite in expressions of congratulations and good wishes. The following extracts from the city papers will indicate something of the love and esteem that were bestowed upon him, and in which his closing life rejoiced, as a deserved tribute to a life well spent.

One of the Baltimore morning papers remarked, on November 14, 1893: "Dr. John G. Morris, who claims to be the only man living who had a father in the Revolution, will be ninety years old to-day. It was announced at the meeting of the Maryland Historical Society last night.   Resolutions of congratulation were offered and adopted, and on motion it was decided to send the Doctor a bouquet of flowers to-day.   Dr. Morris was present at the meeting. He arose and said: 'This is a surprise to me.   I have received congratulations, and expect many more in my mail to-morrow.   I must tell you that this is exceedingly gratifying.   It is difficult for me to believe that I am ninety, and I sometimes believe that the recorders of my birth have set the clock ahead of time.   I expect I shall be wished many happy returns of the day, as the new bride was, but the clock will soon stop its ticking.   The will of the Lord be done.'"

In speaking of the anniversary noted above another

paper said: "One of the most notable men of the Lutheran Church in the United States is celebrating the 90th anniversary of his birth to-day. That man is the Rev. John G. Morris, D. D. Not only does Dr. Morris hold a notable position in the Church on account of his learning and piety, but he occupies a unique place by reason of his extreme age. For some time past the Lutheran ministers of Baltimore, of whom Dr. Morris is chief, have been considering in what way they could best observe the birthday of the venerable preacher, and a committee was appointed to take charge of the matter. After many plans had been suggested, it was decided to present Dr. Morris with a group picture of all the Lutheran ministers in Baltimore. Taking the picture with them, the ministers went in a body to Dr. Morris' residence. The Rev. Dr. Chas. S. Albert in a few words congratulated Dr. Morris on his venerable age and good health. He also thanked him in the name of the Lutheran ministers of Baltimore for what he had done for the Church in this city and for the Church in general. Recognizing his deep interest in the Church, and his solicitude for the welfare of Lutheran preachers, it gave him great pleasure, he said, to present the venerable head of the Lutheran Church in Baltimore with a group of his fellow-preachers.

" Dr. Morris made a feeling response, in which he expressed love for the Church and an unabated interest in the success of all Lutheran ministers. During the day the Maryland Historical Society sent a magnificent basket of ninety roses. The German Historical Society proposed giving the Doctor a dinner, but he declined the honor."

Among the many letters of congratulation that were received by Dr. Morris on this ninetieth anniversary the kindly feeling expressed by all showed the extent of the regard for a man who had almost rounded out the century of work. Said the Rev. H. Louis Baugher, D. D., " Allow me to join my congratulations to the many that will reach you on the *scores* you have made in life." The Faculty of the Seminary of the Evangelical Lutheran Church at Chicago said, among other pleasant things: " We congratulate Dr. Morris upon what his eyes have seen and his ears have heard in the development of the Lutheran Church in this country; upon the good work he has been enabled to do, and upon the honorable place he has taken in her growth and history."

From a number of entomologists, of Washington, D. C., there came this sentiment: " Your friends and fellow entomologists send heartfelt greetings on your 90th birthday. We connect you with the very beginning of entomology in this country, and hold you dear, not only for your works, but also for your big heart and jovial nature."

The Faculty of the Theological Seminary at Gettysburg wrote: " Your colleagues in the Faculty of the Theological Seminary send congratulations on the 90th anniversary of your birth. They rejoice with you in the good Providence that has given you so many happy years of prominent, distinguished and efficient service in the church of our Lord Jesus Christ, and hope that many more years may be granted to you."

Judge Albert Ritchie, of the Superior Court of Baltimore city, wrote: " I most cordially congratulate you on your birthday, and unite with your many friends in the earnest hope that you may long be with us, and that good health, happiness and prosperity may wait upon you."

On the occasion of Dr. Morris' ninety-first anniversary, November 14, 1894, from the Maryland Society Sons of the American Revolution was received the following, through the Secretary, Mr. John R. Dorsey: " Allow me to extend the congratulations of the Maryland Society S. A. R. to its honored member who to-day celebrates his ninety-first birthday. May you, the *son* of a Revolutionary soldier, be granted many more years of usefulness to your friends and happiness to yourself."

The same anniversary brought this from the officers of the House of Refuge, a reformatory school of the city, of which Dr. Morris was long a manager, on the part of the city: " Permit us to offer our congratulations on this 91st anniversary of your birth. We who have so long experienced so many tokens of your kindness, so many words of sympathy and encouragement in our work, feel grateful to our heavenly Father that He has prolonged your life to this time."

President D. C. Gilman, of Johns Hopkins University, thus expressed his interest in the 91st anniversary of Dr. Morris: " Allow me to offer you my very warm congratulations on having reached another birthday with vigor unimpaired; and let me beg you to impart to others the secret of good health and good spirits that you obviously possess."

The sunshine that brightened the life of Dr. Morris was dimmed in the last days by clouds of sore affliction and of loss which shadowed his pathway in 1893.   This affliction was the sudden death of two persons from the inner circle of his regard, one from out the very centre of his love.   From that time the strong man was bowed down, and the life forces began to go out.   His tender heart was sadly wounded, and he turned more than ever to that place where his treasures were held in eternal safety, waiting his enjoyment of them.   To all who knew and loved Dr. Morris, the inevitable change that was fast coming over him was easily perceptible.   But the unflagging interest in everything—all the former objects of work and study—the development of the Church—this was, to the casual observer, as strong and bright as ever.   The forming of the Academy of Lutheran Church History was one of the achievements of his closing life upon which he loved to look with commendable pride.   Some one, writing in the *Workman* of April 25, 1895, said of him: " The most prominent and most interesting figure at the recent meeting of the Academy of Lutheran Church History in Philadelphia was its venerable President, Rev. J. G. Morris, D. D., LL. D. His erect form, strong and clear voice, prompt and vigorous rulings, brusque wit, intimate personal acquaintance with all, both young and old, and complete devotion to present interests of the Church, almost made one doubt that he could be any other than one whose ministerial activity was parallel to the average of those who were present. But the records show that when he was a student the entire Lutheran Church in America was no larger than the number of communicants now enrolled within a radius of forty miles from Philadelphia. His memory goes back to beyond the formation of any Synod but the Ministerium of Pennsylvania and New York and the Synod of North Carolina, and of course that of the General Bodies. Time seems after all not to fly rapidly when such vigor belongs to one who was a leader in the Church before men who are now decrepit were born.''

The summer of 1895 found Dr. Morris in poor physical health. Always accustomed to great exertion without apparent discomfort, little things easily tired him now. But on the 22d of February, 1895, he was able to perform a series of duties that would have taxed the strength of a much younger man, and then came home and secured a night's rest that was as undisturbed, sound and refreshing as that of a little child. The day was spent in this way: In the morning Dr. Morris attended the funeral of an old friend, and took part in the obsequies. After the funeral he went to the Johns Hopkins University and participated in the annual exercises peculiar to Founder's Day at that great institution. In the afternoon of the same day he was present at and took part in a celebration at the House of Refuge, a few miles outside of the city, remaining nearly all the afternoon. After the evening meal with his family he went to the regular meeting of the Society for the History of the Germans in Maryland, presided at the meeting with his accustomed vigor, and came home alone about eleven o'clock, fresh and apparently unharmed by the day's work. All this in February of the year in which he died. From that time bodily vigor began to decline. Infirmity of body grew apace, and yet the wonderful brain remained unclouded—wonderfully active. The busy pen kept moving, and columns of the Church papers gave repeated evidence of Dr. Morris' literary activity, even on the day that the news of his death flashed through the Church. Dr. Morris held a pen up to the last. The articles that appeared in the Church papers in October, 1895, over the ever familiar letters, "J. G. M.," were written by him, some of them not longer than three weeks before his death. The end came painlessly, at his summer home, Lutherville, Md., October 10, 1895, at 11:10 p. m. The weary wheels stood still. Nature gave up the struggle, and the giant soul passed out of life here to the perfect life beyond, for which it had been longing many weary years.

The Synod of Maryland was celebrating in Baltimore the 75th anniversary of its organization at almost the precise moment of the departure of its oldest member. The President of that Synod, the Rev. E. H. Delk, in his annual report, said: "There is lying dead in our midst one of the great men of our Synod and the whole Church. Rev. John G. Morris was the nineteenth-century incarnation of Luther. His intellectual attainments, his fine literary taste, his virile temper, his wit, his indomitable energy, his warm and tenacious affections, his conservation of our doctrinal beliefs, his masterful address, his large hope of our denominational prestige and his childlike trust in God, have left an ineffaceable record upon our synodical and church life. His work and spirit can never die."

On the morning of October 12, 1895, after brief services at the Lutherville home of Dr. Morris, conducted by Rev. Dr. Dunbar, pastor of St. Mark's church, Baltimore, the body was taken to Baltimore, where appropriate services were held in the presence of a very large assemblage of friends and acquaintances at St. Mark's church, of which the family of Dr. Morris have long been members, and where Dr. Morris himself worshiped during his winter residence in the city. The members of the Synod of Maryland, which had adjourned for the purpose of being present, occupied the front pews. Rev. Drs. Dunbar, Studebaker and Valentine took part in the preliminary service, and addresses were delivered by Rev. Dr. Benj. Sadtler, Rev. Dr. Chas. S. Albert and Rev. O. C. Roth. Rev. Dr. Dunbar closed the service with a few appropriate remarks, and borne by a special train the body, accompanied by representatives of the Synod of Maryland and the family of Dr. Morris, was taken to York, Pa., and there interred, according to the request of Dr. Morris, beside the bodies of his wife and daughter. The services at the grave were conducted by Rev. Drs. Dunbar and A. W. Lilly.

This brief summary of the closing scenes of so useful and honored a life will not be complete if it omits some recognition of the kind words that were spoken and written and printed concerning a man who had hosts of friends in all classes, in all sections of the Church, that were so dear to him. This list is well begun with the words of one who was a long-time friend of Dr. Morris, Hon. Chas. A. Schieren, ex-Mayor of Brooklyn, N. Y. Mr. Schieren wrote: "I always revered Dr. Morris as one of God's chosen men. His great age seemed phenomenal; his exuberant spirit, ready wit and natural humor made him popular, and drew men to him. He was fond of young men. He was possessed of good sound common sense, and well calculated to be a leader and a counsellor. Dr. Morris enjoyed the rare privilege of living to see the fruit of his early planting. He was considered the Nestor of Lutheranism in Baltimore. The marvelous growth of the Lutheran Church in Baltimore is largely due to his energy, sagacity and wise counsel. He believed in pushing the work forward, and was untiring in his effort to accomplish it. He loved the Lutheran Church, and his name will ever be connected with that Church as one of her foremost sons. His love and ardent spirit will ever be remembered and live long in the hearts and minds of the people of the Church.''

Dr. Morris' best work was along church lines, and particularly Lutheran lines. No man was better known than he among the rank and file of the laity. The Synod of Maryland appointed a special committee to prepare a memorial upon the death of Dr. Morris. It follows here:

IN MEMORIAM.

REV. JOHN G. MORRIS, D. D., LL.D.

"Know ye not that there is a prince and a great man fallen this day in Israel?"

In the inscrutable providence of the all-wise God this session of our Synod, as it marks the rounding out of three-quarters of a century of its history, has been impressively overshadowed by the manifestation of the Divine Presence in the closing of a life identified with its work from its earlier years. In the very hour when we gathered to recall the past, in which he had so prominent a part, the spirit of John G. Morris passed serenely and calmly into the eternal future. Into the music of our anniversary joys came the notes of the minor chord, not to bring discordant sound, but to make it more sweet and tender and rich and heavenly.

With full hearts and bowed down with sorrow, with a profound sense of our loss, we yet reverently recognize the hand of divine love in this dispensation, and rejoice in the triumph of faith which sustained this servant of God through his long life, strengthened him in his declining years, and made him victor over death.

As a Synod we desire to express hereby our high regard for the character of him who has thus been summoned from among us. Rugged and sturdy, we were made to feel again and again the force of a sincerity of purpose which would not stop to compromise or hide itself under the duplicity of soft words. To all of us he was a father, and we have often felt the throbbing of the tender heart as with cheering words he encouraged us in our work.

It is only proper, too, that we should give recognition to his mental endowments and acquirements. He was indeed " our Gamaliel," at whose feet we sat in attentive attitude as learners. A mind well cultivated and stored with knowledge in many departments, he stood pre-eminent among his brethren, and was the intimate companion and associate of scholars.

Nor should we fail to bear testimony to his service to the whole Church. A leading spirit in many of her most important renterprises, the touch of his hand was felt upon all. A staunch Lutheran, a very Luther in spirit, his Church was dear to him, and its every movement was a matter of concern to him which even old age could not diminish.

For what he was to us in the Maryland Synod it is only proper for us to bring our special memorial of loving esteem. Ordained to the ministry in 1826, to this Synod belongs the honor of having his name enrolled through all his long ministry, reaching to the eve of three scores and ten. He was the connecting link with the past, and at the same time one of the most potent factors of our present. He loved his Synod as his Synod loved to honor him.

In the deliberations of this body his voice has always been heard with profound respect. His vacant chair no other can fill.

In this solemn hour, and in the presence of this dispensation, our hearts are tender, and we feel the touch of the divine finger. Into the silence of our sorrow comes the summons to greater devotion and more earnest consecration to the trust committed to our keeping by the fathers who are passing away. We pray for grace that in our inefficiency we may be made strong and faithful. Our days are numbered. No man knows the number of them. It is for us to " do the work of Him that sends us while it is called to-day."

We do not forget those whose loss is greater than our own. Our hearts go out in tender sympathy to those who sit in sorrow in the home. We commend the bereaved family to the God of all consolation, whose hand can apply the balm of Gilead to the bleeding heart, whose grace is sufficient for us, upon whom we may cast all our cares, for He careth for us.　　　　　Respectfully submitted,

W. H. DUNBAR,
CHAS. S. ALBERT,
WM. H. DAVIS.

One institution of the Church appealed most strongly to Dr. Morris; the Seminary at Gettysburg was a source of interest and anxiety to him. He gave it his time and his prayers and his efforts. He loved it. The resolutions of the Faculty on his death are here recorded:

"WHEREAS, The summons to depart and to be with Christ has come to our venerable colleague, the Rev. John Godlove Morris, D. D., LL.D., who for a period of nearly seventy years has been connected with this Seminary, having been enrolled as a member of the first class, and having served almost continuously as a director and lecturer, holding to the day of his death, at the ripe age of ninety-two, both positions with undiminished interest and with unimpaired faculties; and,

"*Whereas*, He sustained the closest personal relations to almost every professor of the Seminary from its foundation to the present.

"*Resolved*, That in the ample endowments of our late distinguished colleague, in his scientific tastes, his literary culture, his voluminous authorship, his biblical and theological learning, his eloquence in his pulpit, his devotion to the Church, his tireless labors for her educational institutions, his outspoken love for her doctrines, his exemplification of her life, his childlike faith, his virile spirit, tinged by kindly affection and sprightly humor, his sturdy independence, united with a sincere catholicity, his buoyant temper, keeping his youth perennial and his versatile mind in perpetual activity, we recognize that extraordinary combination of gifts and powers which have challenged the admiration and wonder of the entire Lutheran Church and left a noble and ineffaceable impress upon her history.

"*Resolved*, That we place on record our gratitude to God for the uncommon measure of life and vigor by which he was enabled to continue for so long a period his labors for the Church, our appreciation of his great and sanctified personality, and of his manifold services to this institution, and our profound sorrow over the void in it left by his decease.

"*Resolved*, That we tender to the family of the deceased our heartfelt condolence, and that a copy of these resolutions be forwarded to their address.

The Board of Trustees of Pennsylvania College adopted the subjoined resolutions:

"WHEREAS, Since our last meeting it has pleased God to call home at a ripe age our venerable brother, Rev. Dr. John G. Morris, and we desire to give fitting expression to our sense of his great usefulness and worth, and also of the loss which we and the Church at large have sustained by his departure. Now, therefore, be it

"*Resolved*, 1. That the death, at the advanced age of ninety-two years, of Dr. Morris, the sole survivor of the founders and patrons who participated in the incorporation in 1832 of Pennsylvania College, is an event well calculated to arrest the attention of every one bearing any relation to this institution. For more than half a century we have enjoyed his devoted service and profited by his friendly counsel. He alone of the faithful band whose sagacity and zeal founded the College lived to see it attain the present flower of its success.

"*Resolved*, 2. He was possessed of fine natural endowments, which he enriched by extensive and varied culture. He invaded many fields of knowledge, and earned some laurels in every field. He was honored with well-merited titles and degrees at the hands of numerous learned associations of his own and foreign lands. The labor of his love, however, was spent in adding to the store of information relating to the founder of the Church of his choice and the literature of her sons.

"*Resolved,* 3. Our sense of grief at Dr. Morris' death is mitigated only by our consciousness of his great usefulness and gratitude for his long life.

"We commend to the divine care those immediately afflicted by his demise, and tender to them that measure of consolation which our sympathy can afford.

"S. D. SCHMUCKER,
"W. H. DUNBAR,
"JERE CARL."

The General Council of the Evangelical Lutheran Church in North America was in session at Easton, Pa., at the time of Dr. Morris' decease. In that body of men there were very many friends, warm and life-long, of Dr. Morris. As soon as the news of the sad event reached the delegates a committee was appointed to draft suitable resolutions, of which the following is a copy:

"*Resolved*, That we have learned with sorrow of the death of Rev. J. G. Morris, D. D., LL.D., the personal friend of many members of this General Council, who has filled so important a part in the history of our Church in this country; that we are thankful for his preservation in active usefulness to an age so unusual; and that while we rejoice in his distinguished services so long continued, we deeply sympathize with his sorrowing family and friends in their bereavement.

"*Resolved*, That a copy of this minute be sent to his family.

"JOS. A. SEISS,
"S. LAIRD,
"A. SPAETH."

For a number of years an informal association of

the Lutheran clergy of the General Synod residing in Baltimore and vicinity has had semi-monthly meetings. During the winter these gatherings were at the home of Dr. Morris, the honored President. He was always fond of such social assemblies, and his death removed the inspiring spirit of the association. As a very imperfect expression of appreciation and reverence, as well as of regret, the following was adopted by the members:

"*Resolved*, That as an association we have met with no ordinary loss in the removal from us of our 'brother-beloved' and our honored President. Rev. John G. Morris, D. D., LL.D. Known so long and so intimately by our entire Zion as one prominent in the councils and conduct of our Church, yet to us who met him so frequently and knew him so intimately 'his loss is the more deeply felt.' And more than once have we, as we have come together, recalling his cheerful, kindly, hearty interest in all that pertained to us and ours, been prompted to cry:

> "'O, for the touch of a vanished hand
> And the sound of a voice that is still.'

"Yet much as we miss him, we have reason for profound gratitude for his long, honored and useful life. And when it drew near its close he was spared from pain and anguish. In the evening of the long day he

> "'But stepped out into the shadow,
> The weary wheels of life stood still.

"We shall meet him again. We shall know him again It were a double grief if the true hearts who loved us here should on the other shore remember us no more.'

"Dr. Morris had no guess for his dying pillow. He 'knew whom he believed.' Our hearts hold to the confident hope that we shall, in the Church triumphant, meet, greet and renew the friendship and the fellowship here severed.

"Our hearts go out prayerfully for those in closer touch with our brother, 'fond friends' and loved ones. And our prayer is that the Infinite Hand may lead and keep them.

"G. W. MILLER,
"F. PH. HENNIGHAUSEN,
"I. C. BURKE,
"Committee."

One of the subjects of study of which Dr. Morris was especially fond, and to which he devoted a very great deal of his leisure time, was entomology. His work in this branch of science has won world-wide praise and recognition. He numbered his friends among the foremost entomologists of the world. Upon information of his death the following paper was prepared by the Brooklyn Entomological Society:

At the meeting of the Brooklyn Entomological Society held Tuesday, November 5, 1895, formal announcement was made of the death of Dr. John G. Morris, an honorary member.

Of the members present several spoke of the work done by him in the Lepidoptera in the early days of entomological science in the United States, and others of pleasant personal recollections. Upon motion it was unanimously

"*Resolved*, That in the death of Dr. John G. Morris the society loses an honored member, upon whom we all looked with love and regard; that Entomology, and especially Lepidopterology, loses its pioneer in the United States, whose work, when work was difficult, lightened the burdens of others, and formed a foundation upon which they builded.

"*Resolved*, That this memorial be spread upon the minutes of the society, and that a copy of it be transmitted to his representatives.

> "JOHN B. SMITH, *President.*
> "GEO. D. HULST, *Rec. Sec.*
> "ARCHIBALD C. WEEKS, *Cor. Sec.*"

The entire active life of Dr. Morris may be said to have been spent in the city of Baltimore, to which he came in 1826, a young minister. He became prominently identified with many public enterprises, and especially with those of a scientific as well as of a philanthropic character. One of the first sort was the Maryland Academy of Sciences, which took the appended action on the death of Dr. Morris:

" At a meeting of the Maryland Academy of Sciences held November 4, 1895, upon motion of Rev. Geo. A. Leakin, it was unanimously resolved that a committee of three members, of whom the President should be chairman, be appointed to prepare resolutions of respect to the memory of Rev. John G. Morris, D. D., a President and one of the founders of the Academy."

"The committee therefore submit: That in the death of our respected and beloved President, the Reverend Doctor John G. Morris, the Academy deplores the loss of one who in the vigor of his manhood was one of the chief promoters and friends of the institution.

As one of its founders he engaged with earnest self-sacrifice in every measure calculated to advance its welfare.   During many years he was a regular attendant at the meetings, and his genial remarks and eloquent addresses always contributed to the interest and pleasure of these occasions.   His kindness of heart and willing helpfulness were recognized and appreciated by all the members who knew him. As an observer of natural objects he was most assiduous and painstaking, and by constant activity he accumulated vast stores of information relative to the insects, animalcules and plants which occur in the neighborhood of his home at Lutherville.   Other institutions and societies have dwelt upon his ability and acquirements as theologian, scholar and historian.   It is ours to recognize his value as scientist and writer upon natural history.   In this department he will continue to be best known as the author of the ' Synopsis of the Described Lepidoptera of North America,' and a ' Catalogue of the same,' published by the Smithsonian Institution.

" He was also a member of many scientific societies, both in this country and Europe, and in none was his presence more highly appreciated than in our well-known American Association for the Advancement of Science.   His friendship was valued by such men as Silliman, Agassiz and Henry, and he was welcomed by the most eminent scientific minds of Europe and America.   It rarely falls to the lot of a man, however gifted, to have lived so long and experienced so much in all that is high and best, and to have left such a wide impression for good in a rapidly growing community, as our deceased friend. His whole life spans the greater part of a century, and leaves behind a precious legacy of good example worthy of perpetual remembrance.''

As already told in this book, Dr. Morris was one of those actively interested in securing the magnificent statue of Luther that adorns the Capital of the United States. The Luther Statue Association has placed the following tribute to his memory on record:

" The Rev. Dr. Morris, whose Lutheran and Christian loyalty has been so conspicuous and consistent for so many years, reflecting honor upon the Lutheran Church, and always exalting the Christ whom he served, born in the third year of the century now closing, lived until October, 1895, retaining to the very closing months of his long, brilliant and useful life the full vigor of his robust and well-rounded manhood. Distinguished alike in the world of letters and of science, but always exalting Luther and 'the Name that is above every name,' he has left upon the generations whom he survived, as upon the generation that now survives him, an imperishable record of labor and faith in the gospel.''

A very marked characteristic of Dr. Morris was his interest in the young. Young people, especially children, were a source of great concern. His heart was full of tenderness for the growing generation, whose laudable efforts he frequently applauded, while he discouraged and despised anything that had the appearance of meanness or deceit. It was this trait that drew young people to him, and none more so than the members of that unfortunate class who, often lacking the correcting influence of parental love, became, temporarily, wards of the city and State. For many years Dr. Morris was one of the Board of Managers of the House of Refuge, a reformatory for boys, in the city of Baltimore, and after his death the following action was taken by the Board:

"At a meeting of the Board of Managers of the House of Refuge, held this 11th day of October, 1895, the following was unanimously passed:

"WHEREAS, In the dispensation of an all-wise Providence, it has pleased his Creator to remove from amongst us our late beloved associate, Rev. John Godlove Morris, who, like a sheaf of wheat fully ripe, has been gathered to the harvest, it behooves us, his late colleagues and friends, to give expression to our sorrow and regret at the sad bereavement; be it, therefore,

"*Resolved*, That in the death of Rev. John G. Morris we recognize the great loss sustained, not only by the managers and inmates of the House of Refuge, but by the community at large, of which he has been for so many years a conspicuous and useful member.

"*Resolved*, That with a sturdy independence of spirit, inherited from his Revolutionary ancestors, he combined a gentle and kindly heart, always awake to the impulses of charity and humanity, and so lived that his words, acts and walk in life were a complete demonstration of that noblest work of God— an honest man and a Christian gentleman.

"*Resolved*, That as a profound scholar, a liberal and devout theologian and pastor, Dr. Morris has left his mark upon the record of his times, and his death has left a void in the many circles in which he moved that will be long felt and difficult to fill. 'Blessed are the dead which die in the Lord from henceforth; yea, saith the Spirit, that they may rest from their labors, and their works do follow them.'

"*Resolved*, That this testimonial of respect to his memory be inscribed upon our records, and a copy be forwarded to the family of the deceased, and published in the papers of this city.

"JOSHUA LEVERING, *President.*
"MAURICE LAUPHEIMER, *Secretary.*"

At the regular monthly meeting of the Society for the History of the Germans in Maryland, held November 19, 1895, after a number of appropriate addresses on the part of members, all eulogistic of their late President, Rev. John G. Morris, D. D., LL. D., the following resolutions were adopted by a rising vote:

"WHEREAS, It has pleased Almighty God, our heavenly Father, in His wise providence, to remove from our midst, to His eternal home, our late venerable President, Rev. John Gottlieb Morris, D. D., LL.D.

"*Resolved*, That whilst we mourn and deplore our loss, we record our gratitude that he was spared so long beyond the usual allotment of human life to adorn a career of signal usefulness as the Christian pastor, the student of science and of historical research, the prolific author, the sincere philanthropist, the trusty citizen, and the tender and genial friend.

"*Resolved*, That he had especially endeared himself to us, as an organization, for his deep and abiding interest in all our pursuits and aims, and that as the descendant from an honorable and worthy German parentage, he not only had a just pride in that fact, but that he cherished with a deep and personal gratification whatever he could discover of honorable or heroic conduct, or of eminence in art or science or literature, in any that bore the German name, especially in those that were citizens, by birth or adoption, in our own beloved city and State.

"*Resolved*, That this record of our appreciation of his worth be entered upon our minutes, and that an engrossed copy be given to his bereaved family, with the assurance of our sincerest sympathy with them in their sorrow.

"B. Sadtler,
"Chas. Raddatz,
"Otto Fuchs,
"*Committee.*"

Words of sympathy and of appreciation were not wanting from many all over the Church and beyond. In addition to the resolutions given above, similar action was taken by the Lutheran Ministerial Association of York, Pa., by various conferences of the Synod of Maryland and of other Synods; religious and secular newspapers contained more or less extended notices and reminiscences, and there was a general and generous outpouring of sorrow at the death of one of whom it was said " How hard it is to realize that he is gone. How much we shall miss him. There is no one left to take his place."

INDEX.

A

C

D

E

F

G

H

M

R

S

T

V

W

Z